THE

MW01001183

BEYOND DECEIT

DEBRA DELANEY

POOLBEG

Published 2022
by Poolbeg Press Ltd
123 Grange Hill, Baldoyle,
Dublin 13, Ireland
Email: poolbeg@poolbeg.com

A catalogue record for this book is available from the British Library.

ISBN 978178199-483-2

www.poolbeg.com

Acknowledgements

As always, I would like to thank the extremely talented Claire Dean of The Editing House. When you contacted me in 2019 suggesting that I take the opportunity of the Covid lockdown to fulfil my long-held ambition to write a novel, I had no idea that it would lead to a saga and the unleashing of a great passion for writing fiction. Our collaboration on this project is testament to what can be achieved through hard work, commitment and true friendship.

Many thanks to the entire team at Poolbeg Press for having faith in us and helping to bring the Faredene saga to life.

Much love and gratitude to my husband, Ian, and daughter, Rose, for always believing in me and supporting my endeavours – however crazy they may be.

And finally, a huge thank you to my readers. Your lovely messages and enthusiasm for my characters and stories is what keeps me writing on the tough days.

DEDICATION

To all of my readers. With thanks for your support, wonderful reviews and inspiring messages.

Book Three of the Faredene Saga

Prologue

Faredene, Christmas Eve 1912

Bella Caldwell had been raised by doting parents who adored each other, shielding her from the many harsh realities of life. She'd believed most people were good at heart – that the world was a beautiful, exciting place. Not any more, though. Every day, she forced herself to get out of bed, wash and keep up the pretence that she was enjoying life. Showing up on the doorstep of her parents, Edward and Victoria, was another delaying tactic, but she rang the bell.

Poking her head round the parlour door, she smiled. Her mother was sitting on the burgundy chesterfield, bent over her embroidery. Her thick dark hair was so like her own, although now streaked with grey. Somehow, she looked contented.

Her mother looked up. "Sweetheart. I didn't expect to see you today."

"Am I disturbing you?"

"Not at all. What's the point of having your parents living at the bottom of your drive if you can't pop in whenever you feel like it?" She patted the space next to her. "Take off your coat and come and sit by the fire."

Still dressed for outdoors, Bella sat, wobbling on the arm of the chair. "Where's Father?"

1

"He's had to go to the office. Although I can't imagine what can be so urgent that it needs to be dealt with today. So, if you fancy a natter and a pot of tea, I've got plenty of time. And Cook has a batch of mince pies in the oven."

"That's a tempting offer. They smell delicious, but I can't stop. I'm on my way into town."

"Are you mad, going into Faredene today? The shops will be heaving with all the husbands who have left it until the last minute to buy their wives a Christmas present."

It was no wonder her super-organised mother looked appalled – as usual, all of her gifts were already wrapped and stacked neatly under the tree in the bay window.

"Perhaps that's where Father has gone and the office was simply a cover story. He may be scouring the shops and return with just a box of hankies and marzipan fruits for you," Bella said teasingly.

"I never thought of that. If he has, he'll have bigger problems than my being disappointed. He'll have to explain who the emerald earrings are for that are hidden in his sock drawer."

"Mother! I'm shocked. Don't tell me you went hunting for your present again."

"It was a purely accidental find."

"You use the same excuse every year."

"It's not my fault I can't resist peeking. But there's no harm done. I've perfected my surprised expression."

"Poor Father has no idea, does he?"

"No, and don't you go telling him. Now, are you sure I can't tempt you to stay? What's so important that you need to do it today?"

Bella stared at the ceiling.

"Surely not! Don't tell me you've not finished your shopping . . ." said Victoria.

"Not quite."

"Bella, you really are the most terrible liar."

"Are you suggesting that I'm always telling fibs?"

"Not at all. I'm saying you're no good at it."

Despite how low she was, Bella couldn't help laughing.

"Exactly how many gifts do you have left to purchase?"

"Erm . . . All of them."

Over the past few weeks, although Bella knew participation in the season was compulsory, she'd been unable to summon any enthusiasm and had refused her mother's many invitations to join her on shopping trips. She'd even resisted her half-sister Kate's urging to take herself off to Chester for the day to do her Christmas shopping, which was something she'd normally have loved doing. Then, when all the pupils had returned home for the holidays, Bella had produced an urgent pile of sewing.

Suddenly serious, her mother made to rise. "Would you like me to come with you, darling?"

"Stay where you are. I need to buy you something, as well. It would spoil the surprise."

"Are you sure?"

"Don't look so concerned. I'll be fine."

Last summer, Bella had discovered that her husband, George Bristow, was in fact a bigamist and their marriage a sham. He'd walked out on her without a word, stealing the money her parents had gifted her from the sale of their mill. What pained her most was the cruelty of his lies – convincing her he was suffering from a weak heart and was dying . . . Despicable. She was sure

3

it was the shock of his betrayal that had caused her to miscarry, obliterating her dream of being a wife and mother.

Amid the heartbreak, Bella had welcomed the opportunity to set up Caldwell Grange for Girls with Kate. They may only share one parent, their father, but they had a deep bond. And Bella didn't know how she'd have coped without Kate. Their school had proved a wonderful distraction, but to her dismay, once it was open and they'd settled into a routine, each night she'd collapsed into her cold bed exhausted from another day spent hiding the depths of her despair.

Bella felt as though her whole family were involved in a bizarre game of charades, where she acted out the part of a cheerful person and they pretended to believe her. After the first few weeks, they barely mentioned George. It was as though even his name was taboo and the very mention of it might bring some great evil into their midst again. At times she'd needed to talk about him and what he'd done, but she'd caused them enough pain, so she hid her sorrow. She did an excellent imitation of living a life, but really, Bella was no more than the pheasants and rabbits hanging from hooks outside the butcher's – a carcass, a shadow of her former self. She was here in body, but he'd destroyed her soul.

Breaking away from her thoughts, Bella stood abruptly.

"You're quite right. I was silly to leave it so late. No time to waste. I'd better get going."

Her mother's eyes clouded. "If you're certain you don't need me to come along?"

She kissed her mother's cheek. "Absolutely. You're a treasure, so I'll get you an extra-special gift."

Loaded on top of all of her other misery, she was now also feeling guilty that she'd caused her mother to worry.

In his stylish monochrome office at his clothing factory, Bella's brother, Sean Kavanagh, was fighting his own demons. He'd not taken a drink since last October – the day after his best friend, Charles Brakenridge, had committed suicide. Even now, the memory of those first weeks without alcohol fuelling his system were uncomfortable. The shakes, the nausea, the blinding headaches – they'd all passed. But the cravings still tore at him.

Only his valet, Max, was aware of the extent of Sean's suffering, having sat up for the first four nights playing cards with him, distracting him, defying his demands to fetch a bottle of wine, whiskey . . . anything. He'd even held him back by force when Sean had tried to go to the cellar himself. Bleary-eyed, he'd stoically endured both Sean's flares of temper and his pitiful whimpering. He seemed to understand why Sean kept his battle secret. Perhaps it was because Max had to spend his life hiding his own true nature.

Leaning forwards in his black leather chair, Sean rested his elbows on the desk and supported his chin in both hands as memories came unbidden of another Christmas Eve two years ago. He'd returned from America penniless, having been swindled by a man he trusted. That fateful night, he'd been looking to ease his sorrow with champagne. Had he been sober, he'd never have allowed Yvette Clarkson to seduce him, resulting in her pregnancy. She was Matthew's daughter, for Christ's sake. The man had been his mother's business partner and had offered him a job at the mill, a lifeline. That drunken tryst had also led to him becoming trapped in a loveless marriage . . .

Yvette didn't even try to mask her contempt any more. "Why don't you do us all a favour and drop dead, Sean," she'd said this morning.

How could she hate him so much? He'd tried hard to love her, to make her content. Nothing worked. Sean pulled at his tight collar, pushing the thoughts away. He didn't want to dwell on the mistakes he'd made.

Why did he always turn to liquor when things were difficult? He wasn't an alcoholic. Was he? He owned a successful factory. Managed a home – although, admittedly, it wasn't a happy one. But he was a good father – apart from the night Pierre was born, which would haunt him forever. Sean had been sinking a bottle of Irish in The Tanner's Arms, the pub run by Kitty Nelson and her husband, Albert. Then later, he'd been throwing up in a bucket in her parlour when he should have been at home. Perhaps then he could have prevented a drunken wet nurse from shaking his boy like a rat. Now, a silent world enveloped the innocent mite. All because Sean hadn't been man enough to deal with the possibility that the child might not be from his loins.

He picked up the bottle. It was almost full. There was enough in there to make him feel good – great – at least for a short while. He unscrewed the lid, holding the rim under his nose. God, he missed the aroma – the promise it made that everything would be easier if he took a drink . . .

"You're a pathetic bastard," he mumbled.

Sean raked his hand through his dark wavy hair, his brown eyes riveted on the amber liquid, enticing him, daring him to take a swig. What harm could it do? He ran his finger around the top of the bottle, fighting temptation. It was foolish to keep whiskey in his desk drawer. Arrogant. Just for visitors, he'd told himself.

Liar.

Having it close by had given him a strange sense of comfort, oblivion never far. His need for alcohol lurked like a spectre in the back of his mind, sapping his strength. But he couldn't go back to using his favourite blend as a crutch. Not now he had the prospect of happiness. Jane Kellet had agreed to be his wife once he was free. And Yvette had finally consented to a divorce, providing he met her demands that they wait six months and he give her the financial settlement she wanted. This was basically everything her father left them in his will, including the house – and most of what Charles had bequeathed Sean. It would be worth every penny to be rid of her, to be free. The hard part was the waiting – sometimes he wasn't sure he'd make it.

He slammed the bottle down with a thud, the liquid sloshing up the sides. Then he swiped it from his desk, sending it crashing to the floor, single malt seeping into the carpet. He would be strong for both of his sons, Pierre and Joshua. Whatever he had to face in future, no matter how strong his longing for liquor, he'd never give in to his desire.

Chapter 1

India, Christmas Eve 1912

On the veranda of a vast tea plantation, George Bristow relaxed in a cane chair, sipping his drink and admiring the view of the distant mountains. When he was alone enjoying the splendour of wealth, all the tough choices he'd had to make to get here seemed worth it.

He'd left his ma when she was dying, hurt Bella and, before that, dumped his wife, Pearl, and daughter, Daphne. It still played on his conscience. Not Pearl – she was a slut. Yes, he'd asked her to go on the game, but she could have said no. He was glad he'd sold her to Moby – a pub landlord and pimp. Whereas Daphne was a different matter. She'd be growing up and before long, Moby would decide she was old enough to be set to work whoring. She'd been a sweet child, with eyes like his mother . . .

He groaned as a wheedling voice caught his attention.

"Georgie, are you coming to bed?"

George sank his drink and went into the room, where an overweight naked woman in her sixties lay propped against several brightly coloured cushions. There was a price to pay for everything, George thought as he went to work, his revulsion hidden behind a sly smile as he caressed the parchment-thin skin stretching over Marjorie Rawlings' neck. Despite the open doors, the heat in the

8

sumptuous bedroom was stifling, intensifying the faint unpleasant odour that emanated from her.

"So, my darling, are you going to agree to become my wife? I don't think I can bear waiting any longer. I need to know you're entirely mine," George said.

"Oh, Georgie, there's no need for us to wed. I'm yours in *every* way," Marjorie said as she stroked her own dark nipples.

Did the old bag think he found her provocative?

"I still find it hard to believe you love me," she added.

"How can that be, my darling, when I shower you with affection every day?"

"You couldn't be more attentive. But you're a handsome young man, whereas look at me, Georgie." She jiggled the roll of fat around her bare stomach. "I'm over thirty years your senior."

"Age doesn't matter. To me, you're beautiful."

He poked his tongue into her belly button, cringing as he tasted salty perspiration. As his lips moved over Marjorie's damp skin, he closed his eyes and pictured Bella's youthful, sexy body. Thoughts of Bella never failed to excite him. Grasping Marjorie's sausage-like fingers, he curled them around his aroused manhood.

"That should be proof enough of how much I desire you."

"Oh my!" Marjorie sighed as he continued to stroke her.

George had never had to try this hard to manipulate a woman and his patience was running out. He'd spent most of the fortune he'd stolen from Bella trying to convince Marjorie he was extremely wealthy in his own right, having inherited from a fictitious grandfather who owned a cotton mill. To his relief, Marjorie wasn't particularly sharp-witted or much of a conversationalist and hadn't asked many questions. And he'd picked up enough snippets around the Caldwells' dinner table to validate his story. Back then, it had irritated him when Sean had prattled on about the mill as though he were the only man in the world to do a full day's work, but the knowledge had come in useful. George prided himself on being smarter than most. He remembered information and used it to his advantage.

If Marjorie wasn't so wealthy, he'd have given up on her long before now and left this hot, stinking, fly-ridden country. But he'd seen the accounts from the plantation – it was worth a vast amount and if they were married, everything would be his once she was dead. Finally, after years of struggling, he'd have enough money to last him the rest of his life.

Marjorie's voice interrupted his musings.

"Georgie, darling, you're not listening to your little Margie."

"Sorry, precious one. Your body is the only thing on my mind," he said, parting her legs.

"I said *yes*."

"What? I mean pardon, my beloved?"

"Yes, let's get married. I've been foolish to deny you for so long."

He thrust himself into her several times before crying out. That was the first time he'd climaxed inside the old hag without imagining he was with Bella, or the little Indian maid he occasionally took down by the lake. There was nothing so arousing as coming into a fortune.

Wandering around the department store, Bella deliberately averted her gaze from the bauble-decked trees. They were another unwelcome reminder that it was the time of the year when being jubilant was compulsory. Everyone, even the poorest who had nothing to give their bedraggled children but a few nuts and a newspaper kite, seemed to rejoice. Wives hiding unpaid bills behind the clock on the mantel, pretending their husbands hadn't pissed their wages up the wall when the rent was overdue. And the miners who rarely saw the light of day, laughing and joking with their mates while black dust coated their lungs, choking the life from their worn-out bodies.

How, she asked herself again, could all these people push aside their troubles, yet she wallowed in a pit of misery and self-loathing? Bella was ashamed of her weakness – her bitterness. Maybe everyone else was pretending to be joyful . . . If that were the case, she wished they'd be honest. Perhaps then her despair wouldn't be so isolating. If she had her way, she'd hide under her bed until January, when all the smiling faces and season's greetings would revert to complaints about the weather.

Not that anyone had greeted her cheerfully. Mainly, she'd received pitying glances and with each one, she'd acknowledged the decision to visit town today was a huge mistake. What's more, now she was going to die surrounded by tinsel and paper chains, and she had no one to blame but herself.

Her demise today on Christmas Eve would surely make it worse for her family – having to mourn her every year when all around them others were celebrating. Her death wasn't something she'd anticipated often, but her preference would be to pass away quietly in her sleep, loved ones by her side. Instead, it appeared she was going to expire while gasping for air in a toy department. She wasn't religious but, as her vision blurred, her breath coming in gulps, she implored a higher power to save her. Because despite the number of times she'd thought that joining her child in heaven would be a relief, she now knew that she wanted to live.

The spinning top she was intending to buy for Sean's youngest son, Joshua, clanged against the glass display cabinet as she stretched out to steady herself.

The blonde shop assistant dropped one of the lead soldiers she was arranging around a wooden fort.

"Goodness, miss, are you all right?"

Unable to speak, her other hand pulling open the top button of her coat and clutching at her throat, Bella shook her head.

The woman cupped Bella's elbow as she led her behind the counter.

"We keep this seat handy in case any of our elderly customers need to rest for a few minutes."

Bella's breath hitched. So, this is what she was reduced to – being treated like an old dear.

She pressed Bella into the chair, taking the spinning top from her and placing it down. Scrutinising Bella, her brow furrowed.

"Don't move, miss. I'll fetch you some water."

Bella wanted to grasp the woman's arm, plead with her not to leave, but the assistant hurried away before Bella could utter a word.

Wild thoughts swam through her mind. She wasn't entirely out of view of the ardent shoppers. Would anyone care if she slid to the floor? Unconsciously, she patted her face with the back of her kid-gloved hand, mopping the perspiration. She struggled to inhale, her breathing ragged, increasing her panic, her vision blurring.

The assistant returned, holding out a glass.

"Sip this water if you can, miss."

Bella ignored the proffered tumbler. Surely the woman could see she was in no fit state to drink.

"C-c-can't b-breathe," she stammered.

The woman placed the glass down, then kneeled beside her.

"Don't talk. Deep breaths."

"D-dying." She fought for air, her lungs burning.

"You'll be all right. It's an attack of nerves. I've seen something similar before. My father was the same when he came back from the Boer War. It'll pass, but if you're still off colour in a few minutes, I'll send for a doctor." She picked up the spinning top and placed it in Bella's lap. "Now, do as I say, miss. Focus on this – see, there are pictures of animals . . ."

Bella's thoughts were distant, hazy, as though she were listening from outside a window. Had she heard correctly? How could a child's toy help when she was drawing her last breaths?

"Come on, miss. See how bright the colours are? The elephant is blue. Wouldn't it be strange if they really were that colour?"

Bella nodded.

"I've got no medical knowledge and I realise it sounds daft, but my father recites the multiplication tables – try that," the woman said.

Despite thinking the woman insane, Bella did as she was bid, blocking out everything else.

The woman patted Bella's shoulder.

13

How long had she been staring at the animals, reciting multiplications? Five minutes? Ten? Bella didn't know.

"Deep breaths, now."

Bella inhaled deeply several times as the woman gave her another reassuring pat.

"Good, you're breathing easier already."

Was she? Bella wasn't sure. She gasped, her chest tightening.

The woman tucked a stray strand of Bella's hair back under her hat.

"Steady now, miss."

Bella ran through the times tables again.

The woman pointed. "The water is there when you want it. I've got to carry on with my duties or I'll be in trouble. You sit quiet until you're up to going home. There's no rush, miss – I'll keep an eye on you."

Although still dazed, Bella was feeling slightly better. The tightness in her chest was easing. Was it possible it was nothing more than nerves? Yes – and she knew what had caused it.

After purchasing a silk scarf for her mother, she'd examined her list as she waited for the gift to be wrapped. Next to get were presents for her nephews. As she'd pondered what to buy them, another wave of despair had come over her as she'd wondered how different today would have been had she been purchasing a present for her own child – had she not miscarried.

Perhaps her melancholy was the reason the encounter with Ethel Hornby-Smythe had distressed her so much. She'd groaned as the dreadful woman had waddled down the aisle between the accessories and perfume counters, her girth blocking Bella's path. She was wearing a lime green coat with a fur collar and a hat adorned with too many feathers to be tasteful. Ethel's beady eyes were sunken within folds of flesh and they'd glinted cruelly as she shook her head at Bella.

"*Miss* Caldwell! How brave of you to be out and about during this time of celebration and reflection. You have the sympathy of the whole town. People have spoken of nothing else for months. Everyone is appalled, although not entirely surprised," Ethel had boomed, causing nearby shoppers to glance at them.

Bella's brows knitted. "I beg your pardon – not surprised?"

"Your mother's modern ways and defying of convention were bound to lead to scandal one day. She was alone far too long before she married your father. Completely ignored my warning that it was unseemly for a woman to remain a widow and run a business. Rather than putting her energy into finding a new husband or selling the shop, she became a *partner* in a mill."

"M-Mrs Hornby-Smythe, m-my situation is *not* the fault of either of my parents."

Ethel ignored Bella's remark.

"You'll never live this down. It's ruined your chances of a respectable life. How are you bearing the disgrace?"

"I'm sure it'll be easier once people stop reminding me," Bella said, hoping with little optimism that Mrs H-S would take the hint.

This wasn't the case, because Ethel had blundered on.

"What are you – twenty? Such a waste. You're an attractive girl, but no decent man will ever take you now."

"Then I'll be content to remain a spinster."

"Have you considered a nunnery?"

"Certainly not."

"Well, you should, my girl. By doing good works, the

15

Lord may forgive you for sleeping with another's husband. As Chair of the Women's Guild, I could put in a word for you at the convent."

Bella balled her fists, crumpling her shopping list.

"Mrs Hornby," she said, deliberately dropping the second part of Ethel's name, aware it would irritate her. "I have absolutely no intention of hiding away or being ashamed of having been duped by an unscrupulous man. Now, if you'll excuse me, I must finish my shopping."

Before Ethel responded, Bella had pushed past her and stalked towards the stairs, pleased that she'd coped with the vicious gossip. It was only as she'd emerged into the toy department and her elation had subsided that the shortness of breath and panic had overwhelmed her. Ethel was right. No man would ever want her. Not that it mattered. To love someone deeply, you must be able to trust, and she was no longer capable of such faith in anyone outside her family.

Images of meeting George when he'd rescued her from an assailant during a suffrage march flashed through her mind. He'd been so handsome. She'd thought he was a hero. How naïve.

Aware her chest had tightened again, she shook her head, dislodging thoughts of the past. She was grateful no one was looking in her direction. Stretching forwards, she peered round the corner to where the assistant was now busy serving a customer. Bella took a sip of water. A little more rest and perhaps she could make her way home. She wouldn't allow herself to become one of those ladies who were slaves to their hysteria, swooning at the slightest provocation. One day, she'd be as strong as the image she portrayed.

Attack of nerves be damned!

Chapter 2

A lmost three weeks later, as smoke billowed and a loud bang emitted from the engine of Bella's motor car, she careered into Station Road, managing to stop before she hit the wooden gates of Faredene Motor Repairs.

Bella plucked at her hatpin with trembling hands, heart pounding, her breath rasping as she dragged her woollen scarf from around her neck, throwing it and her navy feather-trimmed hat on the seat next to her. She clutched at her coat as a searing pain stabbed at her chest.

You're not dying – you're safe, she told herself as she pulled off her gloves and then rummaged in her bag for a handkerchief. She dabbed her forehead before using the embroidered cotton to rub her sweating palms.

Come on, Bella. Calm down.

This was the second bout now. Was it simply as she feared – a case of hysteria? Or was she ill?

Don't think about it – breathe, breathe.

She closed her eyes, willing herself to believe that it would pass.

After what seemed an eternity, her breathing slowed. Bella glanced at her wristwatch. It was eleven thirty. She shivered. She must have been sitting here for fifteen minutes or more – she needed to move.

After taking her mirror from her bag, she checked her appearance before donning her hat and gloves once more. Ready to face the world again, she stepped onto the icy cobbles, her legs unsteady as she negotiated her way through the small yard towards the building. She desperately wanted to go home, but she couldn't abandon the car. Could she? No. Thankfully, the garage owner was one of the few with whom she was entirely comfortable. He was a nice man – a widower in his late sixties and with no interest in town gossip.

At the open doors, she took a deep breath and made her way inside. Tyres and mechanical parts were dotted haphazardly around the floor and on every wall, tools hung on hooks. Bella looked towards the black automobile in the centre of the room, spotting a pair of legs protruding from underneath. He was hard of hearing – if she wanted to attract his attention, there was only one way to do so. Stooping, she tugged at his blue overalls.

The legs jerked. "What the hell!"

A short, stocky man in his early thirties slid from beneath the vehicle. He got to his feet, his glasses dangling from one ear.

"Sorry, miss, I didn't mean to curse. You gave me a fright," he said as he straightened his spectacles.

Bella looked guiltily at the small gash above his eyebrow.

"I'm the one who should be apologising."

The man pressed his fingers to the cut. "It's nothing that will kill me."

"I thought you were the owner."

He grinned, showing slightly uneven teeth. "And he's as deaf as a post, so that was the only way to get his attention."

Reluctantly, Bella returned his smile. "Exactly."

"Well, what can I do for you, miss?"

"Isn't he here? I'm afraid my car has broken down."

"He retired. I'm the new owner. Richard Yates." After using a rag to wipe off the oil, he offered his hand.

Bella tentatively extended her gloved fingers. "He never said he was leaving."

"It was all quite sudden. As he wanted a quick sale, I got a bargain."

He had a friendly face, but she didn't like dealing with men – especially not a young one who smiled at her.

With no thought as to how she'd get home or what she'd do about the car, Bella said, "Right, well, I wish you every success, Mr Yates." She turned to leave.

"Don't you want your car fixing?"

"No, thank you. It's quite all right." She was being foolish, but she didn't care. "I'll telephone my father."

"Is he a mechanic?"

"He's a semi-retired solicitor." Her cheeks burned.

"Perhaps not the best person to help, then. I assume that's your vehicle?" Smiling, he pointed to her automobile blocking the gates.

"Yes, but—"

"I'm a first-rate mechanic."

"It's not that. I'm sure you're very competent."

"What's the problem, then?"

"I'm just used to dealing with—"

"Aye, well, if you let me fix your motor, you'll be used to me. I don't want to sound desperate, but if all his customers take your stance, I'll be out of business in a month. And I don't mind admitting – I've sunk every penny into this place."

How would she explain to her father that she'd abandoned the car rather than deal with a man?

"It was fine last time I drove it, but this morning it started making a grinding noise." She made a stirring motion with her fist. "Then there was a loud bang and smoke poured from where the engine is."

Richard smiled again. "Can you leave it with me for the rest of the day? I'll look at it this afternoon."

"Hmm . . . I have a couple of errands to run in town, but they won't take long. Is there any way you could fix it sooner?"

"Well, if that's the level of service you're used to, Miss . . .? Sorry, I didn't catch your name."

"Caldwell. Bella Caldwell."

"Right, Miss Caldwell. I'll tell you what – you do your shopping and come back in about an hour. I'll push your motor into my yard and look at it now. If it's something simple, I'll sort it. If not, you may have to wait, but I'll do my best."

"Thank you, Mr Yates," Bella said, backing away, wondering what on earth she'd do for an entire hour in town. Perhaps after she'd posted her letter and finished her shopping, she could brave the tea shop.

The post office was situated round the corner from the garage and she joined the small line of customers. The problems with the car had left her jittery and she fiddled with her handbag as she waited to go inside.

As she was served, she kept her gaze to the floor until, from behind the counter, the post mistress said, "You're looking peaky, Miss Caldwell. How are you keeping?"

"Very well, thank you."

The middle-aged woman checked the pearl buttons on

the cuffs of her white high-necked blouse then, after wetting the stamp, she used a ruler to align it to the top right-hand corner of Bella's letter before sticking it down.

Finally, she said, "I'm glad, dear. There's nothing wrong with being a spinster. Don't let the nasty gossips get you down. I never have."

"I, er, won't, thank you."

Bella knew the older woman meant well, but she wished she'd shut up.

"It's good you're not hiding away. Someone jilted me at the altar, you know. But I hold my head up. Still, I don't suppose it's as bad as what happened to you. At least he didn't take my virtue. Never trust a man, dear."

Bella heard the woman behind her in the queue snigger. Nodding, she pushed her payment across the counter and scurried out, her heart racing, breathing rapidly, her head swimming. She'd intended on visiting the haberdashery to purchase some new stockings but discarded the idea. All she wanted now was to be away from the post office before the sniggering customer came out.

Forcing herself to walk, she made her way back to the garage. As she crossed the yard, her foot slipped. Pain shot through her ankle and tears threatened.

When Bella entered, Richard placed his mug of tea on the long workbench.

"By heck, that was quick."

Bella stumbled forwards.

"Are you unwell, Miss Caldwell? Hold on a minute while I fetch you something to sit on." He dragged a battered spindle-back chair from the far side of the room. "It might be mucky, but your coat's dark, so it won't show."

Bella flopped onto the seat, took a few deep breaths and then rubbed her ankle.

"Are you hurt?"

"It's only a sprain."

"I'd better call for a doctor. You're as pale as a gallon of cream."

"No, please don't bother. I'm fine."

"If you don't mind my saying so, you're far from all right."

Bella's breath hitched and she burst into tears.

Richard hovered uncertainly as she rifled in her bag for her handkerchief. Then he pulled a large, clean linen square from his pocket and handed it to her.

As she mopped her face, he said, "I've got just the thing for you in my flat." Then he dashed through the door at the back of the workroom.

He returned holding a glass of dark liquid.

"Sherry – perfect if you're upset or under the weather, so my old mam says."

Bella took it, giving him a wan smile.

"Thank you, Mr Yates. You don't look like a sherry drinker."

"To tell you the truth, the previous owner left it behind in the pantry, but it all goes down the same way."

Bella sipped. "It's rather nice, actually."

"Right, well, if you won't let me fetch a doctor, have one of my sandwiches – I don't need both. It's only potted meat. You can watch me while I repair your engine. How does that sound?" He pushed a small metal lunch box nearer. "Go on – take one."

The last thing she wanted was to eat, but he was being kind and she didn't want to offend him. She nibbled at the edges as he worked. Somehow, sitting quietly, no one expecting her to be strong, was surprisingly calming.

After a while, he said, "You're getting some colour in your cheeks now. You can tell me what's upset you, if you've a mind to. I'm a good listener."

Bella dithered. He was nice enough. Honest. But then, George had taken her in, so clearly she was no judge of character. No – she mustn't suspect every man she met. Most of Faredene knew of her shame, so he'd find out soon enough. And she'd prefer it if he heard the basics from her, not one of the embellished stories that were circulating.

He focused on the engine as he listened. Perhaps that was what made it so easy for her to talk. Eventually, he looked up and wiped his hands on a rag that had been hanging over the bonnet.

"Well, my mam says there's a fool around every corner. And it sounds to me that this George fella was the biggest one you could meet."

"I'm well rid of him, I suppose."

"No doubt about it, if you ask me."

"It's more the loss of what I believed we had that still upsets me. Does that make sense?"

"It does. I was courting a lass back home until she died of tuberculosis. It was five years ago now and I often wonder about what might have been."

"I shouldn't complain. After all, what happened to me was my fault."

"We've all got to take responsibility for our choices, but there's no shame in loving someone. Even if they turn out to be a wrong 'un."

"I thought I was coping with it all, including the gossips, until I had my first attack."

23

"Attack?"

"Yes. I rarely go out these days because I feel everyone is whispering about me. Coming into town is the most difficult – that's what caused the problem. I'm not sure if I'm ill or if I've suddenly become one of those ladies who suffers with their *nerves*." Bella explained about the two episodes where she'd fought to breathe. "The first time I thought I was going to die."

"Best thing you can do is see your doctor."

"Do you think I'm unstable?"

"No, of course not. I hear there's a decent fella in town. Doctor Feral or some such."

"It's Farrell. Actually, he's a family friend."

"There you go. Don't your folks think you should see someone?"

"I'm sure they would, but I'm not telling them."

"Are you worried they'll cart you off to one of those sanatoriums? Is that why you're keeping schtum?"

Despite how she was feeling, Bella laughed. "Heavens, no. They'd be very supportive. But I don't want to worry them."

"They'd probably prefer to know. I would."

"The thing is, my sister and I run a girls' school. I've caused enough scandal without making it worse. If this got out, people might say I'm deranged."

"See your doctor. He'll keep it to himself."

She suspected there was no need to ask, but said, "*You* won't say anything, will you?"

"Not a word. You can trust me. Mechanics are like doctors – we take an oath to keep secret anything we learn."

She cocked her head to one side, then laughed as she realised he was joking.

"I'll make us a brew, then get this finished. I can do a temporary repair, but I'll need to order some bits to fix it properly."

"Oh, I see."

"Would you like me to come out to the school to put it right when the parts arrive from the manufacturer?"

"Would you do that?"

"Aye. I wouldn't have said it otherwise."

When she left the garage two hours later, Bella grudgingly accepted that Richard Yates was a good man.

Chapter 3

Sean glanced out of the French doors of the small breakfast room overlooking the large formal gardens of their home. Rain again. January was coming to a close and so far, the year had been as harsh as their marriage – endless dark skies and bleak nights.

Yvette took her seat at the table. He'd hoped that by getting up early this morning, he'd have avoided her. After saying good morning and receiving no reply, he opened his newspaper. It was a practice his mother would disapprove of, but mealtimes with Yvette were so uncomfortable. If he didn't read, he ended up bolting his food down and suffering from indigestion for hours. Either that or they'd become embroiled in another slanging match.

He watched his wife serve herself a kipper from the silver salver held by the butler. Her ebony hair was swept up in a loose chignon and curls framed her heart-shaped face. She was beautiful – sexy – but he no longer desired her. Indeed, he disliked everything about her. But he should try to be civil.

Closing his paper, he said, "How are you today?"

Yesterday, she'd returned from the home of her closest friend, Louise Mason, claiming to have a headache.

"Fine," Yvette said, glaring.

26

"Did you enjoy your stay with Louise and Peter?"

"As usual, Louise behaved as though she were the only woman to give birth. Yet, their son is the plainest child I have ever seen and he's not particularly bright, either. He takes after her, so it is lucky he will inherit a fortune, or he would struggle to land himself a wife."

"He's still a toddler – there's plenty of time for him to develop his looks and brains."

"I'm sure you deliberately disagree with everything I say. It's little wonder we quarrel so often."

Masking his exasperation, Sean glanced outside. The rain had turned to hail, but the atmosphere inside was bleaker. He continued to eat in silence for a few minutes. Then, unable to bear it any longer and hoping current affairs would be a safer topic, he said, "According to the paper, the House of Commons has passed the Third Irish Home Rule Bill. I suspect the House of Lords will reject it. That won't squash it entirely, but it'll cause delays and that could stir up trouble."

At the other end of the Spanish mahogany dining table, Yvette eyed him disdainfully.

"Do you really expect me to care about the goings-on in Ireland? It is of no interest to me if they get to govern their own pitiful little country."

"That will be all, Harris. We can finish serving ourselves," Sean said.

The grey-haired butler placed the dish of eggs on the sideboard and left the room. As the door clicked shut, Sean spoke again.

"I was merely being affable. Why eat with me of a morning if you don't want to talk?"

"There are more important things for us to speak about

other than what is happening in some place I have never been."

Sean's knife scraped along his plate. He suspected he'd regret asking but did so anyway.

"What *do* you wish to discuss?"

"Why you want a divorce. Because I don't believe your reasons."

"Are you telling me you don't believe we're miserable together?"

"We are no different from most couples."

"I don't want to live the rest of my life this way."

"*You* are the one who makes us both miserable. I am far more attractive than any of the other wives in our social circle. Perhaps if you appreciated me more, we would get along better. There are times I can hardly bear to be in the same room as you."

"Fine, I won't argue with you. I'm to blame for everything. Regardless, we'll be free of each other in a few months."

"Not necessarily."

Sean jolted. What was she up to now? Although initially shocked at the idea of divorcing, she'd admitted it would be for the best for them to go their separate ways.

"Yvette, we agreed – our marriage has been practically dead since we walked out of the church. And I, for one, don't see any reason for a delay. You must find keeping up the pretence of being happily married as difficult as I."

She raised her long dark lashes. "We hardly need to put on a show in our own home. Anyone working here for more than an hour will know there is no affection between us."

"Our servants might know what's going on, but

keeping the decision we've made from my family is deceitful."

"Pfft. Your precious family. Bella is a simpering idiot and Kate is a bitch. It is no wonder one made a laughing stock of herself and the other is a dried-up spinster."

"Keep your spite to yourself. If Bella has any faults, it's that she only ever sees the good in people. As for Kate, she's clever, funny and attractive. Any man would be lucky to be her husband."

"Pity you didn't take up with the marvellous Kate, then, rather than me."

"I can't argue with you on that score."

"Is she the reason you are divorcing me? Because I will kill you before I let you take up with her."

"Don't be ridiculous! There's nothing between Kate and me."

"I suppose that is something to be grateful for, because I hate her even more than the rest of them."

"If you'd made any effort at all with my family, they'd have embraced you. Particularly my mother. She couldn't have been kinder after your parents' death."

"That is *not* how I remember it."

"Well, it's how it was."

"Yes, she fawned over me, but nothing more."

"You make her compassion sound like a fault. She wanted to support you because you're my wife, and out of respect for your parents. Particularly your father – they'd been friends for years."

"He was another man who let me down."

"Your father adored you."

"Then why did he bequeath *you* his fortune, leaving me alone in the world and penniless?"

She looked about to cry. Although she infuriated him, he didn't like to see her upset.

"Matthew put the money in my hands because he trusted me to manage our affairs and look after you," Sean said. "You already know that."

"Then he was a fool, because you care nothing about what happens to me as long as you get your freedom."

"You wanted to end our marriage, too. And once things are finalised, you'll be a wealthy woman with control of your own future."

"But what will become of our children, left without a mother's nurturing?"

Yvette was indifferent towards the boys. She rarely saw them and had readily agreed to them remaining with him.

"What's brought this on?"

"When I popped into the nursery, Pierre started screaming yesterday for no reason. I think he senses he is going to be parted from me."

"He's not even eighteen months old – it'll have been a tantrum."

"Children need their mother. Especially one like Pierre."

"What are you saying?"

"I have been mulling things over. It would be wrong of me to leave them."

Sean called her bluff.

"Perhaps you're right – they should be with you. Do you want custody so you can take them back to America with you?"

"Oh, you would like that, wouldn't you? Banish your wife and sons. Start a new life without a defective child. Well, I won't stand for it."

She was so irrational, lurching from one opinion to another. He could only assume she wanted to rile him – it worked.

"Don't refer to him that way. Pierre is *not* defective! You take no interest in him. You've still only learned a few words in sign language. How can you hope to communicate with him if you don't try?"

"It upsets me to hear him trying to speak. He sounds as though he's not all there. I would be humiliated if any of my friends heard him."

Sean clenched his teeth. "That's a terrible thing to say. And what's your excuse for ignoring Joshua? When was the last time you even glanced at him?"

"If you must know, I can't bear to look at him because he is the image of you."

Sean unconsciously ground his teeth.

"Let me make myself clear. There's no way I'd leave our boys at your mercy. They're staying with me. You don't deserve to be their mother."

"Deserve! You have never been worthy of me. You would not be where you are today without my support."

"If you're referring to my using the inheritance from your parents to match Charles' investment in the factory, I was incredibly grateful. It allowed us to expand our plans. But it's irrelevant now. What Charles left me in his will covered that and far more besides."

"I am talking about all the emotional support and encouragement I have given you."

"Have we been living in the same marriage? The only encouragement you give me is the need to earn more because of your constant spending."

"Tight-fisted toad."

He sighed. "This is getting us nowhere. For God's sake, tell me what it is you want and then we can end this farce once and for all."

"Fine. Surely as the mother of your children, you can grant me some respect."

"In what way do I disrespect you, exactly?"

Yvette ignored his question. "Apart from the emotional distress of a divorce, I have arrangements to make for my future. Have you any idea how much I have to organise?"

"Perhaps I can assist. What is it you need to sort?"

"Saint Sean . . . how kind. However, as you will not be part of my new life, I don't need to tell *you* anything. Just ensure you transfer my money into my account when I need it."

"I'll do as we agreed. I'd never steal from you. As long as I have enough to keep the factory going and to rent somewhere for myself and the children, you can have the rest."

Yvette raised her eyebrows, her head tilted. "No price too great to be rid of your wife?"

"Come on, Yvette. Be honest. We were both trapped by your pregnancy. A divorce will be better for us all."

"Don't pretend you are doing it for me or the boys. You are completely selfish."

"Perhaps I am, but I'll do everything in my power to ensure my sons feel loved and make the most of their lives."

"And what about me? How am I expected to live with the shame of divorce?"

"You'll be in America. Besides, I've agreed to be photographed entering a hotel room with a prostitute so you can sue me on the grounds of adultery. I'll go to Liverpool next week and get things sorted."

"Have you no pride? Your mother might not be too pleased when she hears you have been whoring."

"What I'm going to do is common practice – my mother will be supportive of my decision."

Yvette picked up her coffee but didn't put it to her mouth.

"Aren't you the lucky one! Mummy – always forgiving of her precious son, regardless of how badly he behaves." She slammed her cup down, dark liquid spilling onto the white tablecloth. "What *is* the hurry, Sean? Have you got some little tart waiting to jump into your bed?"

If she had any inkling about Jane, she wouldn't be able to resist using it to ruin both him and her. And she'd insist on having Jane dismissed as Pierre's governess.

"Yvette, I give you my word. Since you and I have been together, I've never lain with another woman."

She waved her hand in a dismissive gesture.

He wasn't lying to her. Kisses weren't adultery. No matter how he longed to take Jane to his bed, he wouldn't cheapen the woman he loved by making her his mistress.

"That is so insulting." Her face contorted with anger.

"What have I said now?"

"If you don't have another woman, then clearly you would rather be alone than be with me!"

Yvette's chair tipped over, clattering on the parquet floor as she rose. She grasped the plate containing the remains of her breakfast, launching it across the room. It hit the wall behind Sean, the food splattering against the burgundy-and-gold flock wallpaper. He was surprised they had any crockery left. Like a child stamping its foot, Yvette would throw things whenever she was annoyed.

"I hate you, Sean Kavanagh. I wish I had never married you."

Sean groaned – he'd heard this so many times.

Resting both hands on the table, she leaned towards him.

"I have been trying to do the decent thing and give you what you want despite how I will suffer leaving my children. You won't be satisfied until you have driven me to my death." Her expression suddenly calm, she added, "Maybe *that* would make life easier for you. Perhaps I should follow Charles' example and take my sons to the grave with me."

Sean gasped. "Yvette! How could you threaten such a thing? Promise me you won't harm yourself or the boys."

"Why should I?"

"Because if you're serious, you need help."

She laughed derisively. "Grow a backbone, Sean. I was angry. People say things they don't mean in an argument."

"It was a wicked thing to say. Either you're ill or evil."

Should he call the doctor out? Remove the boys from her? Surely it was an idle threat. Or was this what he'd brought her to?

Yvette flinched as Sean stood abruptly. She looked nervous as he approached her until he said gently, "Yvette, please don't say such things. This situation isn't healthy for us or the children. We all need to move on."

Her lip trembled. "You will have your divorce. Now, I am going to my room to rest. You have brought on another of my headaches with your constant picking at everything I say."

Alone, Sean was reeling. There was no logic to their disagreements. Yvette took any standpoint simply to oppose him. In his more fanciful moments, he wished they could part as friends, as it would save them both a lot of misery. When he was being realistic, he accepted that Yvette's hatred of him was probably so deeply embedded in her soul that the quicker they separated, the better it would be. April and freedom felt a long way off.

Chapter 4

The rocky outcrop by the top of the waterfall on the eastern edge of the plantation was the best place to see the sunrise and this bright February morning was no exception. As the sun's first rays peeked above the distant mountains, the water glistened and the lush green tea bushes came to life at its touch.

A petite raven-haired girl wearing a burnt orange sari draped over her right shoulder and gold earrings stared into the distance. Suddenly, she covered her face, sobbing.

Standing two feet away, his arms folded, George hissed, "That's enough now. There's no need for this carry-on." He moved closer, his voice softening. "I don't like to see you upset."

"Then please, please, you must marry me and take me to England as you promised."

"Things have changed. I have to marry Marjorie – you know that."

She turned and grasped his hand, pressing his palm to her wet cheek. "But you love me. I have disgraced myself for you."

George placed his hands over hers. "I do, and if I had the power to change things, I would. There was no way I could know that my investments in England would fail," he lied. "Without Marjorie, before long I'll be penniless. You'll marry some lad from the village and forget all about me."

"No man will take me now I'm spoiled. I-I'm . . . I'm having your child. It'll show soon and my whole family will be shamed." She wiped her damp cheek with the back of her hand. "Please, I beg of you to take me away."

"I can't help you."

"Then I must beg Mrs Rawlings for mercy. Perhaps she will protect me." She dropped to her knees before him, her hands held as though praying. "It's impossible for me to return home. I-I'm afraid for my baby." Her hand moved instinctively to her flat stomach.

"Don't be silly."

"A woman in our village – her husband accused her of adultery. They stoned her . . . What I've done is worse."

"That's barbaric. No woman deserves to die in such a cruel way."

"Then you'll protect me and our child?"

George pulled her up so that she was standing pressed against him. She was so small that the top of her head fitted neatly below his chin. He stroked her hair.

"My precious, I won't allow you to suffer such a terrible fate."

She leaned her head against him, her tears soaking his white shirt. George placed his fingers under her chin, lifting her face to his. Bringing his lips down on her mouth, he kissed her passionately as he scooped her into his arms, cradling her like a child.

"You'll never have to be afraid for you or your child again, I promise."

"Thank you. Thank you," she said.

"There, there, now. No more tears," George murmured into her silky hair as he moved towards the edge of the falls.

He halted, suddenly dropping his arms to his sides.

Then he watched as her tiny frame smashed against the rocks . . .

The small card bearing a poppy and a heart slipped from Bella's fingers to the desk. She snatched it up again, tossing it in the bin. Who sent her a Valentine? George? Surely not.

Bella peered through the window. Outside the five-storey red-brick building, Richard Yates was wearing a cap and a thick black jacket over his overalls and was leaning against the car, smoking. She took the damask shawl from the back of her chair and draped it round her shoulders.

"Good timing," he said, stamping out his cigarette. "I've just finished."

"Thank you. I was wondering if you could look at the furnace for us."

"Giving you problems, is it?"

"Not at the moment, but it's temperamental and breaks down at most inconvenient times."

"I can pop back tomorrow. But you're not just being kind by putting jobs my way, are you?"

"Heavens, no. Our handyman clearly doesn't know how to solve the problem."

"Right, then, I'll be here in the morning. I'm grateful for the work. I looked at the books before I bought the business and the turnover was excellent, but I didn't realise that much of it came from repairing other machinery and furnaces."

"You were misled?"

"No, just stupid. I should have realised a small town like this wouldn't have that many automobiles."

"Are you worried?"

"Not really. I'll work on anything I get offered. And cars are here to stay, so the number will increase over time."

"I'm sure you're right. All of Father's clients seem to be buying one. As you've finished out here, would you like to come in for a spot of lunch? You must be frozen. I've asked Cook for a plate of sandwiches and some hot soup as a small thank you for your trouble."

"If you're sure."

"My sister, Kate, will join us," she added quickly, afraid of giving him the wrong idea.

"I don't wish to impose."

"When you've come all this way, it's the least we can do."

"Well, then it's appreciated."

Bella led the way down a narrow corridor and into the parlour. It was a femininely decorated room with pale grey walls, and dusky-pink carpet and curtains.

Doris, the housemaid – a plain girl of fourteen – took Richard's outdoor things.

"Miss Kate asked me to offer her apologies. She's been detained with a pupil and suggests you begin without her."

Richard blew on his fingers then rubbed his hands together to warm them.

"Did she say how long she'd be?" Bella said.

As innocent as the situation was, she didn't want any of the pupils running to their parents with tales of her entertaining a man alone.

"No, miss."

Richard turned. "I don't want to cause you a problem."

"No, please – sit. Doris, leave the door ajar, please."

"Yes, miss," the girl said as she scuttled off.

"Do you take sugar, Mr Yates?" Bella asked.

"Three. And would you mind calling me Richard?"

"Very well, Richard, and you may call me Bella."

She didn't want to be overfamiliar, but it was the natural response.

"Do you know who owns the big estate next door?" Richard asked as Bella handed him his tea.

"Faredene Hall? Yes, that's the Gibbs. They're practically family."

"I bet they've got a nice motor."

"Would you like me to recommend your services?"

"I wasn't hinting."

"I'm sure you weren't. All businesses need personal recommendations. Even we rely on parents telling their friends about our school."

"Do you enjoy teaching?"

About to serve the potato and leek soup, Bella paused, the ladle balanced on the tureen.

"In truth, when I was young, I never imagined being anything other than a wife and mother, or perhaps a nurse. But never a teacher. I'm a bit of a dunce. I only teach music and art. Initially, I helped with French, but my pronunciation is abysmal. We now employ two full-time teachers, as well as Kate. She's the clever one."

"It must be rewarding, though, to pass on knowledge to youngsters." Richard tucked in. "This is delicious. One problem of living alone is the lousy food. I struggle to boil water."

"I'm no better."

He looked at her quizzically before saying, "I was

going to ask why your mother never taught you, but of course things are different for ladies. Where I grew up, girls were cooking as soon as they could hold a pan. I don't suppose any of your pupils learn, either."

"Heavens, no. We're a progressive school, but their parents would have the vapours. Talking of which, thank you for your kindness when I was unwell."

"How have you been?"

"Not too bad. Only one incident, really. I hate to speak ill of a pupil, but let's say Clara can be cruel when she sets her mind to it. She asked me to explain to the class what a bigamist was, even though all the pupils were already aware of my history."

"She's lucky you didn't clip round the ear."

"We cultivate free-thinking young ladies, so questions are generally encouraged. I knew she was a nasty cat, but it was the others giggling that I found upsetting. I thought they liked me." Bella's bottom lip trembled.

"You don't need to give me the details."

"It was fine in the end. I managed to gain control of my breathing."

"Have you not told your folks or spoken to your doctor about your nerves?"

"No. I'm determined to overcome it and enjoy life."

"If you really mean that, do you fancy a trip to the theatre on Saturday afternoon?"

Was the card from him? If so, she needed to put him straight.

"*Someone* sent me a Valentine this morning," she blurted, her tone harsh.

"Steady on, Miss Caldwell. It wasn't me. I'd never do such a thing."

It was obvious he was telling the truth. He looked horrified. How could she have been so full of herself to assume he was attracted to her? No wonder her cheeks were burning.

"Richard, forgive me. I'm terribly embarrassed. It was kind of you to offer. However, this weekend is my turn to supervise the girls' leisure time."

"Say no more about it. I've not had much opportunity to make friends in the area and as you told me you don't go out often, I thought you might enjoy the jaunt."

Kate entered the parlour and Richard stood to greet her. She was tall, slim, with a neat blonde bob. Her black skirt and high-necked striped blouse emphasised her figure.

"I hope you haven't waited for me." She extended her hand. "You must be Mr Yates. Thank you for coming out here today."

"You're welcome, Miss . . ."

"Please, call me Kate."

"Richard," he said, bowing slightly.

"Now, did I hear someone talking about a jaunt?" Kate asked.

"I was asking Bella if she'd accompany me to see *Dick Whittington* in Chester. If I can get us a couple of tickets, that is."

Kate smirked. "I expect she refused."

Bella tried to keep her face passive while attempting to send Kate a message that she was *not* to meddle. "I'm working."

Kate pulled out a chair and helped herself to a bowl of soup.

"Sure, I'll be more than pleased to work this weekend in your place," she said in her soft Irish lilt.

"Kate!" Bella said.

"No need to thank me. You'd do the same for me."

What a pity sororicide was a crime. Surely anyone who had a sister trying to matchmake would understand the urge one might have to stab a sibling. No new excuses presented themselves. They were both waiting for her to respond. She'd seen Kate's determined look before. The woman was as tenacious as a bulldog – she wouldn't let the matter rest until Bella agreed to go. She hadn't been to a pantomime for years and hadn't she said she was going to enjoy life?

"Thank you, yes," Bella said before she had the chance to talk herself out of it.

Richard nodded warily.

Smiling, Kate picked up her spoon. "Marvellous."

For the next hour, Bella listened as Kate and Richard chatted. She was regretting her impulsive acceptance, planning how she might cancel their outing without offending him.

As she showed him out, she was about to make an excuse – an appointment she'd forgotten – when Richard said, "I've been right lonely since moving here. But if you only accepted because your sister made it difficult for you to refuse, I'll understand if you want to change your mind."

Goodness, he was blushing.

Bella bit her lip. She wanted to end his obvious discomfort – and hers. He'd been so kind, she couldn't bring herself to decline the invitation now.

"I'll be happy to go with you," she said.

After closing the door, she leaned against it. Thanks to Kate, she had to go out with him now. She marched back down the corridor.

"Kate, you're an interfering madam."

Kate shrugged, grinning. "Harsh but true."

"I don't want to go out with Richard. With any man. But I have no choice if I don't want to offend him."

"Sweet pea, don't frown at me – your face might get stuck. I'm not asking you to elope with him."

"I could still cry off."

"Nonsense. You're going if I have to drag you there myself."

"Kate! I'm serious."

"So am I."

Bella glared.

"Be honest – you're looking forward to it." Kate held her index finger an inch above her thumb. "Just a little."

"That's not the point.

"Then what is? Would you prefer it if he took you to see a moving picture?"

"That's not the problem and you know it. I'd rather stay home and you shouldn't have interfered."

"It's a sister's right. I'm unrepentant, I'm afraid, so you may as well admit you love pantomimes."

"Hmm, it might be enjoyable."

"There you go, then. You can thank me later."

Bella folded arms, glaring at Kate. "If I go, it's as friends, nothing more."

"That will do for now."

"Forever."

"Even beauty like yours fades. And I have no intention of letting you wake one morning years from now filled with regrets. So, listen to your older and wiser sister – and loosen your corset while you can," Kate said.

Reluctantly, Bella returned her smile.

"I'm concerned he might get the wrong impression. He's sweet in a rough sort of way and I don't want to hurt him."

"Bella, a trip to the theatre isn't a weekend in Paris. If you don't lead him on, where's the harm in having a few outings? You need more in your life than our school."

"There's no reason you and I—"

"No. That won't do at all. If you cancel – because I suspect you're thinking up an excuse – I'll invite the butcher to tea. It hasn't escaped my notice the way he sizes you up like a side of beef."

"You wouldn't."

"Make sure you go out on Saturday and enjoy yourself and we won't need to find out."

"Have I ever mentioned how helpful your involvement in my social life is?"

"Not that I recall."

"Good, because it's not."

Laughing, Kate cut off another piece of walnut cake. "Love you too, sis."

Chapter 5

Sunday morning, Bella snuggled further down under her covers.

"The fire will soon have the room warm," Doris said. She paused, her hand on the doorknob. "I'll come straight up and check on you when we get back, miss."

"Thank you, but there's no need."

Every Sunday, the teaching staff, Kate and Bella included, took the pupils into Faredene for the service. Despite feeling guilty, Bella had pretended to be off colour. It was worth it to get out of the mile-and-a-half walk to St Mary's and then having to sit in the draughty church during what would undoubtably be a long and boring sermon. And it gave her time to ponder her trip to the theatre yesterday.

Richard had behaved like a gentleman, opening doors for her, wrapping a thick rug over her legs, providing a flask of tea and a bag of bonbons for the journey. She'd had fun. He amused her in the same way as Kate and Sean. Also, she could talk to him about anything: politics, religion, art . . . Or, to be more precise, argue. With George, she'd always ensured she never appeared more intelligent or been seen to out-quip him. However, with Richard, she'd taken the opposing position on some topics simply so they could enjoy a lively discussion.

The crucial aspect of their excursion was how at ease she'd felt. No, that was the wrong word. Richard made her feel safe. There was no fluttering in her tummy when he glanced at her. Nor did she spend the entire time in his company longing for him to press his lips on hers. Or imagine she'd drown in his eyes. In fact, there had been none of the heart-stopping emotions that George had invoked in her and she couldn't be more pleased. Friendship . . . jaunts with a male companion, with no other agenda . . . Bliss! No more romance or heartbreak for her.

In the palatial dining room of The Taj Mahal Palace Hotel, India, George stroked the gold band on his wife's finger.

"Mr and Mrs George Bristow. I like the way it sounds," he said.

"How did you manage to stay single for so long, Georgie? You must have had lots of young women chasing after you," Marjorie said.

"There were plenty of opportunities, but I never saw myself as the marrying kind."

"Were you *never* tempted?"

"I wasn't about to throw my life away on the wrong woman. Besides, I focused on earning my fortune."

"Handsome, rich and virile. What more could a girl ask?"

Girl! She was so old that she looked like a week-old stew, ready to slide off the plate and into the bin.

George caressed her wizened face. "Are you enjoying yourself, my beloved?"

"How could I not when we're in this superb hotel, with people attending to our every whim?"

"We have servants at the plantation."

"Yes, but these last weeks have been special."

"It's been marvellous. But unfortunately, my funds are running a little short. Only expecting to be in India for a brief holiday until I met you, I tied up my capital in long-term investments before I left London and we've been extravagant of late, my precious one. So, we may need to curb our spending for a while until I can liquidate some of my assets."

"Georgie, we're married. Leave your cash where it is. I have enough for both of us."

"I wouldn't hear of it."

"Do it for me."

"It wouldn't be right living off my wife."

"Nonsense. What good is money if you don't spend it? I'll settle the hotel bill and any other expenses we've incurred with local suppliers."

"I can hardly let you buy my new suits."

"Let me spoil you for a while."

"If it'll please you, my darling."

Marjorie caressed his hand. "What I have to leave is probably pocket change compared to your fortune, but before we travel back to the plantation, we'll call in at my solicitor and I'll make a new will, leaving you everything."

"Only if you're sure, my precious."

Marjorie was clearly waiting for him to reciprocate. He hesitated, trying not to show how thrilled he was to be getting the fat old bag to give him access to her funds.

"I have no blood relatives, so if anything should happen to me, I want you to have every penny," he continued. "There's no need for us to list our assets. We can simply name each other as sole beneficiaries."

That should keep things nice and simple, eliminating

the need for him to invent investments he didn't own. It was vital she believed he had a significant amount to bequeath to her, as well.

"If I die first, you'll be an extremely wealthy woman, so you'll need to be careful of fortune hunters," he added.

"Georgie, that won't happen. You're a young man."

"None of us know how long we'll live. I could go first. Promise me you won't allow yourself to be taken in by opportunists."

"Oh, Georgie, I hate to think of you going first, but should the worst happen, I give you my word."

George kissed the tip of her nose.

Now she was going to be paying for everything, he could really relish life. Nothing but the best from here on in. As for feminine company, he'd have to be cautious. He couldn't bed too many of the locals. Marjorie wouldn't get suspicious – she was too thick – but their fathers were worse here than in England. And he didn't want any more stupid girls on his conscience – he'd been lucky that the maid's family had assumed she'd accidentally slipped and fallen to her death. Instead, he'd leave the plantation to find some willing young thing to satisfy his needs. A couple of bogus business trips to the city each month, that should be easy to manage.

Marjorie caught his attention by stroking his face.

"Good, that's settled." She beamed, her neck disappearing beneath her chins. "Why don't we skip dinner and go to bed. This is the last night of our honeymoon, after all."

"Shall I have some food sent to our room?"

"Yes, I need to keep my strength up for our night of passion. I don't want to be fading away." She giggled as she waddled towards the lift. "That's if these damned mosquitoes don't eat me alive first," she said, rubbing at the unattractive red blotches on her arms.

Much longer of having to plough her flabby body and he'd go crazy.

Victoria covered her lips with her fingers, attempting to hide her amusement as Kitty ranted. Kitty and her sons – Jake, who was ten and Brian, eight – had arrived at Victoria's home shortly after breakfast and Kitty was still pacing the ornate rug in front of the fire in the parlour an hour later. If not for the jagged scar running from under her left eye to her collarbone, Kitty would have been incredibly beautiful with her thick Titian hair and in her tailored turquoise skirt and lace blouse.

"I'm as surprised as you are, Kitty, but if Milly is happier living in Blackpool, even though we're going to miss her, we must be glad for her," Victoria said.

It was only the previous evening that Victoria had received the news that had Kitty so riled now and she hadn't fully accepted the implications herself. Milly, Kitty's sister, was Victoria's oldest friend and she was going to miss her terribly, but Milly had been desolate since the death of her husband, Bob, so Victoria was putting her own concerns to one side.

Kitty paused in front of her. "I *am* blinking pleased for her and it's right nice she's going to be living with our Agnes. But our Milly was only meant to be there for a few weeks while Agnes' arm got better. I thought she was settled when she got her little cottage and had Jane livin' at home full-time."

"She was happier, but when she spoke to me on the

telephone, she explained that Faredene holds too many memories of Bob."

"Milly said Jane can carry on living in her place, so I suppose at least Milly will still have somewhere to live when she comes back. But then Sean said he's given Jane time off in March so she can take the last of her mam's clothes and stuff over there." Kitty sighed. "So I'm probably kidding myself and she's never coming back."

"She seems to be set on staying there."

"So, you and I *aren't* getting the next train to Blackpool to drag her back here?" Kitty asked, arms akimbo, balancing on one foot, reminding Victoria of the scruffy, spirited waif who had first walked into her kitchen all those years ago.

"I'm afraid not."

Kitty raised her hands, dropping them in a hopeless gesture. "It's such a bloody shock."

Gasps came from the two strawberry blond boys, who were sitting on Victoria's sofa munching on large slices of sponge cake.

"Mam, you're always tellin' us off for swearing," said the smallest.

Kitty glared at him, then her face softened.

"Aye, well, Brian, love – you're little 'uns and I'm a grown-up."

"Bloody unfair," mumbled the taller boy, his cheeks bulging.

"Any more language, Jake Nelson, and there will be no puppies."

"Aww, Mam, yeh promised," said Brian.

"I can change my mind like that." Kitty clicked her fingers.

"Come on, Kitty. Sit down and have some cake. It's your

favourite – lemon drizzle," said Victoria, cutting a slice.

"Aye, all right. At least I've got you. And Jess. She's a smashing sister-in-law. And the way she spoils these two, you'd think they were hers. She'll make a lovely mam, but I've told her and our Harry they need to get a move on before she's too old."

Most residents of Faredene, including Harry Gibbs' own siblings, still assumed Jess was his wife. Victoria, however, knew that Jess had been unable to marry Harry because her brute of a husband was alive – though, hopefully, he was back in America by now, never to return to England to blackmail more money from them. She also knew that after taking a beating from her husband, Jess had lost the child she'd been carrying and still felt the pain of that loss.

"Boys, why don't you go into the kitchen and ask Cook to put Kirby's lead on him for you," Victoria said. "You can take him for a walk in the grounds. Not too far, mind – he's too old to go tearing about."

Jake stood. "Come on, Brian. Mrs Caldwell wants Mam to herself but is too polite to tell us to shove off."

"Can I take another slice of cake with me?" Brian asked.

"Honestly – they act like I never feed them," Kitty said.

Victoria cut two slices and wrapped them in napkins. "They're all gannets. Sean was permanently hungry. He's still the same." She handed them to the boys. "No slipping some to Kirby – he'll be sick."

As the door shut, Kitty said, "Were yeh getting rid of them?"

"Yes. I wanted to tell you something in confidence."

"Sounds serious."

"It'll be best if you don't mention to Jess about having

children of their own. She can't have a child. Please don't ask me to explain. I'm only telling you this, Kitty, so you don't say anything out of turn. She doesn't mention it often – normally only ever to express her regret at not being able to give Harry a son or daughter – but I know she longs for one."

"Me and my big gob. Thanks for telling me. Poor Jess. Has she seen Doctor Farrell?"

"There's no point. Apparently, a doctor in America told her there was no hope. Speaking of Owain Farrell, I have some news about him and Anne."

Kitty licked her fingers. "Go on, then. What's old stick-it-up-her-drawers been up to now?" She'd never been keen on Edward's widowed sister.

"She's convinced Owain is going to propose to her."

"Blooming heck! Is Owain cracked? She's hard work, that one – toffee-nosed as they come."

"Kitty! Don't be unkind. She genuinely cares for him."

"How can you be so nice to her? I've not forgotten that her shoving her neb in was the reason you and Edward spent so many years apart."

"All that was such a long time ago – and she gets lonely."

Kitty made a humph sound. "What makes her think he's going to pop the question?"

Victoria affected her best imitation of Anne's voice.

"Victoria, at your age you have probably forgotten what romance is like, but I can tell by Owain's gaze that he is a man in love. Last night, he said he envies Edward having a supportive wife and how he sometimes regrets devoting his life to his medical practice instead of settling down."

"Well, if she's as bossy with him in the bedroom as she is about everything else, he'll feel like he's on military manoeuvres. He'd better stand to attention." Kitty spluttered, spraying cake crumbs.

Chapter 6

The last Thursday in February, as she had done for many years, Victoria attended the monthly Women's Guild meeting. Unlike many of the ladies, she didn't regard it as an important social event. For her, the occasions had served two purposes: making necessary business contacts and ensuring that the wealthy of the town helped the poorer residents of Faredene. Since her retirement, the latter had become her sole reason for attending.

As usual, Chairwoman Ethel Hornby-Smythe presided over the meeting in a manner befitting royalty, hammering on the oak table at the front of the room with her gavel to ensure she had everyone's attention before she spoke.

"If there are no other matters, ladies, we can commence our luncheon."

"Actually, I have some other business," Victoria said. Ignoring Ethel's disgruntled look, she stood. "This is a topic I've raised before. I'd like to discuss the streets known as the Rows." She heard Ethel groan but continued undaunted. "The houses there are now nothing more than slums."

One of Ethel's cronies, a thin, hard-faced woman, piped up. "We've agreed before – it's up to the landlord to sort them out."

"Exactly, but as they're derelict in their duty, perhaps the committee can work together with the owner to improve conditions."

Ethel heaved herself to her feet and banged her gavel once more.

"It isn't our place to interfere in the private matters of businessmen. We're a charitable organisation, not suffragettes."

Kate said, "Surely the welfare of the town's residents *is* our business."

"As you're a relatively new member, Miss Caldwell, may I remind you we already do a great deal for the less fortunate of our community," Ethel said.

"We can do more."

Victoria could tell her stepdaughter was enjoying the exchange with the chairwoman.

Jess Gibbs, a curvaceous dark-skinned woman with tight black curls and a ready smile, joined the discussion.

"Slums are hardly good for the town's image."

Ethel's enormous neck was blotching, giving the impression she was about to burst a blood vessel.

"We are all grateful to you and your husband for your generous contributions to the town's poor fund, Mrs Gibbs. However, meddling is out of the question."

Victoria bit her lip to suppress a smile. She, Jess and Kate had agreed earlier on how they'd challenge the objections Ethel might make.

"Ladies, you must tire of hearing about the appalling conditions," Victoria said. "I'm certainly fed up with raising the topic only to be fobbed off. Take a drive down there and see the state of the streets for yourselves. The squalor is all too apparent."

"We don't need to hear about such a vulgar matter today, Mrs Caldwell," Ethel said.

"I'd like to understand more about it," a new member at the back of the room ventured.

Victoria seized her opportunity. "It's terrible. Everywhere you look there are broken windows, rotten frames and peeling, blistered paint on the doors. Picture, if you can bear it, your own children – filthy, their hair matted . . . with no gardens, forced to play on cracked, uneven pavements, a foot away from open drains." She let her words sink in. "I have no wish to spoil your appetites, but let me tell you – the stench from the sewers is overwhelming. As for the disease they must carry, it doesn't bear thinking about."

"I must protest. There is no reason for their offspring to be dirty. It is simply poor parenting," another member said.

"How would you keep clean with only a solitary standpipe and toilet per street?" Victoria said. "Although, one can hardly call it a toilet when it's little more than a bucket beneath a wooden plank with a hole."

There were several gasps from around the room and Victoria hoped she was getting through to some of them. Ethel fumed beside her, drumming her fingers on the table, but Victoria continued.

"While many of us are considering installing electric lighting, their homes don't even have gas lamps. Many have only an open fire over which to heat water – if they can afford the coal after paying rent for their hovel."

"God hasn't blessed me with any of my own, but it breaks my heart to think of the little ones growing up in poverty," said Jess.

After the murmuring of agreement ceased, Victoria

said, "You all have warm, comfortable homes, whereas the hardworking occupants of the Rows are forced to live in primitive, squalid conditions while making a heartless landlord rich."

The glass of water in front of Victoria quivered as Ethel gripped the tablecloth.

"I insist we let this matter rest. There may be a dozen or more landlords. You can't be suggesting we harangue them all," Ethel said, leaning heavily on the table, her chest heaving.

Kate smirked. "Are you're proposing we sit back and do nothing, madam chairwoman?"

Ethel grasped her gavel, holding it like a weapon before slamming it down again. "I'm bringing this session to an end. Yet again, Victoria, you have sabotaged our meeting and lowered the tone with uncouth talk. I rue the day we allowed you to become a member of the Guild. Whoever the landlords are, we should allow them peace in which to conduct their business as they see fit."

Her voice wavered with anger and ladies around the room appeared shocked by her outburst, shaking their heads in disapproval.

"If you insist, Ethel," Victoria said. "I'll leave the matter for today. However, my husband, Edward, has investigated and established that all the houses are indeed owned by one person, through a company registered in Leeds, giving him anonymity. If the committee doesn't wish to intervene, I'll take matters into my own hands to help his tenants."

Ethel blanched, thudding into her seat.

"Who owns the properties?" someone called.

"Ladies, if I may ask for your patience. It's only fair that I speak to the person concerned first before I reveal their name," Victoria said.

Ethel remained uncharacteristically quiet during the meal, scurrying from the room as quickly as her bulk would allow as the meeting ended. Victoria, Jess and Kate hung back while the hall emptied.

"Did you see Ethel's face?" Kate said. "She's in no doubt now that we're aware she's a bare-faced liar."

"How she stood there claiming there might be several landlords when her own husband owns the lot is beyond me," Victoria said.

"I nearly blurted it out in front of everyone. The woman's a sack of bile. Why are you protecting her?" Kate said.

"I'm glad you resisted. We need to handle the matter with finesse. We need her husband's cooperation," Victoria said.

Jess grinned. "There won't be any need for that, Victoria, honey."

"Jess, what do you know?" Victoria said.

"My Harry said for me to wait until he was certain, but I've been bursting to tell you, so I'm sure he won't mind. Mr Hornby-Smythe has been losing at poker to one Harry Gibbs at The Jubilee Club since that first week when Harry joined when he came back from America. Hornby hasn't paid a penny back and Harry's been storing Cyril's promissory notes in our safe until he can use them to his advantage."

"How much does Mr H-S owe?" asked Kate.

"A sizable fortune," Jess said. "Hornby-Smythe seems to think Harry will never ask for the money, but he's in for a shock. Harry's seeing him today and is going to call in the debt. If Cyril can't pay up immediately, he's going to insist Hornby-Smythe hands over the deeds to the Rows. The houses were bad enough when Harry was a lad growing up there, but now he's disgusted by the state they're in."

"What's he intending to do with them?" Victoria asked.

Jess touched Victoria's arm. "Well, the best part is he wants Edward to do the transfer legally. Then he's going to renovate every house."

"Jess, that's tremendous news," Victoria said.

"It is, doll. And what's more, Harry wants you to oversee the project. If you will, that is."

"Me?"

"Yes. Harry likes a peaceful life. He's happiest when he's wandering the grounds with his dogs. And I wouldn't know how to manage businesspeople and organise folk."

"I'm flattered. Perhaps Owain will advise on sanitation and such."

"So you'll do it?"

"Well, let's see if Harry gets them first and then I'll speak to Edward. I'm supposed to be taking things easy."

She should consult Edward first. They were trying to spend more time together now she'd retired, although he'd retained his stake in his legal practice so that he could handle a few cases to occupy himself while she was doing charity work. But the Rows overhaul would be an enormous commitment. She'd have to ensure she didn't neglect him.

"Edward won't object. I'll do it," Victoria said impulsively.

After saying goodbye, Victoria made her way to Sean's factory.

* * *

Sean had spent the last twenty minutes lying to his mother. Worse still, from the way her brow was furrowed, she knew he was hiding something. He cringed at her next words.

"I came here so we could speak privately. So, I'll ask one last time. Look me in the eye and tell me again that everything is fine between you and Yvette."

He stopped rolling his pen around his desk and peered at her, struggling to keep his voice steady.

"There's nothing for you to fret about."

"Do I look like I was born under one of this year's cabbages?"

"No."

"Then please don't treat me as though I'm stupid, Sean. I was at your house yesterday and for the umpteenth time, Yvette commented on how I'd soon find out that my precious son isn't the saint he pretends to be. She's desperate to tell me something. If it's bad, I'd rather hear it from you."

What was Yvette playing at? It was at her insistence that they keep their plans to divorce secret. He desperately wanted to confide in his mother. Tell her that the situation was ripping him apart. Explain the strength it took to refrain from drinking was exhausting. Perhaps it was best that he couldn't tell her – in the past, he'd caused his mother enough worry.

"Did you ask her what she was hinting about?" he said.

His mother sipped her tea and placed the china cup back on its saucer on his desk.

"Of course not. I wouldn't give her the satisfaction. I ignored her comment. She was furious."

Half of him wished Yvette had told her. Then he'd be able to talk to her about it.

"I don't know what she was suggesting," he said.

"Are you drinking again, darling?"

"Not touched a drop since Charles passed away."

"Is it the card tables? Do you have debts?"

"No, and I'm not gambling, either. Why do you assume the worst? Am I such a disappointment?"

"Not at all. Please forgive me. It was wrong of me to ask. Especially as you've done so well, despite mourning Charles and coping with Pierre's disability. And as for this business, you've made a tremendous success of the place."

"I've had a lot of help. Kitty barely needs my input on the production side and Darius' designs practically sell themselves."

"You're being modest. You're the driving force behind it all. I burst with pride when I think about your clothing lines being sold in stores up and down the country."

"Then please take my word for it. Everything will be fine."

"At least I know it's not a woman. When you're not working, you spend all of your time with the boys."

"I certainly have enough to keep me busy."

Was lying by omission as bad as an outright lie? When his family and friends found out about Jane, he doubted they'd believe nothing had happened between them beforehand. He scarcely believed it himself. Hopefully, his mother would understand why he'd kept up the pretence that his marriage was working, when he was praying for it to end.

His mother's voice broke into his thoughts.

"I'm silly for calling into Yvette's sitting room. I only do it out of politeness. Perhaps I should just visit the boys in the nursery."

"That would be for the best. She appears to take pleasure from provoking you. I'll speak to her when she gets back. She left this morning to stay with Louise for a few days."

"Frankly, I'm surprised she doesn't move in with them permanently. I pity Louise Mason. Yvette barely has a good word to say about her."

"Louise isn't being singled out. Yvette criticises almost everyone. And she enjoys riding on their estate."

"Do you mind her being away so often? Don't you miss her?"

He shrugged. "Not really."

"My poor boy – that breaks my heart. I wish you had someone you adored."

He longed to tell his mother he worshipped someone, just not his wife.

His mother pursed her lips. "I'll not get any more out of you, will I?"

"What more could there be?"

"Whatever is going on, remember – I'll be on your side. You can rely on me."

"Do you realise how much I love you, Mother?"

Her cheeks flushed. "Yes, darling, but I never tire of hearing it, so you can tell me as often as you like."

"Please don't worry."

"That, my dear boy, is something I've never been able to master. It's part of being a parent. And as you'll discover, the constant fear your children might come to some harm gets worse as they get older."

"Marvellous. I'd best enjoy them while they're little, then. Did you notice how well Pierre is doing with his sign language? And he's speaking the odd word."

"He's a determined little chap, like his father."

"It's difficult to understand what he's saying, but he's trying – that's what matters. Jane says that because he's never heard anyone else speak, he has nothing to imitate."

"Jane's a marvel with him. Incredibly caring."

He was glad his mother was fond of her goddaughter, Jane. It would make it easier for her to accept the situation when she found out they were together.

"Unlike his mother," Sean said.

"Sadly, I can't dispute that. Thankfully, Jane isn't courting, because once she's married, I expect she'll leave. Then again, perhaps what happened with Charles has put her off getting involved with anyone for a while."

Fighting his desire to tell her that Jane had found someone – him – he chose his words carefully.

"She blames herself for his death. I get it, because there's no denying that it was finding out that he was in love with his half-sister that drove Charles to suicide, taking his father with him."

"Jane wasn't to blame for James Brakenridge raping Kitty! If Milly and Bob hadn't adopted the twins, who knows what would have become of Kitty. As for Jane and Robert, they might have had terrible lives because poor Kitty was nothing but a girl when that savage attacked her. And I for one am glad he's gone."

Sean understood his mother's instant flare of anger. Even after all these years, it was the same whenever Charles' father was mentioned. Her reaction was understandable because within weeks of her marriage, she'd almost been widowed when Brakenridge's henchmen had attacked Edward, leaving him for dead in the park. Then a few days later, they killed Teddy Gibbs and left Kitty scarred for life. Sean hated to see pain etching his mother's face.

"Mother?" he said.

She spoke slowly. "Sorry – I was just remembering. As for Jane, eventually she'll realise she wasn't responsible, so you need to be prepared for her resigning. Although, after she visits Milly in Blackpool, you might have a problem sooner than expected. From what I hear, Jane said she wants to remain in Faredene, but let's hope her mother doesn't convince her otherwise."

"How was your Guild meeting?" Sean asked, changing the subject.

"Eventful. Ethel was furious." She told him about Harry's plans for the Rows.

"There's no better person to be in charge of the scheme."

"Ethel looked horrified when she realised that I know her husband is the current owner. Hopefully, it'll subdue her for a while."

"Perhaps you *should* tell the other members. You're too nice, Mother."

"I expect it'll come out eventually, but not from me." She grinned. "And it might be fun watching her squirm."

Sean laughed. "It's good to see you have a wicked side."

"If Ethel annoys Kate again, I don't think I'll be able to stop her from blurting it out. They didn't realise what they were letting themselves in for when they allowed her to join the group."

"I bet they didn't."

"She says it's her duty as a local businesswoman to be

a member, but I suspect she also enjoys having something else to do apart from running the school."

"I get the impression The Grange is all Kate and Bella want for the moment."

His mother smiled. "Men are hardly the most intuitive beings."

"Have I missed something?"

"Probably many things. When was the last time you visited the girls? You know I like you all to keep in touch with each other."

"It's been at least two weeks. I'll pop in on my way home this evening."

His mother drained her cup. "You're such a good boy."

He grinned. "You make me sound like I'm still in knee-length shorts."

"You'll always be my boy. Well, I must be off. I've been out far too long. Remember, I'm always here if you need me."

When she left, Sean leaned back in his chair. Perhaps he should talk to Bella or Kate. Not Bella – she'd been through a difficult time and was too young to be burdened with his problems. But he felt sure Kate would understand. He trusted her completely and would value her opinion. Once again, Sean wondered why someone as attractive and intelligent as her had never married.

Chapter 7

Kate was tidying her bookshelves while one of her pupils filled the inkwells, when Sean arrived. At ten years old, Abigail Tyler was small for her age, her long mousy hair tied back with a green ribbon. Kate noticed Abigail's cheeks flush as he entered. She could hardly blame her. Her own pulse still quickened at the sight of him. She unnecessarily patted her hair into place, wishing she'd known he was intending to visit – she'd at least have changed into a clean blouse.

"Run along now, Abigail. You need time to wash before supper."

The child grasped the edges of her pinafore and bobbed her knee before rushing out.

Kate turned to Sean, her eyes ranging over his smiling face. No man should be that attractive. Aware she was staring, she resorted to her usual method of hiding her feelings.

"You've set yet another of my pupils' hearts fluttering. Though what they all see in you is a mystery."

He folded his arms, giving her a lopsided grin, and slouched against one of the desks that were arranged in four neat rows.

"I can always rely on you to stop my head from getting too big."

"I'm doing you a favour. With so much hair, you'd never fit through the door if your head grew as well."

Sean laughed. "A fine way to treat your stepbrother. Perhaps I should visit Bella."

"She's with the other teachers supervising the girls' evening meal, so you're stuck with me."

"I suppose I'll have to make do. Are you too busy for a chat?"

"Ack, I'll still have a list of things I didn't manage to get done when I go to my coffin, so I may as well have the craic now you're here. Look at this letter. It arrived this morning from the parents of two of our girls." She removed a folded piece of paper from the pocket of her straight ankle-length skirt and passed it to him.

"Am I reading this correctly? They're taking them away because you're half Irish?" he said.

"So it seems. I spoke to them on the telephone earlier. They have an estate near Dublin and with the troubles brewing over home rule, they're worried about their position there because they're English. Even though I think the Irish have a point, nothing in the school or what we teach suggests disloyalty to the crown. We even have the obligatory portrait of the king in the assembly hall."

"Why are they holding you responsible for the Irish situation?"

"They're making some sort of protest. Not putting money into the hands of the Irish was how the husband explained it."

"Idiots."

"Exactly. But they're collecting the girls at the end of the week. I only hope it doesn't cause a stampede."

"Could it?"

"Yes, if other parents decide I'm not English enough. People need little excuse to remove their custom or, in this case, daughters. I'm worried. We've worked hard to reach this stage and we're still not full. Living down the George scandal was more difficult than I expected."

"You've never mentioned anything before."

"I play it down for Bella's sake. Most of our pupils' parents are understanding – they wouldn't have put their daughters in our care otherwise. I do everything I can to prevent Bella from hearing the odd derogatory remark, but I can't protect her from everything."

Sean wandered to the back of the room and placed his hand on the globe, which rested on top of a long, low bookcase. With an angry swipe, he spun it.

"It infuriates me. Why can't people understand she was an innocent victim? She's not culpable for George conning her – he took everyone in. Bella did nothing wrong. Nothing at all."

"Society doesn't care about that. George ruined Bella's reputation – and mine by association."

"People can be narrow-minded. How is Bella? She's been quiet since Christmas."

"Honestly? I'm not sure. I suspect only time and her realising that not all men are treacherous pigs will help."

"She needs to meet a good man."

"Richard Yates from Faredene Motor Repairs has taken a shine to her. And the butcher sent her a Valentine's card."

"The butcher!"

"Bella was horrified when he delivered this week's order and hinted he'd sent the card. The man must be nearly fifty."

"Poor Bella. I hate to think of men thinking that because of what happened to her in the past, she'll settle for any fool. If she needs me to have a word with him and set him straight, just let me know."

"From what she told me, she looked so appalled, I suspect he got the message."

"What about the other chap?"

"I persuaded her to go out to the theatre with him."

"I'm surprised she braved the Faredene gossipmongers."

"They went to Chester, so I doubt anyone saw them."

"What's he like?"

"Decent."

"Not like George, then?"

"I'm pleased to say he appears to be nothing like that rogue."

"Does she still harbour feelings for George?"

"She claims not, but she's keeping something from me. I had to twist her arm to get her to accept Richard's invitation. Even if they're only friends, it's better than nothing. Because regardless of how she tries to hide it, one thing is certain: she's not the carefree young woman she once was."

"I never mention anything about George to her or what he did, as I figured she doesn't need to be reminded. I know that when people ask how you're coping, they're only being kind, but what they don't realise is that everyone else is asking the same question, meaning you're spending half your life talking about the very thing you're trying to forget."

"Is that what happened after Charles died?" Kate said.

"Yes. All the staff and every supplier or customer I spoke to, even though most of them hadn't even met him."

"Sorry – I was probably as guilty as the rest."

"You're different. If either you or Bella ever need anything, you can come to me – I hope you realise that."

"Can you teach? Deportment, perhaps."

Once again, Sean gave her that lopsided grin she adored.

"I have other skills," he said.

"I'm sure you do. They're just buried – very, very deep."

"Cheeky madam. Me working here would *give* them something to complain about, but in case you get desperate, throw me that book – I'll stick it on my head and get practising my posture."

"Thanks, but I'll pass on your kind offer."

"Fair enough. If you change your mind, you know where to find me. In the meantime, what are you going to do about losing your pupils?"

"There's not a lot I can do. But I can't let it escalate, so I'm going to curb the way I speak even more. I'm already careful, because although this isn't a typical finishing school, they don't want their little darlings picking up an Irish twang."

"You don't normally give in so easily."

Kate deliberately thickened her accent. "Now, for sure, I'm not giving in at all. I'm fierce mad about it. But I'm a mature woman of business and The Grange comes first, so it does."

Sean roared.

"Now, you said you wanted to chat. Is it about married life?" Kate said.

"How did you guess?"

"Frankly, although I only see her now and again, God help me, but I struggle to stop myself from throttling your wife."

"You and me both."

71

"Your mother told me about Yvette dropping hints the size of boulders that something is amiss. Come on – let's go into the parlour. I'll ask Cook to make us some tea – or coffee, if you prefer?"

Kate poured, watching as Sean devoured three scones. At times like this she was glad the table was between them. He looked so vulnerable, the barrier would stop her from doing something stupid like kissing him and ruining their friendship forever.

"What did you say?" she said, realising Sean had been speaking.

"My fault – I launched into it. I was explaining that the month after Charles' death, Yvette agreed to a divorce. Providing I comply with her terms."

"Blimey. You kept that quiet."

"It was part of her demands. That we tell no one and wait at least six months."

"Why the delay? I'll help her pack her bags. Heck, I'll carry them to the station for her. The woman is a gombeen – as shady as they come. She must be a nightmare to live with. You'll be well shot of her."

"It must be difficult for her, too."

"I should have more compassion for her." Kate shrugged. "But I can't stand the banshee, so I don't – and there's no point in my pretending otherwise."

Sean laughed nervously. "After her initial shock that I'd want to leave her, she agreed to the divorce readily enough. In fact, she was positively eager. I don't want to rush her and there's only a couple more months to wait – April, hopefully – but I wish it was over now. Not having any booze isn't easy. And living in a disaster of a marriage isn't helping any."

"Those weeks immediately after Charles' death, when you told everyone that you had a stomach bug, were you dealing with the effects of not drinking?"

Sean nodded. "Yes. At first it was terrible. Until I gave it up, I hadn't admitted even to myself the hold it had over me."

"You don't have to talk about it if you'd prefer not to."

"To be honest, it'll be a relief to tell someone in the family about my struggle. Yvette seems oblivious. Either that or she simply doesn't care enough to ask. The only person who knows anything is Max. He was terrific and sat up with me all night for days." Sean briefly explained about the cravings and effects of withdrawal.

"I suspected as much. But for once in my life, I was being tactful and didn't ask you outright. I wish you'd told me – I could have helped."

"You've had enough to do supporting Bella. And to be honest, I didn't want anyone to pity me, not even you."

"You're over the worst now?"

"Occasionally, I still long for a glass – it may always be that way. Thankfully, so far I've resisted."

"In future if you have a problem, with anything, ask for my help. Promise?"

"Thank you. You're a brick."

"Not the most flattering description a woman can ask for, but I'll take what I can get."

"Sorry – I'm not great at giving compliments."

"Ah, forget it. I forgive you."

"Seriously, we may not be blood relations, but we're far closer than many siblings – or husbands and wives, for that matter. Your friendship is incredibly important to me."

"Away with you. I'll be crying in a minute," she said, hurriedly tidying the tea tray before he noticed her desperation.

They had a strong connection and if only Sean could see that they could be more than friends, Kate was certain they'd be happy together. But she wasn't good enough for him. She wasn't ugly, but she was no beauty, either. Whereas in her eyes, Sean was perfect.

"Kate, have I embarrassed you? I didn't mean to."

"Not at all."

"Good. May I have the last scone?" he said.

"I can hardly refuse when you're already taking it off the plate."

He grinned as he spread it with butter.

She fiddled nervously with her brooch. Why had he confided in her? If only her love were reciprocated.

"As for your divorce," Kate said, "hold on a while longer and Yvette will be out of your life. Or as much as she can, as she's still the boys' mother. I assume they'll remain with you?"

"She's returning to America once matters are settled."

Kate clapped her hands. "Perfect. The further away she is, the better it'll be for everyone. Yvette divides our family. Most of us hate her, whereas your mother just dislikes her immensely."

Sean laughed again. "Pierre and Josh might miss her."

"They can't miss a mother they've never had. Bella spends more time with them than Yvette does. Besides which, growing up with a mother who doesn't love you properly can do far more damage than not having one. When they get older, you can take them to visit her."

"I will. It's not my intention to shut her out of their

74

lives. Yvette was the one who said she was longing to go back to America. Why, I'm not sure. She left there as a young child, so I doubt she can remember much."

"If it's what she wants, let her go. I joke about her, and I probably seem heartless, but I've always suspected that she trapped you into marriage. And then from the moment you put that ring on her finger, she undermined your confidence and belittled you at every opportunity."

Sean stopped eating and shook his head slowly. "It takes two to make a child – I was as much to blame. Yvette thought I'd returned home a rich man and when she found out that her uncle had swindled me out of my fortune, I was a disappointment."

"Did you claim to have money?"

"We never discussed it and she crept into my room that first night we met. At the party, I'd overindulged and she said I should stay over. There's no excuse for my behaviour, but I didn't mislead her about my financial situation."

"As I said, you'll be better off when there's an ocean between you."

"I'm concerned she might change her mind or try to delay matters. I suspect she's not being truthful about something."

"Like what?"

Sean shrugged. "She claims Pierre is aware we're separating. I admit he's occasionally temperamental, but it's only to be expected at his age and being deaf must isolate him."

"I doubt she'd give a second thought to either Pierre or Josh if it suited her, so I'd ignore anything she says regarding them. What other demands did she make in return for your freedom?"

"That I shoulder the blame for the breakdown of the marriage and give her almost every penny we have."

"It'll be worth it. You can make more money, but no one can get back lost years of their life. I suppose I'd better do the right thing and ask – are you certain there's no hope for the two of you?"

"None."

"Good. That saves me having to beat some sense into you."

"The thing is, I'm in love with someone else."

Kate's heart pounded in her ears. Please let him say he loved her . . .

"With Jane."

No. No. No. Her words strangled her. "*Jane*?"

"You'll think I'm a rat. But once I'm divorced, we're going to marry."

She heard herself gasp. "You're having an affair with *Jane*?"

"Not exactly. We've shared a few kisses, nothing more. Things might easily have gone further, but I couldn't do that to her. I love her too much."

Kate swallowed, fighting the urge to vomit. She rubbed her fingers across her mouth. Why the hell was she reacting so badly? She'd always suspected Sean cared for Jane, but dear God, this was unbearable. She mustn't cry. He didn't realise she loved him. She'd played her part too well, continually acting the fool and joking with him. To him, they were friends, family.

"You're shocked?" he said.

"No. Erm, Sean, I-I . . . I'm not sure why you're telling me this."

"Because I'm a selfish swine."

"So, we've established that you're a swine. Sorry, that was meant to be funny. You're nothing of the sort."

"It's true, though. I needed to say the words out loud, other than to Jane, but I shouldn't have involved you in my deceit."

Her heart practically broke every time she thought about never being held by him, being able to feel his lips on hers . . . How much more was she expected to cope with?

"I've loved her from the moment I saw her," Sean said. "You must think I'm mad. But if you'd experienced the intensity of the emotion, you'd understand."

If she spoke now, she'd break down. Her mind shot back to that first day in her father's house when Bella had introduced her to Sean. She understood exactly what it was like to fall for someone instantly. Kate listened as he explained about how his relationship with Jane had developed, nodding at appropriate points until she felt composed enough to speak.

"Sean, we've always been able to talk to each other, but Jane may be furious that you and I are discussing your involvement."

"Jane admires you – she wouldn't mind. And I had hoped you might understand."

"Why? I've never been in a relationship with a man."

Thankfully, he didn't know about her liaisons or her affair with Garrett Ackerley. Sean might not love her, but she needed him to respect her.

"Apart from Edward, you're the smartest person I know and I need some advice," he said.

"Go on."

"Jane wants me to tell Yvette about us. Should I?"

"Definitely not. You can't ruin Jane's reputation for the sake of a couple of months. After the divorce, people may say you got together too soon and suspect something was going on before, but they'll overlook it. Whereas Jane being called an adulteress is another matter entirely. You must sit Yvette down again and make it clear you won't wait longer than previously agreed."

"I told Jane the same thing. Thank you, Kate. We'll bide our time. But it's obvious from your face that you don't approve. I should have realised that you'd be scandalised. All I can do is apologise for overstepping the boundaries of our friendship. I don't want to spoil things between us."

Kate's mind whirled. She'd never dreamed anything could hurt this much. Regardless, she beat her own emotions into submission.

"You haven't affected our relationship. I could hardly tell you to come to me if you had a problem and then act as though you've offended my sensibilities the first time you do."

"You're not angry?"

"Of course not. Does Jane know about your difficulties with alcohol?"

"No – I don't want to put her off before we even get together. Besides, it'll never be an issue in the future."

"*Really*? You've acknowledged the desire may never go away."

"What I mean is, I won't allow it to become an issue. My drinking started after I found out that my real parents dumped me in a church, close to death. Not that I'm making excuses, but it made me feel worthless. And when James Brakenridge took me to the races without my mother's knowledge and got me drunk, I realised that for a short while, booze stopped the questions and the turmoil in my head. With Jane, I'll have no reason to drink. Life will be pleasant – joyous."

"Secrets are rarely a good idea."

"Once I'm divorced, I'll tell her everything. I'm not completely stupid. I don't want to be married to another woman who regrets our union."

Kate waited as Sean pushed his hand through his dark hair, glad that he was doing most of the talking, giving her time to compose herself.

"I can't tell her yet because we've not been sneaking around, meeting up away from the house. So apart from the night Charles committed suicide and we talked nearly all night, Jane and I have only had a few snatched moments together. I can hardly pop in while she's teaching Pierre sign language and say, by the way, I'm a raging alcoholic. But don't worry – hopefully I've got it under control."

"I take your point. So, all you can do is wait for your divorce. And in the meantime, you need to stay out of Jane's bed. If you sleep together, someone will find out. Sure, they always do."

"You're right, of course. The anticipation might kill me first, though."

Kate dug her fingernails into the palms of her hands. She mustn't cry. Until today, buried in the cobwebs at the back of her mind, she'd still harboured the hope that Sean would eventually realise she was the woman for him. Now, she had to kill that hope forever.

"Kate, have I said something wrong?"

She stood abruptly. "Not at all. But tomorrow's French lesson won't plan itself, so I must get on."

Sean looked nonplussed. "I won't keep you any longer.

Shall I pop into the dining hall and say hello to Bella?"

"The last thing I need is my pupils swooning over their tapioca. I'll tell Bella you called round. Now, off you go and keep Yvette sweet, so she doesn't mess up your plans."

"I knew you'd be supportive." Sean walked to the door and paused. He looked back over his shoulder. "Kate, you do like Jane, don't you? Your opinion matters."

"She's a dear. How could anyone not like her?"

"You look . . . well, strained."

"Now away wi' yeh, you eejit. Me head's in a jangle at the thought of havin' to drop me accent to save my school, so it is."

She was aware Sean was laughing as he walked down the corridor towards the front door and she buried her face in her hands. Had she told him to stay out of Jane's bed for his sake? Or to give herself time to accept it? She wasn't sure.

"Lord, give me the strength," she murmured.

Chapter 8

O n a wintry afternoon in March, Victoria entered the nursery of Faredene Hall with Jess. It was a bright room with green curtains and matching eiderdowns on the two beds. Kitty was kneeling on the floor dropping books into a packing crate. She brushed a stray strand of hair off her face as she looked up.

"Victoria, what do you think of this blinkin' weather? The daffodils are buried under a foot of snow. If I was a brass monkey, I'd be shaking in me tree. And it's as windy as our Brian when he eats peas."

"You crease me up, Kitty," Jess said.

Kitty might dress like a lady now, but her turn of phrase and sense of humour was still that of her childhood.

"Kitty, you're incorrigible," Victoria said.

"True, but everyone loves me as I am, so there's no point in me trying to change at my age."

"Do you need a hand with your packing?" Victoria asked.

"No thanks, love. Our Jess offered to get the maids to do it, but I asked Tatty Head for the day off so I could make sure we're ready for our move tomorrow."

"I trust you didn't call Sean that when you were asking for time off," Victoria said, smiling.

"He loves my little name for him. If you've got time

for a natter, park your behind on the chair by the fire for a few minutes. Sit yourself down on Jake's bed, Jess, if you're sure you won't wet yourself laughing. I don't want him moaning about sleeping in a damp patch."

"You've no worries there, hun. I've a bladder the size of a hot-air balloon."

"Jess, Harry and I have had an extremely productive meeting," Victoria said, hoping to move the conversation away from bathroom habits.

"Victoria's got everything in hand," Jess said. "The first lot of residents have already moved out of the Rows and into temporary accommodation, and work to renovate the properties starts Monday."

"All thanks to you and Harry. If you weren't being so generous, I doubt the building firm would have been willing to start so soon. Although we need a thaw or the workmen will spend most of their time breaking ice off their tools," Victoria said.

"Sounds painful." Kitty giggled.

"Aww, Kitty, you're a tonic." Jess laughed. "They'll find a way to get started. They know Harry won't skimp and will pay their bills on time because they're the same firm that did this place."

"And our new place," Kitty said. "They're making a fortune from our Harry. He could have built a palace with the amount he's spent."

"Harry says there was no point making all that money from the oil strike then letting it sit in his safe or at the bank. He'd rather use some to improve folks' lives," Jess said proudly.

"The residents are in for a pleasant surprise when they move back in. Some of them still don't believe that they'll all have running water and a water closet in their own backyard," Victoria said.

"It's a flaming disgrace Hornby-Smythe didn't sort the problem long before now, if you ask me. If I'd known years ago Ethel and her husband owned them, I'd have sewn itching powder into her corsets while we were making them. I'd have loved seeing her run around like she'd got fleas," Kitty said.

"Are you looking forward to moving into your new home, Kitty?" Victoria asked.

Kitty glanced at her sister-in-law. "No offence, Jess. Living with you an' Harry is great, but I've got to admit, I can't wait to have our own place again."

"I understand, honey. You can't beat having your own fireside. Mama died sleeping in the hayloft on the farm she worked on . . ." Jess paused. "It's not right, people having to live like animals."

"Aww, Jess, I never realised," Kitty said.

"No point in talking about the past," Jess said.

"We'll never be able to repay you an' our Harry for yer kindness, renovating that old farmhouse for us. Or Harry becoming a partner in Paynes Brewery with Albert, 'cos he couldn't have managed it on his own. But most of all, I'll never forget that you didn't hesitate to take us in when we turned up on your doorstep after the burglary at our pub. A lot of women would have resented another woman coming into their home. Especially one wi' a gob on them like me. Whereas you did everythin' you could to make us feel welcome."

"We've loved having you all here. And we're grateful you're still going to be close by. If I had my way, you'd stay with us permanently," Jess said.

"Aye, family should stick together. Speaking of which, our Milly telephoned to say Jane arrived safely. Hopefully, she won't persuade her to emigrate to Blackpool an' all," Kitty said.

Victoria decided the best option was not to engage Kitty on the topic of her sister and remained silent.

"It's daft, because your place is on our grounds and I can see the chimney from here," Jess said, "but I'm going to miss you. David and his family are just as near, but they hardly ever come round." Her normally smooth skin crinkled as she appeared to struggle to hold back tears.

Kitty, who had her head bent over a pile of books, didn't notice. Victoria moved to join Jess on the bed so she could squeeze her hand.

"This place is too grand for our brother," Kitty said. "David likes the quiet life. Whereas my lot, we'll never be away – and our boys will still play in the grounds. Although why you'd want them outside your door with all the noise they make is beyond me."

"Jake and Brian are the nearest thing I've got to children of my own. You'll eat with us sometimes, I hope?"

"You've got no worries on that score. I'm like the smell of month-old haddock – there's no getting rid of me."

Albert Nelson's bulk filled the doorframe as he entered the nursery. He hoisted an enormous trunk off his shoulder onto the floor beside this wife.

"Shove it over by the wardrobe, will yeh, big fella? That one is for their clothes," Kitty said.

"The footmen could have fetched that down from the attic for you," Jess said.

Albert's smile softened his hard features as the burly man flexed his biceps. "I've not reached the stage where

I need someone fetching an' carrying for me yet. Thanks all the same, Jess."

"I'm probably wasting my time packing," Kitty said. "Those two will no doubt want something the minute I've closed the lid." Her eyebrows came together. "They should be in by now. I told them we were having a special supper for our last night living here."

"They won't be far. They popped in earlier to borrow my cap to put on a snowman they'd made. Said they were going to look for animal prints in the woods next," Albert added.

Kitty shook her head. "If the little monkeys aren't in soon, I might smack their backsides for them. Don't roll yer eyes at me, Albert Nelson. There's a first time for everything."

"If you say so, my love." Albert lit his pipe while his wife continued to pile books into the trunk. "I'll leave you to finish off here. Perhaps 'Arry will take a walk wi' me to see if we can find 'em."

Hours later, Victoria watched as her friend once again moved towards the French doors in the morning room.

Pressing her nose against the glass, Kitty peered into the blackness cloaking the grounds of the Hall as she spoke. "Nine o' bloody clock!"

Unnecessarily, because she was fully aware of the time, Victoria glanced at the carriage clock that stood on the marble mantel below a huge gilt mirror.

"Do you honestly believe they're safe?" Kitty asked.

"They'll come scurrying in any minute now, demanding to be fed and claiming they got so carried away playing in the snow that they didn't realise the time."

"They'll be soaked through – it's turned to sleet. They

can be little buggers, but they'd never stay out this late 'cos they know I worry. Besides, he won't admit it, because he wants Jake to think he's as fearless as him, but Brian is afraid of the dark."

The sound of voices coming from the hallway halted Victoria's response and Kitty shot to the door.

"If they're safe, I swear I'll never raise me voice to them again," Kitty said.

Victoria followed, her fingers crossed behind her back. Her heart sank at the sight of Albert standing alone in his greatcoat, unwinding his muffler from around his face. He stroked his moustache before clasping Kitty's arms.

"No sign of 'em. Sorry, love."

Kitty glared up at him. "What the bloody hell are yeh doing back here if you've not found them? Where's those brothers o' mine?"

"Harry's nipped to the kitchen to feed his dogs an' make sure the servants have a bite to eat, so David and his lad went home for an extra pair of socks. Their feet are like ice."

"I'll bleeding kill those two. Their nephews might be dying in a ditch an' they're complaining about being cold and fussing over blasted mutts."

"Stop talking tripe. Yer brothers are worried an' all. They love those lads. You know that as well as I do."

"Sorry. I'm beside myself. If it was summer, I wouldn't be so concerned. Was there no trace at all?"

"The dogs picked up a scent down to the river but lost it there."

"Aww, Jesus! You don't think they've fallen in?"

"Calm down – the trail could be days old. The boys spend half their lives in the woods." He crossed to the fire, holding his hands out to the blaze. "I hope they've had the sense to take shelter somewhere, 'cos the wind is making it feel ten times colder than it is."

"As if I need you telling me that, yeh great useless lump. If *you're* freezing, what the heck do you think it's like for them?"

Albert turned his back to the fire and stared at Kitty.

"There's hardly a pick on either of them," Kitty added. "An' they've nowt to warm their backsides on."

"I understand well enough what danger they're in, so there's no need for you to be glaring at me and throwin' insults around."

Kitty's tears flowed unchecked. "I just want them home, so I can hold them in me arms."

"That's what I want an' all," Albert said, kissing his wife's forehead.

"Edward was here while you were out, Albert," said Victoria. "You've not long missed him. He's driven round to the school to help Bella and Kate check the outbuildings, but before he went, he telephoned the police. They're sending some men to assist with the search in the morning."

Albert lit his pipe. "Thank him for me, Victoria. We'll be going back out in a few minutes."

"I'm going with yeh. I can't sit here any longer tearing me hair out," Kitty said.

"Stay here with Victoria in case they come home," Albert said.

"No bloody chance."

"You're not traipsing round the woods in that get-up."

"Since when do you tell me what I can and can't do, Albert Nelson?"

Albert raised his eyebrows and Kitty glanced down at her skirt and silk blouse.

"Fine! I'm going upstairs to change, but don't you dare leave without me, 'cos if yeh do, I'll go out on me own."

Albert sighed, tapping his pipe then emptying it into the fire. "All right – there's no point in arguing wi' yeh."

Less than ten minutes later, Kitty clambered down the stairs wearing a thick skirt and a plain blouse, wrestling her arms into her brown woollen coat.

Victoria reached out to fasten Kitty's top button. "I want no arguments. Jess has brought this scarf and some gloves from her room for you because you're so stubborn, we knew you'd come down without."

"I know yeh mean well, but give over, will yeh? How can I wrap up when my babies are freezing? I only changed 'cos Albert was kicking up a fuss," Kitty snapped.

"I can be just as stubborn as you. Now, put these on. When they're found – and they will be – you'll be no use to them if you've got pneumonia or frostbite," said Victoria.

Kitty knuckled away a tear that was escaping from her puffy eyes.

"Aww, Victoria, forgive me. I'm an ungrateful bitch. Once Edward gets back, you must both get off home and have some supper. You've had nowt to eat."

"Neither of us will leave until Jake and Brian are safe and sound. Jess is organising some food for anyone who's hungry."

"We shouldn't be involving you in our troubles."

"You're talking daft, Kitty. We're as good as family. This is where we want to be, helping in any way we can. Even if all we can do is provide moral support," said Victoria.

Once the search party had set off again, Victoria

telephoned Sean from Harry's office and asked if he and his male servants could be available at first light, explaining that she'd let him know if they found them overnight.

"Harris isn't up to tramping round all day, but I'll bring the others. Are you sure you don't want us to come now? I won't rest knowing they're missing," Sean said.

"Wait until morning, darling. Harry told Jess that no matter what Albert said to Kitty, it's too dark to find them tonight and they'll be forced to give up soon."

"Do you think the boys will be all right?"

"Honestly, Sean? I don't know. But anything else is unthinkable. All we can do is pray."

After putting the phone down, Sean went into Yvette's private parlour, where she now spent every evening while he was in his study. It was a lonely way for them both to live but preferable to being around each other.

She laid her embroidery beside her on the pink chintz sofa, eyeing him suspiciously.

"What's the matter with you?" she said.

Nothing that putting you on the next ship to America wouldn't solve, Sean thought.

"I'll probably be taking Max and the other men up to the Hall tomorrow. Apart from Harris, that is."

"Why, pray tell? With their wealth, if Harry Gibbs needs extra servants for the day, he can hire them."

"Jake and Brian are missing. They were playing in the woods earlier and haven't come home."

"Hardly surprising. They're practically feral. No doubt they'll turn up before long. That woman has no control over them."

"Kitty's an excellent mother. She adores her boys."

"Unlike me, you mean."

"You said that, not me."

"I suppose I should be grateful you've got the decency to leave me the butler."

"Believe me, if Harris didn't have gout, I'd be taking him as well."

Yvette glared. "Well, as long as all this fuss doesn't affect our dining at the Masons later in the week. We've not been seen in public together for months. People are talking. Now, if you've finished, I'd prefer to be alone."

Sean left without responding.

Chapter 9

Victoria poked angrily at the dying embers, asking herself yet again if Jake and Brian could survive the night outside in freezing temperatures. How would Kitty cope with losing two children? Plenty of women got through it. Surely it changed you, though – made everything that followed pointless.

Jess, unable to stem the flow of tears, was keeping out of the way. Although she proclaimed they'd waste most of it, she was still in the kitchens watching the cook and the maids prepare warming food.

As the clock struck midnight, Victoria heard Kitty shouting in the hallway.

"Youse lot can carry on with life as though my boys don't matter, but this is killin' me."

"No one will give up until they're found," Albert boomed. "But it's too dark. Even with the lamps, you can't see more than a yard. That poor lad from one of 'Arry's farms has broken his wrist. We can't risk someone else getting hurt. Our best chance of finding our boys is if we have a couple of hours' rest and go back out first thing."

"I don't bloody care about anyone else," Kitty bellowed. The door opened and she marched in alone. She tossed her filthy hat and coat on a chair and pulled a twig from her tangled hair. "I can't believe Albert has called off the bleedin' search until dawn. If owt happens to my boys, it'll be the finish of me. And him, because I'll swing for him."

Victoria brushed a piece of fluff off her own beige skirt as she considered how to respond. She couldn't think of a single reason to tell the truth. A lie was the only viable option.

"They'll find them alive and well, I'm sure of it." Even to Victoria's own ears, the words sounded insincere.

Kitty plucked at the fingers of her soiled kid gloves and threw them on top of her coat. "Yeh can't be sure – no one can. They might both be at the bottom of the quarry."

"You've got to stop thinking the worst."

"I'm trying, but I can't help it. You'd be the same if it was one of yours."

There was no point Victoria denying it. She'd have been frantic in Kitty's position. She picked up Kitty's outdoor things, moving them off Harry and Jess' elaborate upholstery.

"It looks as though you've been dragged behind a galloping horse. What on earth happened?" Victoria asked.

Kitty pulled at her navy skirt, which was ripped, the bottom sodden.

"It's nowt. I just slipped a few times."

"You look as though you lay down in it."

"The sleet isn't heavy now, but it's been coming down for hours and now it's like a flaming quagmire in the woods. Me boots kept getting stuck. And even with the lanterns, it's hard to see the tree roots. I wanted to carry on, but Albert practically carried me back here."

"Get them boots off, and your stockings, then come over here by the fire. You're fro . . ."

"Frozen?" Kitty said sharply.

"Oh, Kitty. Sorry, I shouldn't have—"

"Don't be. I didn't mean to bite yer head off again. You're here wi' me, but my sisters ain't."

"Would you like me to telephone Blackpool in the morning and let them all know what's happening?" Victoria asked.

"No, they can't do anything to help, so there's no point troubling them. I don't want to set our Milly off fretting – you know how she worries."

Victoria crossed to the rosewood sideboard and poured a sherry. She handed the glass to Kitty.

"Drink this – it'll steady your nerves."

Kitty downed the dark liquid before she spoke again.

"Me lads aren't bad 'uns, are they?"

"Far from it. They're like you. Full of fun and mischief. You could never meet two more loving boys." Victoria touched Kitty's sleeve. "Your blouse is wet through, as well. Please slip upstairs and put on a dry one."

"In a minute. What do you suppose has happened to them?"

Poor Kitty had asked this same question so many times.

"One thing I know is that Jake is extremely resourceful. No matter what, he'll be taking care of Brian."

Kitty wrapped her arms around herself. "He's a smart one, is our Jake. Me head is in bits. One minute I'm convinced they're dead, the next I'm certain they're alive."

"If you won't get changed, then sit down. If you're determined to go out again tomorrow, you need some rest."

Without argument, Kitty slumped onto the chintz chair.

"Jess is still belowstairs. There's hot soup, venison pie

and sandwiches for everyone. It should be ready now. Can I fetch you something?" Victoria asked.

"No thanks, love. Where's your Edward?"

"He's fretting that he can't go out looking with the other men. He never complains about the discomfort his leg and hand cause him, but on occasions like this, he says his deformities make him feel useless."

"There's no need for him to feel bad. He can't go out in this weather with his limp. He'd be falling all the time." Kitty pointed at her legs. "You can see the mess I got meself in. I'll not admit it to Albert, but he spent most of the time hoisting me out the mud."

"Edward's in Harry's study examining old maps of the estate for places the boys could be trapped."

"If they've fallen down an old mine shaft or the like, we'll never find them." Kitty pulled at her hair. "You're not saying it, but you've all given up on me lads. I can tell by your faces."

The door to the morning room opened once more and Albert entered, still dressed for outdoors and carrying a lantern. Kitty sprang to her feet.

"You promised to search all night. You bloody liar! If they die, I'll never forgive you," she screeched as she pummelled his broad chest.

He slammed his lantern on the coffee table. "You're being unfair, love. I'm at me wits' end, as well. Listen, Edward has identified some caves on the other side of the woodland. 'Arry and me are going to take his dogs over that way first thing to see if they can pick up a scent."

"What are we waiting for? Let's get over there now."

"Kitty, love, talk sense. We can't be stumbling around searching caves at this time of night."

As Kitty opened her mouth to speak, Albert held up his hand.

"I let you have your own way in most things, but I'm firm on this, me darlin'. You're coming into the kitchen for a bite an' then you're lying down and at least trying to nod off for a couple of hours – that's all there is to it."

"But it's so bloody cold. And they'll be starvin'. They eat more than a grown man an' they've had nowt since lunch."

Albert skirted Kitty and walked towards the fireplace. "One day won't harm them," he said reasonably.

"They'll be scared. I'm supposed to keep them safe. This is my fault. I'm a lousy mother."

Victoria went to Kitty's side, draping her arm around her shoulder.

"You're a wonderful mother – none better. As for Jake, he's been playing explorers and whatnot since he could walk. If I know him, he'll have found somewhere for them to sleep. You need some food and rest, as well. At dawn, you can be back out there. No one will give up, I promise you."

Victoria tried to turn Kitty from the door and guide her to the sofa, but she held firm until they heard a gut-wrenching sob from behind. Albert was resting his hands on the mantel, his shoulders shaking.

Kitty rushed forwards. "Oh, Albert, love."

"It's n-n-not your pla-place to protect them," he stammered. "It's m-mine. I'm so ashamed, I can hardly l-look you in the eye."

"Don't talk daft," said Kitty, reaching up to place her hand on his shoulder. "You shouldn't listen to me when I'm ranting. I don't blame you."

Victoria was shaken by the sight of the hulk of a man breaking down and moved to the far side of the room to give the couple privacy as they talked.

Albert said, "You married me to p-protect you."

"I wed you because I love you."

"Aye, now you do. B-but I'm no fool. If you'd not been through hell, what with the rape, then your Teddy being murdered by Brakenridge's men . . . Well, you'd never have looked at me, a widower with two small boys."

"I love your lads and so do Jake and Brian. We've all missed them since they signed on as sailors."

"Aye, but you picked me because I had a bit of brass and because I'm built like a brick outhouse, so you thought I could keep you safe. I didn't mind 'cos I wanted you. But now I've let you and our sons down," he said.

"No, you haven't." Kitty wrapped her arms around his waist and leaned her head against his chest. "Our Jake will get them through. Now come on – let's get that bite to eat you mentioned."

As they left the room clutching hands, Victoria was once again astounded by Kitty's ability to put her own fears and pain to one side and think of others.

The following evening, after a fruitless day of searching, Victoria watched as Kitty chewed her nails to the quick. Sean had once gone missing for a short while when her housekeeper, Bridie, who had been suffering bouts of memory loss, took him for a walk and couldn't find her way home. Victoria had been beside herself. If he'd been gone for this long, she'd probably have lost her mind. She was sick of lying to her friend. Of hearing herself say they'll be fine, don't worry, when she knew that with each passing hour, the chances of discovering two bodies increased.

The grounds of Faredene Hall stretched for several miles and once you left the formal gardens, they became a mixture of pasture and woods, crossing the river in the east and the quarry to the west, both of which would be deadly if the boys had fallen in. After this length of time, they all admitted, out of Kitty's hearing, that the best hope of finding Jake and Brian alive was if they were injured or trapped somewhere, unable to call for help.

"That bloody policeman needs my boot up his arse. Fancy stopping the search when it's only ten o'clock," Kitty said.

"It's been a long day. Everyone set off before it was light this morning and we'll all be back out again when the sun is up. You'll do a better job when you've rested," Victoria said.

Kitty sprang out of her seat, gripping her skirt as though wringing water from it.

"They could have sent a bobby whose chin has seen a razor. He can't be more than eleven."

"Kitty, he's older than he looks. And he said the sergeant will be out in the morning."

"Morning! He should be here now. It's obvious the daft young 'un thinks Albert has hit one of them and they've run away."

"No doubt you put him straight."

"I said what the hell do you take me for, yeh stupid git. Do I look like the kind of soft mare who would stand by and let someone knock holes in me sons? Besides, my Albert never even raises his voice to them. What's more, no one else has ever laid a hand on them, either."

"I'm sure he didn't ask any imprudent questions after that."

Kitty gave her a sad smile. "You'd think not, but the gormless lump asked me if I can think of any other reason they could have scarpered. So I said why the hell would they do that? They've loved living up at the Hall here with their uncle and auntie. Jess spoils 'em rotten an' they want for nowt. They're right excited about moving into our new house. We've promised to get them puppies of their own once we're settled. So instead of asking daft questions, he should go out an' bloody find them." She pulled a handkerchief from her pocket and dried her tears.

Jess, who had been curled up on the sofa staring blindly into space, said, "I suppose they must look into all possibilities, honey."

"He'll be looking at the end of my fist if he tries to suggest once more that Albert has hurt them," Kitty said.

Victoria would never admit it, but if she didn't rest soon, she'd fall asleep standing.

Tentatively, she said, "Kitty, dear, perhaps we should all try to get some sleep."

"You get yourself upstairs, love. Edward looks worn out. An' I'm right grateful to you both for stopping over again."

Jess stood. "I doubt any of us will drop off, but the maids have lit fires in all the rooms. If you don't mind, Kitty, I'll go up and make sure Harry gets a hot drink and into bed after he's washed."

"Aye, you go on up," Kitty said.

Once the door had closed, Victoria said, "Come on, Kitty. You need to lie down. Do it for Albert's sake. He won't go to bed if you're down here."

"What's the point? Last night I didn't get a wink. When I close me eyes, I conjure pictures that terrify me."

"At least sit in the chair in your room so he knows where you are. You never know – you might manage an hour."

Victoria knew it would take a minor miracle for Kitty to rest while her children were missing but supported her friend as the two women slowly made their way upstairs.

At six the next morning, following several hours of worrying and about ten minutes' sleep, Sean yawned as he climbed out of his motor car. Normally, it was thoughts of Jane that kept him awake, but for the last two nights, instead of fantasising about her sharing his bed, he'd thought of nothing but the missing boys.

"Wait here. I'll find out which direction they want us to go today," he said to Max, his tall red-headed valet, and the other three men he'd brought with him.

Leaving them on the driveway with the rest of the search party, he made his way into the spacious entrance hall where the family were assembling. He approached his mother, who immediately used her fingers to tidy his hair in the same way she had when he was a child.

"Morning, darling. You look drained," she said.

"No more than anyone else."

"Most of the snow has melted, but I expect it's going to pour and that won't make the task any easier."

"There's even more men turned out this morning."

"Every man from the estate and the farms is here again," Victoria said. "And David got word to the town, so there's a few others turned up. Some can't help because they're working, but if we've not found them by the time the mills and factories finish for half-day closing, more are coming."

"Have Kate and Bella arrived yet?"

"They can't both keep leaving the school at the same time. They need to keep things as normal as possible for their pupils. Bella's here, though, and she's brought their gardener and handyman again."

"Where is she?" Sean asked, glancing around.

"She's taken some chap called Richard Yates through to the kitchens to fill a flask with hot tea before he sets off. She seemed pleased to see him. Do you know anything about that?" his mother said, wearing her interrogation face.

"Not a thing," Sean lied.

His mother eyed him sceptically.

"Is Kate coming over this afternoon?" Sean asked.

"Yes. And this morning she's going to check their cellars and outhouses again."

"Is there any point?"

"We're prepared to try anything. Even Anne's offered assistance. She's gone to Wiltshire visiting a friend, but she's sent some of her servants over."

Kitty descended the ornate curved stairs unsteadily. There were dark circles under her bloodshot eyes and she was gripping the bannister, each step seemingly taking immense effort. As she reached the bottom tread, she crossed the room to Sean's side, pecking him on the cheek.

"Thanks for coming again, Tatty Head," she said wearily.

"Where else would I be?"

"*You* believe they're still alive, don't you, Sean?"

"They're tough, like their mother."

"I'd feel if they were dead, wouldn't I?"

Sean pulled her into a bear hug. "I'm certain you would. We'll find them today, you'll see."

100

She gulped. "If anything has happened to them, I'll end up in that asylum where they took our Teddy that time me dad let him take the blame for stealing."

Albert came to her side, nodding in greeting to Sean.

"Kitty, darlin', can I not persuade you to stay here this morning? You've not slept again an' yer in no fit state to be trudging about all day."

"No bloody chance. I'm not sitting here being tortured by what's going round in me head. Victoria, Edward and Jess will be here if they come back. Besides, I can't drop off. If I don't get me lads back, I'll never sleep again."

"All right, love." Albert shrugged, his face drawn, anguished. "Come on – we'd best get started."

As they made their way outside, Sean put his arm round Kitty's waist. She rested her head against him as they walked.

"What's the postie doing up here this early? He's peddling like his life depends on it. Maybe he's seen my boys," she said, pulling away from Sean's side.

The young man jumped off his bicycle, allowing it to crash to the floor.

"Mrs Nelson, this has got no stamp on it and the post mistress was about to put it in the dead mail box," he said, waving a crumpled envelope on which "Faredene Hall" was written in a scrawled hand. "I heard about your sons and, well, who would be daft enough to mail a letter without a name and without paying the postage?"

Kitty's hand clutched at the collar of her coat. "You open it, Sean. I've got a horrible feeling."

Sean read the note.

"Jesus Christ. Someone has abducted your boys. I'm so sorry, Kitty."

Chapter 10

Although it was early in the day, the brief winter was over and the Delhi heat was stifling. In a cramped, stuffy office where every surface was littered with stacks of documents and files, George held a handkerchief over his face as he pretended to sob.

Marjorie Rawlings' solicitor shifted uncomfortably in his seat. "We must be thankful the memsahib is no longer suffering. Malaria is a bad thing – it takes many good people. It is the putrid air."

"It's been heart-wrenching burying her after such a brief marriage." He shook his head dolefully. "Somehow, I must find the strength to carry on without her." He blew his nose. "So if we may get down to the issue of her estate . . . I hate financial matters and want this sordid side of things sorted as soon as possible."

"Indeed. It all appears to be straightforward."

"Neither of us expected it to happen f-for years." Once more, George pretended to wipe a fake tear. "If you remember, my wife and I b-both updated our wills immediately after our marriage, leaving everything to each other in case of a tragedy such as this."

"The memsahib had little to leave, but it all goes to you."

"I beg your pardon?"

"Mrs Bristow had little of her own—"

"My wife owns . . . owned an enormous tea plantation. What the devil are you talking about, man?"

"It has never belonged to her. It was only hers to enjoy during her lifetime. As she and her late husband had no children, it now passes to his nephew. He will arrive in one month to take possession. We have received a telegram from him insisting that you vacate the house immediately. As you have private means, would you like me to look for a suitable house?"

George gripped the edge of his chair. Thanks to that deceitful bitch, the future he'd planned had evaporated.

"I won't be staying in this godforsaken hellhole. How much *did* my wife leave me?"

As the solicitor slid a piece of paper across the table, George snatched it. It was nothing like what he'd believed Marjorie to be worth.

"How soon can I have the full amount in cash?"

"Three days."

"Good. I'll be here by nine thirty. And book me a passage on the next ship back to England."

George marched out of the office, slamming the door behind him. He gesticulated angrily to a skeletal, bedraggled man standing by a rickshaw.

"Take me to The Taj Mahal Palace Hotel and be quick about it."

He wanted a drink before returning to the plantation to collect his clothes and any valuables that were small enough to carry and that the new owner wouldn't miss. Blasted women. You couldn't trust any of them.

In the bar, George ordered a bottle of brandy. He'd

received a blow and needed to think – plan his next steps. That old trout wouldn't beat him. If he had her here now, he'd happily squeeze her fat neck until the blood vessels in her eyes burst. How dare she hide all the facts about her financial status! The conniving crow.

Half a bottle later, he was calmer. This wasn't what he'd hoped for. He should have guessed it was too good to be true when the old crone corked it only weeks after their marriage without him having helped her on her way. There was enough for a first-class ticket home and for him to live modestly for a year. Perhaps if he got a couple of tarts working for him, he could stretch it out. Hmm, it might work out all right. Women on tap and not having to pander to their stupid whims . . .

It was pointless the search going ahead now and as the estate workers and townspeople dispersed, Victoria was pleased when Mr Yates offered to drop Bella, who looked badly shaken by the news of the boys' kidnap, back at Caldwell Grange. Since her miscarriage, Bella had been particularly emotional where matters relating to children were concerned. She'd telephone to check on her later, but for now, the Gibbs family needed her support.

Victoria sat next to Kitty, and Harry, a stick-thin man, stood on the oriental rug in front of them. The police sergeant placed his helmet on the yew side table and cupped his chin.

"It's fortunate I was here this morning. This is a criminal act now. Us professionals will handle it. From what the note says, we've got four days to find them," Sergeant Roper said.

Kitty, who was sitting with her elbows resting on her

knees and her head buried in her hands, shot up, throwing up her arms, knocking Harry out of the way.

"Yeh should have been here before, yeh useless maggot. So stop wasting time and get out there hunting down the evil bleeders."

Roper glared at Kitty.

"I'm sure you understand their mother is distraught. She means no offence," Victoria said, catching Kitty's arm and pulling her back into her seat.

He nodded tersely.

"Why are they making me wait to get my babies back?" Kitty said. "If I get me hands on the vermin who's got them, I'll string them up meself."

"They'll be allowing you time to pull the sum together and let the situation sink in. In case you were thinking of not paying," Roper said.

"We'll get the money. More if needed, even if we have to sell everythin' we've got," Albert said.

"Don't talk daft, Albert. I've got the cash in the safe," Harry said.

"I'll have my men watching the gate. We'll nab them when they pick up the ransom," Roper said.

"You flaming well won't. If yeh grab 'em, they may never tell us where they've left our lads. We've got to do whatever they say." Kitty jutted out her chin.

"You should allow us to handle this our way."

From a chair towards the back of the room, Edward spoke up, his tone quietly authoritative.

"With respect, Mrs Nelson is right – the boys' safety must be priority. We don't know how many are involved. Watch them by all means, but surely the most sensible approach is to follow them at a safe distance. If someone comes for the ransom, they might have arranged with an accomplice what actions are to be taken if they don't return by a set time." He looked apologetically in Kitty's direction as the remaining colour drained from her face.

"I take your point, Mr Caldwell," said Roper.

"It's not mine and Albert's brass, so why target us?" Kitty said, jumping up again.

"Because any effing idiot could work out I'd stomp up for me nephews. Let's organise some fellas and track down anyone we think might be involved. Put the frighteners on – see if we can flush out whoever it is." Harry's angular face contorted with anger.

"Taking the law into your own hands would be a mistake. You could end up the one behind bars. I'll speak to our new inspector about you paying the ransom and make some discreet enquiries. In the meantime, I must insist you do nothing."

"Harry, you need to listen to him. If we spook them, the consequences could be dire," Edward said.

Kitty whimpered.

Once the police officer had departed, Albert led a sobbing Kitty to their bedroom.

Victoria choked back her own tears. "There's nothing you can do here for now, Sean. I'll show you out."

"In that case, I'll check on the factory. But I'll telephone later to see if you have any news or if there's anything I can do to help. Are you staying, Mother?"

"You've seen the state Kitty and Albert are in – and Jess and Harry aren't much better. Edward and I will be here until the boys are home."

*   *   *

"Doris, when Kate's finished teaching her lesson and the girls are on their break, can you please ask her to come in here?" Bella said.

"Yes, miss. And I'll fetch a pot of tea through, shall I?"

"Please."

As the parlour door clicked shut, aware that Richard had draped his arm along the back of the sofa, Bella sat forwards.

"Someone holding them hostage is dreadful, but after all this time, a lot of us men thought we were looking for bodies," he said. "At least now there's a chance of getting them back alive."

"Do you think so?"

"I wouldn't have said it otherwise. I'll never give you any flannel. It's not my way."

"Jake and Brian aren't the type to sit quiet. They'll be giving cheek to whoever has them, I'm sure of it. If the kidnappers get angry, they might kill them – if they haven't already."

"Best not think that way. The things we imagine might go wrong are often worse than what happens. The Gibbs family have money and I expect they're willing to pay up, so the kidnapper has no need to harm the boys."

"They will if they think Jake or Brian could identify them."

"True. But not every criminal is capable of murdering children. That takes a certain kind of evil."

"Growing up, I went to church because it's what my parents did. And now we have to take our pupils. But I hate going. I sit there trying to shut out the words of the sermon because it's nonsense, isn't it? If there was a God, He wouldn't let bad things happen to children. Even ones who never get the chance to take a single breath, who never get to feel their mother's arms around them or to know how much they're loved. And why doesn't He strike down the people who hurt them, like the woman who shook poor Pierre or the monster who's taken Jake and Brian?"

"I won't give you all that guff about it being part of God's plan, because none of us knows, not really. But to my mind, God doesn't judge what's good or evil and deal out punishment. He lets us all find our own way through life and at the end, we have to account for the way we lived."

"Hell, you mean?"

"Aye. Surely hell is facing up to the wrongs we've committed."

"When George left, I-I lost a baby – before it was born. Now, there's a hole in my heart that I don't believe will ever heal. I feel so guilty. Everyone said there was nothing that could have been done and it wasn't my fault, but if I hadn't been so distraught, maybe I wouldn't have miscarried. I'll never forgive myself for allowing my child to die inside me. That's the hell I'll have to face."

"Aww, Bella, then millions of women will have to suffer the same torture, because far too many babies die."

"I wish I could stop it from happening or at least ensure more of them live."

"When the girl I was courting died, my guilt was terrible, because the only doctor we could afford was a drunken old fool. A better doctor might not have made any difference, but it took me a long while to accept that. I suppose sometimes there's nothing we can do to save the ones we love."

"Do you believe we can ever make a difference?"

"I hope so, because I intend to grow my business and

make money so if anyone I love is ever sick again, I can pay for decent care."

"I had one of the best doctors in Harley Street, but it didn't help my child."

"Not everyone can be saved, Bella. Even doctors aren't infallible."

"When I was younger, I thought I might become a nurse, but when I met George I forgot about everything else."

"It's not too late."

"There's no way I could leave Kate. She rescued me from a pit of despair and made me a partner in this place. But running a school was her dream, not mine. Do I sound terribly ungrateful?"

"Not to me."

She leaned back again against Richard's arm.

"I'm glad you're here," she said.

Chapter 11

Although he struggled to stay awake or concentrate, Sean put in a full day and sorted out several matters at the factory that Darius didn't have the authority to resolve. When he returned home that evening, he found Yvette in her bedroom wearing a stunning royal blue low-cut satin dress. She was spinning round while her maid admired her.

"Do you like my new gown, Sean?"

"It's lovely, but aren't you overdressed for dinner?" he said.

"You had better hurry – we are going to be late," Yvette said.

Sean knuckled his eyes wearily. "Are you going somewhere?"

"*We* are dining out. Don't tell me you have forgotten?"

Her maid reached out to adjust the beaded neckline and Yvette smacked her hand away.

"Leave us."

"Please don't slap the servants," Sean said as Yvette's maid scurried from the room. "We've discussed it before – it's simply not acceptable to treat them that way."

"It is your fault I am so upset. This dinner has been arranged for ages."

110

Sean groaned as he remembered.

"Yvette, I'm sorry, but surely you can't still expect me to take you to the Masons'?"

"I reminded you the other day," she said, her voice rising. "Louise and Peter are expecting us. It is Peter's birthday."

"Yvette, the boys aren't missing – they've been kidnapped!"

She sprayed perfume on her long neck. "I gathered that when the servants returned."

"Then why on earth didn't you cancel our arrangements for this evening?"

"You promised me," she said. "Most men fall at my feet, yet my husband won't even take me out to dinner. What is *wrong* with you, Sean?"

She was right. He could see the desire in other men's eyes. Especially when she turned on the charm, as she often did. Perhaps he was naïve to assume she was faithful to him. But then how could he expect *her* to be when he'd broken his own vows. Not physically, but a thousand times in his heart.

"I'm sorry," he said calmly. "I'd forgotten about our plans. But under the circumstances, it would be wrong to dine out. Besides, I'm far too tired."

"You were quick enough to go to your precious factory."

"I don't have much choice. Since I set most of our capital aside for your divorce settlement, the factory pays for all of our expenses, including your gowns."

She grasped her gilded hand mirror, slamming it down on the dressing table.

"I bought one dress! A lot of women would be filling their wardrobes at your expense before the divorce goes through."

"You had three others last month."

She glared at him through the mirror.

"Penny-pinching doesn't suit you. And as you no longer need to spend every minute searching for the Nelson brats, there is no reason for us not to go out this evening."

"Don't call them that. Jake and Brian must be terrified – if they're still alive, that is."

"If they are dead, our letting Peter and Louise down won't help anyone."

"For Christ's sake, woman. Don't be so bloody callous."

"Children die all the time."

"What's got into you?"

Her attitude shocked him. Yvette had always been spoiled and selfish, but since the death of her parents, she'd also become hard and uncaring. Whether it was grief or disappointment at being married to him that was changing her, he didn't know. Whatever the cause, she was only in her twenties, but if she carried on this way, by the time she reached middle-age, Sean suspected she'd be an extremely bitter and lonely woman. Then again, perhaps freed from a marriage that clearly brought her no pleasure, Yvette would find something in life to make her happy.

"Think how we'd feel if it were our boys," he added.

Picking up the mirror again, she slammed it down for a second time, cracking the glass.

"The point is, they're not ours. Besides, I wouldn't allow my sons to run wild like Kitty does, so they wouldn't be abducted."

"No – you let some drunken hag shake Pierre senseless."

"Sean! Why do you always throw that in my face? There is no proof she even caused his deafness. Perhaps

112

he was always going to have problems. As I have said before, given that your father died before you were born, the fault could have been in his lineage."

Yvette's eyes glistened and he regretted his outburst. She infuriated him, but he didn't like to upset her. Besides, she could be right. Yvette believed Victoria was his birth mother and that she was widowed before Sean was born, whereas he was actually a foundling, so he knew nothing about his bloodline – other than his mother suspected his real parents were Irish and had emigrated to America.

"I shouldn't have said that." He rubbed his face. "But I need some sleep and I'm in no mood for socialising or playing the doting husband."

Yvette sniffed, twin tears making their way down her cheeks. "But it isn't my fault that you have been traipsing the countryside when you could have been resting. Can't you do this one little thing for me? Nobody cares about my needs."

Was this part of her games?

Yvette covered her face with her hands. Sean liked Peter and Louise and hadn't seen them for a long time – since Charles' funeral, in fact. Their parties were always entertaining, but he couldn't imagine laughing at trivial conversation while Albert and Kitty were going through hell.

"You will be more alert after you bathe," she said.

"It doesn't seem right. Just explain why I'm not there."

Yvette allowed her hands to drop dejectedly. "Please, Sean. I can't go without you – not to a formal dinner. You haven't attended anything with me for months. At first, I explained it away by telling people you were grieving for Charles. Over Christmas, I said you were unwell. Part of our deal was that you would ensure our friends didn't suspect that our marriage was in difficulty." She approached him, placing her hands on his chest as she gazed up at him. "Give me this one last evening. I was going to tell you later when we got back, but I have decided you can arrange your trip to Liverpool to obtain evidence of your infidelity and I will give you your divorce in April as we discussed."

"No delays?"

"It will be over as soon as we can make the arrangements. I have been looking into a passage to America and will stay in London until the divorce is granted."

"I have your word?"

"Yes, providing we go tonight. It would be a shame to waste the effort I have made getting ready."

He sighed. "Only on condition that we come home early."

"I think it would be best if you were cold towards me this evening. That shouldn't be too difficult for you. As we will be telling people soon, they will remember how beautiful I looked and how badly you treated me. It will make the tale of your adultery more believable."

"If that's what you want."

He made his way to his dressing room, wondering if giving in to her would prove to be a mistake.

Sean had been so exhausted earlier that he hadn't considered how friends and acquaintances would react to him abstaining from liquor during a social occasion. Despite a few raised eyebrows and joky comments from the other dinner guests who knew he enjoyed a tipple, he covered his glass once again as the butler brought round more wine.

Yvette spoke loudly from down the table, causing a dozen faces to turn in his direction.

"Sean, darling. You've been so secretive of late. Have you taken the pledge without my knowledge?" She giggled, her long dark lashes fluttering.

He shifted in his seat. There was no way he was going to explain that he feared that one sip might set him back months. He patted his stomach.

"I'm a little off colour. I don't think alcohol is the best thing for me."

Yvette turned to the portly man in his fifties who was sitting to her side.

"What do you think, Doctor Greeves? Will it harm my darling husband? I would hate for him to be unwell."

The man's gaze flicked to Yvette's cleavage, as it had done several times during the meal.

"What a delightful wife you are. Don't you worry your pretty head about him. Fetch the man a large brandy. You've no objections, I take it?" he said, looking at their host, Peter Mason, a tall blond man on the opposite side of the table.

"Of course not," Peter said.

"I'd rather not," Sean said.

"Nonsense – it's medicinal. Perfect for a dicky stomach," Greeves said.

Moments later, the Masons' butler presented Sean with a silver tray holding a glass of brandy.

"I *really* don't think I should," Sean said.

"Drink up. Doctor's orders." Yvette said slyly.

To Sean, it was now perfectly clear she was aware of his struggle.

"I don't think alcohol will help."

Peter said, "Leave it if you don't want it, Sean. You look like you've lost a little weight. Are you all right, old chap?"

"I'm fine – just tired. Not much chance for sleep during the last couple of days."

"Drink up, man," Greeves said.

Yvette gave Greeves a dazzling smile, leaning closer to him.

"I am so glad you are here. My husband and sons are all I have, and Sean has been so distant, so temperamental of late." She rubbed the top part of her arm that was covered by her sleeve, wincing as she did so. "I hate to make him angry. I-if I were to lose him . . ."

Was she trying to give the impression he hit her? How could she be so devious? Many of the men here had mistresses or used the services of women who came in through the back entrance of the Faredene gentlemen's club, but violence was another matter entirely. Some of the other guests were customers of his factory and another, his bank manager. Although no one knew what went on behind closed doors, publicly they'd take a dim view of brutality and he couldn't afford any loss of custom, not when their divorce would leave him with little capital.

"Come on, man. Can't you see this beautiful young wife of yours is concerned about you?" Greeves said.

With her hand resting on the doctor's arm, Yvette turned to Sean.

"Please drink it, darling. Doctor Greeves is a respected physician. Surely you don't doubt his advice."

To Sean's surprise, he didn't want or need a drink. Not now, when his life with Jane was about to start. Perhaps he should refuse churlishly. After all, Yvette had told him to be cold towards her. Somehow, he sensed that if he did, she wouldn't react with her usual anger. Instead, he imagined her sobbing, possibly falsely accusing him of striking her.

One or two people had resumed their conversations, but most of the party were still staring at him. Irritation prickled. He'd beaten the booze before – surely one drink wouldn't make much difference . . .

Sean reached out to take the glass. The liquid burned the back of his throat gloriously. Within minutes, he felt the difference – he was calmer, happier.

By the time the men retired to the library for port and cigars, Sean had already had two more brandies.

At eleven o'clock, Sean made his way back from the water closet assigned to the male guests to rejoin the party, which had now moved to the drawing room. He scanned the room for Yvette, but she was nowhere to be seen. For most of the evening, her well-rehearsed tinkling laughter had filled the room as she'd flirted with the men. As this was their last social engagement, he was pleased she was enjoying herself, although he wondered why she'd found it necessary to put him in a position where he'd felt forced to take a drink.

It shouldn't surprise him. She was probably hoping he wouldn't be able to stop again. She was wrong. He'd not drank much, not compared to what he used to consume, but after a dry spell, it was certainly having an effect. It was time to leave before he succumbed to the temptation to down more.

He made his way towards Louise – a quiet and plain but pleasant woman. As he approached, she excused herself from the man she was speaking to.

117

"Sean, you look exhausted. Peter and I would have understood if you'd cancelled tonight."

"To be honest, I suggested we telephone and explain, but it's Peter's birthday and Yvette insisted."

Louise frowned slightly and placed her hand on his arm.

"And Yvette always gets what she wants in the end. Perhaps you were right not to fight it. I hope your poor friends get their sons back unharmed. You will let us know?"

He nodded. "Actually, if you don't mind, I think it's best if we get off home now."

"Not at all, Sean. Peter should be back in a moment. He's gone to fetch a book on architecture from the library – there's a diagram he wants to show one of the guests." Her hard features softened. "I'm afraid my husband thinks everyone shares his passion for buildings."

"I can't see Yvette, either."

"She wandered off a while ago. Perhaps she has one of her headaches."

At that moment, Yvette entered the room and strode over, her eyes dark.

"Yvette, is anything wrong?" Louise asked.

"Should there be? What are you two *whispering* about?" she said sharply.

"No one is whispering. I was explaining to Louise that we need to leave," Sean said.

Yvette pouted. "If we must. Goodbye, Louise dear. Sean, I am going to say goodbye to everyone else. You won't deny me *that*, surely."

Half an hour later, as footmen held umbrellas to shelter Sean and Yvette from the torrential downpour, there was no sign of her pleasant smiles or laughter as she shouted at him.

"If you had let Max bring us like I wanted, rather than insisting on driving yourself, you could have gone home earlier and sent him back for me. Instead, you had to give him the night off."

"He's shattered after spending two days searching for Jake and Brian. He deserves a break."

Without waiting for the footman to assist her, Yvette yanked open the car door.

"You are the most selfish person I have ever met. How can you drag me away from my friends when I may never see them again once I am in America? And all because you are worried about some boys who aren't even yours!"

"They're *my* friends' children," Sean retorted.

"And I'm giving up *my* sons so you can have *your* freedom."

Sean gritted his teeth, determined not to respond. The last thing he wanted was for her to delay the divorce out of spite. He inched the car down the drive, wet gravel crunching under the tyres, the rain pounding on the soft roof. He peered into the night. Even with the wipers, it was almost impossible to see through the silver sheets that bounced on the windscreen.

For a mile or so, Yvette silently fiddled with the trim on her coat, her head bent. Then she reached out and placed her hand on his thigh.

"Sean, I have changed my mind. Let's stay together for another six months. If we both try, it might work."

What! The alcohol may have dulled his senses, but he wasn't drunk. He must be mistaken.

"Yvette, you can't be serious."

"Neither of us have anyone else. We have nothing to

lose. I can make you happy. You know I can." She walked her fingers up his leg.

Taken by surprise, he shoved her hand away.

"There is no need to hit me," she said.

"I-I didn't. You know full well I'd never strike you."

She placed her hand back on his thigh.

"We have had some wonderful times," she said.

Had they? Not to his memory. What was she up to?

She leaned closer to him. "You still want me. I can tell."

He gently but firmly removed her hand again.

"Stop it, Yvette. Please. We're toxic. If we stay together any longer, we'll destroy each other."

"Sean, don't leave me alone. I won't be able to bear it. You promised Papa you would take care of me," she wheedled.

Keeping his eyes on the road, Sean said, "I can't do it. If there is any way I can help you to start your new life, I will, but we can't stay together."

"He would be furious with you."

"Matthew would understand that I've done my best."

"Does it ease your conscience to believe that?"

Sean didn't answer.

"Surely you don't want to be alone, either. Why do you want a divorce so badly? I am beautiful and you enjoy our intimacy. What more could a man ask?"

"Someone who wants to share a life with me and doesn't hate me. As for bed, I can hardly remember what it was like."

Her voice was harsh. "Well, I wish you luck finding another woman, because as husbands go, you've been inadequate to say the least."

"It's impossible to satisfy you."

"Only because you are a pathetic excuse for a man."
She dug her nails into his thigh.

"Ouch! Jesus, Yvette. You're behaving like Jekyll and
Hyde."

He'd had enough of her mood swings over the years.
He'd be glad to be rid of her.

Yvette thumped his arm.

"Stop it. You'll have us spending the night in a ditch,"
he said.

"Good. If we do, I hope you freeze to death, you heartless
good-for-nothing. You have failed at everything. Eventually,
you will bankrupt your beloved factory, as well. And as
for the boys, when they realise what a pathetic, spineless
drunk you are, they will despise you as much as I do."

"And you're nothing but bitterness and spite hidden
under an attractive cloak. But the veil has worn thin and
this joke of a marriage is at an end. As for Pierre and Josh,
I'll take my chances, because I'll do everything in my
power to be the father they deserve."

"I want my sons."

"This is ludicrous."

"Things are different these days. Mothers have rights."

"You don't give a damn about them!"

What a mess. He'd never expected ending their marriage
to be easy, but couldn't it be amicable? She'd been
discontented since their first day together. Apart from
believing that he was rich, he didn't understand why she
crept into his bed that first night.

"Why did you seduce me the night of your parents'
Christmas party?" He wasn't sure why he'd asked but
now he had, he wanted an answer.

"You were convenient. Nothing more."

121

"Well, I won't be convenient any longer. I'm in love with someone else," he blurted.

He'd not meant to say it, but relief flooded him. It was liberating to admit it finally.

"Who is she? How *dare* you sleep with some little tramp!" Yvette spat, emphasising each word by punching his forearm.

"I've never slept with her."

"Is it Kate? I have seen the way you two are always laughing together. You are not throwing me over for that sow!"

"It's not Kate. And please don't insult her."

Through the corner of his eye, Sean could see Yvette fuming beside him, her chest heaving. He'd seen her working herself up like this before and waited for the torrent of abuse. To his relief, she remained quiet.

Then as they passed Caldwell Grange, she snarled, "Tell me who the little tart is, or I swear tomorrow morning, I will tell your precious family and friends what an adulterous rat you are."

Sean gripped the steering wheel tighter. He couldn't let her do that.

"You don't know her."

"Where did you meet her? Is she some common tart from the factory?"

"No, but I'll tell you this – she's no tart. She's perfect."

"You have been unfaithful with some dirty trollop behind my back and you call the bitch perfect!"

Should he try again to reassure her he'd never slept with anyone else? What was the point? She'd never believe him. Desperate for the journey to be over, he pressed the accelerator to the floor.

"I have been such a fool," she shrieked. "You have been at it right under my nose. It is that conniving whore you brought into my home under the pretence of teaching my son." Yvette grabbed at his hair, yanking his head to the side, shouting, "I will ruin her. After I have finished with Jane Kellet, no one in Faredene will ever fall for her sweet, innocent act again. Everyone will know she is nothing but a filthy whore."

"Leave off, you mad bitch." With one hand, Sean tried to prise her fingers from his hair.

As they turned the next bend, she pulled again, dragging Sean towards her. The Rover swerved, skidding on a patch of water, aquaplaning directly at a tree.

"Sean!" Yvette cried, letting go of his hair.

He fought to control the car, swerving at the last minute, his heart pounding. As he tried to straighten their path, two slight figures shot out from the woods.

"Jesus, no!" Sean jerked the wheel again to avoid hitting them, ploughing into the bulky figure who was a few strides behind the boys, giving chase.

Yvette screamed as they careered off the road, the car turning over several times as they rolled down the hillside, dragging the limp form with it, finally crashing into an old oak tree.

The last thing Sean heard before he passed out was Yvette whimpering.

Chapter 12

In the panelled billiard room of Faredene Hall, Victoria wept uncontrollably against Edward's shoulder as he rubbed her back. Two men, with sacks draped over their shoulders to keep the rain off, entered carrying a makeshift cloth stretcher, trudging mud across the polished floor. Jess pointed to the green baize table.

"Put her down there and then there's a hot drink and food for you in the kitchen."

Edward's hand stayed Victoria's head from turning.

"You don't want to see her like this, Vicky, darling."

Jess grasped one of the folded crisp white sheets that had been placed on the sideboard in readiness before closing Yvette's stony eyes and covering her still form.

"She looks like she's sleeping now. What a waste, to die so young and beautiful," said Jess.

"For all her faults, she didn't deserve to end her days like this," Edward said.

To Victoria, their voices were distant yet piercing. She wanted to scream at them to shut up yet beg them to comfort her. To tell her it was all a mistake.

Why was life so cruel? Jake and Brian were home safe – had Kitty's sons' lives being spared been the trade-off for Sean and Yvette's lives? To her, it felt the same as years

124

ago, when God had answered her pleading, sparing Edward but taking poor Teddy Gibbs instead. Perhaps everyone's collective prayers had returned the boys, but at what cost? The men were bringing up bodies – including her precious son?

Silence echoed until Harry trudged in, removing his sopping overcoat.

"Honey, you look done in," Jess said.

"I'll be all right, my sweet." Harry cleared his throat. "By the looks of things, the fella chasing the lads is dead."

"And?" Edward said.

"I've told them to leave his body till last. The bastard's lucky I don't let him stay out there and rot. They're bringing Sean up next—" Harry's words halted as Victoria let out an anguished cry. He shot to her side. "Mrs Caldwell, Victoria. Effing hell. I'm so sorry – I told them to let you know straightaway. Sean's still breathing. It seems he was thrown from the car and escaped the worst of it."

Her boy wasn't dead!

"Edward, Sean's alive!" she said.

"Yes, darling. Harry, why didn't they bring him up first?"

"I sent them up to get a door to make a proper stretcher. I thought that was best. If I'd realised the daft sods weren't going to let you know the situation, I'd have come back myself."

"It's not your fault, Harry," Edward said.

Relief and fear battled in her brain. Sean wasn't dead. But did he have injuries that weren't obvious at first glance? Would he be disabled? That would destroy him.

"Doctor Farrell should be here soon," Harry said.

"Kitty's got the boys in the bathtub at the moment, so I'll send him straight to the bedroom they're preparing for Sean."

Victoria allowed Edward to lead her upstairs, her mind in turmoil. Please, God, don't take my boy. I'll do anything you ask. Did He grow tired of her prayers? Were only so many granted in one lifetime?

A fire was burning in the grate, taking the chill off the green-and-gold bedroom. The housemaid had turned the covers back and a hot-water bottle was warming the bed.

"Is everything to your satisfaction, Mrs Caldwell?" the maid asked.

"Y-yes, I think so. No, wait – could you bring up a jug of water for him? And some warm water and a cloth in case he has any wounds that need bathing." Victoria shuddered as an image of his handsome face, cut and bruised, appeared in her mind.

The young woman curtsied and hurried from the room.

"It looks like Yvette died swiftly," Edward said.

"You can't be certain. Although, it's what we must tell Sean. And Pierre and Joshua once they're old enough to understand. It might be selfish, but if one of them had to die, it's better that it was her. Not for my sake – for the boys. If they're to grow up with only one parent, it should be the one who genuinely loves them. Am I terrible?"

"Not at all. What has happened is tragic. But it doesn't change who Yvette was."

When they carried Sean into the room, Victoria held her breath, fighting the need to run to her son until the men had gently transferred him to the bed. Then she dived forwards, taking his hand between hers. He was mumbling, but apart from a short gash on his forehead, he looked relatively unscathed. Though, she wouldn't be reassured until Owain had checked him over – not until he'd recovered fully.

"M-Mother," Sean mumbled, his voice barely audible.

"I'm here, darling."

Victoria bent over him. She could smell alcohol on his breath. Why had he been drinking? He'd not taken liquor for months.

Sean dug his elbows into the mattress, wincing as he tried to sit. She placed her hands on his shoulders.

"Yvette?" he murmured.

"No talking. Lie down. Don't move until Owain has examined you," she said.

Sean clutched her fingers. "P-please. Yvette . . . the boys – are they hurt?"

Victoria perched on the edge of the bed and kissed his cheek.

"The boys are fine." She stroked his unruly hair as she spoke. "I'm sorry, Sean. Yvette didn't make it. But the end was mercifully quick. She didn't suffer."

"No! Not like this." Sean's face contorted.

"My darling, it might not feel like it at the moment, but time will heal the pain," she said.

What a hypocrite she was. She doubted any amount of time healed loss. You merely learned to accept it. Victoria knew his marriage had always been difficult, but Yvette was his wife, the mother of his children, so he was bound to be distraught.

"It was m-my fault," he said between sobs.

Her heart missed a beat. Had it happened because he'd been drinking? It wasn't an answer she wanted to hear. If he really was to blame, how would he live with himself? Before she could question him, Owain bustled into the room in his usual brisk manner. He was of medium height and had a slight paunch, his once sandy hair and beard now sprinkled with grey.

"Evening, Victoria, Edward. Nasty business. I'm sorry for your loss. Now, Victoria, if you can step back, please. Better still – leave me to it and let me inspect my patient."

She trusted Owain with her son's life, as he'd cared for Sean since Sean was a boy, but said imperiously, "I'm staying."

Owain tutted and, shaking his head, began his examination.

Sean lay still, tears tracking down his cheeks, groaning as Owain removed his clothing.

Victoria squeezed his fingers gently. "It's all right, darling. Everything will be fine." It was banal, but what else could she say?

Eventually, Owain returned his stethoscope to his bag. "You can stop worrying. He has a few cuts, bruises and cracked ribs, but he should make a full recovery."

"Are you certain? Don't you need to check him again tomorrow?" she said.

"Victoria, my dear, I don't make a habit of giving my patients false hope. Not even when they are my closest friends. Naturally, I'll call again in the morning. And if you have any concerns before then, I'll come out straightaway."

Once Owain had left, she and Edward sat on Sean's bed while Sean told them what had occurred. As she wiped his tears and heard the anguish in his words, Victoria vowed that regardless of how much he'd had to drink, she wouldn't let her beloved son take the blame for the deaths.

* * *

Sean's head pounded. Yvette was dead. He'd killed her.

Despite how many times he told himself she hadn't loved him, it didn't change a thing. He'd broken his wedding vows before he'd made them by marrying her when it was Jane he wanted. He thought he'd been doing the honourable thing, standing by Yvette because she was pregnant, but what chance did their union have? He'd tried to make his marriage work, but how could you love someone you didn't like? He should have found a way. Her pregnancy had trapped her every bit as much as him.

His mother kissed his cheek again.

"Try to rest now, darling."

Why wasn't she listening? If she railed at him, that would be better – perhaps it might even ease his conscience. He deserved to be punished for the loveless life Yvette had lived because of him.

"You're not hearing what I'm trying to tell you. I was overtired. And I'd been d-drinking. Not much, but it was the first time in months, so it went to my head."

"It doesn't matter. Hush now."

"But I need to explain. W-we were arguing. Yvette was hitting me. She g-grabbed my hair and we hit a pool of water as they ran out," Sean said for the umpteenth time.

"We understand, darling. You've explained it all. Let yourself drift off to sleep. You'll feel better after some rest."

"How am I going to tell my sons I caused their mother's death?"

"*Never* say that to them or anyone else," she said. "All that Pierre and Joshua need to be told is that there was a terrible accident, nothing more. Do you understand me,

Sean? No more talk of drinking and arguments. It won't bring Yvette back or help the boys. They need you."

"What about the man? I can't believe I didn't even ask about him. Is he alive? Who was he? Jake and Brian appeared from nowhere. He seemed to be chasing them."

"He is dead, I am afraid. When we came upstairs, they still hadn't brought the body up, but they may well have identified him by now," Edward said.

"I mess everything up. My life in New Orleans . . . our marriage, my future, Pierre and Joshua's lives."

"What nonsense. I won't allow you to blame yourself for everything," she said. "You were doing well in America until Claude Dupont cheated you and gambled away your money. As for Yvette, it takes two to make a relationship work. And from what I've seen over the years, you were incredibly tolerant of her behaviour. Perhaps too much so. The more we all pandered to her after her parents' deaths, the worse she got."

"Y-you don't understand. We were g-getting a divorce. It was my idea, but she agreed to it months ago. Then suddenly, out of nowhere, when we were driving home tonight, she changed her mind and wanted to try again. I couldn't do it, Mother. There was no w-way I could s-stay with her."

"You were separating?"

"Are you ashamed of me?"

"Never. Though you should have told me. I could have helped. Either way, it still doesn't make what happened your fault."

Sean fought against the laudanum the doctor had given him, lifting his heavy eyelids. "Do you honestly believe that?"

"Absolutely. We might not share the same blood, but you certainly have my habit of blaming yourself for everything. If you insist, we can discuss it more when you're fully recovered. For now, rest. Harry was sending for the police, so Edward and I need to go downstairs and speak to them. We'll explain to them the boys ran out as you were skidding."

"They should be told the truth. That I've had a drink and Yvette and I were arguing. I'll come down," he said, trying once more to get out of bed.

"Sean, you are in no condition to talk to anyone yet. Besides, I expect they will be more interested in hearing what Jake and Brian have to say," Edward said.

"Will they want to q-question to me tomorrow?"

"Not if I've got anything to do with it. I'll deal with the police. Now sleep – Mother's orders."

Sean tried to fight it, but the opiate won the battle.

Victoria joined the family, who were seated in the morning room. Quickly sitting on a chintz chair, she clenched her hands in her lap to stop them from trembling as Sergeant Roper took out his notebook. She was going to protect her son no matter what.

"Right, first, does anybody recognise the deceased man?" Roper said.

Harry spoke. "He's another of those effing Charnocks."

"It's a good thing the bastard's dead, or I'd ring his bleedin' neck for taking our boys," Albert said.

"I'm aware of the unpleasant history between yourselves and the Charnocks, but it was all a long time ago," said Roper. "And there are plenty of wealthy families about who he could have targeted. Is there any other reason you can think of that made him take your sons?"

"He was working for James Brakenridge," Kitty said. "When James and Charles died, Charnock lost his position. In his warped mind, p'rhaps he blamed me, because it was summat I said that led to Charles' suicide and James' murder."

"Which was?"

Kitty hesitated. "Why the flaming hell do you need to be told that?"

"With respect, madam, I realise you're distressed, but it's my job to say what information is important."

Kitty had told Charles that James had raped her, making Jane Charles' half-sister. Kitty was right – there was no point in bringing all that up again. Victoria glanced at Edward, hoping he was going to stop this line of questioning. Thankfully, he spoke up.

"No resentment towards Mrs Nelson and her family can justify kidnapping Jake and Brian," Edward said. "As the matter won't be going to trial, perhaps we can leave it there."

"Hmm, if *you* think it appropriate, Mr Caldwell . . ." Roper turned to Kitty to continue his questioning as the others listened. "How was he able to kidnap the boys?"

"They were playing in the woods, when Charnock approached them saying he'd found a fawn that was injured, so they followed him to see if they could help."

"Why didn't they come back here and fetch an adult?"

"My lads think they can take on the world an' they wanted to save it themselves. And they were worried Harry might say it had to be put out of its misery."

"Hmm, very rash of them."

"Aye, well, rash or not, they got away from him. Now,

if you'll let me finish explaining . . ." Kitty glowered at him. "He led them to an old workman's hut on the far side of the quarry, just outside Harry's estate. That's why we never found them. We never went over that side looking, 'cos they know not to go playing on someone else's land. When they got there, there was no fawn. He pulled a knife and tied them both up. The poor kids have had next to nothing to eat. Most of the time, he kept them bound and gagged."

"How did Charnock know the lads would go with him?"

"If the rotten bleeder was still alive, I'd ask him. But as he got what he deserved, we'll never know. He told my lads he'd been watching the Hall for months, poaching on Harry's land, waiting for his chance to get back at us."

Roper nodded. "One last thing. How did they escape?"

Kitty said, "They've always liked playing at escaping and suchlike. As it turns out, all that practicing came in handy as they managed to get the ropes off their hands. The doc's given me some ointment for them. Not that it'll do much good – their poor little wrists are raw."

"Didn't Charnock notice?"

"His family are as thick as pig shit and my lads are crafty. They held the ends of the ropes while he was watchin' them. Jake said Charnock untied their legs whenever they needed to go out to do their business, so they didn't stink the place out. And tonight Charnock had been on the ale and was kaylied, so once they were outside, Jake tripped him up and they legged it."

"Brave lad. Can I speak to your sons to clarify all this?"

"No bloody way. Don't you think they've been through enough? You'll have to come back tomorrow. Although they'll tell you the same as me. Now, if you've finished with me, Jess is watching over them, but they need their mother," Kitty said firmly.

"You have procedures to follow, Sergeant, but as the perpetrator's dead, there will be no case to answer," said Edward.

"Indeed, Mr Caldwell. We'll leave it at that. No need to bother the lads."

As Kitty left the room, Roper turned to Victoria.

"Has Mr Kavanagh been able to explain how the accident happened?"

The policeman scribbled in his notepad as she relayed Sean's story, leaving out his drinking and the argument.

"So if I've got this right, the boys were running across the road as your son's car hit a patch of water. The car skidded as he tried to avoid the children, instead colliding with their pursuer."

"Correct," Victoria said.

"Anything else you can tell me?"

"Nothing."

"It all seems straightforward. I'm glad the little chaps weren't harmed."

"That remains to be seen. If they don't have nightmares, I for one will be surprised," Victoria said, her voice steely.

Edward stood, holding out his hand to the policeman.

"Sergeant, we don't want to take up any more of your valuable time now Jake and Brian are home. And my family need to grieve the loss of my daughter-in-law. She's left two small boys behind."

"I understand, Mr Caldwell. I'll leave you all in peace."

⌒◯◯⌒

Chapter 13

It was almost a week later when Victoria prepared to take her son home from Faredene Hall. Sean was finishing his breakfast at a small table in the guest-room, his face a mass of purple and yellow.

"Please, Sean, come back to the Lodge House. You're not fit to look after yourself yet," she said.

"I have a small army of servants to take care of my needs."

"Servants can't give you emotional support. And we can make room for the children, if you're worried about that."

"Mother, I appreciate the offer, but I need to be in my own home and the boys don't need the upheaval of a different house."

"Jane's back and I've no wish to be cruel, but the way she and Nanny tell it, neither Pierre nor Joshua appear to have noticed Yvette's absence. They were so used to her being away, it's hardly surprising."

"That's not the point. This time, she won't be coming back and it's down to me."

Victoria struggled to keep the exasperation from her voice. "Sean, for goodness' sake, stop this. We've been over it – far too many times already. The crash was *not* your fault. You've admitted that even though you'd taken

135

a drink, you weren't inebriated. It was simply the result of badly timed coincidences."

"My conscience isn't clear and nor should it be."

"You can't control the weather and couldn't have had any influence over the timing of the boys' emergence from the woods. Nor did you make Yvette attack you."

"If I'd not been arguing with her—"

"As Kitty would say, Yvette could have picked an argument with a plucked chicken. And you can take that expression off your face. She's dead and I'm truly sorry about that. But the woman was no saint. And I refuse to allow you to ruin the rest of your life because of a misplaced sense of guilt."

"If I'd loved her as a husband should, then she'd have been different."

"I doubt it. She was the image of her mother, both in looks and personality. Matthew adored Sophia, but she was never happy. Some people are made that way."

"Matthew worked too much."

"So do most men."

Sean sighed. "Mother, you may be right, but you've barely left my side since the accident and you're exhausted. If you're afraid that I'm going to drink myself to death . . ." He held up his hand to stop her interruption. "I don't blame you for your concern. As tempting as the prospect is, my actions – or at the very least my inability to love my wife – has robbed my sons of their mother, such that she was. A drunken father is the last thing they need. In a perverse way, the crash has helped me to overcome my drink problem – hopefully, forever. So there's no need to worry about me."

"Sean, that's impossible. My happiness is tied directly

to that of my children. If one of you is hurting, then I suffer with you."

"Then you're doomed to a life of misery," he said. "Mother, I'm incredibly grateful and you can come round whenever you wish, but I need to navigate my own way through this."

Sean examined his mother's face. The fine lines around her eyes had deepened over the last few days. She'd always protected him. Supported his decisions. But he was a grown man and it was time he stopped causing her anguish. She should be with Edward at home, resting.

"Mother, you've been wonderful, but I need to get back to normal."

"You're not going back to the factory . . ."

"Not for a while. Darius will be keeping things going as best he can. I'll go back after the funeral."

"Edward has taken care of everything. We thought you wouldn't mind. There are only the final arrangements for you to approve."

"It's a relief not to have to attend to it myself. Thank him for me, please."

The first thing Sean did when he got home was read through the letters of condolence. There were dozens, although many were from his business associates who didn't know her. The most heartfelt was from Louise Mason, who had written that she and Peter were both shocked and deeply saddened for him and the children, offering to assist in any way she could. They'd all need responding to at some point, but they could wait. As soon as they'd eaten their lunch, he wanted to see Pierre and Joshua.

His ribs caused excruciating pain when the boys tried

to climb on his knee. Even so, he leaned forwards and kissed their curls. They were so different. Pierre's hair was fine and straw blond, while Joshua's was so like his own dark mass.

As they showed him their toys and he played with them, there was a lump in his throat. His poor sons would be deprived of the opportunity to get to know their mother. Would they grow to hate him if they knew how she died? Sean felt as though his guilt would strangle him. And it was about to get worse.

A short while later, as Nanny ushered the boys from the room for their afternoon nap, he said, "Could you ask Miss Kellet to come in? I need a word with her."

Sean pressed his head back against the chair, exhausted. He was longing to see Jane yet dreading what he felt compelled to do. Moments later, there was a gentle tap on the door and Jane entered. The sight of her brought an instant reaction in his gut – longing and sadness.

She shut the door softly then rushed across the room, dropping to her knees beside his chair.

"My darling, I've been so worried about you. When I got back from Blackpool yesterday, I was so desperate to see you, I nearly marched up to the Hall and demanded my rightful place to be by your side. As your future wife, I wanted to be the one to care for you. But I thought you might be cross if I behaved so brazenly, so I stayed with the boys. Did I do the right thing?" she said, barely pausing for breath.

Sean stroked her white-blonde hair.

She reached up and gently kissed his swollen lips. "Your poor face. It's dreadful about Yvette and I know she's not yet buried, so this will sound wanton." She glanced away shyly. "But I'm here to help you in whatever way you need. To hell with the gossips."

It was too difficult to look at her. He turned his head away. How was he going to find the strength to do this? If he could just spend a few hours alone with her before he had to give her up forever . . . But there was no point in delaying.

His words were slow and halting, each one crushing his dreams as it left his mouth.

"I'm so, so sorry. But you and I – we . . . we can't be together."

He stared at her. He had to be man enough to face the suffering he was causing the only woman he'd ever truly loved. Confusion crossed her face.

"Not straightaway, you mean, surely. But eventually. I'll wait, if it's what you want. You know I will. We can keep up the pretence."

"No. I'm sorry. For you and me, there can be no future now. Everything has changed."

She gasped. "No. No. You can't mean that. You're grieving. It's understandable that you still have feelings for her."

"If only that *were* the case, but the truth is, I never loved her. If I had, she might still be alive. You must understand – I can't be with you. Not now, not ever. Yvette's death was my fault. My sons are motherless because of me. I can't replace her with another woman. I need to dedicate myself to raising them."

"But you're not making sense. When Yvette was planning to move back to America, you were happy for me to be their stepmother."

"Exactly. Before, I imagined she'd be enjoying life.

Now, she'll be rotting in Faredene Cemetery."

"You can't intend to stay alone forever. I'll be here when you're ready," Jane said.

"No, my darling. I can't let you wait for me. You'll find someone else. Someone who deserves you. There are things you don't understand."

"So make me understand. Because it seems like you're punishing me for some crime I didn't even know I'd committed."

"Hurting you is the last thing I want."

"Well then explain to me why you're doing this."

"It was wrong of me to hide it from you before. I'm a drunk."

"Do you think I'm blind *and* deaf? I work in your household – your drinking and marital problems have been the talk of the servants' hall for years."

The thought of being gossiped about shamed him.

"I'm convinced I'll never touch a drop again, but I won't take that chance with your happiness, or your life."

"I can help you."

Sean shook his head. "No. You're not wasting your life on me. Try to understand that I'm letting you go for your sake."

"How about asking what I want?"

"Jane, please . . ."

"You can't end this now. I've waited months already because you promised we were going to be together. It may surprise you to hear, but I have had other proposals, which I've turned down."

"I'd have been shocked if hordes of other men weren't clamouring for your affection. But it changes nothing. Eventually, I ruin everything and I won't drag you down with me."

"And what do you intend doing with your life? Are you going to sit around mourning a woman you claim you never loved?"

"My boys need me – I must focus on them."

"And am I supposed to carry on teaching them?"

"I hope you will, but I understand if you don't want to."

"It's not a case of not wanting to. If I had to see you, talk to you, all the while knowing we have no future, it would crucify me."

"Then I must look for another tutor."

"Just like that?" She snapped her fingers. "That's all it takes for you to get over me?"

He wanted to tell her he'd never get over her. She'd captured his heart since the first moment they'd met. Telling her would only give her false hope.

She stood abruptly. "I won't beg – I have some pride left."

Nothing he could say would make things better.

She glowered at him. "This is it, Sean. The end. If I walk out of this room, I'm leaving this house immediately and going back to Blackpool until I decide what to do with the rest of my life."

His voice flat, Sean said, "It's for the best."

Chapter 14

Below a sky of indigo and coral, Kate climbed into her car. As she went to place her bag on the seat, Bella jumped in next to her.

"What are you doing?" Kate said.

Bella's face was full of concern. "I don't want to interfere, but I can't help myself. You've been at Sean's every evening for weeks."

"He needs me."

"No, he doesn't. I went over lots while he needed nursing. But he's back to full health, so why the nightly visits?"

"Do you have a problem with it? Most of the time we were closed for the Easter holidays – you didn't have to cover for me."

"That's a hurtful thing to say. I'm not bothered about you getting out of supervising the pupils for a few evenings, and you know it. Tell me the truth – are you hoping something more might develop between you and Sean?"

"I'm not completely stupid. To Sean I'm a friend, nothing more."

Kate didn't think she was lying to Bella. Then again, perhaps she was fooling herself.

"The fact that you're being aggressive and defensive tells me I'm right," said Bella.

"This is about more than my feelings. What matters to me now is supporting Sean."

"Kate, it's me you're talking to, not some stranger. Now Yvette's not on the scene, are you planning to swoop in and steal his affections while he's grieving?"

"I'm aware who I'm speaking to and believe me, if it was anyone else, I'd have slapped them sideways after a comment like that. I'm helping him, and anyone who doesn't understand can mind their own business," Kate snapped.

"Including me?" Bella said, her neck and face blotching.

"If you're suggesting I abandon Sean when he needs me, then yes."

"What happened to you and I being able to discuss anything? Or does it only count when it's my life under a microscope?" Bella turned away, but not before her lip trembled.

"Of course not." Kate caught her arm. "I'm sorry, sweet pea."

It was wrong of her to get angry – Bella was worried about her. Victoria had also cautioned Kate to be careful.

"Sean is my only son and I'd gladly die for him," Victoria had said. "If there is a future for the two of you, no one will be happier than I. But you mean as much to me as Sean does, so please don't lay yourself open to more pain. There are enough of us to support him. It doesn't all have to be you."

It did, though. Kate felt compelled to help him.

"Bella, Sean's grieving and blaming himself for the accident," Kate said. She could have added "and breaking his heart over Jane", but Bella knew nothing of that relationship.

"The accident wasn't his fault."

"Guilt isn't always logical, Bella. I'm worried he might start drinking again."

"Sean's fine. He's back at work and he's found a new tutor for Pierre and Josh." Annoyance flashed across Bella's face. "Though why Jane chose now to leave at short notice is beyond me. I thought she cared about the boys."

Kate felt she had to defend Jane. It wasn't Jane's fault that Sean had ended things.

"I'm certain she does. Don't judge her harshly. We can never know what's going on in someone else's life, but I expect Jane had her reasons."

"Then *I*'ll spend more time with Sean," Bella said. "I don't want you to get hurt. And I don't want either of you doing something that you'll regret. Because if you fall out, I can't choose between my sister and brother."

"You'll never have to pick one of us. Bella, whether I'm there with him or sitting here pretending to read, he's all I think about. I'll be back by midnight. Please try to understand that I just need to help him through this."

Kate was only half lying. There had been a dozen times when she'd imagined him pulling her into his arms, smothering her with kisses, undressing her . . . But so far, compassion had outweighed everything else. She admired his strength. He was fighting on all fronts: his guilt, his crushing need for alcohol, juggling his business while finding time for the boys, as well as sacrificing his own happiness to protect Jane. In Kate's opinion, that aspect of his plan was misguided, as she was sure Jane must also be going through hell.

"What do you do all evening?" Bella said.

"Talk. Read to him. We play cards or chess. It's all perfectly innocent. All I'm doing is offering him support. And you can take that look off your face. There's nothing improper between us – I've told you how we spend our time."

"If I can't stop you, be careful. Please."

"I will. I promise."

In Sean's study shortly after eleven thirty, Kate stifled a yawn.

"If you're not making your next move, I'd best be off and we can carry on tomorrow evening," she said.

He looked up from the chessboard that he'd been staring at for the last fifteen minutes.

"Kate, what am I going to do?"

He obviously wasn't referring to chess, but she said jokingly, "Well, you could move your knight to king four."

The right side of his mouth twitched upwards.

"You're going to be fine. Look at how far you've come," Kate said seriously.

He held up his bruised hand. "If I keep putting my fist through wardrobe doors, we won't have any furniture left."

"Admittedly, it might be a good idea to find a better way to manage your frustration."

"No one *really* understands. Everyone keeps saying Yvette wasn't a good wife or mother as though that makes it all right. But it doesn't. Pierre and Joshua shouldn't be motherless. Even if she was across the Atlantic, they could have written to her, visited. More importantly, if I'd not got her pregnant or if I'd loved her, then perhaps our marriage might have worked and she'd still be here. That way, our sons could have decided for themselves how they felt about her. As it is, Joshua probably won't even remember her."

"That might be a good thing. The boys have you and they're loved."

"If I was a good father, they'd be all I care about. I'm tormented by guilt and even worse, self-pity, because I've lost my chance of being with Jane. I heard from Kitty that Jane has accepted a job teaching for a family in Fleetwood. She's going to be a governess for a couple with six young children, so she's settled there for years. Unless she gets married."

"Settled, but will she be happy?"

"It's for the best. She's better off without me. I'll tell the temporary tutor I engaged that he can stay on."

"Sean, stop being stubborn. Go to Blackpool and fetch her back here."

"No matter how much I want to, I can't." He swiped the back of his hand across his face. Then he stood, his back to her.

In two steps, she was at his side. Placing her hands on his arms, she turned him round. His face was awash. This was the first time she'd seen him shed a tear since he'd come home. It had been a long time coming. She held him close as great racking sobs escaped.

"Hush now." Her lips brushed his hair as she spoke. "Come on, let it out. There now, my love."

"Kate, I'm not sure I've got the strength to get through without Jane. I adore my boys, but life without her is unbearable. Yet, I can't risk being with her."

"Give it time. One day you'll feel differently and then you and Jane can talk things through."

She shouldn't be holding him so close while he cried over another woman. But she couldn't help herself. She wanted to ease his suffering. To her shame, even though it was Jane he wanted, Kate knew that at this moment, she'd comfort him in any way he needed. Even if he tossed her aside afterwards, destroying her in the process, so be it.

Despite it being three in the morning, Sean was still wide awake. He thumped his pillow into submission as though it alone had caused all of his problems. As with every night since Yvette's death, his mind had been jumping from one disturbing thought to another. Tonight, though, another terrifying train of thought had been added.

Kate had been a terrific support over the past weeks. In fact, she'd got him through the worst. Things had been getting easier – at least that's what he'd told himself – but this evening he'd broken down and she'd held him.

Her body had been so close – soft, inviting. Her perfume was light, flowery . . . and alluring when her cheek had pressed against his. Neither of them had said anything, yet he'd felt that if he'd turned his head, she'd have let him kiss her – and more, much more. Kate!

It would have been so easy to take comfort in her warmth, her strength. But it would have ruined their friendship. Kate didn't have feelings for him, he was sure, yet he suspected she'd have allowed it to happen out of sympathy. Thank God he'd pulled away. From now on, he'd have to ensure his emotions didn't overwhelm him while in her company. It had been wrong of him to allow her to come round to his house every night. He had to stop relying on her for support. It wasn't fair. Either he was man enough to get through this or he wasn't. Either way, he cared for Kate far too much to take advantage of her.

It was a cool, crisp April morning when George's ship docked. He couldn't understand how a dullard like Marjorie had managed to deceive him. It had affected him so much that he'd spent much of the journey from India secreted in his cabin, unable to bring himself to play the part of the wealthy businessman or look for women he could target. Now he was back in England, things would be different, he told himself.

As he walked the short distance through the Limehouse area towards Glebe Street, George was smiling. A few nights being looked after by his ma and he'd be ready to start again.

To his dismay, the door of his childhood home was opened by a slovenly woman with greasy hair and two filthy brats clinging to her skirts.

"Who the hell are you?" he said.

"You the son I heard about?" the woman said as she hoisted the smallest of the urchins onto her hip and bared her breast for it to suckle.

"Where's my mother?" he said angrily.

Unperturbed by his tone, the woman dragged the back of her free hand under her nose.

"Sorry, cocker. From what the neighbours said, the poor old dear what lived here went into the work'ouse a month back and didn't even make it through the first night."

George gripped the doorframe, his knuckles whitening. Why hadn't his ma hung on a bit longer instead of shaming him by going into that place?

Apparently misreading his anger, the woman spoke hurriedly.

"None of her bits o' furniture were left, if that's what yer thinkin'."

George stalked away without answering. He didn't believe her but had no interest in his mother's battered and broken furniture. Even his ma had let him down. She was gone. He was alone in the world. But at least he'd never have to come back to this dump. He'd always been ashamed of where he'd grown up. Now, he could reinvent himself and make enough money to wash away his past.

By the end of the month, George had settled in a suite of comfortably furnished rooms in a fashionable area surrounded by theatres and restaurants. But it was expensive and so far, he'd done nothing about securing the services of two prostitutes. He had, however, realised he needed to be more ambitious than the initial scheme he'd thought of in India. A couple of tarts wouldn't earn him sufficient income, even if they spent all day servicing punters. His new plan was to open a whorehouse with gaming tables and once it was established, he'd open more until he had a string of them.

George suspected Moby would have Pearl working the docks and didn't want to risk running into her, so he kept his search to the Covent Garden area. Before lunch, he'd spotted the perfect woman: tall, slender, good bone structure. And despite her cheap clothing and rouged cheeks, she held herself with dignity. She was wasting herself by working on the streets.

"You after some fun, guv'nor?" she said.

"How long have you been on the game?" he asked.

"If you're a flaming God-botherer, my soul is my business, so shove off."

George gave a wry laugh. "I have no interest in saving you. Answer my question," he demanded.

"What's this all about? I've got a living to earn. If yer not payin', sling yer hook."

George held out some money. "If you answer my questions, this is yours."

She took the coins. "All right. I've been working the docks for nearly a year."

"Are you clean?"

"Course I am."

"Good. I have a proposition."

"You a pimp?"

"Such an unpleasant term. If you work for me, you'll not refer to me in that way again."

"What you harpin' on about?"

"You'll find out soon enough. How old are you?"

"Twenty-four."

"Why are you whoring?"

"I had a gentleman – set me up in a house and everythin'. He came to visit me regular – twice a week until he died sudden. Then his wife sold the house and turfed me out."

"Was there no other employment you could take up?"

"I'd been with him since I were nowt but a girl. I've no training other than how to entertain and there was no way I was charring. Besides, I'd rather be lying on me back than breaking it scrubbing floors for a pittance."

"I'm setting up a respectable establishment for gentlemen who want to enjoy the company of clean, attractive ladies. How would you like to run things for me?"

"Who are you?"

"From now on, you'll refer to me as the guv'nor."

It reminded him of colonial governors. It would suit him well.

"All right, guv'nor it is. Buy me a drink and we can talk," the woman said.

George offered her his elbow.

Chapter 15

The late-afternoon sun fought to break through cumulus clouds over Faredene's graveyard. Although Sean wanted to tell Max to drive past and take him home, he braced himself for the task he'd been putting off for too long. The guilt was still a crushing weight. Consequently, this was the first time he'd visited Yvette's burial plot since the funeral.

He'd struggled to think of an appropriate inscription, so they'd only erected the headstone yesterday and he was duty-bound to check the stonemason had done it correctly. Max pulled the car to a halt and after getting out, opened the passenger door.

As though sensing his employer's reluctance, he said, "Would you like me to accompany you, sir?"

"No thank you, Max. This is something I must do alone. But I appreciate the offer. You've been a great help since the accident."

"Only doing my job, sir."

"Even so, I won't forget your loyalty."

Max handed Sean a spray of amaryllis.

"Sometimes I feel like I hardly knew my wife, but she once told me she liked them," Sean said.

Sean made his way through the cemetery, his step

slowing as he neared the place where they'd laid her to rest. Was she resting, or was she unable to find peace – unhappy in death as she had been in life? He hated the thought of her lying beneath the cold earth. Alone in a dark coffin – where he'd put her, if not entirely by deed then by thought. That wasn't true. He'd wanted her gone, but in America – as far from him as possible – never dead.

Sean was tired of making blunders, hurting others. At least Jane was safe from his stupidity. No matter how painful, letting her go had been the right thing to do. She deserved better – none of this was her fault. He'd written to her many times, each unfinished letter resulting in a crumpled ball in the waste bin. There was nothing to say, because he hadn't changed his mind. The shame was his to suffer. Once again, the same tormenting thoughts came. If he hadn't longed to be with Jane, could he have made Yvette happy? Would she have grown to care for him? Perhaps then she'd still be alive.

Sean dragged his mind to the present as he laid the flowers on the grave next to a rose. He picked up the crimson bloom, turning it in his hand. It was fresh – someone had placed it here recently. He was glad someone cared enough to visit her grave.

Perhaps it was his mother. Her collection of rose bushes was extensive. She visited Bridie's grave regularly and leaving flowers for Yvette as well was the type of thing she'd do, but she'd not mentioned coming this week, and why a rose?

He read the inscription on the black marble: In memory of Yvette Kavanagh, loving wife and mother. It was untrue, whitewashing the past, but it was the way he preferred people to remember her.

As he returned the stem to the ground, a question formed. Red roses were for love – had Yvette had a lover? It would mean that at least someone had loved her, as he'd never been able to. Hope crept over him. What sort of husband wanted his wife to have been unfaithful to him to ease his own conscience? He wanted her to have had some joy, even if not with him. But who?

One name came to him instantly. Sean tried to dismiss it, but it wouldn't budge. Peter Mason.

Surely not. He was a friend of his – and Yvette and Louise were best friends. They'd dined together on the night of the accident. So why was it the logical answer? Had Sean unconsciously been dismissing signs of intimacy between them?

He recalled both Louise's and Peter's faces at the funeral. She'd appeared stony, impassive, and Sean had assumed she was trying not to break down. But her words had struck him as strange.

"You will find the happiness you deserve. Perhaps we both will."

Whereas Peter had looked far more distressed than one would have expected, embracing him without a word.

Sean walked back towards the motor car, his mind reeling. He needed the truth.

Back at home, he opened the floral curtains in his wife's bedroom. He hadn't been in here since before she died. Cowardly, he'd asked his mother to select a gown for Yvette to wear for her burial and then ordered the door to be locked. He'd kept the key with him, not wanting the maids to erase her from the house, as she had been from life.

Although now covered in a thin layer of dust, everything was as she'd left it. The mirror she'd slammed down and broken was lying on the dressing table, her jewellery case open . . . An image of Yvette admiring her reflection as she often had transformed to one of her lifeless face, her skin porcelain cold as she lay in her coffin.

Sean forced the vision from his head. For the sake of his own sanity, he needed to prove to himself that he'd not ruined her life, that she'd known love. Yvette had always written a diary, but where did she keep it?

When a search of her chest of drawers and trunk revealed nothing, Sean flung open the doors of the wardrobe, pushing gowns aside, pulling them out. Next, he dragged out the shoe and hatboxes, scattering them across the floor.

"S-sir, can I help you?"

The upstairs maid had entered the room without him noticing. Sean's gaze followed her eyes. Shoes and clothes were strewn over the carpet. She probably thought he'd gone mad. He smiled, hoping to dispel the wariness he'd detected in her tone.

"Where did my wife keep her journal?"

The plump young woman shifted uncomfortably.

"I'm not sure, sir. Her lady's maid would have known."

"Of course. Thank you."

Sean sighed. Yvette's maid had left shortly after her mistress' death.

"There's a chest under Mrs Kavanagh's bed, which she didn't permit me to polish."

Sean bent and pulled out a long, thin mahogany casket and after placing it on the bed, he used his handkerchief to wipe it then tried to lift the lid.

155

"I believe madam kept the key in her jewellery box, sir."

Sean was tense – nervous about what he may discover.

"Could you please light a fire in my study?" he said.

On the north side of the house, his private office was chilly regardless of the season. He placed the casket next to the armchair and selected the volume dated 1913 from the top. As expected, the first entry was January the first this year – scarcely half a page:

New Year's Day and I am alone. The dunderhead is downstairs, but he doesn't count. Normally, he'd be holed up in his study until he was too intoxicated to stand, but he appears to have stopped drinking! Perhaps I may find some amusement in encouraging him to partake.

How I loathe him. I am more than happy to oblige him with a divorce. If my plans work out, I will be free of him. This will be the year I put myself first.

Hadn't she always put herself first?

He read a few more entries at random, a smile twitching as it occurred to him how often she'd criticised him and referred to him as the dunderhead. She *really* had despised him. But she'd filled most passages with trifling domestic matters that irked her. And a verse about how misunderstood she was. He turned to the last few pages containing Yvette's neat copperplate handwriting, made the night before her death. His heart missed a beat.

Even though I have assured Peter that my settlement will be enough for us both if his mother cuts him from her will, he still insists he can't leave Louise and their dreadful child. Why is he being so stubborn? His love for me is clear whenever our bodies are entwined.

I fear if I am unable to persuade him, I will be forced to delay my divorce for longer to maintain the respectability it affords. She is too much of a mouse to say anything, but I believe Louise has finally become suspicious. Her friendship matters nothing to me and wiping that asinine smile from her face would be satisfying, but I must ensure Peter leaves her first. Tomorrow evening, I will dazzle him by wearing my new gown, which is his favourite colour.

He is the only man I have ever wanted. I come alive at his touch. If only he would see sense, he and I can start our lives again in America. I will make him happier than he ever dreamed possible.

Irritation flared – she *was* having an affair! He wanted her to have been happy, so why was he annoyed?

It was Yvette's duplicity – her refusal to give him a divorce straightaway when she'd been asking Peter to take her away all along – that angered him. Her pleading for the marriage to continue and her attempt to seduce Sean had been a ploy to manipulate him and buy herself more time. All she was interested in was Peter.

He rummaged in the box to find the diary dated 1910 and flicked through the December entries. There was nothing of interest – mainly complaints about her mother – until he reached the tenth:

Mama is such a hypocrite. She has betrayed Papa so many times. Yet, she is furious because she discovered Peter in my bedroom last night. I hoped she would insist he end his engagement to that mealy-mouthed Louise and marry me.

*Instead, she said he must honour a betrothal made by his
parents when he was a boy!*

*I may tell Louise myself. It would devastate her to discover
Peter and I are lovers . . . She deserves to suffer. He should not
be hers. But Peter might hate me and I couldn't bear that, so I
will remain silent – for now. Even if he marries Louise, his heart
will always belong to me.*

He turned a few more pages:

*This morning, Mama said I must find another man willing to
accept me now I am no longer pure. She is insisting I act
quickly in case I am with child. I spoke to Peter and he agreed
with her. He actually said Louise is the innocent party and he
would never forgive me if I hurt her by telling her about us!
How can he treat me this way? I hate the thought of another
man touching me. I hope it tortures Peter. Perhaps then he
will understand how it has been for me, watching him fawn
over Louise.*

Sean thumped the arm of his chair. Yvette had deliberately
duped him, all because she feared she was carrying
Peter's child. He thumbed through to Christmas Eve:

*Sean Kavanagh was the talk of the ball. Everyone was chatting
about the eligible rich American. Naturally, he could not resist
my charms. He is a drunkard, but a handsome one. And his
lovemaking was certainly skilled, so it will be bearable if I find
out I am expecting and must marry him to protect my
reputation. But he will never compare to being with Peter. And
once I have the safety of a wedding band, Peter and I can
continue to enjoy time together.*

The conniving bitch. His mother had been right about her all along! Yvette was as manipulative and cold-hearted as her own mother, Sophia. Sean grabbed the 1911 volume and found the entry made shortly after Pierre's birth:

My son is born. He is blue-eyed and blond, like his father. He is going to be extremely handsome. I am so clever – I have used the French version of the name Peter without arousing suspicion. People say he looks like Papa. Everyone except Mama, of course – she knows the truth.

Because of her comments to the dunderhead, he suspects he is not the father. How could she be so spiteful when it is her fault I am married to the wrong man? And now he claims the wet nurse has injured my child – it was such a cruel thing to say. I will never forgive him.

So, she named Pierre after his real father. Sean was sickened. Who was Joshua's father? Again, he rooted through the box, grabbed a diary and skimmed through until he found the entry he was looking for:

His son was born yesterday. He has our colouring – dark hair and brown eyes – as I knew he would. I have done my duty, as Peter insisted – given the dunderhead a child of his own. I can only hope the boy does not inherit his father's annoying ways.

So, Joshua was his. But not Pierre. It had dented his pride, yet Yvette's infidelity eased his conscience. He'd not been the reason Yvette was cornered in a loveless marriage. They hadn't been arguing that night because she genuinely wanted to save their relationship.

Did he feel differently towards the boys? The answer

came instantly: no. They were both his. Nothing had changed. Pierre was his son. No one would ever take him away.

If Sean was to move on and rebuild his life, he needed to learn more about Yvette. He rang the bell and asked Max to arrange for a tray of sandwiches, then he settled himself once again to read through all the diaries.

By the time he'd finished reading all the way back to when she'd started keeping a journal as a thirteen-year-old girl, it was past midnight. Finally, he understood his wife. He doubted she'd ever been genuinely content.

From what he'd gleaned, Yvette believed her mother had blamed her for being the one to survive whooping cough as a child when her brother had died. Perhaps she was right – now, he'd never know. Either way, Sophia had a lot to answer for. She'd taught Yvette to view her role in life as an ornamental, adored creature with the right to sleep with another man as she saw fit.

Yvette fell for Peter when she was a girl and her love had never faltered. The entries that saddened him most were those where she wrote about having little maternal affection for Pierre and none for Joshua. She refused to accept Pierre's disabilities were anything other than a cruel trick of nature. Perhaps it eased her conscience.

One thing was evident from the diary entries: Peter was aware he was Pierre's natural father. It was unlikely Peter would ever want to make the knowledge public, but if he did, he had no proof. Sean should have been furious with Peter, but he wasn't. If Yvette's diaries were to be believed, then Peter had also allowed himself to be manipulated into a marriage he didn't want and had spent his life longing for Yvette. Sean pitied him. And

Louise. She'd been betrayed by both her husband and her best friend.

Pierre or Joshua might want to read these diaries one day, but he couldn't let that happen. They could never learn how little she cared for them.

One by one, he dropped them on the fire. If Pierre ever discovered Sean had withheld the truth from him, would he be angry with his father, as Sean had once railed at his own mother for keeping his origins secret? Perhaps. It was a chance he was prepared to take. Because now Sean appreciated what his mother meant when she said her love for him wasn't lessened because she hadn't given birth to him.

He wanted to tell his sons only the good things about their mother, but it pained him that right now, he couldn't think of anything. No one was all bad. With time, pleasant memories would surface, surely, and he'd build on them. Isn't that what everyone did? The graveyard was overflowing with faultless people. Posthumous saints.

She'd had a tinkling laugh . . . Yes, he'd tell them that and assure them she *had* adored them. It would be a lie, but one intended to protect them. They were his priority. He'd devote himself to raising them, securing their future and helping Pierre to make the most of his silent world.

The next morning, Sean woke early. Somehow, he felt cleansed, empowered, changed. More of the man he'd hoped to become before he'd found out about his own birth. He hadn't ruined Yvette's life – that was an enormous relief. Most importantly, the realisation that he didn't care about Pierre's parentage was cathartic.

Perhaps now he could stop punishing himself and be

with Jane. Would she still want him? Sean needed her, there was no doubt about that. But he'd always been too impulsive. He was in control right at this moment, but it would be selfish to contact Jane now. He owed it to her to learn to be happy while alone first.

Chapter 16

Kate pressed the piece of chalk so hard against the blackboard that it snapped. Had William Tyler *really* had the gall to say that to her? She rounded on the man sitting casually on the edge of a desk. He was tall and good-looking, with fair hair that flopped forwards charmingly.

"Mr Tyler! Abigail is an extremely bright girl. But no one can excel in every area. Her French is more than passable for a girl of her age."

"If you can't teach her, perhaps someone else can."

"For you to put Abigail's poor French accent down to my teaching is incredibly insulting."

"I have no wish to offend you, Miss Caldwell, but my niece should be fluent by now. During the last holidays I insisted we spoke French at all times and she barely uttered a word."

"Perhaps it was more to do with the company than her ability to converse."

"You do realise I pay her fees?" He smirked.

"Of course."

"Then perhaps you should speak to me in a more respectful manner."

He was so irritating. She'd like to respect him with a punch on the nose. Kate breathed deeply.

"If you focused on getting to know her, you'd notice that she's a lovely kind girl with an inquisitive mind and a great sense of fun. Surely that's more important than worrying about what you referred to as her provincial French accent!"

"Are you questioning my ability to be her guardian?"

"I rather thought I was defending my skills as a teacher."

His attractive green eyes smouldered. They wouldn't look so sexy if she blackened them for him.

"Mr Tyler," she continued, "the weekends and holidays where the pupils spend time at home should be enjoyable – an opportunity to reconnect with their families. In Abigail's case, it's especially important. She needs to be loved, having suffered the loss of her parents."

"I do love her."

"Does she know that?"

"I hope so." His face softened. "My apologies for the way I spoke to you. I never saw myself as being a father. And I'm unsure how to guide the girl. She'll be a young woman before long and it terrifies me."

She understood his concerns. Abigail's mother and father had died in a sailing accident when she was five years old and her uncle had suddenly found himself caring for his niece. He was raising a child alone, so despite how annoyed she was, she felt a grudging respect for him.

"Be patient with her," she said. "When she's here at school, she'll be able to feel almost like all the other pupils, but when she goes home, it must magnify what she's lost. After the holidays or any home visit, all the girls exchange stories of the things they did with their parents or siblings. Abigail is always quiet."

William glanced out of the window. "That makes me so ashamed."

"It shouldn't. No doubt you're doing your best. Try to have fun with her. With summer approaching, there's bound to be some celebrations you can enjoy together."

"There's a fair on Sunday. Would you come with us?"

"Excuse me?"

"Come with us."

"Pardon?"

"Would you prefer me to invite you in French? I'm inviting you to attend the fair with Abigail and me."

"With you . . . and Abigail?"

"Is that such a horrific suggestion? You appear to understand my niece better than I do. She likes you. You can help me to interact with her."

"Are you serious?"

"Naturally."

"You want me to come along to teach you how to behave with her?"

He smirked. "A few tips here and there wouldn't go amiss. But mainly, I'm asking you because I'm incredibly attracted to you and want to spend time with you."

"Oh."

"Well? How about it? I'll pick you up at say . . . ten o'clock?"

As Kate gaped at William, her thoughts returned to Sean. Regardless of how she'd longed for him in the past, she'd finally accepted that he'd never be hers. If there was a time when it might have been possible, it had passed. He'd been so vulnerable after Yvette's death and helping him to come to terms with what had happened had been a torturous mix of pain and pleasure. He'd needed her.

And it had been wonderful, intoxicating. But seeing him suffer had hurt more than she'd imagined possible.

The night Sean had broken down and she'd held him had been a turning point for them both. She was certain that if she'd kissed him, he'd have responded and she'd finally have found out if the reality of making love to him lived up to her fantasy. And Sean was a gentleman, so he may have felt obliged to propose. He could have been hers. Although really that was nonsense. She may have been his wife, but she'd never have held his heart. She'd have trapped him in a marriage just as Yvette had. And one day it would have been Jane to whom he turned.

Following what Kate thought of as their near miss, the next few times she'd visited Sean there had been an awkwardness between them. Clearly, he'd also realised how close they'd come to taking their relationship to a more intimate level. She'd taken their mutual embarrassment as a sign that they weren't meant to be together in that way. She still visited him, although with less frequency, and Sean appeared to welcome the new arrangement, the distance. As for her, she'd come to her senses, realising it was stupid to waste her love on a man who would never be able to reciprocate.

"Miss Caldwell, have you forgotten I'm here? Do I need to raise my hand to get your attention?" he said, smiling.

Kate's attention was jolted back to the man in front of her. Even though she wanted to stick her piece of chalk up his left nostril, William Tyler was eligible, challenging, exciting.

"Make it ten thirty," she blurted.

"Wonderful. Now, I'll collect my niece if she's ready."

"All the girls are waiting in the hall for their parents."

"Right. Oh, and wear something blue."

"I beg your pardon?"

"Dress in blue."

"Blue?"

"That suit you wore for the parents' assembly last month would be perfect."

"Why?"

"It sets off your eyes." He grinned.

What a cheek!

Despite herself, Kate was smiling as she finished tidying the classroom. Then she went to find Bella, who was on the driveway waving off the last of the girls.

"You'll never guess. I'm going to a country fair with Abigail and William Tyler on Sunday."

"Never? He's dashing in a stern sort of way. He terrifies me."

Kate laughed. "He invited me while we were bickering about my teaching methods and Abigail's French pronunciation. He's quite assertive."

Bella giggled. "If you ask me, he's just what you need to keep you in check."

"Impertinent madam."

"You're flushed. If he's had this effect on you, I like him already. Ooo, he owns a plane, doesn't he?"

"So I understand."

"He might take you up in it! How exciting."

"How terrifying, you mean. My feet are staying firmly on the ground. Anyway, talking of exciting things, when are you going to admit that you care about Richard?"

"When did we start talking about me?"

"When I changed the topic. Come on – confess."

"I don't have feelings for Richard Yates or any man."

"Your eyes tell a different story."

"I'm admitting nothing. But I was thinking – Yvette's death made me realise nothing is hopeless unless you're dead. I don't want to waste my future – not that it's being wasted, exactly. Our school is diverting and you're marvellous. And I adore spending time with Pierre and Joshua."

"Yes, I understand all that, but what I'm interested in is how you really feel. Not what you think we all want to hear."

"The thing is, I've not been as happy as I pretend."

"Tell me something I'm not aware of."

Bella glanced over her shoulder then lowered her voice, even though they were alone.

"George ripped my heart apart like an old newspaper. Twisted it into pieces and used it for kindling. The humiliation I can cope with – just about. But even after all these months, I feel as though the agony of his betrayal might kill me."

"Sweetie, eventually you'll get over it. No one dies of a broken heart if they fight it."

"There's no fight left in me. I've never been clever like you and Father. Or determined to improve people's lives in the way Mother is. But I felt I still had a place in the family and the world. It wasn't much, I suppose, but Mother always said my optimism brought out the best in people.

"I genuinely believed that everyone had good in them. And I care about people, I really do. Occasionally, I considered training to become a nurse. No one knew, because I wasn't sure I was brave enough to face watching people in pain. But then George came along and suddenly, he was my only dream."

"And now? Because if you don't want to stay at the school, I'll understand."

"Now, I've lost sense of who I am." Bella hesitated. "When I'm around lots of people, or even a few, I get panicky. It's terrifying, as though I can't breathe."

"You're not ill?"

Bella took Kate's hand, leading her back inside, walking as they talked.

"No. Give me a chance and I'll explain. I put it off for months, but after the kidnapping, I finally saw Owain. It's caused by nerves. If I were a more gentile lady, I'd be fainting every time someone upset me. Pathetic, really. All I know for sure is that there's no way I'm going to let it stop me from getting back to who I was before George."

In the parlour, Kate poured them both a sherry.

"What George put you through was bound to have an effect. The Irish let out their rage. You should have screamed at us all like a banshee and not pretended everything was fine."

"I'm not the screaming sort."

"More's the pity. So, what are you going to do about it?"

"I've found ways to cope."

"Are you deliberately being obtuse to torture me? How are you going to find the old Bella?"

"Even though I've allowed Richard to escort me to the theatre and the picture house, he knows we can only ever be friends. And, well, I've just had an idea. It's rare *all* the pupils go home. We generally have one of two who stay over at the weekend and now you're going out—"

"Heavens, Bella! The suspense is torturing me."

"Now I'm tempted not to tell you."

"Bella!"

"I might invite Richard for a picnic in the grounds on Sunday afternoon."

"Hardly running off to Marrakesh, but at least you won't be on your own for the day."

Overall, Sean was coping better. For the last two weeks, he'd bounced from being annoyed at Yvette's deceit to being pleased that she'd experienced real love while also being incredibly relieved that not everything was his fault. Their marriage was a result of her scheming. She'd planned it all. As for the crash, it wasn't a case of him easing his own conscience – he'd been drunk enough times in the past to know that he'd still been in control of his faculties.

Countless times he'd been tempted to contact Jane and beg her forgiveness. But good sense had prevailed and he'd resisted. Jane had a new life now and his focus must be on building his business and ensuring his sons had a happy, stable home. How happy it could be with a father who was lonely remained to be seen.

There was a sharp tap on his office door.

"Can I have a word, boss?"

"I've always got time for you, Kitty," Sean said.

She frowned as she stalked towards him, waving a yard of emerald taffeta.

"You might not be so welcoming when you see this bloody thing."

"Sounds ominous."

"The quality of this latest batch is a blinking disgrace. It all needs to go back." She spread the material on his desk. "This fault runs all the way through the lot."

"Have you got enough other fabric to be going on with, or will it affect production?"

"I'll switch the girls over to making the plum-coloured two-pieces. Then they can go back to the dresses when the replacement cloth arrives. Will you ring Marshalls, or do you want me to give them the length of my tongue?"

"I think we'll save your wrath for if they don't get it sorted."

"Righto. I'll get back in there and give them their new orders. We don't want them sitting idle."

"As if they'd have the opportunity with you around. Is everything else going to plan? I worry I put on you."

"Aye, yeh feed me through the mangle every day. But I wouldn't want it any other way."

"Get back to it then, woman, before I dock your wages," he quipped.

Laughing, Kitty walked to the door. There, she paused and leaned against it, her face serious.

"Oh no. What have I done now?" Sean said.

"How are you doing, Tatty Head?"

He managed a half-smile. "Could be worse."

"By the look of you, not much."

Sean shrugged. "Are Jake and Brian still having trouble coping with what happened to them?"

"When you consider what Charnock put them through, they're not doing too bad. Brian hasn't wet the bed for the last few nights. Not since I let the puppies sleep on their beds."

"The dogs are bound to make them feel safer."

"P'rhaps, but Albert said the little devil might have been pouring water on his mattress so I'd give in. The spaniels didn't like being made to stay in the kitchen and kept crying."

171

Sean gave a half-hearted laugh. "I wouldn't put it past him."

"How's Pierre and Josh doing?"

"Not bad. If Josh is awake, he's smiling. Pierre kept pulling at his ear last week. Owain thought he had an ear infection, so he prescribed something for it and he's as right as rain now."

"I'm proud of you, Tatty Head."

"Me?"

"Aye, you, yeh daft lump. You'll not often get a compliment off me, but you've impressed me and that's more than most ever manage."

He pulled at his tight collar. "Don't, please. You can't possibly mean that."

"You're my gaffer, but you can't tell me what I think. For a start, you've built the factory from nothing. And since the accident, you've stayed off the booze. That's surprised me, I don't mind admitting."

"It's hardly something I should be praised for. I should never have let liquor get a grip of me in the first place," Sean said ungraciously.

"Aw, Tatty Head, love, don't be ashamed of making mistakes. That road leads to misery. The important thing is that despite having a rough time of it, you've come through. The only ones who make no mistakes are those who end up in the ground before they can talk."

"You might have a point there."

"Course I blinking do. When are yeh gonna learn I've got more sense than folk give me credit for. It might not be my place to say anything—"

"Something tells me that won't stop you."

"No, it won't." She strode towards him. "I've kept quiet

172

and told no one about me catching you an' Jane together at our Milly's the morning after Charles died. But if you ask me, you're not grieving for Yvette. It's misplaced guilt – you love Jane and you're pining for her."

Sean drummed his fingers on his desk absently. There was no arguing with that.

"Happiness is waiting for yeh, if you've a mind to take it," she added.

Sean stared at her.

"Don't look at me as though I'm knitting on one needle. Haven't we just established that I'm nowhere near as stupid as I look? You know full well I'm talking about you and Jane. You should be together now and instead, you're both miserable."

"It's how it has to be."

"Look, Sean, I've never said this to anyone, not even my Albert. But giving up Jane and Robert when they were babies was the hardest thing I've ever had to do. Many a time I've regretted it. And I've lost count of the nights I've lain awake wondering what it might have been like if I'd kept them. But I've never tried to be anything more than an auntie to them – it wouldn't have been fair on our Milly. But in me heart . . ." She pressed a clenched fist to her chest.

"It must have been so difficult for you, Kitty. I can't imagine losing my boys."

"I love Jane and Robert as much as I do Jake and Brian. Maybe I'd have felt the same about them if our Milly had given birth to them, what with me an' her being so close, but there's no way of knowing." She gulped as though swallowing her emotions. "What I'm trying to say is that Jane's my only daughter an' it breaks me heart to think of her being miserable. And if you stay off the drink, I can't think of a better husband for her."

"There are worthier men than me. Jane can have anyone she chooses."

"Perhaps, but she loves you and when the women in my family love, it's for life. What's more is I know you'd never hurt her. If you were with the right woman, you could achieve anything."

"I can't talk about Jane."

"Bottling things up won't do you any good. You and me have always been mates."

"I know that, Kitty." Sean hesitated. "Is she really still unhappy?"

"I'm glad you asked. I spoke to our Milly last night on the telephone and according to her, Jane comes home every Sunday, but she hardly speaks, which isn't like Jane. O' course Milly, like everyone else, has got no idea what's happened, although she suspects Jane had a fella on the quiet and summat went wrong."

"You said nothing, did you?"

"Did I blinking heck."

"It'll all work out for the best."

"Flaming Nora! Is that all you've got to say? Whatever's gone on, put it behind you and fight for her, Sean."

"My sons and the factory are all I can cope with. Just let it drop, please."

"Jane could help you with the boys, so I'm sorry, Tatty Head, but I'm going to keep reminding you that she loves you and you're throwing away your chance of happiness."

"You won't give up, will you?"

"Not as long as I've got a hole in my backside."

"Then can we stop talking about her for now? I don't

want to sound ungrateful, but I need to focus on getting through each day."

"Fair enough. I'm here *when* you change your mind. But Jane might not wait forever."

In the months since the accident, sometimes he didn't think he'd have been able to keep the factory running without Kitty.

"I do appreciate you, Kitty. Your friendship and everything you do to help run this place . . . I don't know what I'd do without you. Do I pay you enough?"

"Not even close, lad. I'm a fool working for a pittance. I'd earn more selling my body." She did a little wiggle.

"Albert might object to you taking up that line of work."

"You're probably right, so I'd best put up with things here then until summat better comes along like cleaning out privies."

When Kitty closed his office door behind her, Sean leaned against the back of his chair, stretching his shoulders back to ease the tension. Whenever he thought about Jane, his chest knotted. He grabbed the telephone. God help Marshalls if they refused to replace the faulty goods within the next few days.

Chapter 17

Victoria was already standing in her hallway when she heard Owain's car coming up the drive. Not wanting to keep him waiting, she quickly checked her appearance in the mirror before donning her lace gloves. She was proud of her contribution to the Rows renovation project. Decisions regarding paint colours and selecting suppliers had been left to her and she liaised with the site foreman daily, ensuring that problems such as delays in the delivery of materials and sanitation issues were addressed swiftly. However, she was sure Owain was the best person to manage this latest situation.

"It was good of you to collect me. Normally, Edward would have driven me into town, but he has an appointment," she said.

Owain bowed slightly. "My pleasure, Victoria. You look very fetching."

"Thank you." Her cheeks pinked. Even at her age, she still found it difficult to accept a compliment. "Am I overdressed? Should I change?"

She glanced down at her lightweight dove-grey two-piece. During the time she'd been working on the Rows project, she'd struggled to choose the right outfit when meeting the residents in their homes. Despite dealing with the poor when she owned the mill, somehow her well-cut clothing caused the shabbily dressed women to apologise for their own standards of dress. Which, frankly, had made her feel terrible.

"As always, you've struck the right balance between elegance and businesslike."

"Thank you," she said, reddening deeper. "Shall we go?"

As Owain drove off, she said, "I didn't want to drag you away from your practice when you're so busy, but I understand from the foreman that Queenie says she's not budging. As she's been a patient of yours for years, I'm hoping she'll be less suspicious of your motives."

"She's quite a character and can be stubborn, but we'll convince her."

"I certainly hope so, because there are only these last few and all sixty houses will have had a complete overhaul."

"Don't worry. We'll soon sort it," he said.

"Your help on the project has been invaluable."

Owain reached out and patted her hand. She felt the warmth of his touch through the lace. It was intimate. Wrong. Victoria wondered if it was her imagination, or was Owain looking at her strangely again?

Over the last couple of months, she'd detected a change in his manner towards her. Nothing untoward – just different, more familiar. Fleeting moments where she'd been uncomfortable but couldn't explain why. Such as when his fingers had touched hers as he'd passed her an article relating to sanitation. She'd assumed it was accidental, but now she wasn't sure.

"Don't play down your part in this. You've worked tirelessly. Besides, we're a first-rate team, you and I," Owain said, his head cocked as he gazed at her.

Again, she was unnerved.

"Yes, yes, we've done well."

He should have been focusing on the road, not looking at her with that daft grin on his face. Now she thought about it, there had been other occasions, too, where his eyes had lingered on her slightly longer than they should. This was preposterous – they'd known each other for over thirty years, since Sean was a baby. He was a kind man, and she liked his no-nonsense attitude and work ethic. She'd always been relaxed in his presence.

Perhaps Owain was less formal with her because he was almost part of the family. Back at the start of the year, Anne had been convinced he was going to propose to her. Although recently, she'd told Victoria that she was losing patience with him.

"What's the matter with the man? I have made it as clear as I can without humiliating myself that I will accept his offer," Anne had said.

Then last week, when Victoria and Edward had joined Owain and Anne for dinner at Latimers, Owain had made several remarks about what a fortunate man Edward was. Edward had simply agreed with him, whereas Anne had glared at her.

Victoria was brought back to the present as Owain parked outside a small terraced house in Farriers Row.

"Before we go in, I want to say how much I'm enjoying working with you." He reached out to touch her hand again. "You're a remarkable woman."

Victoria inched her fingers from under his. Perhaps it was her imagination – surely it must be . . . She was acting like a young girl.

"Er. Yes, well. It's been pleasant," she said finally.

178

"I hope Edward realises how blessed he is."

Goodness. There was definitely something odd about his manner.

"I'm the fortunate one. Edward is wonderful."

Victoria exited the car door, not waiting for Owain to assist her as she normally would. She rapped on the battered door of number nine and it was opened by a young woman wearing a hairnet and a floral wraparound pinny.

"Morning, Rene," Victoria said.

"Hiya, Mrs Caldwell, ma'am. Queenie is in the back kitchen." Rene leaned forwards to whisper. "Don't sit down. The place is riddled wi' bedbugs."

Victoria flinched.

"Don't worry – you'll smell them before you see them," Rene added.

Victoria hesitated, her nose wrinkled and her brow furrowed.

"They have an odour similar to coriander," Owain explained, smiling. He put his hand to the small of her back. "After you, my dear."

There was no need for him to touch her. Should she mention her concerns to Edward? No. He enjoyed his weekly game of chess with Owain. She didn't want to affect their friendship because she was imagining things. Pushing it from her mind as she entered the cramped kitchen, she jolted, stifling the instinct to cover her nose, and gave the old woman a tight smile.

"This is Mrs Caldwell. She's come to talk to you about doing up yer house," Rene said.

Queenie returned her curled sandwich to the plate, folded her arms across her sagging breasts and glared.

Owain sidestepped Victoria to enter the room. "Hello, Queenie."

"'Ow are yeh, Doctor?" Queenie replied with a gummy smile. "Do you wanna cuppa or a biscuit?" She gestured to the table.

Victoria's eyes moved to the brown tablecloth. Her stomach lurched as she took in dozens of flat creatures wandering across it and over the biscuits.

"Not today – I don't have time," Owain said.

Today! Victoria shuddered. Surely he'd never accepted something to eat or drink here before . . .

"How are your aches and pains?" he asked.

"Creasing me, Doc. At my age, I don't s'pose I can expect owt else." She held up her knotty fingers. "It's these buggers that get me down. You'd think with summer upon us that they'd ease off, but the slightest bit of cold weather makes 'em worse. I can't fasten me buttons to get dressed decent, never mind keep on top o' this place."

Owain opened his bag. "Here . . . I'll leave this with you. Take a drop when we've gone. It'll ease them."

Queenie flicked her cloudy eyes towards Rene. "Can yeh see me purse? I can barely see owt these days. Still, I s'pose it means I can't see the mess. What do I owe yeh for the bottle, Doc?"

"Now, Queenie, after all the years you helped me to birth half the occupants of the Rows, you know me better than to think I'd take a penny from you."

"Aww, Doc. God created a good 'un when He made you."

"Now, Queenie, what's this nonsense about you not moving out?"

"They claim I'm to go to a boarding house while they do me place up. But I know their game, Doc. They're trying to get me out and into the workhouse. I'm havin' none of it. Not while I can still pay me rent. You know me son sends money from Liverpool – regular as clockwork – don't you, Doc? You can vouch for me."

"I can. Now, have I ever lied to you, Queenie?"

"No, Doc. I'd be a liar mesel' if I said yeh had. You've always been straight wi' me, even when you had to tell me my lass were dying, an' I know how hard that was for yeh."

"Good. Remember the Gibbs family who used to live in Halton Row?"

"Aye, Doc – nine kids I helped bring into the world. Plain bunch, 'cept the youngest girl."

"Well, Harry is a rich man now and he owns the Rows."

"I've been hearing the same from others. Richer than Midas, they're sayin', but I don't believe it. They couldn't afford newspaper to wipe their arses, never mind ownin' houses." She cocked her head towards Victoria. "Begging yer pardon for me language, ma'am, but I speak as I find. Always have an' always will. Ain't that right, Doc?"

"You have, Queenie. Though what you've been told is true. He is your new landlord."

"The youngest, Harry, was a quiet lad, if I remember right. Always knew how to make a bob or two. Had an entire army of kids collecting firewood for him to sell during the winter."

"Well, Harry's never forgotten where he came from and wants people to have decent homes. He acquired the houses so he could renovate them. Also, as you're the oldest resident, we've chosen you to have all new furniture, bedding and curtains."

"By heck. That would be summat, 'cos I've got a few crawlers. I've not been able to do much since I hurt me hip."

Rene stepped forwards. "An' when you move back in, I'll come round once a week to give the house a good bottoming for yeh."

"Will you have time with your own house to do, now you're wed?" Owain asked.

"I'll manage. We take care of our own round here. Queenie used to look after me an' my sister when we were kids. She'd always slip us a slice of bread if our dad had no work."

"You're a good lass, Rene," Queenie said.

"I'd have done summat before now, Queenie, if I'd realised you were struggling." Rene turned to Victoria. "She never said owt an' has let no one in here for years. The only reason I'm here now is 'cos I stuck me nose in when the foreman were banging on her door yelling that she had to move out."

Victoria scratched her arm absent-mindedly. "He shouldn't have done that, Queenie. I apologise. However, if you're happy for the work to go ahead . . ." She paused, fighting the urge to scratch her head, her leg, her neck. She needed to leave before she ran out screaming. "We can get you into a boarding house next week and you'll be back home before you know it."

"If the doc says I can trust yeh, I will. Aye, all right."

"I'll make the arrangements and send a messenger with the details."

"Tell him to come to my house, if you don't mind. I'll sort everything," Rene said.

Back in the street, Victoria gave free rein to her desire to scratch.

When Owain and Rene smirked, she said, "It's not funny. I can't stop."

182

"Victoria, don't move." Owain reached out to her shoulder. "You had a little passenger."

"Eww." Victoria shuddered. "Errgh."

Rene laughed. "I'll wash some of her clothes this afternoon an' help her sort the stuff she's keeping. Don't worry – I'll throw away owt infested."

Still scratching, Victoria said, "I appreciate that. So will the owner of the lodgings. He certainly wouldn't be pleased if Queenie caused an infestation."

Once they'd completed the arrangements and Rene had gone back inside Queenie's house, Owain drove Victoria home.

"If you don't mind, I won't ask you in for tea. I'd like to change," she said.

In truth, she didn't know whether it was her imagination or not, but she was no longer comfortable alone in his company. It was strange how a relationship could be altered so quickly.

Martha, their housemaid, opened the door.

"Is everything all right, ma'am?"

"Please run me a bath and once I've undressed, burn all of my clothes, including my hat."

"But, Mrs Caldwell, this grey coat has got years left in it. Don't you want it laundered or sent to charity?"

"I hate waste, Martha, but please do as I say – they might be infested," Victoria said, shuddering as she made for the staircase.

Fire might get rid of the bugs, but it wouldn't expunge her uncomfortable thoughts about Owain.

Chapter 18

The August sun burned white hot, but under the shade of a large oak tree, Victoria and Edward spent the morning reading in companionable silence, surrounded by a mass of colourful blooms and intoxicating scents. A bee hovered above Edward, who had nodded off, his mouth hanging slightly open. Then it moved away and settled in a patch of delphiniums.

She couldn't imagine life without him. He was far more than her husband – he was her rock. How much longer would they have together? The thought of losing him or leaving him behind were both equally terrifying. Why was she being maudlin on such a glorious day? It was typical of her. She was worrying about the future instead of making the most of a period where, for once, life was relatively calm.

Sean appeared to be settled, running his factory and raising his sons. Of course, she still hoped that one day before long he'd meet someone special. Because despite his devoted parenting, they needed a mother and Sean, a wife. Still, there was no hurry – she didn't want him to rush into another mistake.

After the crash she'd noticed Kate and Sean growing closer, and her feelings had been mixed. If they had found happiness together, she'd have been delighted. On the other hand, if they'd become romantically involved and it went wrong, the family would have been rent apart. Now, it seemed unlikely, as Kate was courting William Tyler. She claimed it was all very casual, but he'd brought a flush to Kate's skin and an enthusiasm that had been missing for years, since Sean became engaged to Yvette. Could it be that Kate hadn't realised she was falling for William? She wouldn't be the first woman to be blind to her own feelings.

As for Bella, now her smiles and laughter seemed more genuine. Although adamant that their relationship wouldn't develop further, Bella had recently admitted that she regarded Richard Yates as a friend. Unbeknown to anyone else, Edward had checked into Richard's past and was confident he had no secrets. They hoped that one day, the pair would marry.

Edward woke with a start.

"Did you enjoy your nap?" she asked.

"I wasn't asleep – I was only resting my eyes."

"So you snore while you're awake? How unusual."

Edward chuckled, straightening his wire-rimmed spectacles. "Maybe I had five minutes. Shall we have lunch? All this reading builds up an appetite."

"All right, then this afternoon we need to sort out some clothes to give to the charity bazaar."

Edward stood. "Come on then, old girl. I'll help you up."

"Less of the old," she said, accepting his outstretched hand.

After a light lunch of ham salad, eaten on the patio, they went to their bedroom. It was dark and stuffy after being outside, so Victoria opened the sash window.

"That's better," she said.

"Perhaps we should have left this job until it cooled down," Edward suggested.

"Best get it over." She held up a shirt for him to inspect. "I assume this one can go in the box. You've not worn it in years and I doubt it'll still fit you."

Edward puffed out his chest and pulled in stomach. "Are you saying I'm fat?"

Victoria smirked. "Just cuddly."

"Cuddly!" He feigned horror, holding the back of his hand to his forehead. "Hardly how a man likes his wife to describe him. I'm going to have to tell Cook not to make any more of her rock cakes, because if I know they're in the pantry, I can't resist them."

Victoria placed the shirt in the donation box and selected another from the shelf. As she inspected the cuffs, she said, "I love you as you are. You look contented."

Edward laughed. "No more, please. It's like a knife to my heart."

"I can see that I've mortally wounded you."

"Perhaps I need to wear stays."

"Your jokes are getting worse as you get older."

"That's crueller than saying I'm getting fat. Being amusing is something I pride myself on."

She laughed. "You should have been on stage. You were wasted on law."

"Such sarcasm. Kirby appreciates my sense of humour. Don't you, old boy?"

The golden retriever, who was lying in a shady spot at the foot of the bed, with his head resting on his paws, did what Victoria could only describe as a canine eye-roll. She returned the shirt to the wardrobe, then halted as there was a tap on the door.

"Come in," she said.

"Ma'am, you have a visitor—"

Her sister-in-law bustled into the room.

"No need to announce me. I am family," Anne said.

Although middle-aged, with a smattering of silver in her blonde hair, Anne was a pretty woman. Over the years, Victoria had come to care for her, but at times she still found her infuriating. She hoped this wouldn't be one of those occasions. Victoria removed a pale grey suit from the wardrobe.

"Anne, what a pleasant surprise. I didn't realise you were intending to visit today. Perhaps we should go into the parlour. Cook can make some tea. Or would you prefer lemonade as it's so warm?"

Anne straightened her collar before plonking herself on their bed and frowning.

"Nothing for me. I wouldn't normally intrude into your boudoir, but I am incensed."

"Thank you. That will be all, Martha," Victoria said.

Whatever had got Anne's corset in a tangle, it would be best to keep it private.

Before Martha had shut the door, Anne blurted, "I can hardly believe it of you, Victoria. Then again, nothing you do should surprise me."

Victoria groaned, glancing at Edward. He gave a "don't ask me" shrug.

"What have I done wrong this time?"

"So, you admit you are at fault?"

"No, Anne. I'm simply assuming that based on your manner and words, you're cross with me. What do you wish to speak to me about?"

"I would have thought it was obvious."

"Anne, it's way too hot for guessing games. Why don't we have some refreshments on the patio? It's lovely in the garden."

"I am fine where I am, thank you. Being outside surrounded by beauty would highlight how my dreams have withered."

Goodness. Anne was always a touch dramatic, but how could Victoria have possibly done anything to cause such despondency? She'd not seen Anne for weeks.

"Whatever is the matter, Anne?" Edward asked, taking his sister's hand.

Anne sighed loudly. "Owain."

Victoria stiffened. "What about him?"

"Months I have been waiting patiently for him to make his intentions clear. Then today we have been for a walk in the park. It should have been romantic, but no. The entire time, all he talked about was you, Victoria. What an inspirational, *caring*, *elegant* woman you are. I mean, what does that make me? An old crone?"

Victoria was unsure if Anne expected an answer.

"We were supposed to be dining together this evening, but I shall have to claim I am unwell," Anne added.

"Come now, Anne. Surely that won't be necessary," Edward said.

"I will not allow myself to be humiliated in this way. As my only brother, I expect you to support me in this."

Edward frowned at his sister. "Victoria is wonderful. I can't argue with Owain on that score. He admires her – I am aware of that. But humiliation? What are you suggesting?"

"Isn't it obvious? Not content with having her own doting husband, Victoria wants to ensnare the only man I am interested in."

Anne's voice was rising and Victoria regretted opening the window. She hoped Cook or Martha weren't outside – she didn't want them hearing.

"While using the excuse of doing charitable works, they have been flirting with each other behind our backs. You can choose to close your eyes to their carrying on, but I refuse to allow them to make a fool of me, even if you don't care," Anne ended.

Victoria's mouth dropped open, but words didn't form.

Edward chuckled. "Don't be silly, Anne. Owain is my friend. He would never make advances towards Victoria."

"I am not being silly, Edward. It is clear now that Victoria is the reason he has not proposed. As Owain and I have no formal understanding, it is impossible for me to say anything to him, but you need to deal with your wife before it is too late."

"Arrgh!" As Victoria shrieked, Kirby ran under the bed with surprising agility. "Anne! How dare you accuse me of being unfaithful to my husband."

Anne jerked, sliding off the bed, pulling the silk eiderdown to the floor with her. As Edward helped up the stunned Anne, Victoria stuffed the suit she was holding in with the charity donations, despite it being one of Edward's favourites.

"As for you, Edward Caldwell, why the hell wasn't your response that my wife would never . . . Arrrgh!" She kicked the box. "Or, Vicky would never behave inappropriately," she growled.

Anne looked nervously from one to the other as she adjusted her clothing.

"Vicky, my love, that was a given. I—" Edward said.

"I don't want an answer yet. Anne, shoo! Go home before I *really* lose my temper and say something I'll regret."

"Charming!" Anne screeched.

Victoria gripped Anne's shoulders and pushed her towards the door. Grasping the handle, she yanked the door open.

"Edward, are you going to allow her to manhandle me?" Anne said as she hovered in the doorway, looking over her shoulder.

Victoria slammed the door and it shuddered in its frame. She was livid with the pair of them. As for Owain, despite wanting to believe she was imagining it all, Anne's comments had catapulted her concerns about his feelings to the forefront of her mind again. Was she to blame? Surely a woman shouldn't have to watch every move a man made.

Edward was standing quietly by the door, watching her. Eventually, he asked, "Victoria, are you feeling calmer now?"

"Do I look calmer?"

He shrugged one shoulder. "A little."

"Well I'm not. Why didn't you jump to my defence and throw Anne out yourself? Don't you trust me?"

"Of course I do. But you are still a beautiful woman. You have never realised the effect you have on men. Perhaps that is why you don't take steps to keep them at arm's length."

"Are you suggesting that if Owain has formed an attachment to me, it's my fault?"

"No. But I can't blame him if he has. What man wouldn't want to be with you?"

190

"Anne's talking nonsense and so are you."

"I have noticed the way he looks at you, but he wouldn't act on it."

"And you think I would?"

"I didn't say that. Nevertheless, it would be prudent if you told him you are stepping away from the project."

"Why?"

"For Anne's sake."

"No, absolutely not."

"Vicky, why would you be stubborn over this? The renovations are progressing well – your contribution can't be that vital."

"It's nice to know how important you think my role is. I've spent months working on this, having meetings about water closets, gagging over filthy open drains while the foreman explained the issues he faced laying the new pipes. Do you have any idea how upsetting it was for me to stand in a bedroom where mould covered the walls and cockroaches swarmed over a bed shared by six children while dead mice rotted in the corner of the room? The only thing that got me through it was knowing that I was making their lives better. So I'm not giving up something so important to me for Anne or anyone else."

"Then you should speak to Owain, or do you want me to have a discreet word?"

"Don't you dare. Thanks to Anne, I'll feel awkward enough next time I see him. The project will be finished before long. Until then, Anne will have to put up with things as they are."

"I would have thought you would have wanted to stop Owain from developing feelings for you."

"So, you *are* blaming me. Not every woman assumes

that all men fall at their feet. This is laughable. Out! Tell Cook I'm not coming down to dinner this evening. I'd like a tray in my room and I'll be retiring early."

"Vicky, you're overreacting."

"Out! And take your dog with you."

Left alone, Victoria fumed, screwing up random garments of Edward's and throwing them in the donation box. Edward was blaming her. As they thought she was a temptress, then perhaps she'd act like one . . . No, she could never behave in that way – it wasn't in her to do so.

She desperately wanted to believe there was nothing more to Owain's behaviour. Despite this, for the last couple of months, she'd done everything she could to avoid being alone with him, which hadn't been easy. If she mentioned his manner towards her now, it would make working together too uncomfortable. Maybe she *should* tell Owain she was too busy to help. No. She couldn't give up before they'd completed the Rows overhaul. It meant too much to her and she'd worked so hard.

Regardless, eventually she must find some way to ensure he realised there could be nothing between them. Then deal with the embarrassment if he thought she was conceited or crazy or both.

Tears threatened. In all their married life, she and Edward had never argued. The occasional cross word, but nothing serious. She didn't want this to escalate, but there was no immediate solution.

Wednesday night after a long, hot day, Kate finally relieved herself of her clothes, which had clung to her skin mercilessly all day. While soaking in a cool bath, she'd decided to retire to her room, throw open the window and lie on top of the bed in her slip while reading a book until she fell asleep. Instead, five minutes later she was back in the office, her dressing gown wrapped around her, speaking to Jane on the telephone and having to make one of the biggest decisions of her life.

"The thing is, I've applied for a vacancy at a school here in Blackpool," Jane said. "I realise I've never worked for you, but I was wondering if you'd give me a character reference."

"I thought you were settled working as a governess. Did the children turn out to be little monsters?"

"No, they were delightful. It's the father who's the problem."

"Say no more. I take it he wanted you to carry out some extra duties."

"Exactly. He was forever placing his hand on my shoulder and insisting I have dinner with them. Then he'd get drunk and sit staring at me or make lewd comments. It was so embarrassing. Yet the wife ignored his behaviour. The cook told me they dismissed the last governess because she was carrying the master's child.

"The final straw was when he came into the schoolroom on the pretext of talking about their eldest son's progress and tried to kiss me. I slapped his face, locked my bedroom door and put a chair under the handle. The following morning, I quit. The mistress wouldn't believe what I told her and refused to give me a reference because I was leaving her in the lurch."

"I'll gladly give you a reference, but isn't Sean the best person to vouch for you?"

"Probably, but I don't want to ask him. I explained he'd been recently bereaved, so as you're his sister and a headmistress to boot, they agreed you may provide one for me. It's a terrible imposition, but will you do it for me?"

"I'll do it first thing."

"Thanks, Kate."

Kate accepted that she had to speak up.

"I hope you don't mind, but Sean told me about the two of you."

"He did?"

"Yes. Now, don't be cross with him about that, as well." Kate made a joke about Sean being a mess without Jane and then said, "Seriously, you shouldn't give up on him. He adores you and always has."

"He gave up on me. You know him better than anyone, Kate. Did you ever guess he could be so cruel?"

"Jane, he wasn't thinking straight. Guilt, like love, makes us act like crazy people. And Pierre needs you. Bella said he was crying yesterday and he's not missing Yvette, of that I'm certain."

"Don't, Kate. You mustn't make me feel worse than I already do about leaving the boys."

"I don't want you to miss the chance to be together."

"Sean did this, not me. I realise you mean well, but if you could post the character reference, I'd appreciate it."

Kate came off the phone filled with mixed emotions. She hadn't entirely squashed her own feelings for Sean, but they'd never be together and she was glad she'd put his case to Jane, because she didn't want him to be lonely.

Sean had been about to undress, when his butler informed him that there was a telephone call from Kate. He dashed from the room and took the stairs two at a time, trying to stem the fear that his mother or Edward might have taken ill. In his study, he snatched up the telephone.

"Kate, what are you doing telephoning this late? Is there something wrong?" Sean asked.

"Not if you see sense. I've just spoken to Jane. She's quit her job and is back living at Milly's. There's no point my lecturing you, I know that, so all I'm going to say is please think very carefully about your future. You're both miserable without each other and remaining apart isn't helping anyone, especially the boys. Not only will she make an excellent mother to them, but she'll also make you happy, and that must be good for Pierre and Joshua as well as you."

"I'm happy enough."

"Rubbish. You'll never be truly happy without a wife – without Jane. You're not the type to be alone."

"Kate, I—"

"Sean, please don't give me all the reasons you should carry on with your self-imposed torture. Be a little kinder to yourself and try to get her back."

"She might say no. I hurt her terribly."

"Yes, she might, and frankly, I hope she gives you hell – before she gives in, that is. Mull it over. If you decide not to take my advice, I won't mention it again."

"Really?"

"No – I can't be trusted to stick to my word." She laughed. "It's late. Go to bed and imagine how wonderful your life can be if you get Jane back. You're a grand fella and it's time you believe in yourself, so it is."

As Sean made his way upstairs, he replayed the conversation in his mind. Surely Kate was wrong. But what if she was right? He was feeling stronger than he'd ever remembered. In all the months since the crash, he'd not taken a drink. He didn't want one. Not even in his low moments when he was missing Jane or dealing with problems at the factory or home.

Sean undressed and held out his waistcoat to Max.

"Are you happy, Max?"

His valet hesitated.

"Sorry, is that question too personal?" Sean added.

"It is, really, but I don't mind answering. Things could be worse. I enjoy working here. The other servants are decent enough and not having any family, it's important to get on with those I work with." Max smiled cheekily. "And you're not too bad as employers go."

"I suppose I asked for that."

"What made you ask, sir?"

"Something Kate said. She believes I'll never be truly happy without a wife."

"Ah, then I'd say Miss Caldwell is correct, sir. If you ask me, human beings aren't meant to be alone. Some of us have no choice. It takes all my strength to deny my unnatural desires, but I do it because I hate who I am." Max squeezed the bridge of his nose. "I told you once I'll never marry. P'rhaps what I should have said is I'll never know love or affection of any kind."

"Could you not marry a nice girl?"

"You don't understand how it is for me, sir – how could you? But it wouldn't be right. No matter how lonely I am, I'd never deceive a lass that way . . . have her spending her life living a lie, as well." Max swallowed. "If the world was a different place and people like me were able to find someone to love and live with without shame, I might feel otherwise. But as it is, there's no hope for my kind."

Sean rubbed his hand across his face. "Jesus. I'm sorry – I shouldn't have asked."

"No harm done." A slow smile spread across Max's face. "But as we're discussing delicate subjects . . . can I speak freely?"

"After you've been so open with me, say whatever you want."

"You and Miss Kellet. Perhaps you shouldn't waste your chance to be with the right person."

Sean's mouth dropped. "Don't tell me all the servants know?"

"Just me. When you have no life of your own, you notice a lot more of what's going on around you."

Poor Max – he'd be alone his entire life.

"I can't find you love, Max, but you'll always have a home in my household."

"Thank you, sir."

Sean climbed into bed, doubting he'd get much sleep but determined to give what Max and Kate had said consideration.

When Sean woke, he was smiling. Turning, he reached out for Jane. Disappointment washed over him to find that she wasn't lying by his side. He'd been dreaming.

Less than an hour later, Sean rushed into the small room at the factory where finished articles were pressed. He paused in the doorway and beckoned to Kitty.

"What's up?" she said, coming over immediately.

Sean caught her arm and pulled her into the corridor. His voice was little more than a whisper.

"I've spoken to the office manager and Darius. They're going to handle their areas. Can you cope with everything on the production side for a day or two?"

"You know I can. But where will you be?"

"I'm going to see Jane."

Kitty flung her arms around his neck.

"Aww, Tatty Head, I'm right made up."

Sean laughed. "I never said why I was going to see her. Besides, she might not forgive me and if she's anything like you, she might clout me over the head with the heaviest thing to hand."

"She's going to give you a rollicking. I'd expect nothing less from her. But it'll be worth it. Don't take no for an answer, or you'll have me to deal with." Kitty kissed his cheek then pushed him towards the exit. "Get going. You don't want to be wasting time here gassing wi' me."

Chapter 19

Sean had lied to Milly, claiming he'd been visiting a fabric manufacturer in the area as the reason for his unannounced visit. Then he'd convinced Jane to take a walk with him, to discuss Pierre's new tutor.

Couples strolled arm in arm, ladies' parasols angled to protect their complexions from the evening sun. Sean leaned against the railings as he watched Jane staring intently at the waves lapping against the legs of the pier. Clearly, they were more interesting than anything he was saying. He was tempted to reach out and trace the shape of her lips but thought better of it. If the look on her face was anything to go by, he'd lose his finger.

Jane hadn't spoken – or, more accurately, berated him – for several minutes. Did this mean she was considering forgiving him? She turned to him, her lips thin.

"How did you know I was here? Did someone tell you I'd left my situation in Fleetwood?"

"Kate told me. But she didn't say why you'd left."

"My position became untenable, so I walked out last week. The father . . . h-he . . ."

"He made advances?" Sean couldn't keep the irritation from his voice.

"Nothing serious. I resigned before he had the opportunity."

199

"The swine!"

A spike of anger shot through him. A woman who looked like Jane would be in danger in any household. Was that man so very different from himself? Hadn't he lusted after her from the first moment? No, damn it, he loved her.

"So, did you really come to Blackpool because you had a meeting?" Jane said.

"No. I came to see you."

"I've spent months trying to get over you. Can you imagine what it was like for me? I couldn't even tell Mam why I was miserable."

"No. But I know what it was like for me. And Pierre and Josh miss you. Especially Pierre. Your replacement is a decent chap, but Pierre has tantrums."

"Sean Kavanagh, don't you dare try to make me feel guilty about them. I can't come back and that's final."

"Please, Jane. Don't throw our chance away."

"You did that, not me. I thought losing you and the boys would kill me."

Sean hung his head. He'd hurt the woman he adored.

"Come back to Faredene for a while and give me the opportunity to show you that I'm sincere," he said.

"You're too late. There was a teaching post advertised. I'm applying."

"Forget about the job – let me look after you."

"You wouldn't let me help you. Your mother and Bella tended to you while you were recovering after the crash. Then according to Mam, Kate was the one you turned to for companionship. I hated you when I heard that."

"Kate's a friend, nothing more – I swear."

"I know that. I wasn't jealous. Just angry that you'd cast me aside."

"It was the guilt. I wasn't in my right mind. I believed that I deserved to be punished – and not only because of her death. It was impossible for me to love her because I wanted you even before I married Yvette."

Her face softened momentarily. "Oh, Sean. You weren't to blame. You never planned it that way."

"I know that now, but it took time for me to accept that everything wasn't entirely my fault."

She turned back to face the sea, her hands clasping the railing.

"No. I can't put myself in that position again. You broke my heart," she said.

He placed his hand over hers. She pulled it free.

"I'm begging you to give me another chance," he said.

"So your guilt has vanished? Disappeared in a puff of smoke? You've not given me a good enough reason."

Sean hesitated. He was loath to tell her about Yvette's infidelity, but she was to be his wife and the boys' mother. At least he hoped she would.

"Well?" Jane demanded.

"I found Yvette's diaries a while back and it was apparent she cared nothing for me. Not even when we were first married."

"Any fool could have told you that."

Sean stifled a laugh and Jane smiled at him for the first time that day.

"The thing is, I've always felt so guilty because I slept with Yvette when I was drunk, forcing us both to marry." He hesitated. "It turns out Pierre isn't my son. And Yvette seduced me so I'd have to marry her."

"May God forgive me, but she was a selfish bitch. Do you know who his father is?"

"Peter Mason. I believe he's aware, but I doubt he'll want it to get out. As for Pierre, there's no way I want him thinking he's anything but my son, so I'm not going to tell him. And I need you to keep it to yourself."

"I won't say anything, but he may still find out one day and be angry with you."

"I pray that never happens, but if it does, I'll have to face it then."

"How do you feel about Yvette now?"

"Relieved that I didn't ruin her life. I could never have made her happy no matter how hard I tried. And I hope she's at peace."

"So when you realised everything wasn't down to you, why didn't you come to find me straightaway?"

"I stopped myself because I was . . ."

"Go on."

"I needed to make sure I was strong enough never to drink again. Coping with the agony of losing you, the guilt, the loneliness, has been the biggest challenge of my life and I handled it. Now, I believe I can be the husband you deserve." Sean grasped her fingers, bringing them to his lips. "Please say you'll marry me. I love you and I truly regret causing you pain."

She snatched her hand away and turned from him.

"You hurt me more than I thought possible. Pushing me away . . . it was cruel, Sean."

"In my own stupid way, I thought I was protecting you. I'm a complete idiot – that's my only defence."

"Don't you think I wasn't racked with guilt, too?"

"*You?*"

"Yes. I wished Yvette out of Faredene a million times. I didn't want her to die, but on top of feeling responsible for Charles' death, her dying like that was too much. I needed you."

"I didn't realise."

"Well, you should have. I love the boys like they're my own. We'd have been a family, yet you were prepared to throw it all away."

"I won't make the same mistake."

"Why today? What's changed?"

He paused. "Last night I spoke to Kate. But really, I think it was Max. He reminded me that people shouldn't waste opportunities, because not everyone has the option to be with someone they love."

"He's right."

"I've come to realise that he often is."

"We should have worked through things. Isn't that what couples are supposed to do?"

"From now on, whatever life sends our way, good or bad, you and I will deal with it together. If you'll give me the chance, that is."

"Kate said I should forgive you. She claims that without me, you'll spend the rest of your life a gibbering wreck. Apparently, I need to save her from having to scrape you off the floor when she has more important things to do."

Sean laughed nervously. "Kate likes to keep me in my place. She rang me straight after speaking to you. She's a good friend."

"Hmm. Probably better than you deserve."

"That's true – and I don't deserve you, either, but I love you. I need you."

"I love you, too. But do I *need* you?"

His stomach lurched – Jane still loved him . . .

203

"If you'll let me, I'll dedicate every day of my life to making you happy," he said.

Jane's lips curled upwards. "Goodness, Sean. How dramatic."

He returned her smile. "Has it convinced you to forgive me?"

"Will it be *every* moment of every day you're devoting to my happiness?"

"If that's what it takes."

"Heavens, no! You'd drive me potty. I want a normal marriage with love and laughter and blazing rows."

"You want us to argue?"

"A little, so we can make up."

"How about we practise?" he said, pulling her to him.

Sunday evening, Sean arrived back from Blackpool and went straight to his mother's house. He wanted to get home to the boys but owed it to his mother to give her his news before she heard about it from another source. Milly and Agnes had been surprised but pleased by the announcement that he and Jane were to be married. Milly's only caveats were that Jane mustn't return to working in his household in the interim and that the nuptials shouldn't take place until a decent period of mourning for Yvette had passed. Frankly, he'd have agreed to anything if it meant Jane was going to be his wife. So it was decided that she'd remain in Blackpool for a while longer and once she returned to Faredene, she'd live in Milly's cottage until the wedding.

Victoria laid down her book as Sean entered the parlour.

"Darling! What a lovely surprise. There's nothing wrong, is there?" she asked.

Sean kissed her then stood with his back to the fireplace, his hands clasped behind him, legs slightly apart.

"On the contrary. Is Edward home? I'd like to speak to you both."

"He's in his study."

Victoria rang the bell and asked Martha to fetch Edward. If Sean hadn't look so pleased, she'd have been extremely worried. Grinning as he rocked back and forth on his heels, she knew he was bringing good news.

Edward sat in his matching chair opposite Victoria. "Sean, you're late calling. Anything amiss?"

"It says a lot about me when you both automatically assume something is wrong. You needn't worry – I have something wonderful to tell you. So please hear me out before you throw lots of questions at me," Sean said.

She'd always thought herself an intuitive person, but as she listened to him explaining that he'd been in love with Jane ever since they'd first met, she realised she didn't know her son half as well as she thought.

"Does Milly know?" said Victoria.

"Yes – she's pleased but wants us to wait awhile before we're married." He cleared his throat. "How do you feel?"

"I'm more than a little surprised. But I'm thrilled you've fallen for someone kind and caring. Were you and Jane involved . . . before? Is that why you've felt so guilty about Yvette?"

"Would it matter?"

There was a defensive edge to his voice. Victoria didn't want him to doubt her support.

"Perhaps it should – Milly wouldn't be pleased if that were the case. After all, Jane is her only daughter. But no, not to me. Your happiness is all that matters."

* * *

Sean felt the tension leaving his shoulders. He explained how he'd confessed his feelings to Jane the day Charles died and how a month later, Yvette had agreed to a divorce, providing he agreed to her conditions. As he spoke, he studied his mother's face. He was a grown man, but he still wanted her approval.

"There's something else I want to tell you. Jane already knows and I trust you both to ensure it goes no further."

"Now you look worried, Sean. What is it?" his mother asked.

"Peter Mason is Pierre's real father."

Sean explained how he'd found out and his mother listened, her face giving away nothing of her thoughts or feelings.

"I'm a hypocrite after the way I treated you," he said. "But now I realise that you were right to keep it from me. And I'm not telling Pierre unless I'm forced to explain to him one day. He's my son and nothing will ever change that. At least not for me," he ended.

Finally, she said, "And I will always be his grandmother, so the matter is closed. But I'm glad you confided in us. As for the wedding, strictly speaking, you should wait at least a year, but a December wedding would be lovely. Where children are involved, society will forgive widowers for marrying sooner than is appropriate. Don't you agree, Edward?"

As Edward hauled himself out of his seat and held out his hand, Sean was shocked to notice how weary he looked.

"Pierre and Joshua are both very fortunate to have you as their father. And December sounds fine to me. Sean, I'm pleased for you. Being with the woman you love is a great blessing. Make sure you don't waste a moment. Now, if you'll excuse me, I'm reviewing a case file, so I'll leave you in your mother's capable hands."

His words had sounded sincere, but something wasn't right. Sean glanced at his mother, who was fiddling with the locket around her neck.

When the door closed behind his stepfather, Sean said, "Is Edward unwell?"

"He's tired, but we're both thrilled for you."

"Are you sure? You would tell me if he, or you, were ill?"

"I promise. So, you'll be Milly's son-in-law. And when little ones come along, our family and the Gibbs will be united by blood."

"I don't think that could make the ties any stronger, do you?" he teased.

They sat talking for a long while. It felt good to speak to her about Jane. There was no hint of condemnation or recrimination.

"You're a terrific mother. There have been so many times when I've let you down and made mistakes. Not lived up to what you must have wanted from me."

"Sean, darling, there's only one thing I expect from you or your sisters. And that is that you live the life that makes you happy."

"Jane's a lot like Kitty. I'm sure our marriage will only grow stronger over time, just like yours and Edward's."

His mother smiled, but it didn't reach her eyes.

"Even the best marriages have to be worked at, Sean."

Had something changed between her and Edward? Poppycock. Nothing could rock their marriage.

* * *

When Sean left, Victoria went to Edward's office, hoping that having something pleasant to talk about would bring them together. After tapping lightly, she cracked open the door and peered round. The study was in darkness.

Saddened, Victoria returned to the parlour, where she nursed a mug of cocoa. Sean and Jane – who would have thought . . . He'd certainly kept that secret.

He said he'd not committed adultery and she wanted to believe him. Either way, she couldn't be more pleased for her son. He was in love and equally important, he also liked Jane – this was no infatuation or simply driven by lust. And there were no concerns about Jane being a mother to the boys, as she already had a strong bond with them.

How would Kate take the news?

After Kate had helped Sean to get over his grief following the accident, Kate had told her she'd realised they'd never be more than friends. But had she really got over him? Because you couldn't force love in a chosen direction. Although, according to Sean, Kate had been instrumental in him and Jane reconciling. So perhaps now she had William Tyler, Kate's affections had finally changed. Victoria hoped so. As for Pierre, she only hoped if he ever discovered the truth, it wouldn't affect him as badly as Sean had been by the discovery of his true origins.

Victoria sighed. Normally, she and Edward would have snuggled up in bed and discussed the development in Sean's life. Instead, Edward had gone up without saying goodnight. And here she was, sitting alone, waiting for him to fall asleep before she went up to bed so she wouldn't be confronted by his indifference towards her.

How had they come to this?

Chapter 20

Autumn brought a swirl of gold and red that danced around Victoria's feet and blew into Kitty's house as the front door opened.

"Come in before half a ton of leaves follow you," Kitty said, smiling.

Victoria wafted a box of chocolates at Kitty. "For you."

"Ta. We'll scoff a few before the boys see them or I won't get a look-in."

Victoria handed Kitty two bags. "I've brought them some sweets."

"They'll still eat mine given half a chance."

The building firm had transformed the old farmhouse into a comfortable home for Kitty and her family. In the centre of a spacious whitewashed kitchen was a large oak dining table covered in a dusting of flour. Victoria leaned over the earthenware dish filled with steak and kidney in a thick gravy.

"Something smells good."

"If you can give me a minute to get my pie crust on, I'll make us a brew."

"Would you like me to make the tea?" Victoria asked.

"No thanks, love. The last time you made me one, it was like pond water. I like a cuppa that my spoon will stand up in. Sit yerself down."

Victoria sat down on one of the wooden chairs, watching as Kitty rolled out the pastry.

"You got yourself a new outfit for the wedding or are you making do?" Kitty said.

"I've bought something."

"What's it like?"

"It's dark blue."

A slight line appeared between Kitty's brows.

"That's not telling me much. What fabric have you chosen?"

"Taffeta. It's a simple design – nothing special."

"You are looking forward to the do?"

"Mmm-hmm."

"You're not feeling like your neb is being pushed out? 'Cos our Harry means well, but he can take over if he's not kept in check."

"Surely you know me better than that."

As she chatted, Kitty placed the pastry over the bowl, crimping it with a fork, her gaze fixed on Victoria.

"I was settled enough livin' at the Hall, but it wasn't cosy like this place. And I enjoy looking after my family for meself. Do yeh think I'm daft?"

"Not at all."

"The staff were decent enough, but it was like I was intruding if I went into the kitchens. And who needs fifteen bedrooms? The four we've got are plenty. We only use two, as the boys still want to share. Mind you, I'm glad Harry insisted on having an indoor bathroom installed, because runnin' out to the lav in the middle of the night is no joke." Kitty bent to slide the pie in the oven, her back to Victoria. "Right, I've rabbited on long enough. What's got your knicker elastic in a twist?"

"Nothing – I'm fine."

"Then some bugger needs to let your face know, because you look like someone put salt in your tea. A surprise visit from you is always lovely, but I can barely get a word out of yeh. You've not even described your frock. And for you to be out visiting on a Sunday afternoon, summat's not right."

"Oh, Kitty. I looked at Edward over breakfast this morning and it was as though I hardly know him."

"That's silly talk. What's brought this on?"

"It's absurd – embarrassing. During the last few months, we've grown apart, and it's all over something so trivial. Anne accused me of flirting with Owain and Edward didn't support me. We had a row and now when he's not at the office, he's either sulking around the house or walking Kirby far more than is good for either him or the dog." Victoria gulped back her tears.

"Blimey, it's not often things get to you. You're normally so strong."

"The whole debacle has grown out of nowhere. I love him as much as ever and I pray he feels the same about me. But even though we've not been arguing, I fear the resentment might be permanent." She pressed a handkerchief to the corners of her eyes. "It's such a mess."

Kitty rubbed Victoria's back. "Aww, don't take on. Let me get you a cuppa. Nothing is ever as bad as it seems once you hash it out with a mate."

"I thought Edward and I had a special relationship that nothing could affect. Never mind something as farcical as this."

Kitty took her copper kettle from the range and poured water into the earthenware pot.

"None of this sounds like Edward. Are yeh seeing a problem where there isn't one?" She placed a steaming cup in front of Victoria.

Victoria's voice hitched. "N-no, I'm n-not. He wanted me to stop working on the Rows project, but I wouldn't and now things are definitely different between us. We used to discuss everything." Victoria could feel her cheeks colouring. "At our age, there's no great passion, but we'd cuddle as we fell sleep every night. Now, it's like sharing a bed with a stranger."

"Bloody hell. If things can go wrong for you two, there's little hope for the rest of us. Is Anne still seeing Owain?"

"As far as I can gather. She hasn't called round to see us since I threw her out back in the summer. I'm determined not to ask Edward about her. And because I rush off without engaging in pleasantries with Owain, I've no way of knowing."

Victoria had become increasingly awkward in his presence, avoiding him whenever possible, because there was only so many times she could claim she had to dash when left alone with him. And given that he and Anne used to dine regularly with them, surely he must have wondered why no invitations were forthcoming . . .

"And all this has been going on for months and the situation is getting worse?" Kitty said.

"Yes. I kept telling myself things weren't that bad and I suppose it was true, but when an apple starts rotting, it doesn't stop."

"You are in a right pickle. Why didn't you tell Jess or Harry? They could have got someone else to organise things. No bugger is indispensable."

"I don't know . . . Stubbornness? Embarrassment?

Also, of late I think Jess has been down. I don't want to make you feel as though it's your fault, because it's not, but she misses Jake and Brian so much, even though they're always popping in to see her."

"Aye, I know. I've sent them over there to play this afternoon. But it's not enough – Jess needs a child of her own." Kitty wandered off to the pantry, returning with a pot of jam. "Jess' problems will have to wait until another day. So, you've told no one except me about all this carry-on?"

"No, and I want it to stay that way. The fewer people involved, the better. And you mustn't tell Jess, either, because she'll insist I step down and the project is extremely important to me."

"More than yer marriage?"

"Of course not. But why should I stop helping when this fiasco isn't my fault?"

"Blameless, are you? 'Cos in my experience, no one ever thinks they've done owt wrong when they fall out wi' someone."

Had Milly still been living in Faredene, Victoria would have confided in her immediately. She'd held off from speaking to Kitty as she was so much younger and she'd always regarded her as on a par with her own children, but Victoria realised she'd underestimated Kitty.

"Oh, Kitty, I know I'm as much to blame as anyone."

"Tell me exactly what's been said."

Kitty rolled more pastry before pressing it into a flan dish while Victoria explained about Anne's visit.

"I can understand why that got yer dander up. I know you won't have been making cow eyes at him, but has he been chancing his arm?"

"Truthfully? I don't know."

"Come on. Be honest with me – and yourself."

Kitty spooned strawberry jam from the pot into the dish, looking at her shrewdly. For the first time, Victoria felt as though she were the younger of the two. She explained about the incidences where she felt Owain hadn't exactly behaved inappropriately but where she'd detected an undercurrent, something unspoken.

"You need to put the randy devil straight and no messin'."

"Kitty, I can't. At first, I was determined to ignore it. But then I saw him on Friday and I *wanted* to mention something . . . You know, hint that his behaviour wasn't fitting and his attentions were unwanted."

"And?"

"I couldn't do it."

Kitty licked the spoon clean.

"Why? You're not a daft young lass."

"Exactly. I felt so embarrassed. What if he thinks I'm a stupid old woman? And the most idiotic part is that because I've left it months without saying anything, it's even harder to broach the subject now."

"With us running a pub all those years, I learned a few things about men. If yeh don't make things clear, they'll see things how they want to. 'Cos no matter how old they get or how long you've known them, all men think with what's in their trousers. They can't help it."

Victoria spluttered. "Kitty, you make me laugh."

After placing the flan in the oven, she said, "I'm a giggle a minute. But this is serious. Things like this start small and before yeh know it, you're hatin' each other. Whether yeh end up wi' egg on your snout or not, you've got to do summat an' sharpish."

214

"You're right, I know you are. But I can't say anything until the Rows are complete."

"What did yeh come round here for if yer not gonna take my advice?"

"I needed to talk to someone about it."

"Fair enough, but that won't make the problem go away."

"The last houses will be finished in less than a month, then I'll set Owain straight. All I can do is hope that the damage to mine and Edward's relationship isn't beyond repair before then."

Pleased with himself, George put his feet up on his desk and admired his panelled office. He'd named the woman he met on the docks Mademoiselle, which was far more exotic than her real name. She'd jumped at his offer to run his King Street bordello, managing the other girls. Not having been on the game long enough to look haggard, with a surprising ability to fake a French accent, she was popular with the customers and had a list of select clients she serviced herself.

She was also proving efficient at bringing in young virgins or those hardly touched. Girls who found themselves on the streets, often to escape fear of abuse in the home and in desperate need of a safe place to sleep. They trusted her because she was a woman and it didn't take long to persuade them that all they needed to do to have a good life was spread their legs for a few select gents. Admittedly, she'd led some of them to believe that if they were lucky, one day a punter would fall for them and whisk them away to a better life. But if they were barmy enough to believe that, it was their problem.

He had four prostitutes working here for him now, all under the age of eighteen. George ensured they had three meals a day, a bath each morning, decent clobber, a clean bed to kip in and pin money. Even though the odd punter might get heavy-handed, neither he nor his doormen ever hit the tarts. He didn't want his assets damaging.

The business was doing well and last week, he'd invested heavily in a second establishment on Ellison Road. A new madam and three girls were now installed there. The policeman on his payroll had warned him against opening a club in that part of town, but George wouldn't let his empire be hampered by the concerns of a bent peeler whose job it was to make sure there was no trouble. He had plans for two more premises by the end of the year. Men needed sex. Put that together with the opportunity to drink and gamble all under one roof and you couldn't fail.

George insisted everyone refer to him as the guv'nor and no one knew who he really was. When he left here to go home to his rooms on the other side of London each night, he could leave all this sordid business behind him, which would be an advantage when he decided to remarry.

The door opened and a short, thin, incredibly hairy man sidled in, rubbing his hands.

"What is it?" George asked.

"There's been some trouble over at the new house."

George frowned. "What's happened?"

"The boy who runs messages is here. It's best he tells you himself."

"Nipper's here? Send him in. And be quick about it. If one of the tarts is causing problems, I want her dealt with swiftly."

A wiry lad of about eight stumbled in, looking terrified.

"Pour him a tot of brandy," George ordered.

The boy gulped the liquid down. "They've ruined everything, guv'nor."

"What *are* you talking about, Nipper? Spit it out."

"A gang burst in. And yer doorman scarpered."

"Bleeding hell. What's the damage?"

"They killed the madam and beat up a punter who tried to stop 'em. The gent will be lucky if he lives."

"Where is he now?"

"Still in the house. He's in no state to go nowhere."

George spoke to the thin man.

"Take a couple of local men with you. Make sure they're trustworthy. Get rid of the madam and get that man out of my establishment."

"If he's still breathing, what do you want done wi' him, guv'nor?"

"Finish him off if you have to. Just make sure he can't lead the police back to me."

"Righto, guv. Shall I get off now?"

"Wait a minute. There may be more clearing up to do. Nipper, where are the tarts?"

"They took all the girls with 'em. Dragged them out by their hair, they did."

George slammed his fist on the desk.

"Who the hell were they? If I find them, they'll regret messing with me."

"They ain't hiding, guv. Brazen, they were. They let me go so I could come here to give you a message."

"Well, what is it?"

"The biggest fella – proper mean-looking – he had the madam's blood still dripping from his hands." Nipper shuddered.

"Get on with it, boy," George said as he refilled the lad's glass.

"He said to tell you that the Lees run gambling and girls in the West End an' if you know what's good for yeh, you'll pack up an' clear outta London. Because if you don't, you'll find out what they do to people who try to steal their territory."

George cursed.

Chapter 21

On the first really cold day in November, Victoria hovered in front of Edward's chair.

Slowly, he folded *The Times* newspaper and removed his glasses. "You look smart. Is that new?"

Victoria ran her hand over her fur collar. "My old winter coat was past its best. I've given it to a young woman in the Rows – Rene."

"Very kind."

There was a coldness to his manner that saddened her.

"We're going to view the final house renovation this morning. You were invited, but you didn't seem interested. I had hoped you might have decided to come along."

"Actually, I'm about to leave for the office."

Clearly, he'd not changed his mind.

"You never said you were going in today."

"I didn't realise we had to keep each other appraised of our movements any more. Is there a problem?"

"Not at all. It's perfectly fine," she said petulantly before stalking out.

Victoria climbed into the back of the Gibbs' Rolls-Royce. Harry nodded briefly and Jess embraced her.

"You look nice, Victoria, honey," Jess said. "Owain's meeting us at the house."

219

Victoria gave a tight smile. Since her discussion with Kitty and as the day grew ever nearer when she'd have to challenge Owain about his manner towards her, she'd avoided him even more. Even so, together with Harry and Jess, they'd achieved something remarkable, something to be proud of. Today was special and she wanted to enjoy it without analysing his every word and action. It might be terribly unfair, as it was possible Owain was oblivious to the entire situation, but she was so angry with him. Which was another reason this mess had to be dealt with soon. Although she had to admit, the only thing that really mattered was getting her relationship with Edward back to where it was before Anne had flounced into their bedroom and driven a wedge between them.

As they drove towards the Rows, they discussed Sean and Jane's forthcoming nuptials.

"Jane's level-headed like her mam. She'll make Sean a smashing wife," Harry said.

Victoria wondered if he was referring to Milly or Kitty. Regardless, all three women were sensible.

"Jane's a delightful girl. She's still young, but I'm certain Sean will take good care of her," Victoria said. "He's thrilled she's finally moving back to Faredene. He and Jane have both found it difficult only seeing each other for short visits. But at least with her living with her mother all this time, the gossips haven't been able to suggest they've been behaving improperly."

"That Yvette, the stuck-up mare, always looked at me and my Jess as if we were a dollop of muck on her shoes," Harry said, his face stern. "Tell her what she said to you that one time, Jess."

"God rest her soul. I don't like to speak ill of her now."

"All that being nice about people just because they're dead is stupid, Jess," Harry said.

"I suppose it can't cause her any harm and you know well enough what she was like, Victoria . . . She said that the problem with the American Civil War was that people like me had ideas above their station and no amount of money could make us fit to socialise with our betters."

Victoria gasped. "Jess, I'm so sorry."

"She didn't mind drinking our champagne and eating our food, though. Jess didn't let on to me about it until after she'd passed away or I'd never have let her through our door. I never pretended to be summat I'm not," Harry said. "We were dragged up in the gutter, but I've made a good life for us and I don't see why I should feel inferior."

"Harry, Jess, I can't apologise enough," Victoria said again.

Jess squeezed Victoria's fingers.

"There's no need – it wasn't your fault. I've heard far worse. Plenty of folk I came across in New Orleans think that way – all over the South, for that matter. I suppose she was raised to believe she was better than me. It's not too bad in England – folk aren't so bigoted."

"It's more likely that it's because we're rich," Harry added.

"Sadly, people are judged by their wealth all too often," Victoria said.

"People tolerate me, nothing more," Jess said.

"You're not tolerated, Jess. Most people respect you. As for Yvette, I wish you'd told me or Sean. We put up with a lot from her, but her treating you like that . . . we'd never have accepted that."

221

"There was no way I'd tell you while she was still alive, doll. Because there was nothing you could have done to change her opinion and the last thing I wanted was to cause problems for you or Sean." Jess patted Victoria's arm. "Don't you go worrying about it. Forget about it now. Look – Owain is already here waiting for us."

Inside 12 Halton Row, a skeletal woman said, "Take a gander at this, Mrs Caldwell. Me with running water in me kitchen!"

Victoria held her fingers under the cold water as it splashed into the large Armitage Shanks sink before drying her hands on the rough towel the woman offered.

"I'm so glad you're pleased," Victoria said.

"Would you like to take the doctor and Mr and Mrs Gibbs through to the backyard to see me privy?"

Victoria glanced at Harry and Jess before answering and they shook their heads.

"No, thank you, dear. I wanted them to view your house, as it was Mr Gibbs' home at one time. We'll leave you to finish your chores."

"People round here won't forget what you've done for us, Mr Gibbs. I never thought washing day would be less of a chore. No more carrying buckets of water from the standpipe. You've changed lives for the better and folk won't forget it," the woman said.

Harry looked emotional, unable to speak.

"Our pleasure, honey," Jess said.

Once outside, the four of them looked back at the house as a feeble sunlight bathed the cobbles.

Owain said, "She's right, Harry, Jess. I've been a doctor in this town for thirty-six years and no one has ever done as much for people as you have."

Harry's Adam's apple bobbed before he spoke. "There's not a broken window or rotting frame in the street." He ran his hand over the new sill. "I wish the house had been this swanky when we lived here. For me mam's sake, like."

"She'd be extremely proud of you, Harry," Victoria said.

"One thing is certain – it smells better round here now the new drains have been put in," Jess said.

"That's probably the most important part of all this, Jess. The new plaster and fresh paint look wonderful, but sanitation is the thing that will save lives," Owain said.

"You've done a grand job, Mrs Caldwell. You too, Doc," Harry said.

"It wouldn't have happened without you, Harry," Victoria said.

Harry studied his feet. "I can't organise everyone like you, Victoria. Working with the builders, getting residents to agree to stay in boarding houses while their street was being done . . . People respect you and listen to what you say."

"I'll grant you that was a challenge. They were understandably concerned about having their meagre belongings stored. And who can blame them? When you have so little, the smallest of items is precious. I doubt I'd ever have persuaded Queenie to move without Owain's intervention. Thanks to you, Harry, she's thrilled with her place and it's bug-free," said Victoria, scratching the back of her hand.

Harry coloured.

"If you hadn't acquired the Rows in the first place, none of this would have happened," Victoria added.

"Hornby-Smythe had no choice but to hand the deeds over," Harry said. "He shouldn't gamble. I noticed he only ever did well if Garrett Ackerley was playing. Then once he'd helped Ackerley get in a position to win, Hornby-Smythe would bow out at the last minute. I've seen that type of cheating before. They were probably splitting the profits. I made a habit of playing Hornby on his own and I fleeced him. Serves him right, but it means I didn't even have to pay for the houses – not really."

"You could have insisted he settle his debt in cash but you didn't. And you paid for all the work and temporary accommodation," Victoria said.

"All I did was stump up the readies. It weren't owt special."

"Gees, honey, enjoy the compliment!" Jess said. "Can we take you home, Victoria?"

"If you'd drop me near the department store, that would be helpful. I want to buy a few more gifts for Jane's trousseau."

"I'll drive Victoria. I'd like a word in private, if you don't mind?" Owain said.

Victoria stifled a groan. Ideally, she'd planned to visit Owain tomorrow and clear the air once she'd had the opportunity to prepare herself mentally for the possibility of making a complete dolt of herself. Still, no good would come from delaying.

No sooner were they seated in his car than Owain turned to her, smiling.

"Do you mind if we make a detour to my office for our little chat?"

She supposed it would be better than broaching such a difficult topic in the car.

"I'll have to be quick. I've a busy afternoon."

"It won't take long, but there is something I want to show you."

Victoria coughed as she stifled a horrified laugh at the thought of what it might be.

"Are you all right, my dear?"

"Yes. Yes, thank you," she spluttered.

Victoria used the brief journey to brace herself. She'd got herself into some difficult situations in the past but had hoped her days of making a fool of herself with men were well and truly behind her. This felt so unfair. There was no way she'd encouraged Owain to foster feelings for her – if indeed he had any.

In the surgery waiting room, as Owain spoke to his assistant, Victoria perused the notices about various health conditions pinned to the noticeboard. Some read: Don't spit and spread tuberculosis. Another related to syphilis and gonorrhoea, with others about rats and fleas spreading diseases. She could imagine the faces of some of his well-heeled patients if they were to see them. Though that was unlikely, as they expected home visits. Most of those who came to his surgery were the poor, whom he rarely charged.

Owain opened the door to his office.

"This way, Victoria."

She sat down, placing her handbag on her knee. Was she imagining things, or did Owain look nervous? It was less than a minute but seemed longer as she waited for him to speak.

Eventually, he said, "The thing is, working with you over the last few months . . . Well, I'd like to think you, too, have found our achievements gratifying."

Victoria shifted uncomfortably.

"I can't remember when I've enjoyed my job more. My assistant is an efficient chap but rather dour and not much

225

company. And a doctor's work is often lonely. You and I can do so much more together. I want to discuss an idea I've had about helping the fallen women of Faredene." He held out a leaflet. "This is a scheme a doctor friend of mine is trying to set up in Manchester. Basically, the aim is to give them a second chance in life by helping them to learn a trade and find somewhere decent to live. I was hoping you'd assist me in starting something here – on a smaller scale, naturally."

Victoria was torn. It was such a good cause. But if she didn't distance herself from Owain, things were likely to get even worse between Edward and her. She adjusted the position of her bag unnecessarily.

"It sounds incredibly worthwhile. However, not one I can spearhead, I'm afraid. I need to back away from charitable commitments. When we started this, I didn't expect to be required to help with my grandsons as much as I have."

His smile fell away. "Sean is to be married. The boys will have a new mother. Surely you'll have more time to spare."

"As adorable as he is, you know how challenging Pierre is at the moment."

"Admittedly, I've been out several times and given him tonics. He seems to have suffered from a few ear infections and has had a difficult time teething, but nothing serious."

"I'm sure you're right. Nevertheless, it's important that Sean and Jane have time for themselves."

"From what I've seen, the boys have a very efficient nanny, a nursemaid *and* a tutor. I'm doubt the King's own children get better care."

"Sean's not comfortable leaving them for long with the

servants. One can hardly blame him after what the wet nurse did to Pierre."

"You have to think of yourself, as well. You enjoy charity work."

"I find it fulfilling. However, there are plenty of younger women who would be of benefit to such projects."

"You're still in your prime and I doubt many of them will have your passion or drive. They definitely won't have your experience. If you were involved in a less time-consuming manner, might you reconsider?"

"No, I can't. Kate would be an asset to any scheme. Perhaps I can speak to her about it on your behalf."

"Without you, I'm not sure I want to go ahead with it. I'm busy with the surgery."

"Of course – you do a great deal for the community."

"Are you sure about this? How will you occupy yourself?"

"I want to spend more time with Edward."

"Edward won't mind you getting involved with my project. He keeps himself occupied with the few clients he retained. And I know he has a mountain of books he wants to read."

"I can't be swayed on this."

"Has something changed? Have I offended you in some way? I have wondered if there is something amiss."

Victoria sighed. If she humiliated herself, so be it.

"Owain, this is extremely awkward for me, but I don't think it's appropriate for us to work so closely. I'm a married woman and recently, I've neglected Edward terribly. He means the world to me and I'd never do anything to hurt him." Her cheeks burned.

"Erm, nor would I. But you and I were . . . I thought

you felt . . . Err, there's no denying it – I'll miss your . . . er, your help. Perhaps . . ."

Victoria stared at him. What on earth was he trying to say?

When it became clear he wasn't going to speak again, she said, "Owain. Edward and I both regard you as a dear friend. Anne cares for you. You realise that, don't you?"

Owain leaned on his desk, steepled his fingers and stared at them. Eventually, he spoke slowly.

"I'm terribly fond of Anne. She's excellent company."

"I was hoping one day you and she would marry. And that you'd be part of our family."

"Indeed, she's a splendid woman. I trust my enthusiasm for our working together hasn't given you the wrong impression or caused you any discomfiture. I assure you, I would never behave inappropriately, or wish to damage my friendship with you or Edward."

Victoria rose. Had she been mistaken about his affections? That seemed to be the impression he wanted to give. Either way, she wanted this tortuous conversation over.

"Not at all," she lied. "I hope we can still be friends."

Outside the surgery, she paused. Thankfully, it hadn't gone as badly as it might. All she wanted now was to be with Edward, to get things back to normal.

When she entered her husband's office, he didn't look up. His spectacles were perched on the edge of his nose. Several thick files lay on the desk in front of him and he appeared to be deep in concentration as he used his pen to guide his eyes down a document as he read.

"Edward, darling."

His head jerked up and his brow furrowed. "Victoria, is something wrong?"

"Can't I visit you at work without there being a problem?"

"You could, but you rarely do."

"Well, I'm glad that after all these years, I can still surprise you."

"You have a beautiful smile, Vicky. I am sorry for letting you down. You have worked hard on the Rows. I should have gone with you today." He gestured to the papers on his desk. "These could have waited."

His voice sounded husky. Victoria wasn't sure if he was going to speak again or break down! She moved to stand beside his chair.

"I've come here to apologise to you. Edward, I'm sorry if my behaviour during the last few months has upset you," she blurted.

His jaw relaxed and Victoria touched her fingers to his cleft chin.

"We have both been at fault," Edward said. "I admit that I have become a stubborn old goat. It happened without my noticing. Rather like going grey. You notice the first few silver hairs, then suddenly the roof is collapsing under the weight of the snow."

Victoria ran her hand over his head.

"It makes you look distinguished. I hope you'll be pleased to hear that now the Rows renovation is complete, I've told Owain I'm not getting involved in any more of his projects."

"You shouldn't abandon your charity work. It was my fault – I should have told Anne immediately that she was in the wrong. I have since made my thoughts clear, so she's not speaking to me either, now."

"Don't worry. Next week we'll invite her and Owain to dinner. Everything will be sorted. Leave it to me."

"I understand why Owain would find you attractive – or any man – but I know you would never encourage them."

"Thank you."

Edward stood, pulling her into his arms. "Vicky, I have missed you – our closeness," he mumbled, his face buried in her hair.

"Me too. I'm so sorry."

"You have always been too good for me and I am grateful you are part of my life."

"Oh, Edward, please don't say that."

"It is true. My life would be miserable without you. I have never believed I am good enough for you and the thought of losing you is terrifying," he added, not lifting his head from her shoulder.

Was he crying? *Victoria Caldwell, you are a selfish, horrible woman. How could you do anything to hurt this man?*

"You mean the world to me," she said.

"And I thank God for it every day."

"Edward, I have to ask. If you thought Owain was attracted to me, why were you never jealous or angry with him?"

"Jealousy should never be mistaken for love. Vicky, darling, I was born a cripple." He placed his finger on her lips to silence her. "It is all right. I have lived with it my entire life. I have a good mind and I believe I am a gentleman who knows how to treat a lady. But if at any stage you don't want me, what hope would I have of keeping a woman such as you? I would rather let you go than see the sparkle go out of your eyes because you felt trapped."

"I-I'd never betray you. Never," she said emphatically.

"Vicky, my dear, I never doubted your fidelity."

"I was angry because I felt you didn't trust me, furious that you weren't jealous and hurt because you didn't think what I was doing was important."

"My darling, I have no need to be jealous as long as you don't want anyone but me. It is irrelevant if other men find you attractive or crave your company, because I am certain you would never be unfaithful."

"I wouldn't. You're all I want – you must believe me. I should have stopped working with Owain."

"No, you should not. I was wrong to suggest it. I am incredibly proud of what you have achieved. I went there last week to take a look. It's marvellous."

"Edward, I'm so ashamed that I've let us drift apart."

"Shush. Enough now. We lost our way a little, but we got through it." Edward pulled back and gazed at her face. "Does this mean you won't be giving any more of my favourite suits to charity?"

"I won't give them so much as a pair of socks without checking with you first. And what's more, I'm all yours now." She grinned.

"*All* mine?" he said, raising his eyebrows comically.

"Well, apart from if our family needs me."

"I will settle for that, because they all appear to be getting their lives on track. At last, we should be able to put our feet up and grow old and fatter together."

"Fatter! Edward, calling me fat is a strange way to ask for a divorce."

Edward laughed. "You have a magnificent figure, and you know it. And we are married for life – don't you forget it, Mrs Caldwell."

Chapter 22

For the past month, George's business had been operating solely from his King Street premises. It rankled that rather than expanding as he'd planned, his income had been severely reduced and his future put on hold.

"What the hell am I paying the bobbies protection money for if you allow scum to wreck my establishment and kill my tarts?" he railed.

The constable, whose only feature of note was an exceptionally crooked nose, looked unconcerned about George's problems as he fondled the breasts of a girl of seventeen.

Not bothering to glance in George's direction, he said, "I warned you against that part of town. The orientals are taking over and they're ruthless bleeders."

"So sort them out," George retorted. "Kick in a few kneecaps, break some skulls. That'll teach them to come over here and try to take over."

"We can't prove it was the Lees, so we can't go wading in there."

"Get your hands off her, Jones, and come into my office. You and your lot will get no more free leg-overs if you don't get things sorted."

The man pushed the girl away. "Less of the threats, *guv'nor*." He sneered but followed George.

"Another of my girls has gone missing without a trace," George said.

"P'rhaps she's done a bunk with some fella."

"The Lees have her. There's no other explanation."

"There's no need for them to take yours. If they need more women, there's plenty available."

"If she's found dead, it'll be another death on your shoulders."

"We do our best. There's not enough of us to patrol every street. The respectable men and women of the city are the ones we need to protect, not some filthy whore."

"It might not bother you now, but my punters are being intimidated. If takings are down, you and your mates on the beat will soon be complaining if your weekly back-hander is short."

"That would be a grave mistake."

"Are you threatening me?"

"Just pointing out that the boys back at the station won't take it well if you short-change us."

"I won't have much choice. I'll have no customers left at this rate."

Sergeant Jones scratched his head. "All right, all right. I'll get back to the station and have a word. But there's not a lot I can do. The problem you've got is that the Lees have some of the big brasses in their pockets."

As the constable departed, George poured himself a measure. He had an uneasy feeling. He didn't trust any of them. Jones would betray him without a second thought.

* * *

Kate was enjoying her second glass of wine while Bella was in the ladies' washroom at Latimers. She'd asked Bella to dinner on the pretext of celebrating, because far from losing more pupils over her Irish ancestry, as a result of their latest advertising campaign their school was finally full. In truth, Kate wanted to be distracted, because she was feeling low. William hadn't fully replaced Sean in her heart, but she'd come to care for him and had recently wondered what it would be like to be his wife. However, William appeared content with the way things were between them. She couldn't deny they had fun together, but she didn't want to be the spinster headmistress with no children of her own teaching other people's daughters for the rest of her life. Although Kate had never told another soul, she wanted a child of her own – and time was running out.

Bella's voice interrupted Kate's rumination.

"Are you all right? You look rather maudlin."

"I was thinking we must grasp opportunities as they come along – we could be dead tomorrow."

"What a cheery thought."

"I'm just saying we should make the most of things and I for one intend enjoying every minute of this evening."

"A meal was a splendid idea, Kate. You're right – we do need to take advantage of our time off."

"Let's face it – we should take every chance we can to enjoy ourselves. Even Aunt Anne has finally managed to bag Owain."

"Mother is being cagey about it all. Not long ago, Anne was claiming Owain was a quack who didn't deserve her. Next minute, their wedding is being planned. If I didn't know Aunt was past her childbearing years, I'd suspect she was carrying a little passenger." Bella grinned.

"Hmm, it's all very suspicious, but I doubt we'll find out what went on. Though Anne might not make it down the aisle if she keeps telling me that as Mrs Doctor Owain Farrell, she'll have a position to uphold. And that if I insist on driving myself around town, then I need to keep my speed down. I wouldn't mind, but I don't go that fast."

"She does have a point. You drive like a mad thing."

"Ack, we all need a little excitement now and then.

I'm even considering letting William take me up in his aeroplane," said Kate.

"Gosh, you're brave."

"Here, let me top up your glass."

"Go on, then. I'll have a drop, but I don't want to be hung-over. We're teaching tomorrow. Whoa, it's all gone over the cloth." Bella giggled. "Are you deliberately trying to get me sozzled?"

"Maybe. I want you to relax because I want to talk to you."

"I know that look. What are you up to, sis?"

"*Moi?*"

"Yes, you. Unless Mother or Father are keeping a big secret, then you *are* my only sister."

"Well, sweet pea. A certain gentleman of our acquaintance mentioned that he's the tiniest, weensy bit desperate for me to plead his case."

"Richard?"

Kate laughed. "Who else? How many other men have fallen for you?"

"We're just friends and Richard knows it can't go any further."

"Don't you feel anything for him, sweetie?"

Bella chewed her bottom lip. "A little. Not in the way I did George. But, well, sometimes I think it might be nice to fall in love with a friend."

"But?"

"I'm fighting it."

"Then stop."

Here she was once again meddling in someone else's romance. Was that what spinsters did? It was definitely preferable to becoming bitter and twisted and wanting to deny others joy.

"He's a good man," Kate added.

"Everyone thought that about George."

"Richard is hardly the same. He lives here. No one can keep secrets in Faredene."

"Mother did. Even now, few know she's not Sean's natural mother."

"Well, as the saying goes, she's the exception that proves the rule."

"Can we truly know what's going on in another's mind?" Bella said.

"Of course not. But if we don't take chances, we'll never find happiness."

"Richard has asked me to allow him to court me officially."

"What did you say?"

"No. Several times, actually. I enjoy his company. He makes me laugh and I believe he's genuinely kind, but we can only ever be friends."

Richard had confided to Kate that he wanted to marry Bella. He might be a quiet, unassuming man, but Kate suspected he was determined and wouldn't give up easily.

"Aren't you going to say something? It's not like you to keep your opinions to yourself," Bella said.

Kate gestured to the waiter. "A bottle of champagne, please. We're celebrating – my sister is going to be courted."

Bewildered, blushing and then offering his congratulations, he scurried off.

"Kate, have you gone mad?"

"You'll want to take things slowly, but being courted is exactly what you need. You can start by inviting him to escort you to Anne's wedding."

"I can't do that! Weddings are significant. He might get the wrong impression."

"Well, I'm going with William and Anne is insisting we both have escorts."

"Humph! I don't suppose I'm left with much choice, but I'll explain we're going together as friends. Now, how about we focus on what you need?"

"Me? I have my torrid affair with William Tyler."

"Do you think he'll pop the question?"

"I'll simply be extra alluring so he does. Neither of us are going to die as old maids. Not if I have anything to do with it."

Straight after breakfast, Bella picked up the telephone, her voice hesitant as she asked to be connected. She'd hoped it might be simple enough, but now she wasn't sure.

"Hello?" a voice said.

"Richard, it's Bella."

"Bella, what can I do for you? Is it the motor car or the boiler?"

"Neither. I'm calling to ask if you'd like to accompany me to my aunt Anne's wedding the first week of December," she said quickly before she could change her mind.

"I'd love to."

"I haven't told you what day it is yet."

"Makes no difference. If I have plans, I'll cancel them. I want to go with you whenever it is."

She knew she shouldn't have listened to Kate. He was taking the invite to signify more than intended.

"Anne wants to keep the numbers of men and women even and is practically demanding Kate and I bring partners."

"No. Right. Well, don't worry – I understand it means nothing. I'd be honoured to escort you."

Richard sounded crestfallen. She wasn't a cruel person and didn't want to hurt him. Feeling awkward, Bella gave him the details of the ceremony and reception, ending by saying she was looking forward to it.

When the call disconnected, Bella stood, holding the wire, the mouthpiece dangling. She was confused, because she had to admit, if only to herself, Richard was the only person who could make attending the gathering bearable. But that was only because he knew about her attacks of nerves and made her so secure when they were together – wasn't it?

George opened the small package and dipped his index finger into the white powder before pressing it to his tongue. It was decent quality. At least his drug supplier wasn't messing him around. Nipper watched nervously.

"Well done, boy. They haven't cheated you. Keep up the good work and you'll do all right working for me," George said.

"You can rely of me, guv. I'm right grateful to yeh for letting me work here after Ellison Road was closed."

"Hmm, you've certainly got more sense than the lad we had before. Go to the kitchen an' tell them I said to give you some stew."

"Thanks, guv. But there's something else."

"What?"

"Outside, there were a couple of geezers hanging around and one of them looked like he was giving the nod to the copper who normally stands at the corner of the street."

"What did the peeler do?" George asked.

Nipper opened his mouth to speak, but his eyes flicked towards the ceiling as a woman's scream came from the salon. It wasn't a cry of pleasure, fake or otherwise.

"If that bent copper Jones has double-crossed . . ." George's words faded as the screaming became louder, accompanied by banging and shouting. "Blast it to hell." His heart pounded as he darted to the door, shooting two strong bolts. "Be quick, boy. Help me shift this."

When the heavy wooden filing cabinet was across the door, George said, "That should slow them, but not for long."

He grabbed his keys off the desk and kneeled in front of the safe, emptying the cash into the leather Gladstone bag he carried to and from the club to enhance his professional appearance. Nipper stood by his side, chewing his fingernails anxiously. When he'd stashed all the money, George crossed the room and pulled aside a heavy burgundy curtain, revealing another door.

"Quickly or I'll leave you to your fate," he said.

After locking the door behind them, he led the boy down a long corridor.

"Where does this lead to, guv'nor?" Nipper asked.

George glanced over his shoulder. "Safety. Always make sure you have a way out, boy, and you won't go far wrong."

"A way to escape a building, guv?" Nipper asked as George unlocked a second door leading into the backyard of an empty shop.

George didn't answer until they were in the back alley.

"Out of any scrape you're in. Always put yourself first." George thrust his hand into his pocket, removing two coins. He threw them at the lad. "Get away from here as fast as you can and lie low for a while."

"What are you going to do, guv'nor?"

"Don't you fret about me, Nipper. I always have a plan."

Chapter 23

Victoria adjusted the lace appliqué a quarter of an inch to the left and pinned it in place. The dress was elegant – a little young in style for a woman of Anne's years, but it suited her.

"My modiste in London ordered the fabric specially," Anne said. "Strictly speaking, it is out of season for December, but Owain always compliments me when I am wearing periwinkle blue and I want to look my best for him."

"And you will. This will only take me a few minutes for me to repair and no one will be any the wiser. In fact, I think it's an improvement."

"You are an angel for coming to my rescue and saving me from catastrophe. I nearly fainted when the foolish girl told me she had damaged the neckline while pressing it."

"The lace is so delicate, it's easily done. The girl is distraught."

"As she should be. I have a good mind to make her pay for it."

"Anne, it must have cost more than she earns in a year."

"Well, if I dismiss her, she will be back to making beds and dusting. No one will employ a lady's maid who ruins her mistress' wedding outfit."

"She's inexperienced. Couldn't you give her another chance?"

"I need to consider it. If I do, I certainly won't be letting her anywhere near my new sable wrap. The only reason I promoted her was because she proved to be skilled with hair, but her needlework leaves a great deal to be desired."

As she undid the silk-covered buttons at the back of Anne's dress, Victoria resisted the temptation to point out that the girl was also working for half the wages of someone more experienced.

"If you keep her on, I expect you'll have her undying loyalty."

"Hmm, you are right. I will allow her to remain. You and I are the same. We are both overly kind to those less fortunate."

Victoria turned away, busying herself by selecting a reel of cotton from her box so Anne couldn't see her amusement.

"Indeed we are."

"I am so pleased we have cleared up our little disagreement regarding Owain," Anne said.

"So am I."

"He is a very eligible man. I will have to be on my guard for other women falling for him."

"*I* didn't."

Anne patted Victoria's shoulder. "Of course not, dear."

"Ouch." Victoria jumped as a pin pierced her finger.

"What is it?"

"Just a prick," Victoria mumbled as she sucked her finger.

"Heavens – you haven't got blood on it?"

"No, everything is fine."

"That would have been all I needed," Anne said as she disappeared into the dressing room to change, leaving Victoria to her thoughts.

Having promised Edward, she'd forged ahead with her scheme to improve relations between the four of them by inviting them both to dinner. Victoria had delivered Anne's invitation personally. Anne had been terse, stony-faced, hands clutched on her knee, claiming she'd be too busy to make it.

"Anne, how many times have you forgiven a friend who's annoyed you? Yet, Edward is family and you've refused to take his calls. If something happened to him, how would you live with yourself? As far as I'm concerned, Owain and I are merely friends with a shared interest in improving the lot of the poorer residents of our town. You must believe me," Victoria had implored.

"And how does Owain feel?"

"That's something you'll need to ask him. All I can tell you is that he's never declared to have feelings for me. For my part, Edward is the only man for me and I'd never deliberately hurt him or you."

"Thank you for apologising."

Victoria drew back in surprise – she'd said nothing about being sorry – but Anne had ploughed on.

"I forgive you and yes, dinner will be the perfect way to let Owain see what a mistake it would be to lose me."

The evening had been tense until Owain spoke about how the improved conditions had already made a difference by reducing the number of unnecessary deaths in the Rows.

Much to Victoria's amazement, Anne had responded,

"Too many ignore the plight of others, but I have never been able to do so."

Which gave Victoria a brainwave and she'd suggested Anne might have time to help Owain with his charitable work.

"Someone of your standing in the community would be of immense value to him," she'd said.

Thankfully, Owain had welcomed the idea and Anne, who had never been one to put herself out to help others, had given him a broad smile as she spoke.

"I would be honoured. One should never underestimate what one can achieve with finesse and social graces."

With that, they'd all visibly relaxed.

Victoria understood that the following day, Edward had spoken to Owain "man to man", as he'd put it. And Anne had since told Owain she wouldn't be dallied with. It was marriage or nothing. Now, Owain and Anne were to be wed in two days' time.

Her reverie halted as Anne returned.

"All done?" Anne asked.

Victoria held out her work for Anne's inspection.

"Victoria, that is marvellous. You always were an expert needlewoman. I hope you can be happy that I am marrying Owain."

"I'm delighted. He's fortunate to have you. Any man would be." Who knew she was such an accomplished liar?

"All Owain needed was a little push. My staying away from him worked beautifully. It was so clever of me. It did not take him long to realise what a wonderful wife I will make him."

"He's very lucky."

"You have Edward and he is one of the best men in the world. If I may say so, you were extremely fortunate to land him."

"I certainly was."

Anne smiled condescendingly. "Good. Then we will put your feelings towards Owain down as nothing more than infatuation."

Victoria pushed her scissors into her sewing box before she gave in to the temptation to hack at Anne's gown and smiled sweetly.

Other than slipping out to buy food and going to the news stand, George holed up in his rooms. On the third day, the papers bore the headline he'd been looking for: Sinner Slain. He read on:

Following the attendance of police at a King Street bordello, they discovered the body of a woman in her early twenties, believed to be the madam. Sources revealed she was stabbed several times in a frenzied attack.

If the paper was correct, the police were claiming both the raid and the murder were carried out by vigilantes and that their intention had been to shut down a whorehouse that was ruining the neighbourhood. Tripe. George thumped the table, rattling his dirty crockery. They'd never admit it, but the peelers knew the Lees' control of the city's underworld was burgeoning.

He was reluctant to go back to King Street, but eventually the owner would rent the building out again or someone would loot the place and nick the rest of his hard-earned cash. George had more money hidden behind the back panel of his replica Chippendale desk, which in his haste to escape, he'd not grabbed. So, in an effort to disguise his appearance, he donned an old overcoat and cloth cap and made his way to the tube station, taking the train to Leicester Square and then making the rest of the journey on foot.

Someone had boarded up the windows – presumably the owner of the building. He considered using the back entrance, but there was no one around, so he removed a bunch of keys from his pocket and opened the front door. Once inside, he turned the key in the lock – he didn't want any surprise visitors – then he made straight for the office.

The desk lay in pieces, fit for nothing but kindling. Someone had taken an axe to it.

Although he doubted they'd have left much, George checked the rest of the house. There had been some decent silver candlesticks and crystal decanters. He wouldn't get a lot for them, but now the cash was gone, he needed to salvage what he could. Wandering from room to room, he kicked broken chairs and card tables out of his path. The Lees had left nothing intact. The mattresses were slashed and curtains torn down or scorched. No doubt they'd attempted to raze the place to the ground.

In the doorway of the main salon, he paused, his eyes drawn to the large rug, a dark reddish-brown mark obliterating most of its bold pattern. He walked slowly towards it, the remains of the ornate mirror from above the fireplace crunching beneath his feet. Absent-mindedly, he stooped and touched the stain. This must have been where she died. The other women had probably been dragged away by the Lee gang. Such a waste. This whole set-up had been perfect for welcoming city gents looking for an evening of relaxation away from their wives and business obligations.

Beside an upturned chair, a glint of silver caught his eye – a snuffbox. George picked it up and pushed it into his pocket. Then he checked the rest of the building. Detritus from the attack lay everywhere. Nothing of value was left. Disappointed, he made his way back outside, twisting round at the sound of hurried feet, only to see a small, bedraggled figure running towards him.

"Are you opening the place up again, guv?" Nipper said eagerly.

"What are you doing back here?"

"I've been watching out, hoping you'd come back."

"You been stealing from in there?" He gestured at the building.

"No, guv, honest. I spent the coppers you gave me on bread and cheese. Couldn't afford a bed anywhere, so I've been kipping in the yard, but it's bleedin' freezing."

"Don't you have a home – parents?"

The boy shook his head. "Both dead. I can nick bits of food if I'm careful, but I'd rather earn what I need. I don't want to shame me mam and dad's memories by ending up in clink."

"Look, Nipper, I can't help. This place is shut for good. I'm moving on."

"Can I come wi' yeh? I'm not asking for charity – I'll work hard. I need some dosh."

He was useful, but George didn't need some kid hanging around.

"Push off before I give you a clout."

The boy's face crumpled. George turned away.

As he made his way home, George was unable to shake the feeling that someone was trailing him. It was probably Nipper. If the boy thought he was going to get more money out of him, he was going to be disappointed.

cலௌ

Chapter 24

On the day of Anne's wedding, Kate marvelled at her own ability to watch Jane gazing adoringly at Sean without experiencing the need to grab one of the elaborate displays of lilies and hurl it at them. Thanks to William, Kate was enjoying herself. He was a few feet away, his legs slightly apart, hands gesticulating as he chatted to Sean.

Over the months, Kate had come to appreciate William's masculine rakish manner and cutting wit. Although he spoke his mind, he was courteous – some might say arrogant. He wasn't – not really. The best way to describe him was supremely confident. He believed in his ability to do everything superbly. Hardly surprising – as well as being able to fly a plane, he'd achieved a first at Cambridge and built up a successful engineering business before he was thirty. Admittedly, he might be the most irritating man she'd ever come across, challenging her views simply for devilment, but William would never be boring.

A tiny part of her heart was still reserved for Sean with his lopsided smile, eternally messy hair and, well, Sean-ness, but she cared for William, too – more than she'd thought possible. There was only one problem. He'd still not hinted at any interest in marrying her. Unlike Richard, who was desperate to marry Bella yet too afraid to overstep the invisible boundaries Bella had imposed.

Kate glanced around and spotted Richard. He looked completely out of his depth. Apart from him, Anne's guest list excluded any who weren't in the higher echelons of Faredene society. Of the Gibbs family, only Harry and Jess had been invited. It seemed Anne believed that extreme wealth could buy breeding.

"Richard," Kate called.

He ambled over.

"Am I glad to see a friendly face. A few of my customers are here and they look none too pleased to see me."

Kate reverted to her Irish accent. "Don't stand for a bar of it. You should see them when I treat them to the auld blarney. Sure, they're nothing special and you're a grand man, so you are."

Richard didn't laugh as she'd expected.

"They don't like to mix with people they trade with," he said seriously. "I hope they don't stop using my services. There still aren't as many vehicles around as I'd like."

"You don't need to worry. If their car breaks down, they won't be able to get to Chester or anywhere else to have it repaired, so you're almost guaranteed their business."

"Aye, but I'm hoping to expand. I want them to buy from me instead of going elsewhere."

"You need to brazen it out. Victoria was in trade and has never tolerated snobbishness. Don't let them see you're uncomfortable."

"Any fool can see that Mrs Caldwell is a lady, whereas I'm just a mechanic. My parents were ordinary working people."

"Being born in a higher class means nothing to Bella. She likes you because you're a good man."

"She *likes* me, aye. Where is she? Have you seen her?"

"While you were talking to Father, she hurried past me saying she needed to fix her hair. I hope he wasn't asking you about your prospects."

"Actually, he introduced a client of his who is considering buying an automobile. It was a good contact, because he's going to pay me a commission for sourcing one and advising him."

"That's excellent. I'm sure more will follow. And I'll protect you from the gossips until Bella comes back."

"Thanks," he said, looking no less anxious.

"Now you're chatting to me, they'll wonder which sister you're after," Kate joked.

Richard laughed. "William is a decent chap. Smart."

"Yes. Too clever for his own good. Oh no, don't look, but Anne is heading in our direction. As she's the bride, I suppose it would be poor form if we make a run for it."

"Mr Yates, are my nieces taking care of you?" Anne said.

Richard bowed his head. "Indeed they are."

"Aunt, you're radiant," Kate said.

"Thank you, Kate. I may be married again, but I still do not want you calling me aunt."

Kate rolled her eyes at Richard. "Sorry, *Anne*."

"It is a small gathering, Mr Yates, so hopefully you aren't too uncomfortable being surrounded by the town's elite."

"Not at all. Thank you again for inviting me."

"I am glad you could attend. Bella and Kate seem determined to be lifelong spinsters. I am relieved they both found escorts for today."

Richard looked nonplussed.

"Well, that snuffed out polite conversation," Kate said. "I'm sure Richard feels better knowing we're a couple of lost causes."

"Heavens, Kate! Don't be absurd. You could have had your pick of men if you had made a little more effort to be agreeable and played down how intelligent you are. And I am sure Mr Yates knows what happened to Bella." She looked directly at Richard. "You are aware?"

"Erm. Yes."

"Dreadful business," Anne added. "George did not come from good stock, but he was devilishly handsome and charming. Although rotten to the core, it seems. I saw through him at once, but no one listens to me. As for Bella, I suspect she will never love again. If he were to click his fingers, I fear the dear girl would fall at his feet."

"Anne!"

"What have I said?"

"Surely you don't need me to explain?" Kate said sharply.

"Even on my special day, I am put in my place and not allowed to speak the truth."

"I'd never want to spoil anything for you."

"Hmm."

"I fear your attention is required elsewhere – Mrs Hornby-Smythe appears to have an empty glass."

"Heavens! If you will excuse me, Mr Yates." Anne stalked off towards an unwitting footman.

"Richard, what Anne said is nonsense. No one understands Bella better than I do. If George were here, she wouldn't look at him twice. She'd never trust him again. Please tell me it won't stop you from proposing in the new year," she whispered.

Richard winked. "No – I've got the ring." He patted his pocket. "I've taken to carrying it round."

Kate's lips curved.

"I'm not planning on doing it yet. I just like having it with me," he added.

She squeezed his arm. "Good man."

Kate's own future might be uncertain, but Bella could be a wife and mother – if she allowed herself to be.

Bella was finally calm enough to rejoin the reception. She was annoyed. For the last few months, she'd been doing well and then today, nerves had almost got the better of her. The wedding was always going to be a challenge, but she'd been fine until her father took Richard away to meet an old friend of his. She'd instantly been conscious of the curious glances in her direction. Particularly Mrs H-S, who was talking to another guest and pointing blatantly at Bella. Panic had surfaced and she'd rushed to the small room set aside for the convenience of the ladies.

Now, she must find Richard. He'd been nervous about attending and she'd left him for far too long. She made her way to the drawing room, a smile forming as she saw him talking to Kate.

"What are you two plotting?" Bella asked as she came up behind them.

"Simply discussing what a delightful day it's been," Kate said innocently.

"Even from behind, sister, dear, I can tell when you're up to mischief," Bella said.

"If we told you, you wouldn't believe us," Kate said. "Now, I'm going to leave you two alone so I can prise William away from Sean."

* * *

Before Kate reached the two men, Jane, looking stunning in lavender, caught her arm.

"Kate, save me from having to go back to those two for a few minutes, will you?"

"Have they driven you away with their dreary talk of machines and aeroplanes?"

Jane pulled a face. "Who knew there was so much to say about engines?"

Kate covered her mouth with her hand and pretended to yawn. "For sure, they're both fine men, but there's only so long you can listen to drivel about cogs and pistons without losing the will to live."

Jane giggled.

"Only two weeks until your own big day," Kate added. "Have you picked up lots of tips from Anne's soirée?"

"Ours will be nothing like this – just family. Between you and me, I'd have preferred Sean and I to do it quietly, the two of us. I'm not one for attention."

"Why didn't you, then?"

"It wouldn't have been fair to others. Mam doesn't like fuss, but she wants to see me married."

"I'm sure Milly will be happy as long as the day is how you want it. So would Victoria."

"I know. But what we're doing is the right compromise. And Uncle Harry and Jess have been incredibly generous, paying for everything. He's giving me away, Uncle Harry. And because we're getting married on Boxing Day, Mam's staying for Christmas, as well."

"Is your brother travelling up from London?"

"No. Robert's too busy. It didn't come as a surprise, but I wish he was coming for Mam's sake."

"It's a good job you're not bothered about all this." Kate gestured to indicate the elaborate reception. "Most brides would have been livid that Anne shoehorned her nuptials in right before their own."

"I don't mind at all."

"Not even when she asked to see your gown, in case it was too similar to hers and she needed you to change yours?" Kate smiled wryly. "Victoria told me."

Jane tittered. "I explained I've not seen the finished article. Mam is bringing it with her."

"I'd have told Anne where to get off."

"I couldn't do that. It's sweet that she was so excited about her plans."

Kate shook her head slowly. "Jane, what am I going to do with you? You're far too nice for your own good."

Jane blushed. "Not really. You're always thinking of others."

"*Me*? It's rare people say that about me. Never, in fact."

"That can't be true and if they don't, they should. Look at the way you helped Bella after George left. And I'll always appreciate your encouraging Sean to fight for me. The world needs more women like you. Strong and kind – you're a lot like Victoria."

"That's quite a compliment, thank you."

"Sean adores her. With you being so alike, I often wondered if you and Sean might have got together if he'd never met Yvette."

"No – Sean was yours since the day you met."

"Will you and William make a go of it?" Jane said. "He's very dashing."

255

"Perhaps. I hope so. It took me a while to realise how special he is."

"They're coming over." Jane jerked her head towards the two men.

William's breath tickled Kate's ear as he leaned in close. "Missed me?"

"You'll find out how much later," Kate whispered.

Chapter 25

In his cold sitting room, George leaned back, rocking his chair on its back legs as he pondered his next move. There was a reasonable amount in the Gladstone bag, but only half of what he'd had when he arrived back from India. Life wasn't going in the direction he wanted. He needed to come up with a plan that would improve his situation quickly. But what?

At that moment, there was a loud crack and the blade of an axe smashed through the door to his rooms. George and his chair fell backwards with a thud. He scrambled to his feet, gaping in horror as three stubbled burly men stormed into his home.

With the first punch to George's stomach, he doubled over. It was immediately followed by another. As he dropped to the ground, they kicked him mercilessly, boots connecting with several areas of his body and head at the same time. Blood trickled down his face. He was barely conscious as a gravelly voice penetrated his mind.

"No one runs brothels around here except us."

George groaned.

"Unless you want another visit, get outta London."

A boot clipped George's jaw. Desperate to get away,

he crawled on all fours towards the corner of the room, splaying as a booted foot stamped on his back.

"Got it?" one thug snarled.

"Yethhh," George mumbled through a mouthful of blood.

The largest of the assailants ground his boot down on George's fingers.

"He won't be going anywhere for a while, the state he's in," another said.

The men gathered the money off the table and tore apart George's home. He lay motionless, terrified to move for fear they'd inflict more injuries. Eventually, with a final kick to his back, they left. George tried to drag himself to his feet using the remains of the table for support. Pain racked through him and he blacked out.

When he woke again, wind was rattling the windows. His skin was goose-pimpled. He lay unmoving then crawled his way to the bedroom, crying out as he heaved himself onto the shredded mattress.

Normally, George didn't like to be bested and would have been plotting revenge, but there was no way he was going up against that gang of lunatics. They'd taken almost every penny, aside from the pittance under the floorboards beneath his bed. Thank Christ he'd had the sense to hide a little there. Every inch of him ached, but some small section of his mind told him he'd live. He fell into an exhausted sleep.

Once a week, Victoria took afternoon tea with Jess. Apart from the splendid array of sandwiches and cakes supplied, she enjoyed Jess' company without fail. Today, however, Victoria was distracted, spending much of the time thinking about her children. For the first time in many years, she finally believed Sean was on the path to true happiness, which was a great relief. Bella had her friendship with Richard and at Anne's wedding, it was apparent that he was a man in love. He was a sensible chap who had ambition and plans to expand his business. Automobiles were definitely here to stay and although there were only a few in the area now, eventually she was sure most middle-class families would own one. He'd make Bella a good husband, if only Bella were brave enough to open her heart to him. As for Kate, William was more than a match for her brains and wit.

Her thoughts were interrupted when Jess said, "Victoria, are you still with me?"

"Pardon? Oh, yes."

"I could tell you weren't listening," Jess said good-naturedly. "I was talking about Hornby-Smythe announcing her re-election as chairwoman at next month's Guild meeting. She's going to stand unopposed."

"It's been the same for the last thirty years. Now, she believes it's her right to hold the post."

"You should do something about it."

"Me?"

"I can't think of anyone more suited to the role."

"No, Jess. I've promised Edward the next few years are all about him and me."

"Being chairwoman can't be hard work or Ethel wouldn't do it."

"You stand, Jess. You're on the committee, as well. And you and Harry have done so much for the area. I'd be pleased to nominate you and I'm sure Kate would second the motion. You could win."

"When I first got here, you showed me how to dress and act more like a lady. Then with your help, I bought my way onto the committee. But if I was poor, half the ladies in the Guild would be afraid to use the toilet after me in case they caught a terrible disease, and you know it. Some probably still are but they don't dare show it."

"That can't be true."

"I've seen it in their expressions. As for Hornby-Smythe, she despises me."

"She hates anyone who doesn't bow down to her."

Jess laughed mirthlessly. "Things are easier for me because I'm the only dark-skinned person for miles. People don't feel threatened that my kind are going to take over. But if I tried to push myself forwards, then it would be a different story."

"Oh, Jess."

Jess toyed with the slice of cake on her plate, her voice heavy. "Besides, I can read and write, because my mama taught me, but I've had no education. Not even one day. I've reached my limit in the world, but I'm happy and there are plenty of well-educated white folk who are miserable."

"*Are* you happy, Jess?"

"Yes, doll. As much as I can be for a woman never blessed with children of her own."

"It's such a shame that so many women have more children than they can cope with or rear, yet others can't have them. Have you considered adopting?"

"If the good Lord wanted me to be a mother, He'd have given me a child. Some things can't be altered, whereas the situation with Ethel we can change."

"Unfortunately, I'm not the answer, so Ethel will reign supreme for another year."

"No, sugar. We should find someone else. After that business with the Rows, she doesn't deserve the role."

Victoria placed her teacup and saucer on the side table. "I can't believe I haven't thought of her before."

"Who?"

"Kate – she'd be perfect."

It was two days before George could stand. Still bruised and sore, hunger forced him into the small kitchen area. He grabbed a tin of sardines and took them back to his bed, where he ate straight from the tin.

The man who also had rooms in the house was timid-looking. If he had heard the commotion, George assumed he'd been too frightened to get involved. There was no one else who would come to his aid. George had told no one where he lived. So how did that scum find his home?

George smacked the heel of his hand against his forehead. Nipper. He must have followed him and then sold his address to the Lees. He should never have been nice to the damned brat. Or perhaps he should have slipped him a few more pennies. There was no loyalty – only what you paid for. Everyone was out for what they could get. That was the trouble with the world.

Now, George needed to find a new patch away from London, and sharpish. It was a hole, anyway. Too much competition. It wouldn't be easy starting again with so little cash and where would he go? Manchester? He'd been there once with Bella. It was big enough that you could remain anonymous and far enough that he could remain away from his rivals. And he'd need new girls. There was a lot of work to do and he wasn't sure he was up to the challenge. Drained just from the thought of it, he slumped back onto his pillows.

But he was a fighter. He wouldn't give in.

What about Pearl? Could he take her with him? It had been a while since he last saw her and Moby worked his tarts hard. She might be haggard by now or perhaps even have caught the clap. Once he was up to it, he'd head over to The White Lion and take a gander at her.

She was bound to be angry that he'd sold her to Moby. Then again, last time George had seen her, he'd told her he was going to Africa on business. And say what you like about Moby – he might be a crook, but the fat slob was a man of his word and had promised not to tell Pearl about their arrangement. So it shouldn't be too hard for George to convince her he'd been stranded abroad, unable to get back to her. Ill? No. In prison. He'd tell her he'd been thrown in jail on trumped-up drugs charges and that as soon as he got out, he'd headed home to her and Daphne so they could be a family again. And he'd claim to be appalled that Moby had forced her to oblige any randy so-and-so with a shilling in his pocket. After all, George had only ever asked her to service the gentlemen he specially selected. He'd tell her he was going to rescue her from the life she'd fallen into. The silly cow would swallow every word. It was easy to lie to people who wanted to believe what you told them.

A smile crept over his face. Pearl was the answer to his current money problems and if he could persuade her to bring another couple of sluts along with her, then all the better. Moby wouldn't be pleased, so George would have to make sure he didn't find out what he was up to. Before he could do anything, he had to wait until his ribs healed, but he couldn't take too long about it. The money wouldn't last indefinitely and he needed to get away from this place now the Lees knew where he lived.

In a four-poster bed in the hotel room of a quaint inn overlooking the River Dee in Chester, Kate turned on her side. She ran her fingers over William's bare chest, adopting a seductive expression. Not that she wanted to arouse him – they'd done *that* twice already. It wasn't every day she declared her feelings to a man, but when she watched Jane walk down the aisle to Sean, Kate wanted to know that she had a man of her own – a future.

"We only have another hour or so before I need to leave to pick up Abigail from the party," William said. "How about we do it once more? I won't get to see you now until Sean's wedding." He circled her belly button with his finger.

She could see he was becoming aroused again. If she didn't ask him straightaway, she'd miss the opportunity.

"William?"

"Yes."

She breathed slowly to stem her growing nerves, then before she could talk herself out of it, she said hesitantly, "Maybe we should get married."

William snorted. Not the reaction she'd wanted.

"Why is that amusing?"

He slid down the bed and kissed the tip of her hip bone. "What's brought this on?"

"I love you."

He looked up at her and laughed again. "You don't. You're overreacting because Sean's getting married on Boxing Day." He moved his mouth lower.

Kate put a hand either side of his head and pushed him away. Surely to Christ *he* didn't know about her feelings for Sean?

"W-why do you say such a thing? Why would I react to his wedding?" she blustered, her cheeks burning.

William lay on his side appraising her.

"Because, my darling woman, ladies of a certain age don't like it when everyone around them is getting hitched. First Anne, now Jane. And if I'm not mistaken, it won't be long before Bella will toddle up the aisle."

"So?"

"You're afraid of being the only one in your family who's not married."

She couldn't deny his rationale. The thought of everyone else spending their life with someone while she was alone was unsettling. Regardless, she wasn't about to admit it.

"That's not true," she said.

"We're fine as we are, aren't we?"

"Don't you care about me?"

"I adore you. But marriage isn't for me."

Kate sat bolt upright and grabbed her cigarette case off the side, lighting one. She rarely smoked, only after sex or when she was nervous or annoyed. At this moment, all three applied.

"So, I'm not wife material but I'm all right for a quick roll in the hay when it suits."

"I'd hardly call the best suite in this hotel a barn," he said.

"Don't be facetious. You know exactly what I mean."

"Kate, darling, we have fun, don't we?"

"Clearly not enough to make me your bloody wife."

"Hey, calm down. If I was going to marry anyone, it

would be you. You're beautiful, intelligent and *very* exciting."
He smiled sexily.

"But?"

William sat up, the humour leaving his face, suddenly realising she was serious.

"I've never seen myself as the type to get married. I had to take on Abigail. And I love her, but I'm not in the market for a wife and more children."

Kate stubbed out her cigarette and began pulling on her clothes.

"Take me home, will you?"

"Kate, don't be like this."

"I'll behave how I damn well want."

"You're being irrational."

"Good. I'm glad we're not spending Christmas together and you needn't come for the wedding."

William climbed out of bed and grabbed his trousers off the chair.

"Fine! Suits me. I've seen enough men get shackled to irrational women to last me a lifetime."

Chapter 26

By the time Christmas grew nearer, George had given up hope of catching Pearl coming or going from The White Lion. He decided a more direct approach was needed. It was possible she'd moved on from here and if so, he couldn't afford to hang around for nothing.

He halted on the steps of the public house as a waif barrelled through the door, colliding with his leg.

"Bleedin' 'ell! Watch where yer goin'! Yeh nearly 'ad me on me arse," she cursed, stooping to retrieve a small parcel from the floor.

She was petite, with long blonde hair tied in a slip of tattered ribbon. Her clothes were tight and patched, her face mucky. She looked up. His own eyes were glaring back at him . . . His stomach lurched – Daphne.

George was stunned. His daughter was a filthy street urchin.

Ignoring him, she glanced over her shoulder, calling, "I'll be back in a jiffy wi' yer money, Uncle Moby." She pushed past George.

He stared after her as she scurried down the road until she disappeared round the corner. Then he entered the smoky, dimly lit pub, immediately spotting Moby, the landlord, his bulk overhanging a tall stool that looked like it could give way under his weight. A tawny woman in a gaudy low-cut gown was emptying some coins from a drawstring bag onto the bar in front of him.

"Blimey! George Bristow. I didn't expect to clap eyes on you again," Moby called.

"All right, Moby. Nice to see you." George hoped his smile masked the shock still coursing through him.

The woman eyed George appreciatively until Moby slapped her backside.

"Fetch me a bottle of whiskey and two glasses through to the back, Flo." He stood, his stomach falling over the top of his waistband like an apron. "Come through to the back, George. We'll have a chinwag."

George took a seat in the cluttered office.

"You can hardly move in here. What's with all the boxes and crates?"

"One of my contacts has pulled off a big job. Knocked off a bonded warehouse. I've not sold it on yet. If yer interested in any of it . . ."

"No thanks, Moby. I'm mainly legit these days."

The woman came in carrying a tray, her hips swaying.

"Put it on the desk. Then get down the docks and see if you can do some more business."

"Moby, can't I wait until I know Daph's back safe? Unless this gent wants some company?" Flo winked at George, licking her lips.

She was scrawny with bird's-nest hair and a black eye.

"Fancy giving her one?" Moby asked.

George shook his head, not bothering to conceal his revulsion. He hoped Pearl was in better condition or it would ruin his plans.

"He's a friend of mine and he doesn't want an old tart

propositioning him," Moby said. "Now, get gone before I get Crusher to have a word with you." When the door shut none too quietly behind the woman, he added, "You sure yer not after a bit o' skirt, George? I've got better than an old boiler if you want to see what's on offer?"

"Not today, thanks. I'm only passing through. Who's this Crusher?"

"My protection. Got that name because they say he once mashed some poor bugger's head to a pulp with his bare hands."

"Nice man."

"You've got to have paid muscle around these days if you're in this game. There's a Chinese gang branching out all over the place. They've not bothered me yet, but it's only a matter of time." Moby poured their drinks, his beer-stained vest straining over his stomach. "Crusher's a vicious piece of work, but I'm getting too old to be playing the hard man. And he keeps everyone in line, punters and tarts alike."

"You must be raking it in. Isn't it about time you invested in some new clobber?"

Chuckling, Moby handed a glass to George.

"No bloody chance. If this lot round here knew what I'm worth, I'd be a target for every worm who fancied chancing his arm. One day I'll sell up and move to Margate – end my days in comfort by the sea. Until then, I'll keep crying poverty."

"You're a smart one, Moby."

"I can see you've done well for yerself an' all. You always dressed like you had a few bob, but now you'd pass for a toff anywhere."

"I can't complain. Life's been good to me."

"So, what brings you back to these parts?"

"I was in London for a meeting not too far from here. It finished early and I had an hour to spare, so I called in."

"Well, it's good to see yeh."

George kept the conversation going for a few minutes, feigning interest in Moby's life and business. Eventually, he asked casually, "So, how has Pearl worked out for you? I hope she's been earning you a fair whack."

"Complete effing washout. The silly mare only got herself killed the first week she was here."

George jerked, the amber liquid sloshing.

"Sorry to hear that. What happened?" he asked, struggling to keep his voice calm.

"I treat 'em right, you know me. So I gave her a few days to settle in, with only me having a go on her. She was a smashing ride, even with all the kicking and screaming – I don't mind a bit of that. Neither did the first punter I put her with. I picked him special, like – a gent. But the second geezer saw red when she scratched his face. Difficult thing to explain to his missus, so he hammered her."

"He beat her to death?"

"Aye – bloody shame. She had a magnificent pair of knockers. Still, the bloke had money and he was willing to give me what I paid you for her an' a bit extra, as long as I got rid of the body on the quiet. So I didn't lose owt."

"I'm pleased for you. What did you do with her?"

"Got a mate of mine to take her out in his boat and throw her overboard."

"And Daphne?"

"Didn't you see her on your way in?"

"The ragamuffin?" George said airily.

"Aye, the little bugger isn't too fond of soap an' water."

"Who's been taking care of her?"

"Flo took her under her wing. I could have had the kid chucked in the water with her mother's corpse, but I'm all heart." He smirked. "Mind you, now she's a bit older, to pay for her keep she helps wi' the cleaning an' runs little errands, delivering and collecting important packages. Ones I don't want the bobbies getting their hands on, if you get me meaning." Moby tapped the side of his nose.

George got what Moby meant all right. The bastard had Daphne carrying drugs. He fought the urge to lean over the desk and throttle the sack of blubber.

"Are you sure that's all she's doing?" George ground out.

Moby's face hardened as he topped up George's glass.

"Yer not gettin' all paternal, are yeh, after I've had to feed an' clothe her?"

Pearl deserved whatever life had handed to her, but George wanted more for his daughter.

Quickly recovering his passive expression and casual tone, he said, "No. I'm merely making conversation. Like I told you at the time, she's not mine."

"Aye, and Fanny's me aunt an' Dick's me uncle. She's got a look of you."

"The last thing I'm interested in is a whore's brat. I've got children of my own who are being raised properly."

"Good, 'cos I'd hate us to fall out about it, George. We've been mates a long time." Seemingly placated, Moby continued, "I think my kindness will pay off in the end. She's got lovely features under all that muck. And if she inherits her mother's tits, she'll be a tasty piece." He gestured with his hands. "I'll have 'em queuing up outside her door an' be able to name my price."

"You'll have a few years to wait yet, but I'm glad your investment will pay off." George raised his glass to Moby.

"Not that long, as it happens. I waited longer than I had to 'cos she's small, but by my reckoning, she must be nearly nine."

"She's just turned eight – I think, based on what her mother told me."

"Aye, well, it makes no difference. I were gonna start her off wi' a few easy jobs, but I've got a seafaring gent. Norwegian sea captain who's real interested in taking her with him to keep him company on the voyage. He likes them young an' unspoiled."

George's stomach pitched. "Isn't it bad luck to have women on a ship?"

"The captain says the beauty of it is that she's not a woman until she needs her monthly rags. Anyway, I told him I'm not selling."

"Are you merely haggling to drive the price, you crafty git?" George said, forcing a smile.

Moby laughed again. "You always understood business. I'll see what he offers. For now, he said he'll settle for breaking her in the next time his ship docks. I'd like to do it meself, but he's offering a pound for a full night with her."

"I assume you've agreed?"

"Not yet. I told him I need to think about it. I'm hoping to squeeze more outta him."

"Do you think he might be willing to pay more?"

"Aye, 'cos he were straining his breeches at the sight o' her. Mind you, Flo, the one who's been mothering her, will moan about it. He's built like a brick shithouse and normally takes two or three girls at a time."

George couldn't keep the edge from his voice.

"The child is too young to be with someone like him."

She was far too young to be near any man. Christ, it had been a mistake leaving her here. George felt compelled to help her.

Moby bristled. "Aye, well, there's nowt of her, but she eats like a flamin' horse. I need to see a bit o' profit from her. If I wasn't so fond of her, I wouldn't have been so patient when she didn't have her mother here to stump up for her bed and board."

"When does the Norwegian ship dock next?"

"Back end of the first week o' January, like as not. Hard to be certain with the weather at this time of year. It's a long trip to the West Indies. He'll be ready for some company."

George said quickly, "I'll double what he's paying you."

"What for? Like I said, I'm not letting her go. She'll make me a fortune over the next few years."

"The night, nothing more."

"You want to be the first and wi' yer own kid? I never saw you as a strange 'un."

Not bothering to deny she was his child, George said, "My tastes are my affair."

Moby eyed him sceptically. George had to allay Moby's suspicions or any plan he came up with to rescue Daphne would fail before it started.

"I've been abroad, remember? There are things I've enjoyed that would curl even your lanky hair."

Moby chuckled again, then knocked back his drink. "Aye, I bet you have. You can tell me about them when

272

you've got more time. I'm always on the lookout for new business ideas."

"Certainly. And the girl – do we have a deal?"

Moby topped up both of their glasses. "Like I said, I've got the captain interested. I've not promised him, but he'll not be best pleased all the same an' he's a regular."

The thought of his daughter with some man made George sick. He'd never forget the terror he'd suffered as a child at the hands of his teacher. Pearl should have protected her. Gone with the men and made the most of it. He'd been stupid to leave Daphne in the selfish bitch's care.

"If she ends up dead like Pearl, you'll be out of pocket. Whereas I'll give her back as good as new. Or nearly. With what I have in mind, he won't even know she's been touched."

Moby rubbed his hands together. "In that case, it's a deal. I knew she'd be a good earner. You can have the first go. Keep it in the family, like. That should shut Flo up an' all, 'cos yer more likely to be gentle than the foreigner."

"I want the entire night."

"Tonight?"

"No. I have to leave town again this afternoon and get back home to my family before Christmas."

"Where you livin' these days?"

"Never you mind. I'll be back on the thirtieth. Make sure no one touches her beforehand."

"She'll be here," Moby said unconvincingly.

"There was another reason I stopped by today."

"Oh aye, an' what's that?"

"Don't cross me over Daphne, Moby, and I'll put a lot more business your way. I'm looking for a business partner

273

who can provide upper-class tarts for parties over Knightsbridge way. You're too good to be dealing with the scrubbers end of the market, Moby. You always have been."

"I've got ambition, but you've got to talk right to supply the gentry, surely?"

"There's no need for you to worry about that. I'll handle the customers. This is your opportunity to earn more money than you ever dreamed possible."

"Smashin' – I'm yer man, George."

"You'll have to find some younger women, though. The likes of that Flo would be no good. An' they'd need to dress the part. Get this right and you could retire far sooner than you expected," George added, hoping Moby's greed would stop him from handing Daphne over to the captain or anyone else before George could get her away from here.

"Righto, George, you can rely on me." He held a fat arm out, sending the stench of stale sweat into the air.

George needed to leave before he threw up or killed Moby. He shook the proffered hand.

"See that the child bathes and is dressed nicely for when I arrive."

"No problem. What time should we expect you?"

"Around eight to eight thirty." George placed some money on the desk. "This should cover the clothes an' I'll want the back bedroom. I assume it's still the best one?"

"It is. Nice and quiet back there, too."

"Good chap. Now, I must be off."

As George made his way back to his rooms on foot, his mind was whirling. First, he must have a foolproof plan to get Daphne away. Pearl was dead. That was a shock. Not his fault, though.

A smile spread across his face. As she'd died in the first week of being at The White Lion, his marriage to Bella had been legal, after all – that changed things. If he left Daphne where she was, he and Bella might start again. Or if she was too stubborn to take him back, if Bella were to die, as her legal husband, would he inherit what she left?

Chapter 27

After the wedding breakfast, Kate slipped upstairs to the guest-room Jess and Harry had allocated to her. She blotted her eyes carefully before the tears could escape. Did weddings always bring your own situation to the forefront of your mind for you to examine? Kate mused. Or was it only when the man you've been besotted with for years was getting married to someone else – for the second time? Or perhaps it was because she was a monumental idiot and had messed up her chances with William. She prided herself on being an emotionally aware woman. Yet, until it was too late, she hadn't even possessed the wit to realise that she loved him. Really loved him – not as a substitute for Sean.

Kate had spent years so immersed in the despair of not being able to have Sean that she never gave other men a chance. In hindsight, she'd deliberately sabotaged her chances of a future with any good man by playing the slut with Garrett Ackerley – a married man who, if she were honest, she didn't even like. Never mind her engaging in other fleeting relationships with men who were equally unsuitable.

In her defence, if someone told her it was possible to love two men, she'd have laughed in their face. William was handsome, exciting and kind, and now she'd scared him away. She'd heaped this misery on her own shoulders and whatever it took, she was going to get through the rest of the reception without making a holy show of herself, she thought as she applied rouge to her cheeks. Not enough so that anyone would notice, but sufficient to mask her deathly pallor.

As soon as she re-entered the ballroom, Sean came over.

"You look serious. No smile for the groom?" he said.

Would his grin ever not make her tummy flip? She doubted it.

She forced a smile. "Are you enjoying the day?"

"It's been perfect, hasn't it? Apart from Jane's father not being here. She's said nothing, but I know she's missing him."

"It wouldn't be normal if she wasn't. Every girl dreams of having their father by their side on their wedding day."

"I wish I could have made it better for her."

"Now don't you shoulder responsibly for things outside your control. Look to the future. There's no peace in the past," Kate said.

"You're right, of course. For the first time in my life, I have everything I could want. And I need to make sure I don't mess it up."

"Are you going to be all right with all this champagne around? It surprised me to see it being served. Was it necessary?"

He pulled a face. "No reason for everyone else to go without. I can't avoid alcohol at social events – it's part of life. The temptation will always be there. But truthfully, it's not been half as bad as I expected."

Kate surveyed him. He looked different somehow. Suddenly, she realised Sean had lost the vulnerable look that she'd always wanted to erase from his face. It had been there the day he returned from America and remained until Jane changed him. Kate felt a pang of jealousy that she wasn't the one to save him, but at least someone had.

She placed her hand on his arm. "Life will be better now. Starting with three weeks in Paris, you lucky thing. What time do you catch your train?"

"Not for a couple of hours yet." He frowned slightly. "It was good of Mother and Edward to pay for our honeymoon, but do you think it's too long to be away from the boys? What if they get upset? Or if they think I'm never coming back, like Yvette? Pierre has been unsettled of late."

Even though his servants were perfectly capable, Sean rarely left his sons overnight in their care. Everyone understood he was frightened one of them might get hurt again in his absence.

"Owain had to give him another tonic last week," Sean added.

"You had Christmas Day with the boys – you and Jane deserve some time for yourselves now."

"I think Pierre gets frustrated."

"That's understandable. He's not unwell, though?"

"No, but even so, I worry."

"Bella already spends most of her spare time with them. And Victoria said she and Father are staying at yours until you get back from honeymoon, so the boys will have a fabulous time. If it helps, though, as the school is closed for another week, I'll pop in when I can."

"Thanks, Kate."

"You're welcome. Once you get away, you'll be too busy to think about anything but enjoying your time with Jane."

Kate flushed. She may have moved on, but an image of Jane and Sean alone in their bedroom wasn't something she wanted. Sean must have sensed her embarrassment, because instead of making an innuendo, he changed the subject.

"Mother said she and Edward will keep an eye on the factory, so I won't be missed."

"I'm sure she didn't mean it that way," said Kate.

"I know. She was just trying to stop me from worrying."

"There you go. Just be thankful you can get away from your business obligations for a while."

"Unlike William – I'm sorry he couldn't make it today."

"Last-minute meeting," she lied.

"I'm glad you're here."

"Didn't I tell you I'd attend all of your weddings? Hopefully, this will be the last one. You're costing me a small fortune in wedding gifts and hats."

"I thanked everyone else in my speech, but I couldn't thank you for what you did with them all listening."

"Sure, it was nothing."

"Don't be coy. Apart from making sure I didn't completely crack up after the crash, you played a large part in getting Jane and I back together. You're a wonderful friend . . . sister."

That was all she'd ever be to him, but now it no longer felt like being stabbed through the heart.

She cuffed him playfully. "I just couldn't face the thought of you moping around for the next decade."

Laughing, Sean moved off to speak to Harry. Sadness swept over her – though not because she wasn't Sean's bride. What irked Kate was that if she hadn't behaved like a blithering fool, William would have been by her side today and no doubt he'd have crept along the corridor to her room tonight. Instead, she'd lie in a cold bed facing a future alone.

"Kate, may I have a quick word?"

"Victoria, what can I do for you?"

"I have a suggestion you might like."

"Go on."

"Jess and I are hoping you'll agree to stand against Ethel for the position of Chair of the Guild."

"I've not been a member for long. Surely the other members would prefer someone more experienced."

"As with a great many things in life, what most people want is for someone else to do all the work. They're willing to give their support and occasionally money to help tackle the things they find unpleasant or distasteful, but they don't want to put in any effort."

"What about you? You're the obvious candidate, Victoria, after everything you've achieved since you came to this town. Building up successful businesses, helping the poorer residents . . . And your work on the Rows has impressed everyone. If you talk to the other members about that and finally tell them that Ethel's husband used to own them, you're bound to get elected."

"Age is catching up with me and my family has to be my priority."

"Do you think I'd be any good at it?"

"Kate, I doubt there's anything in life that you wouldn't be good at if you put your mind to it."

"Victoria, what a lovely thing to say."

"I rarely give false compliments. And never to my children. You're busy with the school, but I don't believe you'd find the Guild will take up a great deal of your time. The secretary does most of the paperwork. The chairwoman is there to guide the group and ensure that their commitment to charitable causes isn't forgotten amid arranging luncheons."

"Ethel will put up a fight."

"Of course she will. That's why we need you. Someone passionate with a sense of social responsibility, which our current chairwoman sadly lacks."

"As she doesn't care about anything but the luncheons, why do you think she's clung on for so long?" Kate said.

"Prestige – it's as simple as that. So, will you do it? I'll assist you unofficially in the background if you ever need me."

"I can't stand Ethel and her pompous ways, but I shouldn't complain about her if I'm not prepared to challenge her for the role."

"Good girl."

"What do I need to do?"

"At the January meeting, I'll nominate you and Jess will second it. In the meantime, you need to prepare your address to the members."

"A speech? I'll probably make a complete eejit of myself and be laughed out of the place."

"Nonsense."

How lucky Bella and Sean were to have Victoria as a mother. Although Kate had to admit, her stepmother never treated her any differently to the others. Impulsively, she kissed Victoria's cheek.

"Thank you."

"For what?" Victoria said.

"You've always been so supportive of me. Even when I've been a twit. You've been more of a mother to me than my own ever was."

"Oh, Kate, my dear girl. I fear I should have said so sooner that I've always considered myself fortunate to have *two* wonderful daughters."

Kate's tears were building again. This time because she was so touched.

Victoria patted Kate's arm gently. "Now, Bella explained Richard is in Manchester visiting his family for Christmas, but is that nice young man of yours really at a meeting?"

"No. We've fallen out."

"Is it something you can overcome?"

"I'm not sure. The thing is, I told him I love him and he didn't react how I wanted."

"Kate, if you mean it, then fight for him. Isn't that what you told Sean?"

"Yes, but that was different – I knew they both loved each other. Whereas William doesn't appear to give a fig about me."

"I've seen the way he looks at you. Not when you're next to him, but when he gazes at you from across a crowded room. At Anne's wedding, William spent a lot of time speaking with Sean, but I noticed his eyes kept moving to where you were."

"Really?"

"Yes. Sometimes we have things in our past that prevent us from acknowledging our feelings, even to ourselves. It took me years of loneliness before I finally admitted to your father that I loved him. Why don't you telephone William and talk things through?"

"Hmm, I'm not sure."

"What could go wrong?"

"How much time do you have? It's a long list."

Victoria laughed. "Then again, everything could go perfectly."

"So, you believe there's still a chance for me and him?"

"Yes, and I'm very wise, so you can trust me. What's more, I'm committed to seeing all three of our children happily married."

That same day in London, George was despondent. He'd had a miserable Christmas. His offer to Moby had been intended to buy time, with no plan behind it. After leaving The White Lion, he'd decided it was too risky to get involved with rescuing Daphne and that his efforts would be better spent winning Bella back. But despite his relentless efforts to convince himself Daphne wasn't his responsibility, visions of her terror as a burly, bearded Norwegian bore down on her tormented him. For the first time, guilt had stopped him from sleeping. No matter how many times he reasoned it was all Pearl's fault, the same disturbing thought crept back into his head – he'd abandoned his helpless, innocent daughter.

So George had decided to approach Daphne if she went on an errand and take her to safety. He had to be careful, though, because if she drew attention to them or escaped, Moby would be on to him. Having watched out for her over a few days, George discovered she rarely went out alone. And it was obvious she was used to predators, crossing the road warily before George could approach her as she made her way through the busy London streets. Uneducated she may be, but she was smart. George was proud of the little scrap.

What would she be like if she'd grown up elsewhere, protected from the foulest elements of human nature? George wondered. How different her life would have been with Bella as a mother – with Victoria and Edward as doting grandparents. Even though she was only a girl and could never hope to compete with a man, perhaps his daughter might have been someone special, achieving the success and recognition George had been seeking all of his life.

He'd tried to think of a future with just him and Bella, but each time an image of Daphne appeared, wearing a white lace dress, sitting on a swing giggling as she called for him to push her higher. And in the background, Bella reading, the sun glistening on her glossy brown hair . . . Surely this proved he was meant to reunite them all as a family.

Occasionally, the woman he recognised as Flo had accompanied Daphne. Twice she'd walked with her, waiting on the corner of a street while the child ran inside one of the buildings to deliver and collect packages. Once, Flo took her to the shop and bought her a cone of chips, another time a twist of barley sugars. On Christmas Day, Daphne was wearing a new blue ribbon in her hair. He suspected it was from Flo, as it was clear she cared for her.

Today, George had once again taken up his position in Alf's Café opposite The White Lion. His table in the corner by the window offered an excellent view of the pub's front entrance and alleyway into which the back gate led. As a precaution against anyone recognising him, again he wore a shabby overcoat and a cloth cap pulled low, and he kept a copy of the *Daily Herald* at hand to hide his face if necessary.

He'd arrived late morning and tucked into a surprisingly tasty meal of steak and kidney pudding and mushy peas, followed by several cups of tea. By four o'clock, darkness descended on the grimy streets. Throughout the day, gaudily dressed women, including Flo, left and returned on the arms of men. Although the alehouse was more than a mile from the docks, many of their customers appeared to be sailors. This was the type of trade Moby had always encouraged his tarts to pick up, as seamen were desperate for the company of a woman. They had money to spend and often no home to go to. That his beautiful daughter may be condemned to a life of servicing bilge rats was now unbearable to him.

Daphne had never appeared after dark before, so he decided he'd come back tomorrow. However, as he rose, on the other side of the road, Flo emerged from The White Lion again. This time, Daphne was holding her hand. They paused under the dim halo of a nearby gas lamp.

George threw some money on the table and hurried outside. Daphne's large eyes were fixed on the woman's face and the child was nodding as though taking instructions. Pausing as he passed them, George pulled out a packet of cigarettes and a box of matches and made a play of lighting up. He didn't smoke but had bought them purely for such an instance, to give him the opportunity to loiter without drawing suspicion.

The woman's black eye twitched as she bent to speak.

"So, yer to go straight there, Daph. No dawdling. I could bleedin' murder Moby, sending you on an errand after dark. And now a ship has docked, he won't let me watch out for yeh. I'm sorry, duck."

"Taint no bovvah. Uncle Moby had to send me. Some filthy git vomited all over the sheets an' the lazy bitch who does the laundry said I had to wash 'em before I could run this errand."

"I know, chick. You make sure you stay in the main streets. No nipping down the back entries. It might be quicker but it ain't safe."

"I'll be all right. If any randy bugger tries anyfink, I'll kick 'em in their unmentionables." She grinned as though she'd made a joke.

Flo stroked Daphne's hair.

"Good girl. Nice an' hard, like I taught yeh. Now, I've gotta get to the docks or I'll get another slap from Crusher. Quick as you can, mind."

"Righto, Flo." Daphne stood on her tiptoes and kissed the woman's heavily rouged cheek.

As Flo moved away, George threw his cigarette in the gutter and without a second thought, hurried after Daphne, keeping to the shadows so as not to scare her. She paused outside a row of shops, glancing over her shoulder before entering the barbers. George got just close enough to see through the window. A tall man was stroking Daphne's face while another stood nearby sneering and probably making crude comments. She wouldn't stand a chance if someone like him decided to take her down.

George grappled with the urge to barge in and tackle him to the ground. Fists clenched, he watched as the leering man slowly tucked a small parcel inside her coat against her chest. The drugs would be worth a packet – more reason for Moby to have his contacts hunt them down if

George grabbed her now. But this might be his only opportunity to approach her. He readied himself to make his move, but as Daphne left the barbers, Flo came dashing up to her, panting.

"Come on, quickly. Crusher will have me guts if I'm caught, but I couldn't get me mind on the job wi' you out alone. I'll take you to the corner of the road an' you can run on from there."

As the pair dashed down the street, George decided he'd enlist the help of Flo and pray her affection for the child would continue to outweigh her fear of Moby's henchman.

Chapter 28

The following afternoon, as a light rain fell outside the windows of Caldwell Grange, Kate was lounging in the parlour and a fire roared in the grate. Her arm dangled by her side as she reached into a bowl on the floor again.

"Has Mr Cadbury been given a peerage?" Kate said.

Bella laid down her book. "What on earth are you babbling about, woman?"

"Anyone who invents something so grand – he deserves some sort of recognition, don't you agree?"

"I think you've eaten way too much chocolate for one day and it's affecting your mind."

"Away wi' you, you soft mare. There's no better way to idle away my time. Sure, I've no man and although I can't claim chocolate is as good as sex, it's a wonderful substitute."

"Kate, you're incorrigible," Bella said in her best imitation of Kate's accent. "If the pupils heard you talking about s-e-x and told their parents . . . sure, they'd have the constables on you and we'd be closed down, so we would."

Kate laughed. "Well, the beauty of the holidays is that I don't have to be careful about what I say. I can be as Irish as I want, because we've no one to teach for nearly a week."

"Are you bored?"

"Something fierce."

"Why don't you work on your speech for the Women's Guild election? You need to be prepared," said Bella.

"Finished it," Kate mumbled as she sucked on another piece.

"Do you want to read it to me?"

"No. That'll make me more nervous."

"You could go round to Sean's and see the boys."

"No chance! Anne's calling there today. If I'm forced to listen to her pontificating about married bliss or the trials of being a doctor's wife, it might throw me over the edge. And I certainly don't want her asking me again why William didn't attend Sean's wedding. The story I gave everyone didn't satisfy our dear aunt's thirst for gossip."

"Yes, she'd want all the details, but I also think she'd feel sorry for you," Bella said.

"Even worse."

Kate moved her arm around, feeling for the bowl. Just before her fingers touched it, Bella whipped it away, taking it back to her seat, popping a piece into her mouth.

"This is for your own good," Bella said.

"Nooo. Give me back my chocolate," Kate whined.

"Answer my questions first."

"That's my kind of tactic – I've taught you well, sweet pea. Go on."

"Are you truly over Sean?"

"As unbelievable as it may seem, I think I am."

"Honestly?"

"I've not gone blind, if that's what you mean. I still love the cut of him and think he's grand."

"But do you *want* him?" said Bella.

"Truthfully? I believe I'd have got over Sean years ago

289

if he'd been happy with Yvette. But with him being so miserable – and that vulnerable look he always had about him – I think I wanted to rescue him. And . . ."

"Good Lord. Don't stop now – I'm agog."

"William is strong and masterful yet kind with it. It's him I want – and not because I'm afraid of being alone for the rest of my life."

"Well that's blooming marvellous, isn't it?"

"It's too late."

"Rubbish. Don't be so stubborn. Go and see him," said Bella.

"Ack, I can't. I made such an eejit of myself, declaring my love when he doesn't give a hoot about me."

"So why did he give you that fabulous necklace after you'd quarrelled and go to the extra expense of sending a messenger with it on Christmas Day?"

Raising her head slightly from the pillow, Kate said hopefully, "Do you think he regrets his reaction? Victoria believes he *cares* for me. But why hasn't he shown up here weighed down with flowers, declaring his love?"

"If you think about it logically, he's not in a position to come charging over here to see you – not when he's got Abigail at home. And he's telephoned daily, even though you've refused to speak to him."

"Hmm."

Over Christmas, Kate had been as miserable as a turkey waiting in a butcher's yard. But she couldn't help it. She'd messed up her life by moving at lightning speed from keeping William at arm's length, insisting their relationship was merely a way of pleasantly passing the time, to proposing, followed by storming off because he didn't want to get married. She should have given the man a chance to warm to the idea.

"I love you far too much to allow you to wallow any longer," Bella said.

"Again, you're taking my role, sis. What should I do, sweet pea?"

"Telephone him now, then go over there tomorrow and see him. He's made the first move at reconciliation, so there's no shame in it."

Kate sat bolt upright. "You have a point. If he seems pleased when I ring and invites me to stay, would you mind if I did?"

"Heavens, no. I'll be glad to see the back of you. Because if you keep eating chocolate at this rate, there will be a national shortage."

"All right, but if I'm going to be brave and risk my last shred of dignity chasing after a man, what about you?"

"Me?" Bella took another piece.

Kate laughed. "See – chocolate is a marvellous comfort when you don't want to face things."

"I don't know what you're referring to."

"We're a right pair, having to drag each other towards happiness. You've known Richard ages. Don't you think it's about time you gave in to your feelings and admit you care for him?"

"Fine. I admit it," Bella said.

"Then why do I sense hesitation?"

"It's not the same as I felt for George."

"That might not be a bad thing. This time you'd be going into a relationship older and wiser. And believe me, people aren't the same, so what you feel for them can't be the same. What I felt for Sean and feel for William is different, but both are real."

"That makes sense. Even so . . ."

"You're too afraid to give yourself permission to love him."

"I am not."

"All right, then, repeat after me. I, Bella Caldwell . . ."

"Where's this going?"

"Come on."

Bella tutted. "I, Bella Caldwell . . ."

"Love Richard Yates and I'm too stubborn for my own good. Only the fear of being hurt is holding me back," Kate said slowly.

"Shut up, will you. I'm not saying that."

Kate laughed as she lay back down. "There you go, then. We're going to die a pair of lonely old hags. Our fate is sealed because I'm stupid and because you, my dear sweet pea, are trapped in the past by the actions of that scoundrel George Bristow."

"I am not."

"Face it – you're in denial."

"If you go to see William, then I promise that while you're away, I'll consider the slim possibility that I *may* be holding back out of fear."

Kate jumped up, smiling. "Deal. I'll ring him and if that goes well, I could throw a few things in a bag and catch the train this evening."

"Clearly my little talk worked miracles. Now you can't even wait until tomorrow to see him."

Kate shrugged. "What can I say? I'll be back to see in the New Year with you, though."

"Don't worry about me," Bella said.

"I'll be back, and if William and I reconcile, it can be a celebration of sorts."

After speaking to William, Kate breathed a sigh of relief. He sounded genuinely pleased that she was going to visit him to talk things through, insisting she allow him to collect her from the station. This might be her last chance at love and she mustn't waste it. She wouldn't let her sister throw her future away, either.

Kate picked up the telephone and made two more calls.

George had followed Flo and Daphne back to The White Lion the previous night and had waited in a side street hoping to talk to the woman, but she'd picked up three customers in quick succession and taken the third into the pub, where she remained. At midnight, when the cold and damp had seeped into his bones, George had given up and gone back to his rooms.

Today when George arrived mid-afternoon, it was apparent that Flo had been badly beaten. Her top lip was a mass of dried blood and her face was grotesquely swollen. Despite how unappealing she looked, she was immediately approached by a man carrying an umbrella and a tattered briefcase and after few words, she led him down an entry.

George left the café and followed. He slouched against the brick wall as he waited for her to finish with her customer in a doorway a few feet further along. After a guttural cry, the man emerged looking pleased with himself as he fastened his flies. Then, spotting George, his expression changed to a mixture of mortification and nervousness before he hurried away.

Flo appeared. She tied the string on a small bag and pushed it down between her large breasts as she eyed

George up and down. She gave him a gappy smile.

"Hello, handsome. Do you want a quick one here or would you want a room?"

She sashayed over, clearly not recognising him from their brief meeting in The White Lion.

"Here's fine."

Flo hitched up her breasts. "What's the world coming to when a looker like you needs to pay for a knee-trembler?"

George held the money between two fingers.

"I ain't got enough change to give you, cocker. I've only had one customer so far today," she said.

"You can keep it all. I just want to talk to you."

She stepped backwards, stumbling in her haste.

"Yer not a bleeding bobby, are yeh?"

George steadied her with his free hand. "It's Flo, isn't it?"

"What the 'ell's goin' on? How do you know me name? If this is one o' Moby's bloody tricks to check I'm loyal, I ain't falling for it."

"You have nothing to fear from me. It's about Daphne."

"Not you an' all. Why can't you mucky bleeders leave her alone? She's nowt but a babe."

"I don't want to hurt her. Quite the opposite – she's my daughter."

Flo's fist smashed against his nose and the back of George's head hit the wall with a thud.

"That's for Pearl, yeh rotten git. I didn't have time to know her well, but that poor girl wasn't a proper whore. An' yeh sold her. She kept crying 'n' saying you'd come back for her. The poor cow is better off dead than livin' the life you left her to face, yeh treacherous gob of spit."

George held his handkerchief to his nose.

"I'll let you get away with that because I've seen that you care for Daphne and I need your help to rescue her."

"What you on about?"

"Moby's putting her to work."

"Aye. He's got two blokes wanting to be the first wi' her."

"I'm one of the men."

"I'll kill yeh before I let you touch her. I had to run away from home because me own dad was forever forcin' himself on me. It's not happening to Daph." She raised her fist again.

George grabbed her hand, squeezing until she winced.

"The only reason I told Moby that I was interested in Daphne in that way was to stall for time. I've been hanging around the streets waiting to approach her so I can get her away from here."

"Well, yer too bleedin' late. Last night, Crusher belted me just 'cos the nasty snake spotted me earlier when I brought her back from an errand she was running. Then we argued an' it all comes out. I found out what Moby's got planned, so when they'd all gone to bed, I tried to sneak out wi' Daph. I've only got a few coppers saved up, but if we'd made it to the station, it would have bought us a ticket outta here."

"You were caught?"

"Aye – lost nearly all me teeth for me trouble. It breaks my effing heart, but she'll never get away now. Moby's got her locked up until one o' youse pays for her. He's a money-grabbing pillock, but I'm shocked he'd do this to her, 'cos he's always claimed to be fond of her."

"Moby would sell his own mother if the price was right."

"You should know – selling yer wife an' daughter."

"I know what I did." George snarled. "The point is, I want to put it right. I've insisted on the back bedroom."

"What's that got to do wi' the cost o' jellied eels?"

"The kitchen roof is below the window. I can lower her onto it before I climb out myself. Then we can drop down into the passage behind the pub."

"You'll never get away with it. Daph is a prized piece. Moby will have Crusher waiting outside the bedroom door making sure she doesn't scarper."

"That's where you come in. You can distract him."

"No bleeding way. Crusher will kill me once he realises I've helped you escape."

George didn't give a damn about Flo, but he needed her cooperation.

"I'll remain in the room the whole night if necessary, making appropriate noises," he lied. "Just so long as she gets away."

"An' how does that help me?"

"All you need to do is distract him for a short while – say twenty minutes – so no suspicion will be thrown on you."

She scratched her head.

"You must have ways of keeping him occupied?" George added.

"I hate that evil bugger groping me and he knows it, but I'll pretend to be drunk – that might convince him. Though I doubt the oaf can keep it up for that long."

"Thank you."

"I ain't risking me life for you. But I'd do anythink for the little 'un. Promise yer gonna do right by her."

"I give you my word."

"What happens when they see she's gone? You'll be for it," she said.

"I'll slip out the window in the early hours. As I'll still be in the room long after you've finished with Crusher, they won't suspect your involvement."

"Hang on a minute – you've missed summat. What'll happen to Daph once she's in the street?"

George raised his eyes to the sky for inspiration. "I'll have someone with me. She'll take her away."

"How can you be sure this woman won't double-cross you? She might make off wi' her."

"She won't betray me."

"Crusher won't hesitate to stick a knife in yer gut, so like as not, you'll end up dead, anyway. An' this piece you've taken up with might just sell Daph. She'll be better off with me if I can get away, as well."

"What you do is up to you. But Daphne is to go with Bella. She'll be safe with her. I'd stake my life on it."

Bella's parents would be furious, but Bella had loved him and with Daphne, they could be a family. What if Bella had remarried? Well, if she had, it wouldn't be legal – she was his wife.

Chapter 29

On the train to William's house, Kate agonised over every word of her telephone conversation with him. Despite how glad he'd been to hear from her, she worried that when she arrived, he might be cold and standoffish. When she changed trains at Chester, she considered catching the next one back to Faredene. Only fear of losing him forever made her catch her connection.

There had been no need for her to worry. William was waiting and as soon as she stepped on the platform, he pulled her into his arms, kissing her passionately until she was practically gasping for air. The drive from the station to his home, Henley Manor, took minutes and he pulled the motor car under the portico of a sprawling two-storey sandstone house.

"This is all yours?" Kate asked.

"Did you think I lived in a shed?"

"It's enormous."

"It would be more flattering if you waited until we're in the bedroom before you said that."

"I never exaggerate," she said cheekily, glancing over her shoulder at him as she climbed out.

He jumped out and came to her side.

"Right, I need to show you who's in charge in this relationship."

He grabbed her hand and they ran giggling through the hallway, past his astonished butler and into the morning room, where he kissed her again, his hands tugging at her clothes, undoing her blouse. Kate reluctantly pulled away.

"Where's Abigail?" Kate was the girl's teacher and it wouldn't do for her to walk in on them.

"Abigail's gone to stay with a friend in the village. She won't be home until morning," he mumbled into her neck as he caressed her.

"William, you've not sent her away because I was coming?"

"No. She finds being stuck here with her old uncle a complete bore. Her friends invited her and she'd refused because she didn't want to leave me alone, so when she found out I was having company, she changed her mind."

"Then let's go upstairs. I feel as though your butler is waiting outside the door listening."

Grabbing her hand again, they raced upstairs, laughing.

Later, they dined, talking about everything but "the situation". She regretted springing it on him and didn't want their relationship to end, but marriage was what she wanted. When they went to bed that night, she lay encircled in his arms as they fell asleep. They'd spent the night together before, but only ever at a hotel. It felt so natural to share his bed, his home.

Sunday morning, Kate studied his face from across the breakfast table. Sometimes it took facing the possibility of losing someone to make you appreciate them fully and she was now certain it was him she wanted. She was afraid of spoiling things but knew that eventually, she'd have to raise the question of their future.

His voice broke into her thoughts.

"Are you jealous of Jane?"

The slice of butter slid off her knife and onto the table.

"Don't be silly." She dabbed at the white tablecloth with her napkin. "I don't think the grease will stain," she muttered.

"You haven't given me a straight answer. And while we were apart, I concluded it was Sean's marriage in particular that caused you to react as you did."

Kate screwed up her face. In a good relationship, there should be no secrets.

"I've seen that expression before when you're dealing with a difficult parent or guardian," William said.

"You should have seen it plenty of times, as you're one of the most challenging," she said, giving him a half-smile.

"Better than being a pushover."

"That's one thing you'll never be. I'm never sure what's going on in that mind of yours."

"Stop changing the subject. Do you care for Sean yourself?"

Kate flinched. "Of course I do. He's like a brother."

"Is that all?"

"You were correct about my not wanting to remain a spinster."

"*Is* that all?" he repeated.

"I admit I was infatuated with Sean at one time."

She shifted in her seat, hoping he wouldn't push the point. She was embarrassed by how long she'd pined after Sean.

"And now?"

"I've matured. Sean will always be important to me, but he's not the one I want – you are." She sounded convincing because it was finally true. "I can assure you that I think Jane is perfect for Sean. I'm thrilled for them both."

"Good."

"Were you jealous?" she said slowly.

"Incredibly."

"Coming from you, that's quite an admission."

"I'll still be possessive when we're old and grey."

Was he hinting they'd be together for a long time? Did he want her to pick up on it?

Before she had the chance, he added, "I rather envy them."

"Who?"

"Sean and Jane."

"Why? You made it perfectly clear that you're not interested in getting wed."

"Only because few ladies have the wit to challenge me."

"You can't have met many intelligent women, then."

William laughed. "Perhaps you and I *should* take the plunge, after all. Get married. Tie the knot."

"Are you serious? Judging from your face, you're even more shocked by your proposal than I am."

"You'll make an excellent mother for Abigail and any other little ones who come along. What do you say?"

It wasn't the most romantic proposal. Certainly not what she'd envisaged when she'd allowed herself fanciful daydreams of romance.

"I won't marry someone who only wants me as a mother for his niece. And I thought you didn't want a family of your own?"

"Kate, I care for you a great deal. I'm not averse to having children. You took me by surprise when you mentioned marriage. I panicked because I didn't think your reasons for wanting to marry me were genuine. No man wants to be a last resort, but you and I together would make a terrific team. And from what people say, even the most ardent passion fades and marriages flounder, whereas when friendship and respect are the basis, tenderness might grow." His words petered-out as though he were pondering what to say next.

Kate couldn't help feeling disappointed. There was no talk of love.

"I won't give up teaching," she said.

"Agreed. Any more conditions?"

"No. Do you have any?"

"I won't give up flying."

"Fine."

"So, are you accepting me?"

"Not yet. Maybe one day, eventually. But not until we're both certain we're doing it for the right reasons."

"I assumed your reasons were avoiding spinsterhood and wanting to start a family before it's too late."

"It's not just that. I want something more."

"Which is?"

"I want to be adored."

He picked up a slice of toast from the rack. "Splendid." What did that mean?

"I have a question," she said.

"Fire away."

"Might your feelings for me develop over time? Or am I fooling myself? Because I don't want to waste my life on a man who will never love me." She stared at her plate as colour crept up her neck, grateful for the high collar of her blouse.

William reached across the table and took her hand in his. "Kate, I'm truly sorry."

She'd embarrassed herself again. Twisting, she made to pull away. His fingers tightened around hers.

"No. Don't withdraw from me. Look at me."

She bit her lip, fighting back her tears. Where was this coming from? She was no romantic. Just because she'd realised she loved him, it was ridiculous to expect him to reciprocate immediately.

"Kate, darling. My proposal was dire and I wish I could take it back and do the job properly. Our father was a general in the army and it was considered a mortal sin in our house to display emotion of any sort – our mother was no better. Neither of my parents showed any affection towards each other, let alone my brother and me. Consequently, we learned to quash our emotions. To get on with making a success of our lives without allowing feelings to get in the way – that was how our father used to put it.

"Will you forgive me for being a blundering idiot? Love can't develop between us because . . ." He paused, clearly struggling to find the words.

Her eyes dipped to her boiled egg. What was wrong with her? First falling for a man who saw her as just a friend, then one who was incapable of deep emotions.

"Please – say no more," she said.

Maybe a marriage based on liking one another and great sex was the best she could hope for.

He stroked the inside of her wrist with his thumb, sending a familiar tingle up her arm.

"*Because*, Kate, I've been in love with you for a long time."

Relief washed over her. "You have?"

He nodded, his eyes holding hers.

"I can't leave Bella to run the school and my whole family is in Faredene," she added. "There's no way I could contemplate leaving there."

"Don't worry – we can sell this place and buy something there or live at the school."

"You'd honestly give this up and move?"

"Yes. I should have told you before that I adore you, but you're not a woman who encourages a chap to lay his feelings out for inspection."

"You *really* love me?"

"Like a madman."

She pressed his hand to her face. "That's the best kind."

"Well, what about you?"

"Me?"

"Jesus, Kate, I'm a proud man. You're the first woman I've ever said I love you to. Don't make this so difficult. Despite the pretty speech I made before about marriages based on respect and friendship, it's not what I want, either. I didn't believe what you said before Sean's wedding about loving me, but do you?"

"Like a crazy woman."

After speaking to Kate on the telephone, Bella trudged into the kitchen, where Doris was polishing the silverware at the large wooden table. Kate and William were to be married. Naturally, Bella was thrilled for her sister, but that didn't stop her from being envious and sorry for herself. Though she hated to admit it, Kate had been right – Bella was too afraid to grasp her own chance to be loved.

"Can you make sure Kate's bed is ready?" Bella said. "She'll be back tomorrow afternoon. You needn't worry about dinner, as Cook will be back by then, as well."

"Yes, miss. Shall I finish the silverware or do Miss Kate's room now?"

"You can do them both later, Doris. Seeing as it's just you and me, what would you say to me driving us both to church?"

"Eee, miss, a treat like that is almost worth having no family to spend Christmas with."

"How old were you, Doris, when you went into the orphanage?"

"I were just a few days old when me mam died. I've always imagined being part of a big family, but who knows – maybe I wouldn't have liked it."

"Did they look after you well at the orphanage?"

"Yes, miss, I guess you could say that. They taught me to clean and do basic sewing. My last couple of years were in the laundry. It's right hard in there and the days are long. The matron didn't let us starve, but it was all slop. Not like the food we have here. And it was lonely – fifteen in my dormitory, there was. But in all the years I was there, I only had one proper friend and she died of a fever when we was both seven."

"Get your hat and coat on, then," Bella said, spinning away, her face crumpling. She was ashamed of feeling sorry for herself.

During the service, Bella's mind kept wandering. Both Kate and Sean were going to be settled, but what about her? She may not have a husband, but she had a loving family, which was far more than poor Doris had ever had. Doris' life had been incredibly harsh before she came into their employ, with no childhood to speak of. She was still young and it must be awful for her, being stuck at school while the rest of the staff were with their families. It was time Bella stopped dwelling on herself and did something for someone less fortunate. If her mother consented, she'd cry off luncheon with her parents and spend the afternoon playing draughts or ludo with Doris.

Chapter 30

Doris' obvious gratitude and delight at receiving Bella's attention and playing board games humbled Bella. It had also allowed her a few hours' reprieve from thinking about her own life – or lack of it.

It was late afternoon when Doris announced a visitor.

"Richard, what a pleasant surprise," Bella said untruthfully. It would be impossible to avoid thinking about him if he were sitting in her parlour.

"Bella, I hope you don't mind my calling unannounced. Kate mentioned you'd be home alone."

"Really? When?"

"We spoke before she went to see William."

The meddling madam. How did Kate know she wouldn't be at Sean's house? Come to think of it, there was also something odd about the way her parents had cancelled their luncheon before Bella had had the chance to mention her plans to entertain Doris.

Bella forced a smile. "Would you like to share my tea?"

"If it's not an imposition."

"Not at all." She turned to Doris. "Add some extra bits and pieces to my tray, please."

"Yes, miss. There's some of that lovely pork pie Cook left us, so I'll put a couple of slices of that on, as well."

Despite agreeing to join her, Richard sat bolt upright, not touching the food and looking as though he wanted to be elsewhere.

"Aren't you eating?" she said, taking another sandwich.

Richard reached out to the plate. "Sorry."

"Was your trip to visit your parents pleasant?" she asked.

"Aye."

"Did all your family get together on Christmas Day as planned?"

"Aye, yes."

"And how are your parents?"

"They're fine. My dad's back is still playing up, but that's nothing new."

Goodness, this was hard work. Richard hadn't even asked her about her Christmas or made her laugh. And he was continually tapping his foot and inspecting his fingernails. He looked more like he was in the dentist's chair than visiting a friend. There was something going on. What was wrong with everyone today?

It hit her like a wet rag in the face – he was going to pop the question, and her entire family knew about it!

"Would you like something stronger to drink?" Bella asked. She needed one, even if he didn't.

Richard puffed out his cheeks and exhaled slowly. "I'd appreciate that."

She wasn't ready for this. How should she respond? He was funny – at least he was normally. Kind . . . honest? Yes, she was sure he was. But was what she felt for him enough to sustain a happy marriage?

A life and family with a good man was what she still secretly longed for. She thought she'd have that with

George. She *wanted* to love Richard, but was she even capable of such depth of emotion any more? Would her body ever respond to another man with the same abandon as it had with George?

Even now, memories of what they'd done made her long to be in George's arms. Shameless as it might be, Bella wanted to experience the thrill and excitement of the bedroom again. If only she could be sure it would be the same with Richard. George had turned her into a hysterical wreck with no outlet for the passion inside her.

Kate had openly admitted to her that she was having intimate relations with William, whereas Bella hadn't even permitted Richard to kiss her. He'd been about to many times over the past year, but Bella had always turned away, too scared to do anything that might lead to her being hurt again. Now, she deeply regretted being so reserved with him. If only she'd allowed herself to relax more, she might have been surer of her feelings.

Bella's hand trembled as she poured them both a drink. If he made a proposal today, she couldn't possibly accept. She wanted time to consider his offer. Although if she was going to refuse him, perhaps she should do so quickly and not drag out his suffering by asking him to wait.

But the point was . . . Actually, she was utterly confused and didn't know what her point was. She settled on the edge of a chair, her hands in her lap, doing her best to look poised and in control, whereas in reality she was a quivering mess.

Richard knocked back his whiskey, the glass clunking on the table as he placed it down. He got on one knee.

This was it!

She grabbed her sherry and took a gulp.

"Bella, I was going to speak to you in the new year, but as you are alone, I decided not to wait."

"Hmm," she mumbled.

"The thing is, we've known each other a while. There was nothing I could do to stop myself falling for you. I'd like to think that one day, your feelings for me might grow. Because although I know I'm not fit to clean your shoes, I love you with all my heart."

He halted, looking over his shoulder at the sound of the doorbell, then Doris' familiar footsteps padding down the hallway, followed by muffled voices, then a tap on the parlour door.

Richard was too slow getting to his feet and was still kneeling as the door opened and Doris appeared, followed by a tall fair-haired, blue-eyed man Bella believed she'd never see again. Her glass slipped from her hand to the floor, sherry soaking her purple skirt.

"George . . ." she murmured.

He swaggered into the room, smiling as though he'd only been gone an hour, his eyes moving from her to Richard.

"Hello, Bella. It looks like I'm just in time," George said.

Richard scrambled to his feet. "I ought to take your arrogant head off."

Richard's fist shot out, catching the taller man's chin, causing George to step backwards into the corner, where his hand knocked a side table, sending a large aspidistra in a brass pot crashing to the floor, soil spilling on the carpet. Doris shrieked, instantly making to clear up the mess. Bella wobbled to her feet and grabbed the back of

Richard's jacket, stopping him from lunging again. George rubbed his chin as Richard glowered at him. Silence stretched between them until Bella spoke.

"You can tidy later, Doris. Go back in the kitchen, please." She turned to George. "What are you doing here?" Her voice was hollow – eerily calm.

"I called at your father's old house and Anne wasn't home, but I told her butler I was an old family friend and he said you live here now."

"That's not what I meant, and you know it. Why are you here?"

"By the look of things, stopping you from making a grave mistake."

"The only mistake Bella ever made was getting involved with you," Richard snarled.

"I presume you were about to ask for *my* wife's hand in marriage."

"She's *not* your wife."

Bella found her voice. "Richard, I'll handle this." She was breathing heavily yet strangely in control. "I met your mother, George. Do you remember her – the one you left to die alone? She told me everything. All about Pearl and Daphne. You're a bigamist. Father wanted to find you and prosecute. If he has his way now you're back in England, he'll call the police."

George shook his head. "Bella, I understand why you're cross with me—"

"Cross! Cross doesn't even begin to describe it. How dare you come back here after the way you treated me!"

"You're angry, understandably so. But I assure you, Pearl died before I married you."

"Liar! Why would I believe anything you say?" Bella

spat. "You wouldn't recognise the truth if it hit you in the face."

"If that were the case, why disappear, taking Bella's money with you?" Richard said.

"I lost our baby because of *you*." Her voice was little more than a whisper.

Shock flickered across George's face but immediately dispersed and he remained silent.

"Don't you have anything to say?" she added.

"You two have hardly given me a chance to defend myself. It's unfair to blame me for what happened. Plenty of women miscarry."

"You heartless bastard," Richard said.

"George, I can't bear to look at you," Bella said.

She wanted him gone. Yet, she needed to know why he'd come back and left her in the first place. So many unanswered questions still haunted her.

"Bella, I'm sorry for your loss. Our child would have been beautiful. It must have been a difficult time."

"You can keep your meaningless platitudes. After the way you behaved, you have a nerve turning up here."

George swallowed. "I can explain everything if you'll give me a chance. If we can speak in private."

"She doesn't want to hear any rubbish from you," Richard said, his normally cheerful countenance twisted in anger.

"Richard, I need to talk to George alone," she said.

Richard looked stung.

"But why, Bella?" he said.

She didn't want to upset him, but her head was spinning.

"Please, Richard," she said softly.

His face pained, Richard stalked out. With leaden legs, Bella followed him down the corridor to the front door.

"Let me stay and protect you. I was about to propose, but I suppose if that swine is telling the truth, he's your husband whereas I'm . . . nobody," Richard said.

She reached out a placatory hand. "Don't say that. This isn't about you and me. Try to understand. I need to handle this myself. And there's only so much I can cope with at one time."

Richard looked concerned.

"Say the word and I'll make him leave. I could kill him for what he's done to you."

"Richard, my head is going to explode. I know you want to help, but the best way for you to do that is to go home."

"Your aunt was right. She said you'd not got over him and I can see it in your eyes."

"No – you're wrong. But I can't deal with your feelings, as well. Please try to understand."

"All right, I'll go if you insist."

"I'm sorry, but I must."

"May I telephone you?" he asked stiffly.

"Perhaps it would be better if I call you."

He looked wounded. Bella instinctively reached out and hugged him. He was rigid. Unresponsive. Bella sighed and turned away. She closed the front door behind him and leaned against it, taking slow, steadying breaths. If ever there was a time when her nerves were going to overwhelm her, it would be now.

Chapter 31

Bella forced herself to return to the parlour. George was standing by the dresser, examining the silver-framed photographs on the side. Without glancing at him, she poured herself another sherry, drinking it before she moved. Then she crossed the room and stood behind the sofa. If she sat down, it might give him the impression he was welcome, and he wasn't.

"The kids in the photograph – are they Sean's?"

"We're not playing happy families, George. Get to the point."

"I've missed you."

She gave a harsh laugh. "Is that why you're back?"

"Yes."

She tutted. "Don't lie to me, George."

"I can explain everything, if you'll just listen instead of glaring at me."

"Oh, you can? I'll be very interested to learn why you didn't tell me I was your third wife. Although, I suppose bigamous marriages don't count."

Good – he looked stunned.

It was a moment before he spoke.

"My ma was wrong about me having been wed twice before you. I don't know how she came up with that load

314

of codswallop. The only explanation I have is that her mind was going. I had a brother who died. It affected her badly. It was as though she only remembered having one son. And because I used to help his family by doing jobs for them and slipping them money when I could afford it, Ma would get mixed up and refer to his widow as my wife."

"Do you expect me to believe that nonsense?"

"There's no reason to lie. I've already lost you."

"And what about Pearl?"

"I admit – I didn't tell you I was married because I thought it might put you off."

"Surely not. And you such a catch."

"Being sarcastic doesn't suit you, Bella."

"Your opinion is immaterial. As for you, you're looking remarkably well for a man who should be dead by now."

"You used to be so sweet. I'm sorry if what happened between us has changed you."

"Changed me! You ruined my life." She stood. "Just go. I've heard enough of your nonsense. I'm not a naïve girl any more who will fall at your feet."

"I can see that. You're even more beautiful."

"Don't say things like that."

For over a year, she'd imagined lashing out, causing him pain. So why instead of detesting him was she trembling like a fool, mesmerised by his eyes?

"We got off on the wrong foot. It was seeing a man here. I was jealous. You must believe me – I'm truly sorry about the baby, my lies, everything. I'm a different man."

She looked away. She wouldn't cry. Not in front of him.

"What do you want?" she asked, her voice flat.

"Perhaps you, one day, if I can prove I've changed and

regain your trust. But for now, I've come to you for help, because you're the kindest person I've ever met."

"Kind? Stupidity, I call it. You hurt me so much."

"I'll apologise as many times as you need."

"Nothing you can say will ever repair the damage you did. So, if this is some mad scheme to get back into my life, then you're wasting our time. Don't you get it? You nearly destroyed me."

"Pain and disappointment are an unavoidable part of life. But your mistrust is understandable."

"You arrogant, cold-hearted bastard."

"I deserve your anger. But I loved you, Bella. God knows I still do. And I swear to you, Pearl was dead when we married."

"Then why did you lie to me? You took my money when there was no need. I'd have given you the lot. You're a horrible person and I'm ashamed to have loved you."

He removed his hat, dropping it on a chair.

"All I can do is tell you again how truly sorry I am."

"Are you? I doubt it."

"I love you," he said.

"You're incapable of loving."

"Things were out of control. I panicked."

"You were calm enough to frame poor Max for stealing petty cash from my parents' house."

"I didn't plan it."

"Pfft. Everything you do is planned, George. If, as you say, we are legally married, I'll sue for divorce."

"Bella, I'll give you your divorce, I swear. But my daughter is in grave danger," he said as he peeled off his gloves.

"Why should I care? *My* baby never got to draw breath."

316

He slumped onto the sofa as though all of his arrogance and energy had seeped out of him.

George couldn't stop looking at her. She was gorgeous, stronger, poised. At the same time, she'd never excited him more. He wanted to throw her on the floor and ride her into submission. But for now, Daphne must be his priority. If he didn't help her, her face would haunt him forever.

So, Bella had met his mother *and* found out about his first bigamous marriage – that had come as a shock. It was a good job he'd been able to think quickly and come up with the story about her being his brother's wife. He needed to win Bella round and she wouldn't be taken in as easily as when he first met her, that much was obvious. Keep your lies simple – that was the key to getting away with it, he reminded himself.

"Bella, if you'll just let me explain," he said.

"Very well – let's hear it."

"I admit I was keeping things from you when we met. I was still married."

"Tell me something I don't know and stop wasting my time."

"You must understand. I couldn't tell you because I was afraid your parents would never sanction our relationship."

"Why didn't you get divorced?"

"It's too expensive. But I would have once I had enough money put by."

"You told me you longed for children, yet you left your wife and daughter."

"Pearl and I were kids when she got up the duff after a quick fumble in her parents' backyard, so we had to get married. We were miserable together from the start. Eventually, she took up with someone else. When I left, she and Daphne were living with another man. Moby, his name is. They were going to be a family and I thought I could be with you."

"Lucky me," she said sarcastically.

"The thing is, once I'd started lying to you, it was too late to go back. There was no malice in my intention, I swear. Pearl died and you and I were legally married."

"If your wife was dead, why didn't you take your child away from this Moby?"

George took a deep breath while he worked out what to say next.

"That was my plan. I went to where they'd been living. There was no trace of Moby or Daphne. None of the neighbours knew where they'd gone."

"Why pretend you were dying? That was so cruel."

"I genuinely believed I had the same condition that finished off my brother. Then when I found out I was all right, I realised it would give me the excuse to be away from home. The times I claimed I was visiting the doctor in London, I was looking for Daphne. That was why I could never allow you to go with me. Lying to you was tearing me apart. But I'd dug a big hole for myself and didn't know how to get back out."

"What would you have done if you'd found her?"

"To be truthful, I planned to lie and say she was my illegitimate child and hope you'd accept her. But I couldn't find her and to my shame, in the end I gave up."

"The last I heard was that you'd scarpered to Africa," she said.

"I did. I've not been back long."

"So, how did you find Daphne when you returned to England?"

"As soon as my feet hit dry land, I started searching for her again. I made a few enquiries around the dock area, without much hope, really. But then I had a stroke of luck. I heard about a fella called Moby running a pub in Spitalfields. It's an unusual nickname, so I checked it out."

Bella was in turmoil. It all sounded feasible. George had admitted lying and she could understand how he'd got into a situation where there was no means to backtrack. Even so, she could never forgive him.

"So if you've found her, what's the problem?" she said.

"I found out that when Pearl died, she was working as a prostitute for Moby."

Bella gasped.

"You're right to be shocked," he continued. "It floored me. Pearl was killed by a punter. And now the man who said he wanted to be a father to Daphne has not only got her carrying drugs around London, but he's also intent on setting her to work pleasuring men."

"She's just a child, surely . . ." Bella rasped.

"She was eight last birthday – an innocent girl. Or as innocent as she can be, given what she's seen in that place."

"But that's appalling – vile."

"There are men who prefer young girls – children."

Bella caught a flicker of something in his face. Was he lying, or was it guilt over abandoning his daughter? Either way, she couldn't allow herself to be taken in again. None of this was her problem.

"It's truly shocking, but why are you trying to involve me?" she said.

"Because I'm hoping that together, we can get her out of there before it's too late."

"Don't be ridiculous. You must go to the police."

"Bella, the peelers don't care about kids like her."

"Is there no one in London who can assist you – someone you can pay?"

"Another of the women working there is going to help me sneak her out, but we need you as well if the plan is to work. I swear to you, Bella, if we don't get to Daphne, she may not survive what he has planned for her."

"And what exactly is that?" Bella asked, already fearing the answer.

As George explained about the Norwegian sea captain, her mind was spinning. The world was a crueller, more terrifying place than she'd ever imagined.

"How long do you have?"

"Moby said the foreigner docks the first week in January, but I've set things up to get her away on the thirtieth."

"Tomorrow!"

"I'm heading back to London on the six thirty train in the morning, with or without you."

"You should never have come here. It might be too late when you get back."

"I've secured her safety for a while."

"How? With more lies, I expect."

"Yes. My God, yes – of course I lied, dammit. I told him I wanted to be the first to bed my own daughter!" he roared.

Bella's knees buckled and she grasped the back of the sofa.

"How could you say such a dreadful thing?"

"Though it sickened me, I had to say it so he'd leave her alone until I came up with a plan. You don't know what that world is like."

Bella wanted to vomit, cry, scream. She covered her face with her hands. The thought of a little girl in that situation . . . But she mustn't make herself vulnerable to George again.

"Why the hell should I get involved in your moronic scheme? Find some other fool."

"You're the only person I can rely on. Bella, my prec—"

"Don't you dare call me your precious!"

The tightness in her chest was threatening to overwhelm her. He was staring at her. Could he see her panic rising? She took slow breaths, counting each one.

"Bella? Bella, are you all right?"

"I'm f-fine. As I said, you must put your faith in the p-p-police."

"One whiff of the coppers and Daphne will disappear forever. Then she'll be suffering worse than what's waiting for her now."

"Could it b-be any worse?"

She was regaining control of her breath.

"Yes. Moby is a shit," George said, "but he's not as bad as some. If she's sold on, there's a good chance they'll drug her until she's so dependent on the stuff, she won't know who's having their way with her."

Bella turned away again. He must be lying. How could there be such depravity in the world and her be completely unaware of its existence?

"You expect me to believe there are men who are so . . . so . . ."

"Perverted is the word you're searching for. There are

321

brothels all over London filled with young girls. Most are older than Daphne, I grant you, but she won't be the first by any means."

"How do you know about these places?"

"You've seen where I grew up. Faredene is like another world. You have no idea. As a lad, I had a teacher once who—"

"Are you telling me a woman forced you—"

"It was a bloke. Someone I trusted."

"Oh, George, didn't you tell someone?"

"No point. No one would have listened. He was respectable and I was a guttersnipe. I told my mam years later, but he was already dead."

How did anyone survive such a thing? She pitied him but, regardless, she couldn't get embroiled. There again, if she didn't, how would she live with herself?

"Daphne's own mother let her down," George said.

"And her father."

"That's true, but with your help, I can make amends."

"Stop. Stop it! I don't want to listen to any more. I pray you manage to rescue your daughter, but I want no part of it. I hate you, George. Now get out." Her voice rose. "Out!"

George slowly picked up his hat.

"All it'll take is a couple of days of your time. Your father can draw up the divorce papers as soon as we get back from London. I'll sign anything and you'll never see me again if you don't want. I'll take Daphne somewhere safe and try to raise her decently."

Bella didn't respond.

"You must forgive me – I feel terrible about what happened between us," he added.

"Are you so selfish that you expect me to forgive you to make *you* feel better?"

"I just want to wipe the slate clean."

"Unfortunately, some things can't be erased."

George gave her one last searching look before placing his hat on his head and picking up his gloves. At the door, he paused.

"I'll have a carriage waiting outside the gates tomorrow morning at quarter to six. At least think about it. I know you, Bella. If you leave Daphne to her fate, it'll plague your conscience."

"Just go, George."

Bella waited until the front door clicked shut, then she flew down the corridor and shot the bolt. She wanted to keep him out and stop the raging battle in her brain. But nothing could bar the conflicting emotions that consumed her: concern for the child, hate, anger and, yes, God help her, desire. She still remembered his kisses, his hands on her skin . . .

"Bella Caldwell or Bristow – whatever your real name is – you disgust me," she said aloud.

Chapter 32

It was five o'clock in the morning when Bella, rubbing her stinging, bleary eyes, finally accepted there was no point pretending that she was going to be granted the mercy of dreamless sleep. All night she'd been taunted by images branded on the inside of her eyelids. She threw off her tangled covers, her mind churning over what she was planning to do today. Madness was the only way to describe it. But if Daphne was in as much danger as George claimed and she didn't secure the girl's safety, Bella doubted she'd ever have a peaceful night again.

With no fire lit, the room was freezing, the ice on the inside of the windows obscuring the view of the grounds. Reluctantly, Bella pulled off her thick flannel nightgown. Shivering, she dipped her cloth in the bowl of cold water on the dresser and quickly rubbed it over her goose-pimpled body before tugging on her clothes. Then she sat at the writing bureau in the corner of the room, her mind as blank as the piece of paper before her.

She had to let her family know where she was going and pray it stopped them from contacting the police. And if the worst happened and she didn't return, she must at least give them some idea where to start looking. The best thing was to write a note to Kate and let her handle everyone else, Bella decided as she picked up her pen.

Dear Kate,

Don't faint. I've gone to London with George. No, I haven't gone mad. And trust me – only a matter of the utmost importance would make me go anywhere with him.

As it would be wrong of me to ask you to keep my absence from our parents, I'm relying on you to stop them from calling out the cavalry. Poor Richard was about to propose, when George waltzed in as though he'd been out for a stroll. I suspect you know more about Richard's intentions than I do, and you and I will be having a little chat about that when I get back.

There's no point in anyone trying to find me, as I'll be home tomorrow, when I promise to explain everything. I'm sorry for putting you in this difficult position.

Love Bella

PS. I'm so pleased for you and William and look forward to hearing about your plans.

PPS. And I haven't taken leave of my senses or been abducted.

Bella read what she'd written. Did it portray what she wanted – that her mission was important but not dangerous? And was it chatty enough to make Kate believe all was well? No. It was woefully inadequate, but it would have to do. Nothing she could pen would stop everyone from worrying or being furious at her recklessness. She placed her note in an envelope and sealed it.

Taking her valise with her, she made her way downstairs, where she paused in the hallway. It would be imprudent to risk being stranded in London with no money. In the office, she opened the metal box and put a roll of notes in her bag, quickly replacing the cash with an IOU so Kate wouldn't assume they'd been robbed by George.

In the kitchen, Doris was bent over the grate.

"Heavens, miss. I didn't expect you to be up this early," she said without looking up as she tried to light the kindling. "The fire's playing up this morning. I've not got the water hot yet for your bath."

"It's fine, Doris. I managed with a quick wash."

"Give me a minute then, miss, and I'll get breakfast started."

"No need. I won't be eating this morning."

"You must have summat in yer stomach to start the day, miss. It isn't good to go without. Miss Kate is always telling the pupils 'n' she's right."

Despite her nerves, Bella was hungry. She had a few minutes to spare.

"I'll have some milk and take some biscuits."

Doris finally looked up and stared at Bella, her mouth slightly open at the sight of her dressed for outdoors, concern clearly showing on her face.

"Miss, you're going out at this hour?" She stood, wiping her sooty hands on her rough apron.

Bella took the large jug from the larder and poured a glass.

"I need you to listen carefully." She laid the letter on the table. "When Miss Kate gets home, please give this to her immediately."

"It's not yet six o'clock, miss."

"I'm aware of the time, Doris. Do you understand about the letter?" Bella said a little too sharply.

"Yes, miss. But where are you going?"

326

"Doris, it's not your place to question my actions." Bella felt guilty. "Can you wrap the biscuits for me – five if we have them?"

Bella stood by the table drinking as Doris rinsed her hands and did as Bella bid, chewing her lip as she worked.

"Here yeh are, miss." She handed Bella the parcel.

"Doris, there's nothing for you to worry about," she said irritably.

"Everyone will be angry 'cos I didn't stop you."

Bella's voice softened. "Doris, no one will blame you. I'll be back tomorrow."

The girl fiddled nervously with her apron.

"Yes, miss. But I still don't think you should go out at this hour. It's not decent for a lady to be in the streets alone."

"I'll have a companion."

"The man as turned up here yesterday? I wasn't earwigging or nothin', but I heard who he was. He's ever so good-looking, but please don't run away with him."

"I'm not running away with anyone. Now, try not to worry."

"But I've never been left in the school by myself before. What if summat goes wrong? They might cart me off back to the orphanage."

"You have nothing to be concerned about. The outside staff are here, Kate will be home mid-afternoon and Cook should be back by teatime. More importantly, I'll never allow anyone to send you away from here." She checked her watch again. "I must go. Now, you carry on with your duties as you normally would, there's a good girl."

Bella retrieved her bag from the entrance hall and walked on jelly legs down the driveway, past her parents' empty house. She opened the gate enough for her to squeeze through. A hired horse and carriage was waiting in the road, its breath misting in the icy morning air.

"I knew you'd come." George leaped out and extended his hand to assist her.

She batted it away. "I want no help from you now or ever again."

He was blocking her way.

"Are you going to move?"

George hesitated.

"Unless you get out of my way, I'm going to turn round and leave you to sort your own mess."

He stepped aside. "Very well."

Bella placed her bag on the floor of the carriage and with difficulty, hoisted herself up on the small footplate, grudgingly admitting to herself that it would have been easier with his assistance.

"If we must speak, kindly stick to the matter at hand – rescuing the child," she said with every bit of coldness she could muster.

"Have it your way," he said, jumping in beside her.

No trace of his weak heart, she thought bitterly.

He settled himself, their knees touching. "Once we're on the train, I'll go through the plan with you."

At the station, George purchased the tickets while Bella was sitting in the waiting room out of the cold. Her decision to go with him was foolhardy, but she truly believed she had no option. Although how she was going to get through this ordeal, she had no idea. Apart from the danger she may put herself in, worse still, she wasn't entirely certain she could trust herself with him. One thing she was sure of – if he was lying to her, she'd make him pay.

Their proximity on the journey to the station had alarmed her. Her heart was skipping from desire to hate and back again. She didn't know if she wanted to kill him or kiss him.

In his absence, she'd tried to convince herself that his eyes weren't the colour of the sky on a sunny day and pretended that his teeth were crooked. It was nonsense, she accepted somewhat bitterly. When he spoke, she found herself watching his lips, remembering them pressed against hers. Or bringing pleasure to her body in ways it made her blush to think about.

Even if you were pricked by the thorn of a rose, you could still find it beautiful. She supposed this was no different. Nevertheless, she wanted to find him repulsive. She wanted to claw at his face with her nails and pound him with her fists. To cause him a little of the suffering he'd inflicted on her. Yet, she also longed to curl her fingers around his hair as he kissed her. Right up until the moment he walked into her parlour, she believed she hated George Bristow. Now, she no longer understood her feelings towards him.

Once they were installed in a first-class compartment, George went to sit beside her.

"No," she snapped. "Take a seat on the other side."

George smirked as he sat down and stretched his long legs.

"I can see you better from here," he said.

"If you want my assistance, George, you'd do well to curb your arrogance," she said, her voice steely.

He had to learn she wouldn't succumb to his charms. At least, she prayed she wasn't going to. Why the devil was he staring at her? She was in half a mind to tell him to find another carriage, but she needed to hear what he had planned.

"Bella, you're magnificent," he said.

"Your opinion of me is irrelevant," she said, sitting up straighter. "Tell me about the scheme to help Daphne."

"I've chosen a quiet hotel – respectable but not too fashionable. It's not what you're used to or deserve—"

"Don't pretend you care about my comfort. I didn't deserve to be lied to, but that didn't stop you. I thought George Bristow wanted only the best, so why not The Ritz?"

"At The Burlton, the staff won't be too inquisitive."

"Why would they be interested in us?"

"We'll be checking in as a married couple without a child and leaving with one."

"I see." She scowled at him.

As George gave her more details of his plan, she listened intently, her mind working things through as she asked questions intermittently.

"There are two tube stations fairly close to The White Lion – Aldgate East and Whitechapel. Once you have Daphne, go to either of them and take the train back to the hotel."

"Whitechapel? Where Jack the Ripper murdered his victims?" she said, alarmed.

"That was years ago. You don't need to worry about him – he's long gone. It's Moby and his thug we need to get you both away from."

If these people were as dangerous as George said, nothing must be left to chance.

"You said you asked for them to dress her nicely," she said.

"The rags she was wearing when I saw her will draw

attention when she's with us in a better part of London."

"Presumably . . ." She struggled to put into words what was on her mind as it conjured scenarios too horrific to contemplate. "Presumably, that Moby person believes the child will remain in the upstairs room with you?"

"That's right," George said, his brow furrowed.

"So they won't have supplied her with outdoor garments."

"Good point. We'll have to buy her something. I can guess her size. I knew you wouldn't let me down."

Bella pressed her lips into a thin line. If he was going to keep up the flattery, it was going to be extremely tiresome. Not to mention more difficult not to remember why she'd loved him.

"Was any of it real? Did you ever care for me?" she said.

"Did it feel false when we were in bed?"

Bella didn't answer. She wished she'd never asked.

By the time the train had reached halfway, George had gone over the plan several times. Bella had eaten all of her biscuits without offering him one. It was petty, but she didn't care. Let him starve. Then she pretended to doze so she didn't have to look at him.

Kate would have the note by now. Had she kept Bella's departure to herself, or had she decided that their parents must be given the facts? If she had told them, their father would be beside himself. Bella suspected their mother would switch between fury and despair. She hated to think she was causing them pain, although they were both kind and had raised her to believe it was important to help others, so they might agree she was doing the right thing.

Who was she kidding? If they'd known, they'd have locked her in her room and thrown away the key to stop her from risking her life, whatever the circumstances. And with George involved, if they could have conjured it from somewhere, they'd have stationed the mythical three-headed dog Cerberus outside to guard the door. She'd have to deal with their outrage when – if – she got back, because she couldn't live the rest of her life knowing she'd condemned the girl to a life of unspeakable misery.

An unwelcome question stole into her mind. Were all of her motives entirely altruistic, or was George pulling her back under his spell? Because there was no denying that when he was close by, her body betrayed her.

Chapter 33

On the journey back to Faredene, the smile barely left Kate's lips. Finally, she was in love and loved in return.

"I'm sorry we can't put you both up here. The gossip would be rife if anyone found out," she said as William pulled the car up outside Caldwell Grange.

"You've already apologised four times. Abigail and I will be more than happy at Latimers. Won't we?"

"The hotel will be nicer," Abigail said.

"Young lady, are you daring to suggest our dormitories aren't pleasing enough?" Kate joked.

Abigail looked horrified. "No, miss."

"Relax, I'm sure you spend enough time in the dormitories without being there during the holidays. You'll have to get used to my teasing now I'm to be your . . . your . . . step-auntie – is that right?"

"Yes, but I can't possibly call you auntie in school. I'll get a terrible ribbing from the other girls."

"Don't you worry. We'll work something out and I'll make sure no one teases you. Will you come in and see Bella before you go to your hotel?"

"Why not," William said.

Before Kate could put her key in the lock, the door opened and a tearful Doris handed her an envelope.

"Aww, Miss Kate, it's from Miss Bella. She's run off with a fella. I've been here all alone an' worried summat awful."

Abigail gasped.

"Away in, Doris. Enough of this nonsense. I'm sure there's a perfectly logical explanation for whatever has happened, but let us over the threshold before I read it. Put the kettle on and make some tea. Abigail, will you go with her and help? You can choose some cake for us. Wait in the kitchen, both of you. We'll join you shortly. Off you go now. And no filling Abigail's head with ridiculous tales, Doris," Kate said, her words tumbling.

As the girls walked down the corridor, Kate marched into the office, William following. She threw her bag and gloves on the desk and without bothering to remove her hat, skimmed the letter.

"Jesus, Mary and Joseph, what now?" she said.

"Bad news?"

"The worst." She handed it to him.

"George? Her husband?"

"The man she thought she'd married, more like. What the hell am I going to tell Father and Victoria?"

"I'll go with you to see them, if you like. Or I can go to London to search for her?"

"You'd do that for me?"

"You're going to be my wife. From now on, I'll support you in all things."

She squeezed his fingers. "Would you check in at the hotel, then come back here for me? I need to telephone Richard. He may have more information, as he was here when George turned up. Then we'll go round to Sean's. This is hardly how I wanted today to go. I wanted it to be

334

about us. But Bella's situation comes first. You understand, don't you?"

"Frankly, I'd have been shocked if you'd said otherwise. If Bella is back tomorrow and everything is all right, we can all see in the New Year together and tell your parents then."

"And if she isn't?"

"We'll cross that bridge together if we come to it. Don't worry about Abigail – I'll assure her that Bella hasn't run off with a man and has merely gone to London on a personal matter. She's a good kid, but I don't want her saying anything out of turn to her school-friends when they return after the holidays."

A footman appeared in the doorway of Sean's study.

"Madam, you have visitors – Miss Kate, a gentleman and a young lady."

"Thank you." Victoria turned to the tall lank-haired tutor. "It's time you were getting home. I'm certain there's nothing to be concerned about. Pierre is merely behaving as most children of his age do, throwing tantrums when he doesn't get his own way. Even so, we can speak again tomorrow, if you like?"

"Yes, madam, I'd appreciate that."

As she made her way to the drawing room, Victoria was grinning. Richard had visited and asked Edward's permission to propose to Bella after church yesterday and although they'd heard nothing from her yet, she was hoping her daughter would accept. Now, Kate and William had turned up unannounced. Surely it meant they'd agreed to formalise their relationship, too. Should she ask for a bottle of champagne from the cellar? Perhaps it was best to wait until they'd given their news.

"What a lovely surprise," Victoria said as she entered the room.

Her smile faded. They all had drinks, yet Kate looked agitated. This was bad.

"I've sent Abigail up to the nursery to see the boys so we can speak privately," Kate said.

Victoria hovered. "I can see something is very wrong. What is it?"

Kate shook her head. "When you're sat down."

Victoria settled herself next to Edward on the striped sofa. His face was a mixture of concern and curiosity. Kate's hand trembled as she placed her glass on a side table. Finally, after taking a deep breath, she spoke.

"I don't have all the facts. However, yesterday, Richard was to propose to Bella."

Victoria's heart sank further. "We know. Has she refused him? I should speak to her. It's a mistake."

"Vicky, darling, let Kate explain. We must understand Bella's reasons before we go interfering," said Edward.

"Sorry, sorry. Go on, Kate."

"I've no idea what she intended to say to Richard, because he wasn't able to finish asking her. This is going to come as a shock. I can scarcely believe it myself. The thing is, while Richard was there, George Bristow turned up."

Victoria let out a strangled cry. Edward reached out to her.

"I'm fine," she said, her voice a mere whisper.

"Where's Bella? She must be distraught. We'll go to her. As for him, I'll have the police on to the scoundrel straightaway. Is he still in Faredene?" Edward said.

"George is . . . Well, as far as I'm aware, he's back in

London – and Bella has gone with him," Kate said hesitantly.

Victoria's vision blurred and for the first time in her life, she swooned.

During lunch at a small restaurant by the river Seine, Sean lifted his chair and moved it around the table, causing several patrons to glance in their direction. Once he was sitting close to Jane, he dragged his plate over and pinched a frog's leg between two fingers. Waggling it in front of his wife, he grinned.

"Go on – try one. They're much better than the snails, honestly. They taste a bit like chicken."

As she recoiled, her nose wrinkling, Sean threw back his head and roared.

She elbowed him in the ribs. "Really, Sean, you're like a three-year-old, taking pleasure in torturing me."

He felt childlike – carefree. Everything about her delighted him.

"What happened to devoting every minute to my happiness?" Jane said, her face serious. "I can see you're not going to be the doting husband I was counting on. We've not been married five minutes and you're changing already."

Sean jolted, horrified that he'd upset her. "Jane, I'm sorry – I was just teasing."

She reached out and tousled his hair. "Ha! Fooled you. You're not the only one who can tease, Mr Kavanagh."

Instantly, his shoulders relaxed and he affected an air of mock sternness. "I've a good mind to send back all those new outfits, including the matching hats and shoes, until you learn your proper place, *Mrs* Kavanagh."

"Surely not – and miss out on the opportunity for Darius to see the latest Paris fashions first hand rather than in *Vogue* magazine? You're too good a businessman to do that."

This time they both laughed and Sean reached for her hand.

"I can hardly believe it's all real," he said. "For the first time since I found out about my parentage, I feel at peace. On top of that, I'm married to the most beautiful woman in the world. *And* she makes me laugh. What more could I ever need?"

"How about a slice of one of those delicious-looking cakes?" With her free hand, she gestured towards the waiter pushing the dessert trolley.

Once they'd been served and were alone again, Jane said, "It's the same for me, you know. I was looking for something – someone – too."

Sean raised his eyebrows in surprise.

"Mum and Dad were wonderful parents," she continued, "but they were so in love, it magnified my loneliness."

"I'd already left home by the time Bella was born, so there were times I longed for a sibling, whereas you're a twin. How come you were lonely?"

"Robert and I were never close. But it doesn't matter – I have you now."

"After what we've got up to during the past few days, you can't compare me to a brother . . ."

She blushed prettily. "Definitely not. You and I will be like my mam and dad – devoted to each other for life. At least I hope so."

"And we have our boys. Are you fine with me calling them 'our' boys?"

"I love it. But we won't let them forget Yvette."

"Thank you," he said gratefully. "And before long, we'll give them a sister."

"You want a daughter?"

"I'll be delighted with another boy, but I must admit, I would love a daddy's little darling."

"Are you missing the boys?"

"A little. Thankfully, I don't need to worry about them – they have lots of people looking out for them."

"We'll be home soon."

Sean winked. "Exactly, so I suggest we head back to our hotel and get to work giving Pierre and Josh a sibling."

As Kate held the smelling salts under Victoria's nose, she fumed internally at her sister. When Kate had moved from Ireland to live with her father, she'd been certain that she was going to find Bella extremely irritating. In fact, she'd wanted to dislike her. After all, Bella had lived with their father all her life, while Kate's mother, when she was alive, had done everything in her power to alienate Kate from her father. But to Kate's surprise and initial annoyance, Bella had been so sweet and welcoming, without a hint of nastiness, that it had been impossible not to love her. That said, if she had her here now, she'd cheerfully strangle her. Why had Bella, who was normally so considerate, behaved so irresponsibly?

Victoria stirred, bringing Kate's attention back to the room. Her father lovingly stroked his wife's cheek as he spoke.

"Take it easy, Vicky. We've left a message with his assistant asking Owain to call here after his rounds."

"Please tell me I misheard," Victoria said as she tried to get up.

"Stay where you are," Kate said. "If Bella were here, I'd give her a dressing down for what she's done. But I don't believe for one minute that she's gone off with George because she's in love with him."

"What's your explanation?" her father asked.

"Her note said there was an important matter she needs to deal with and she'll be back tomorrow."

"Surely nothing would warrant going to London with that miscreant?" her father said.

"I can't fathom it. But every night in those early months, I listened to her sobbing on the other side of my bedroom wall. After the pain he put her through, there's no way she'd take him back."

"I pray you're right, but I'm not so sure," Victoria said. "She worshipped him – and we all know how convincing George can be."

Kate shook her head. "Bella knows how Richard feels about her. She'd never be so cruel as to become romantically entangled with George without at least leaving a note for Richard explaining."

But she wasn't certain. And she'd never dreamed Bella would put her parents through this.

Victoria was lying on the sofa, endlessly twisting the locket that hung round her neck. Her father was staring at the fire as though the flickering of the flames would provide the answers he sought. His skin had taken on a grey hue and he looked broken. Kate loved them both and she'd give anything to take the stricken expression off their faces.

"Even if she hasn't gone off with him for romantic reasons, what if she's not safe with him?" Victoria said. "George may have tricked her into going somewhere with the intention of imprisoning her and demanding a ransom."

"I'm sure that's not the case," Kate said.

"He's capable of anything," her father mumbled without looking up.

"No, George is a chancer. He wouldn't blatantly commit a crime in the open. I don't believe it occurred to him we'd ever find out he was a bigamist. He probably thought we'd assume he'd gone off to die, like some gallant hero, to spare Bella from having to watch him deteriorate, and only stolen her money to survive on."

"Again, I pray you're right. Are you sure you're not worried about her, Kate?" Victoria said.

"I wish it was tomorrow and she was home safe, but I'm not overly concerned," Kate said.

It was a whopping lie. She was frantic, unable to sit still. Despite racking her brains, Kate couldn't justify Bella's rash behaviour in her own mind, but their parents didn't need to hear that.

"Frankly, I'm more worried about you two," Kate said. "Should I ask Sean's cook to prepare you some food?"

"I couldn't eat a thing," Victoria said.

"Father, what about you?"

He shook his head slowly, every one of his seventy years and more showing on his face. Brave, strong Victoria was traumatised. Bella would never forgive herself if her actions led to one of them taking ill. Would Kate forgive her? It was best not to think about that.

"Should we ask Nanny to bring the boys down?" Kate suggested, hoping the distraction might be good for her father and Victoria.

"Yes, Kate. Please ring the bell for me, would you? I

mustn't neglect Pierre and Joshua," Victoria said. "And I'd forgotten about poor Abigail, stuck in the nursery all this time. What must you think of us, William."

"Don't you worry about me or Abigail. If there's anything I can do, anything at all, just ask," William said.

Pride swept through Kate. He was going to be her husband and he was a good man – wonderful.

Chapter 34

George smiled at the buxom middle-aged hotel receptionist, causing her cheeks to flush. It never failed. Bella, who was standing stiffly at his side, tutted. She must be jealous, he thought.

"Do you have a booking, sir?"

"It's under Mr and Mrs George Bristow, but our daughter will join us this evening once we've collected her from her grandparents. We'd like her to share our room, if possible."

"Ah yes, here it is," she said, looking in the register. "Two nights – is that correct?"

"Can we let you know tomorrow? We intend to head home to Kent, but my wife enjoys the sights, so we may linger awhile."

"Very good, sir. We have a lovely room on the second floor with a double bed and a single that we can make up for your daughter."

"Perfect."

"I'll get a boy to help with your bags and show you to your room."

"There's no need. We sent our main luggage on to our home. All we have are our valises and I can carry them. Although, I have a shirt I want laundered. Can you have it back by this evening?"

"Certainly. I'll send someone to collect it," the woman said, her eyes lingering on his face.

When women ogled him like that, they were usually easy to manipulate. Normally, he'd have been wondering how to use her obvious attraction to him to his advantage. Today, however, he had far more important matters to think about.

His explanation about choosing this hotel and the staff not asking questions had only been part of his decision. If his funds would have run to it, he would have preferred to take Bella to a better hotel, where he could have enjoyed their reunion in comfort. But the rooms here were adequate and clean. They'd have to do until Bella accepted that she still loved him and he'd persuaded her that her future lay with him.

She obviously still had access to plenty of money. Perhaps she'd move to Manchester with him and Daphne. Or somewhere on the south coast, like Bournemouth. The three of them could be a family. Eventually, they'd return to Faredene together and win her parents round. If he put another child in her, it should be easy enough, because Victoria and Edward would be desperate to be part of their grandchild's life.

Once he'd unlocked the door, Bella pushed past him.

"How easily you lie and charm people. Watching you operate, it's clear how you deceived me," she said, looking at him with ill-concealed contempt.

"How many times must I say it? I understand why you're angry. But as you're stuck with me for now, try to enjoy it, please, Bella."

"We're not here to enjoy ourselves. We're here for Daphne," she said.

She had more spirit now. He liked it, but it might get

irksome after a while. If it did, he'd soon knock it out of her. Not literally – he'd never been one for beating women – but there were other more subtle ways to subdue them.

"You'll like Daphne. She's attractive – feisty," he said.

The way Bella was scowling at him, she'd take some bringing round to his way of thinking. But surely all he had to do was remind her what she was missing out on by not being with him. Bella turned her back on him and moved to the mirror that stood on the dresser, where she removed her hat.

"It doesn't matter to me what she's like. I won't be with her long enough to form an opinion," Bella said.

Did she need to keep pressing the point that at the first opportunity, she'd be scurrying back to the short-arse she was with yesterday?

"Who was that speccy fella?" he asked.

"Pardon?"

"The one who was down on one knee when I arrived. Surely you're not going to throw yourself away on him?"

With Bella's reflection glaring at him, George instantly regretted asking. She turned from the dressing table.

"Richard is worth a hundred of you. A thousand!" She jabbed her finger at him. "Don't you dare mention him again or I swear I'll get the next train heading north, you bloody crook."

George held up his hands in surrender. "I'm sorry, and I had no right to ask about Richard. Forgive me. I apologise."

Bella jammed her hat back on.

"There's no point in waiting at the hotel. We may as well go to the shops and buy some more clothing for

Daphne. We should purchase some food, as well. She might be hungry when we get her back here."

When she was fiery, it aroused him far more than the obliging, fawning Bella had ever done. Perhaps he could harness all that passion to her antics in bed.

"Don't look at me in that way," Bella said.

"What way?" he asked, feigning innocence.

"Like you used to when we were alone in our bedroom."

She stalked towards the door – a sure sign she was nervous about being around him.

"Once we have the child to safety, I'm leaving immediately. There's no way I'm spending the night in this room with you."

George stifled a smirk. She wanted him as much as he wanted her. He could practically feel the heat coming off her.

"It'll be after midnight," he said.

"Regardless, it'll be up to you to get Daphne away from London. I'll wait on the station all night if I must, because I'm heading home on the first train. You should get away from London, too. And before you suggest it, let me be clear – you're not coming back to Faredene. Write down an address where my father can contact you to arrange the divorce."

"Very well." He removed a calling card giving a false address from his wallet and handed it to her.

If all he had was the rest of the day to persuade her to take him back, he'd best get to work.

How easy it would have been to pretend it was real, that he'd not broken her heart. Thankfully, Bella was no longer that stupid. The address he'd given her was probably fake, but for the moment there was no way she could check it.

They'd spent two hours wandering around Selfridges, purchasing the things they'd need for Daphne. George had been attentive, playing the part of the devoted husband and father. Rather than charming Bella, to her great relief it had helped her to see what a slimy toad he'd always been.

"We should get a meal. There won't be time this evening. Let's go up to The Palm Court," he said now.

Bella considered refusing. Her stomach was in knots and she wasn't sure she'd be able to keep anything down. But the biscuits she'd eaten weren't enough to sustain her and she didn't want to be passing out from hunger. Blast the expense. He'd be paying with money he'd stolen from her anyway.

They made their way to the restaurant on the fourth floor, where the waiter showed them to a small table towards the back of the room. While they ate, Bella allowed George to steer the conversation as she had done on so many occasions during their marriage. She was intrigued by the way he faked such interest in her family. They discussed her parents' health and Kirby. He enquired after Kate, Sean and his children. And he appeared incredibly sympathetic when he learned of Yvette's death and said how glad he was to hear that Sean had found happiness with Jane. Finally, they talked about Caldwell Grange.

"I'm filled with admiration. Few women – or men, for that matter – could have achieved what you have and in such a short time," he said.

In the past, Bella would have been ridiculously pleased by his praise. Now, she mistrusted every word.

"There's no need to flatter me," she said.

He reached across the table and took one of the loose curls that framed her face between his fingers.

"It still feels like silk. You're stunning."

Did he mean any of it? When he gazed at her that way, it was hard to believe his love was a mirage. But that's exactly what it was. Everything about George was fake.

To her astonishment, she suddenly realised that was how he'd made her so besotted with him. He'd charmed and complimented his way into her affections, sealing her fate by appearing to care for her family. He asked questions, lots of them. Said all the right things to make himself seem thoughtful and caring. When all the time he was simply gathering knowledge to be used to manipulate people and only giving the barest of information about himself. By winning them all round, he'd made sure there were no objections from any corner.

He smiled at her alluringly. Outwardly, he was still as handsome, but until today, she'd never noticed the arrogance in his manner. She toyed with her dessert.

"What have you been doing since you left Faredene?" she asked.

He took a long time before answering. No doubt getting his story straight.

"I found Africa too hot and almost immediately moved on to India. Not that it was much better there. I got work in the offices of a tea plantation."

"Why get a job? You'd stolen my money. Surely it was enough to live on."

George cleared his throat. "I thought about buying a small plantation of my own but needed to learn the business first. I figured working at one was the best way."

"Tell me about India."

"It was pleasant enough."

"What about the scenery, the culture?"

"It wasn't to my taste."

"What made you leave there? Why didn't you buy a plantation?"

"A dicky stomach. It put me off settling there. The water isn't clean – you never know what you might catch."

"When did you return?"

"Only a few weeks back. As I've explained, I started looking for Daphne straightaway. There's nothing more to tell."

"You don't appear to have caught the sun out there."

"As I said, I've been unwell."

"Hmm."

Bella put a spoonful of dessert in her mouth so that she didn't have to respond. That proved her point. No details. How had she been so stupid before? There may be *some* truth in what he'd told her, but what had he left out or made up altogether? As for claiming he'd been ill, she'd have to see his dead body and the death certificate before she'd ever believe he was sick again.

She'd spent their short married life pandering to him. Believing that he was going to die long before he should. Everything she did had been to ensure that he was enjoying life, not wasting a moment. She'd lost count of the number of times she'd put her own needs second to his, disregarded her own wishes – anything to please him.

He wasn't to blame, not really. From the moment she'd met him, she'd seen him as perfect, overlooking and dismissing any signs that he wasn't. In fact, she'd blatantly ignored everything she hadn't wanted to see. In her defence, it wasn't until he was sure of her devotion that he'd made her feel she was selfish and foolish if she disagreed with him. She remembered the time she'd practically pleaded to be allowed to travel to London to spend time with him and see where he worked and lived. What was it he'd said while looking hurt and upset?

"There's nothing attractive about the docks where I work . . . The rooms I rent are unpleasant . . . My employer doesn't care about how tired I am . . . Most nights, I don't know what time I'll finish. If a ship comes in late, I can't leave until the paperwork is complete . . . I can't expect you to understand . . . Bella, stop this, please."

At the time, she'd been terribly ashamed of her lack of understanding.

"You never had a job in the dock office," she said now. "I went there and the manager told me. So, how did you earn a living before you met me? Were you even employed at all?"

George put his spoon down and rubbed his hands over his face.

"Bella, I'll never lie to you again. So, here's the truth and if you don't like it, well, I can't help that. I grafted, but not in a way you'd regard as a job. At the docks, part of the consignments can go missing. I acquired those goods and sold them on at a profit."

"You were a thief? A fence?"

"Yes."

"A criminal."

"If you want to put it that way."

"There's no other way to put it. What a fool I am. I was so proud to have married an honest, hardworking man."

"If you'd been born in the East End slums like I was,

350

watching your father work himself into an early grave trying to keep a roof over your head and day-old bread on the table, then you might have done some things you'd regret. Because I'll tell you this – it's a damn sight easier to be a good person when you've never gone hungry or wanted for anything."

"There are plenty of people who have a hard time, but they don't behave the way you did. Richard, for one, came from a poor family," Bella shot at him.

"Then maybe he's the better man. Or perhaps it's some weakness in me. But I was just a lad with a wife and child to support, so I did what I felt I had to do to provide for my family. I can't regret trying to care for my child. Can't you at least concede that was the right thing to do?"

How was it he always made her question her beliefs and feel embarrassed by her comfortable life? How did he manage to leave her feeling so ashamed of the privileges she'd enjoyed? Was that how it was with people who controlled others – they ate away at your confidence until you were so unsure of yourself that you had to rely on them?

Once, Kate had cautioned her, suggesting that it wasn't right that George was stopping Bella from wearing harem pants. Although she'd said nothing to Kate, much to her shame, Bella had wondered at the time if Kate was a little jealous. How wrong can you be! Bella accepted now that George had manipulated her from their first meeting and she'd been too blind to see it. No – she'd refused to see it.

But not any more. Today, she'd viewed his every move with a clinical eye, comparing him to Richard and finding George wanting. Richard didn't need to control her. He worked to increase her self-belief. Made her laugh no matter what the situation. With George, she'd hardly ever laughed.

Victoria checked the clock on the mantel. It was going to be a long evening and night. Neither Kate nor William had hinted if they'd come to an understanding, although their manner towards each other had shifted. Kate was clearly looking at him for support.

Normally, Victoria would have been desperate to find out. Today, she prayed they wouldn't mention it, because she couldn't fake joy. She'd cooed and smiled half-heartedly at her grandsons' antics, but her mind was a barrage of questions. Where was her darling girl? Was Bella in danger? Afraid? Had she succumbed to George's charms again?

"Mrs Caldwell, it's time for the young masters to have their supper. Should I take them back to the nursery?" Nanny asked.

"Of course – we mustn't spoil their routine."

"We should get back to the school. If Bella telephones, I'll get word to you," Kate said.

"Whatever the hour, we want to know," Edward said before Victoria had a chance.

"Likewise, if either of you need me, telephone and I'll be straight round," Kate said.

Joshua, always a pleasant, biddable child, took Nanny's hand, but as she took hold of Pierre's, Pierre screamed and clutched at Victoria's skirt.

"Naa, Ganngan."

"Come along, Pierre. Grandmama is busy," Nanny said, even though he couldn't hear.

"Naa, naa."

Her grandson's voice penetrated Victoria's misery. The lamb was desperate to make himself understood. He used bits of sign language to communicate, but he was still so young and as yet knew so few words. He tried to speak, invariably getting frustrated when people didn't understand him. "Ganngan" was his word for grandmama and every time she heard it from his little mouth, it wrung her heart.

"I'll come up and help feed them," Victoria said.

It had to be easier than sitting here watching the clock, praying for tomorrow and the safe return of her daughter.

"Wait until you've seen Owain," Kate said.

"I'm fine now." She stood and hoisted Pierre into her arms. "I'm sorry we weren't better company, William, but thank you for giving up your time."

"Any time," William said.

Pierre bounced like a ton weight on Victoria's hip as she walked. The sooner she put him down, the better. She was halfway up the stairs, when the telephone halted progress. She turned as blackness descended.

Chapter 35

When they left Selfridges, George was feeling pleased. Things were going well. Since they'd arrived in London, Bella had relaxed. He'd got her talking about her family. That Sean was a lucky bleeder, married to Jane Kellet now. He constantly fell in the mire and came out smelling of flowers.

George hailed a hackney and Bella allowed him to take her hand as she climbed up. On the journey, he deliberately sat close to her and she didn't move away. Despite her occasional barbed comment, he was certain she was still in love with him. And she was definitely a lot easier to look at than the old hag he'd had to put up with in India.

Bella had irritated him, though, when he'd asked her about her pathetic little school. She'd boasted about what an amazing job she and Kate had done setting it up and attracting pupils. What was there to be proud of? Anyone could buy a building and put advertisements in the paper if they had enough money. He'd not felt it advisable to ask, but Bella must have bought it with another handout from her parents. Still, if he persuaded her to sell her share to Kate, that would give them enough to live on for a while. First, though, Bella must accept that she was his wife and that she had a duty to stay with him. If he couldn't persuade her, he wasn't agreeing to a divorce without receiving a large settlement.

It had been a risk telling her about how he'd earned a living before they met, but it paid off in the end. She'd soon shut up when he'd made it clear that she didn't understand what it was like to be skint. That was the thing people like her didn't get. If you had money to start off with, everything else was easy.

He'd forgotten how lovely her hair was. When he'd touched it earlier, he'd had a fleeting image of her dark waves against his skin as she brought him to his peak with her mouth. If he taught her to do that, he might not need to bed other women. And if things got tight, she could earn a fortune with that little trick. She wasn't the type who would ever agree to whore for him. Not unless she was hooked on opium. It was worth considering. There were certainly plenty of possibilities.

Victoria woke to find herself in bed, the curtains closed, her shoulder aching and her arm in a sling. Was it the middle of the night? What had happened? Pierre? Bella? She raised her head half an inch, groaning as she did so.

"Vicky, darling! Thank God you're awake. Don't move – you took quite a fall," Edward said.

He was sitting on the edge of the bed beside her.

"How did I get here?" she asked.

"William carried you."

"I must see Pierre."

"Hush now – everything is fine. Owain thinks it is the shock that caused you to black out, but I want him to see you again now you are awake."

"But Pierre?"

"Owain checked him over and all is well."

"Edward, if I've hurt that child, I'll never forgive myself."

"Don't worry about him for the moment. From what Owain says, children bounce a lot better than adults. You, my love, have fractured your arm, I am afraid. And I suspect the side of your face is going to be black by morning."

"I don't care about me. Has Owain left?"

"No. Kate has asked him to pop back to the nursery." She raised her head again, but Edward shook his head.

"Stay right where you are, missy."

"If you won't let me get up, please find out how my grandson is. And why is Kate still here? I thought she was going back to the school in case Bella calls . . . Before I fell – the telephone call – was it Bella?"

"No, it was Anne. She called to invite us to dinner. When she heard about you, she wanted to come round. Although she means well, I have insisted she stay away and let you rest. William is at The Grange if Bella rings. He is a splendid chap. As for Kate, she wanted to make sure you and Pierre were all right before she went home."

"Edward, why have things gone wrong just when I thought all of our children were going to be happy?"

"Don't go thinking the worst."

"Our daughter might be injured. Or on a ship to Africa with George. I can't believe she hasn't telephoned. Something terrible must have happened to her."

"Vicky, I am desperately worried about Bella, too, but we must remember that although George is a bounder, we have no reason to suspect he would harm her physically. And her note said she will be back tomorrow, so I am hanging on to that. If I don't, I won't be able to cope. Right now, I am just relieved. Because when I

356

walked into the hall and saw you and Pierre lying at the bottom of the stairs, I thought you were both gone."

"I'm sorry I frightened you. My mother killed herself by throwing herself down a flight of stairs. Did I ever tell you that?"

"Yes, my darling, you did. Kate's desperate to see you – can I go and get her?"

Victoria nodded.

When Kate rushed across to the bed, it was clear she'd been crying.

"Kate! How's Pierre?"

"He's grand. Really good. Owain will be here in a minute to tell you himself."

"Could you put some pillows behind me so I can sit up properly?" Victoria asked.

Kate supported Victoria as she moved the pillows from Edward's side of the bed.

"Better?" she asked.

"Much. Lying here, I felt as though the priest were going to arrive to give me my last rites. Oh, Kate, dear, don't look so upset. I was joking."

Kate sniffed. "Your poor face." She touched Victoria's cheek. "Victoria, I adore Bella and Dad. Everyone knows that . . . What I'm trying to say is . . . I know I'm not your real daughter and I don't expect you to feel the same about me, but you mean the world to me, as well."

"Kate, my darling girl, don't cry. I'm fine. I love you, too. Just as much as I love Sean and Bella. I thought you realised that. If you didn't, I'm at fault. Perhaps it's time you called me Mother. Only if you want to, of course."

Clearly overwhelmed, Kate gently pressed her lips to Victoria's unbruised cheek.

"Owain said I'm only allowed in to see for myself that you're all right and to say goodbye because you need rest. So I'll leave you for now, but I'll telephone later, Mother."

At one time Victoria believed she'd never be a mother. And now, although she'd only given birth to one of them, she was blessed with three – and two grandsons. But would she ever see Bella again? And would Sean ever forgive her when she told him what had happened? She'd fallen while holding *his* son. She remembered how angry she'd been with her maid, Bridie, when Sean had been scalded while in the woman's care. She closed her eyes as she tried to work out how she'd find the words to explain, when Owain and Edward entered the room.

"Edward says you won't rest unless you hear it direct from me," Owain said.

A smile was playing around his mouth. That must mean Pierre isn't badly hurt, she told herself.

Owain wagged a finger at her. "Now, madam, no rushing around for you over the next few days. You're not getting any younger."

"Yes, yes, fine. Tell me about Pierre," she said irritably.

"No broken bones. You must have clung on to him as you fell, so he landed on you."

She sensed his hesitation. "No other injuries?"

Owain shook his head. "You mustn't get all excited, because I can't explain it myself . . ."

"What? What is it?"

"It's early days and it might go again."

"Owain, get to the point, please."

He handed her a small glass. "First, drink this laudanum for the pain. It'll also help you to relax."

She snatched it from him. "Very well."

Owain spoke slowly. "It appears the boy has gained some hearing in his left ear."

"I don't understand."

"Neither do I. Perhaps it resulted from his accident today. Alternatively, he may never have been entirely deaf. Maybe the amount he could hear was too minor to detect while he was a baby. Sean's had me out a few times in recent months as he's been anxious about the child being fractious. I didn't pick up on anything apart from a couple of ear infections."

Edward took her hand in his. He was smiling.

Owain continued. "There's also a possibility his hearing has been coming and going, and it was frustrating the lad, possibly even frightening him. Truth be told, despite the advances X-ray machines are helping us to make in many aspects of medicine, hearing isn't one of them. So as I told you when he was first injured after his birth, there's still a great deal we don't comprehend."

"Let me get this straight, because my mind's all over the place. You're telling me Pierre can hear?" Victoria asked.

"So it appears."

"Marvellous, isn't it, Vicky?" Edward said.

"I'm dumbfounded." She was reeling. Pierre was no longer completely deaf. It was the miracle she'd prayed for every night. "Could it improve further?"

"I doubt it, but I suppose it's not impossible."

"Might it deteriorate?"

"Perhaps. Victoria, you're asking questions to which I simply don't have answers. All we can do is wait and see."

"Should we telegram Sean?" Victoria said.

"Best not. Let's see how Pierre gets on over the next

couple of weeks. Make sure there's no immediate deterioration," Owain replied.

"Edward, shouldn't we tell him about the accident?"

"If we tell him, he will come tearing home. Pierre is fine. No sense in ruining their honeymoon."

"He may be angry with us. But if you're sure, Edward, we'll leave it for now, because I don't feel capable of making any big decisions."

"Owain can monitor Pierre and if we have any concerns, we will get a message to Sean," Edward said. "Otherwise, I think it will be best to wait until we have more facts regarding the Bella situation, as well. Because if she hasn't come back, we will have to involve the police and then Sean must be told."

They thanked Owain and he took his leave, promising to return first thing.

There should be so much to celebrate. If only God would allow her beloved daughter to return safely . . .

"Edward, I need Bella home."

"I know, my love."

Edward moved round to the other side of the bed and she settled into the crook of his arm.

After a while, she yawned. "I can't believe I'm saying this, but I'm ever so tired. Do you mind if I take a nap?"

"That will be the effects of the laudanum. I would say rest is exactly what you need, my love. I will wake you if we have any news."

Back at the hotel, Bella folded the small blue coat with a fur collar. If this was the perfect size for Daphne, she was tiny. But so were the children from poorer families in Faredene. George was right about one thing. Wealth created two completely separate worlds. He claimed that in the cities, although they were under the age of consent, it wasn't uncommon for young girls to be working the streets at thirteen or fourteen. But for one of Daphne's age, it was exceptional, and only certain men were so inclined. How could any man possibly want a child in that way? They were animals. If Bella had her way, she'd hang the lot of them. Or at the very least render them incapable of intercourse.

She was examining the matching hat, when George's movements by the wardrobe caught her attention.

"What are you doing?" she said in alarm as George kicked off his shoes then removed his jacket and tie, placing them on the armchair.

"I'm getting changed. Moby believes I'm a successful businessman. I can hardly turn up there wearing the clothes I've had on all day."

"Do you have to do it here?"

"Where else would I go?" he said, removing his shirt and dropping it on the floor. "It's not like you haven't seen my bare chest before. And as I've already explained, we're legally married. If you want, I'll lay you down on that bed and make love to you." He paused as though savouring his words. "We'd be doing nothing wrong."

Bella turned away. She wouldn't give him the satisfaction of answering. She placed the coat, hat, gloves and some stockings on top of the boots in the leather bag they were taking with them later this evening.

Her attraction to George was no different from how she felt when she saw gooseberries. They looked appetising, yet she knew even one would bring her out in a horrid prickly rash. Yes, she could desire something, someone, but as long as she realised they were no good for her, then she was safe. Wasn't she?

George had his back to her and was removing a clean shirt from its hanger. He could have been dressed by now – he was deliberately taking his time covering himself. As though sensing her watching him, he pulled on the shirt and walked towards her with it hanging open. How beautiful he was – muscular, with just the right amount of chest hair.

He stopped in front of her.

"Temped?" he asked as he undid the top button of his trousers.

"Stop. Don't take those off!"

"I have to undo them so I can tuck my shirt in."

"Then I'll leave the room first."

His breath caressed her neck as he whispered in her ear. "You're afraid to give in to your desires. If you don't want to make love, I can pleasure you in other ways. Remember how you used to enjoy that?"

She poked her finger in his chest. "Don't touch me!"

"You don't mean it. I can see the desire in your face."

He tilted her chin with his fingers. Then his lips brushed hers in a feather-light kiss.

Bella tensed, expecting her traitorous body to betray her with that familiar longing in her most private place. Nothing – well, only a little. She sighed with relief. George, taking this as a sign of her desire, moved his lips against hers, his tongue forcing them apart.

Laughter erupted from her and she pushed him away.

"Wonderful," she said breathlessly.

"I knew all the nonsense with the other fella was bullshit. Bella, you're mine and always will be."

"No. I'm not yours. Don't you get it, you arrogant swine? I'm over you."

"You don't mean it."

"But I do, and it's such a relief."

"You can't. I want you back."

"Not my problem," she said.

"But you must give me another chance. We're married and I'm miserable without you."

"What a shame, because *I* don't care. And we'll be divorced as soon as it can be arranged."

"I might contest it."

"Just you try and my father will ensure every aspect of your past is investigated. I'm sure there are plenty of things you don't want unearthed."

He grasped her arms, pulling her so close, his erection pressed against her stomach.

"George, get off me!"

"If you're so confident you feel nothing for me, then lay with me right now." His hands moved to her buttocks, squeezing them. "If I can't arouse you, then you can be sure you're over me."

"What a kind offer," she said contemptuously, "but I'm already certain."

He kissed her neck as one hand cupped her breast, his thumb searching for her nipple.

"You want me – I can feel it," he said.

Bella stamped her foot down hard on his toes and he staggered back.

"Bitch! What did you do that for?"

"Was your story about Daphne a trick to get me here?"

George sat on the bed, rubbing his toes.

"What do you take me for?"

"Someone for whom lying is as easy as breathing. I'm leaving."

"No, don't go. I shouldn't have kissed you – I'm sorry. You're so beautiful, I forgot myself for a moment. Any man would around you. But it's true, I swear. Daphne really is in danger."

"If you try anything like that again, you'll have to find someone else to help you. In case you've forgotten, I'm practically engaged and I intend to become Mrs Richard Yates as soon as possible."

He drew back.

Her words had the desired effect. Although she still wasn't sure she was ready to wed Richard or any man, George didn't need to know that.

Chapter 36

George pulled the chair from under the dressing table and straddled it. As they went through the plan again, he was finding it difficult to concentrate. Bella, looking smug, had plonked herself on the padded armchair. Her rejection had hurt his pride. But he didn't believe she meant it – not for a minute. One thing was sure: she wasn't leaving London without his seed growing inside her. They'd get Daphne first and then he'd do whatever it took to keep Bella with him. He'd lock her up if he had to.

He considered forcing himself on her now, but if he did, she might refuse to accompany him to The White Lion. Would that matter, though? Daphne was a cute kid and she looked like him, but was she worth risking everything for?

Best to stick to the plan for now. If Bella saw him as a hero, she'd find him harder to resist. And as Bella seemed to want a child to raise, when she saw how pretty Daphne was, she was bound to want to mother her.

"It's seven thirty. We need to get going." George went to his valise and removed a gun.

Bella gasped. "Where on earth did you get that thing?"

"You can get anything in London if you know where to shop."

"Surely you can't be thinking of taking that with you. Someone might get hurt."

"If I don't have it with me, I'll get hurt. It's only for protection."

"Please tell me you've never killed anyone."

He shook his head. She'd never understand that sometimes, it was necessary to take a life. The memories came unbidden . . . When he was sixteen, he'd waited outside the church hall, where the teacher who had abused him years before taught illiterate lads to read. It was the same place he'd cornered George in a cupboard and forced him to do unspeakable things. The bastard was a hypocrite. Everyone praised him for his good works, but it was just a cover for finding victims. George had been carrying out a public service – the filthy pervert wouldn't hurt or shame any more innocent boys. Then there was the first woman he'd pretended to marry while he was with Pearl. She'd been no loss to anyone.

His mind turned to Matthew and Sophia Clarkson – Yvette's parents. Sophia was going to tell Matthew that she'd had sex with George. If Bella had found out, their marriage would have been over. When he'd pushed Sophia under a tube train, her husband had fallen trying to save her. George couldn't be blamed for that. As for the young Indian girl, her pregnancy would have shamed her and her parents, so he'd saved her from suffering a worse death.

Sometimes you had to make difficult choices. Even so, he doubted Bella would understand. One day, he might have to hint that he was prepared to do anything to keep her, though. If she believed he might hurt one of her family, she'd be too scared to leave him.

He rummaged in his bag again and pulled out a small silver box.

"Do you want something for your nerves?" he said.

"A drink?"

"Something stronger. A medicine – it'll calm you. You're shaking."

George was right – Bella's hands were trembling so much, she was struggling to get her gloves on. What did he expect? He'd said it might be dangerous, but guns and drugs! She knew nothing about the man she'd once loved.

"Do you take that medicine?" she asked.

"Don't talk daft."

"It's a perfectly reasonable question. If it's not for you, why do you have it?"

"I-I thought I might need to drug that bloke. Crusher – the one who works for Moby."

Bella didn't believe him. He was looking at her as though she'd offended him. That was all part of his tactics. The sooner she got away from him and back to Faredene, the happier she'd be. She placed her hat on her head and secured it with a hatpin.

"Come on," she said. "Let's get this over."

Outside, a thick fog was descending.

"If this gets worse, it's going to be difficult to see where we're going," Bella said.

"It might come in handy if we're trying not to be seen," George replied as they climbed into their cab. "Brick Lane," he said to the driver.

Bella peered through the windows into black streets where dark figures, their heads bent, illuminated by the occasional inadequate gas lamp or shop window, hurried to their destinations. Her heart was thumping so loud, surely George would hear it. She closed her eyes and focused on the rhythmic sound of the horse's hooves, willing herself to relax.

It must have worked, because she jumped when George said, "Bella, if anything happens and I don't make it, get Daphne out of London as quick as you can."

"Don't say such things."

"What is there for me if you don't want me?"

"Daphne, for one thing. You can move away and begin a new life together."

"She's not enough. I want you. Seeing you again has made me realise that."

Was he being genuine or saying this to manipulate her?

"George, I made it clear. I'm going home in the morning – tonight, if possible."

He shrugged helplessly. "Then if I die, it doesn't matter."

"What's the point of rescuing Daphne if she's going to end up orphaned?" she asked.

"Find someone to adopt her. Daphne matters to me, but to get me through this, I need to know that I have a future with you."

If he meant it, she didn't want him on her conscience. For now, she'd lie. When George and his daughter were safe, she'd make it clear that all she wanted from him was a divorce.

"Get out of there in one piece and we'll talk," she said.

He twisted his body towards her. "You still have feelings for me? Tell me you still love me, Bella. Please – it may be the last chance I have to hear you say it."

Damn him. He was so manipulative.

"I do," she said, sounding as sincere as she could while inwardly seething.

George smiled. "I knew it. This can be a new start for us." He brought her hand to his lips. "Tonight will be dangerous, though, so promise that you'll look after yourself and Daphne. If I don't make it, I'd like to think you'll give her a home because she's mine."

Despite her sympathy for Daphne's plight, the idea of raising George's daughter was intolerable. Still, as this was probably all part of his plan to ensure her compliance, one more lie would make no difference.

"Very well."

He grabbed her. His arms formed a tight band across her back as he kissed her hard on the lips, holding her so close she could barely breathe. Finally, he broke away.

"Tell me again that you love me."

Bella nodded.

"Say it. Your man is about to risk his life to make us a family. Tell me you love me."

"I love you."

He touched his finger to the end of her nose. "You'll always be mine, Bella. You have been since the moment we met."

The cab stopped and George helped her out before paying the driver.

"This is where I leave you, my precious. Stay here a few minutes before you follow me. You'll be safe enough if you stand by the steps of this hotel. Remember – wait in the café until nine o'clock. Don't come out too soon – it's too dangerous around there. Then cross into the alleyway next to the alehouse." He handed her the small leather Gladstone bag that contained the coat and boots for Daphne. "My brave wife. Our new life together will be everything you could ever dream of, trust me."

As George turned away, Bella wiped her mouth with the back of her gloved hand. She hated that she'd allowed him to kiss her. She'd never trust him again. Although wasn't that what she was doing by helping him? The whole thing might be an elaborate trick. He was capable of anything. Perhaps she should leave now – go home before it was too late and something bad happened. Bella knew there was no way she could do that. If there was even a remote possibility that George was being truthful, she had to see this through.

Her legs were so unsteady, she wasn't sure she could walk the last mile to Spitalfields and contemplating what lay ahead wasn't making it easier. Breathing deeply, she pushed her shoulders back.

As George approached The White Lion, he could hear music coming from inside. The smoke-filled bar area was crowded, lewd-looking women draping themselves over eager men. He scanned the room. Four men were sitting around a table and the whale-like landlord was amusing them by pushing his head between the breasts of a buxom woman.

"Moby!" George said sharply.

Moby lifted his head, laughing.

"Evening, George. There's a half-crown in there." He gestured towards the woman's chest. "First one to get it out wi' his teeth wins. Fancy a go?"

"No. Is the girl ready?" George said.

He wanted to get out of here quickly and begin his new life with Bella.

"All right, George. I can see yer eager an' I don't blame you. Scrubbed up nice, she has."

"Where is she?"

"Locked in the room. I tried to prepare her for you."

"You what?" George snapped.

If the fat bastard had touched her, he was going to kill him and to hell with the consequences.

Moby took a step back. A gigantic man George assumed to be Crusher stopped drying glasses and placed the cloth down on the bar before cracking his knuckles loudly. George needed to allay Moby's suspicions.

"What did you do? I've paid for her to be intact," George said.

"Steady on. Nothing like that. I just put her in the picture so she'll behave for you."

"I don't want her scared out of her wits. I've got all night. Have someone bring me a bottle and a tray of food, will you, Moby?" George said pleasantly.

"Come through to the back. There's the matter of payment to be sorted first." Moby rubbed the pad of his thumb and two fingers together.

George placed the notes on Moby's desk.

"One o' my girls will take you up," Moby said. "Flo!" he bellowed towards the bar. "Show the gentleman to the back room." He passed her a key. "You'd best warn Daph not to play up or I'll not be pleased."

Glaring, Flo nodded at Moby. George followed her up the narrow wooden staircase. His legs were unsteady – he'd never been so afraid. If he didn't pull this off tonight, Daphne would be condemned to a life of prostitution. Worse, Bella might change her mind about giving their life together another chance and he was almost broke.

As Flo unlocked the door, he tapped her on the shoulder. When she looked at him, he mouthed, "Remember – nine o'clock."

She nodded before walking away with tears in her eyes.

Why was she so upset? He had no intention of harming Daphne. Admittedly, if everything went to plan, Flo would never see her again, but she'd get over it soon enough. Tarts were cold-hearted, he reasoned.

George pushed open the door. Daphne was sitting on a faded pink eiderdown. She was wearing a navy-and-red tartan dress and a matching ribbon decorated her hair. On her feet, she wore satin slippers. She looked tiny, vulnerable. Even from the doorway, it was clear she'd been crying.

"Daphne, don't be afraid. I won't harm you," he said, walking towards her.

Her little body tensed, her lip quivering.

"I know what yeh want and Uncle Moby said I'd better behave," she said.

His girl looked terrified. He was doing the right thing getting her away from here.

Kneeling before her, he said, "I promise I won't hurt you or touch you. We're going to play a game."

"Yeh mean like when Flo plays I spy wi' me? Or the sort she has with her customers?"

"Like hide-and-seek. Are you hungry?"

"Yeah, a bit. But me tummy feels all fluttery."

"Try to eat something."

George opened the door to allow Flo to enter. She placed the tray on the table, glancing towards the open door at Crusher, who had followed her upstairs.

372

Loudly, she said, "Now, you mind what I told you, Daph. No crying or screamin'. I've warned you what'll happen if you're a naughty girl."

"But, Flo, he says—"

She kneeled in front of Daphne, placing her index finger over the child's mouth.

"Hush now. No talking, either, unless the gentleman asks you summat."

Flo jerked her head slightly and George guessed she wanted him to distract Crusher. He blocked the entrance.

"Brandy is too strong for the girl. Bring me a bottle of wine, there's a good chap."

Scowling, Crusher dropped his cig, grinding it into the floor, and took the stairs.

George glanced over his shoulder. Flo was whispering to Daphne, who gaped at him. At the sound of heavy footsteps returning, Flo kissed her cheek.

"Loves yeh, Daph," she said before scurrying from the room, past Crusher, who grunted something unintelligible as he shoved the bottle at George.

George closed the door, shooting the small inadequate-looking bolt. He cut off a piece of cheese and handed it to Daphne. She was staring at him.

"Is it true what Flo said? You're me dad?"

"Yes. But keep your voice down."

To George's amazement, she flung her thin arms around his neck. He held her close, hesitantly at first, then fiercely. She wasn't angry with him for staying away. No recriminations – this was that unconditional love everyone banged on about. Youngsters and animals, they were the only ones you could trust. He kissed her blonde locks. She was his daughter. He'd never let her down again.

⤳⟐⟐⤳

Chapter 37

Dragging strength from deep inside her, Bella walked, fear making her shift quicker than she thought she was capable of right now. As George had explained it would, The White Lion alehouse came into view on the other side of the road. Almost opposite was Alf's Café. A bell tinkled as she opened the door. Inside was tatty, with eight small tables crammed around it. The smell of stale grease and tobacco hung in the air. At the table by the window, a couple were holding hands. At another, an old man was smoking a clay pipe. And in the back corner was a tawny-haired woman in a shabby chartreuse dress with a black shawl draped over her shoulders.

Even though Bella was wearing a simple grey coat, she looked out of place and there were curious glances from the other customers as she walked towards the woman.

"Flo?" she said hesitantly.

The woman gave a brief nod, whispering, "I'm glad yer not late, 'cos I'm shitting meself here. If owt goes wrong, I'll not see morning. You'd best sit – yer drawing attention to yersel'."

As Bella took a seat, the waitress came over.

"Can I get you another cup?" Bella asked Flo.

Flo drained the dregs of her drink.

"Ta, duck. They make a nice brew here – and a meat 'n' tater pie wouldn't go amiss."

"Of course."

"You should get one for yourself an' all, 'cos you've a while to wait and they won't be best pleased if yeh sit nursing a cuppa."

Although she had no intention of eating, she ordered two teas and two pies. As the waitress walked away, Bella spoke.

"Is Daphne—"

Flo hissed, "Shh. Best say nowt until we've been served."

Once the food and pale, unappetising liquid in chipped mugs were placed on the table in front of them, not wanting to cause offence, Bella sipped slowly.

"Coming in here on a frosty night's a real treat when I can have a bite an' a hot drink to warm me fingers. It's a wonder they don't drop off, it gets so cold. Mind you, if I were a bloke, I'd be a sight more worried about my tackle freezing off." Flo laughed.

Bella spluttered.

"Sorry if I've offended yer sensibilities, but you're a married woman, so you've seen at least one in yer time," Flo said.

Bella nodded shyly.

"I'm glad I got to see for meself what yer like, 'cos I've been like a mother to Daph."

"George told me you tried to get her away from here."

"A good pasting I got for me trouble an' all. To tell you the truth, it would have been no life for the kid wi' me. She'd have been living in one room with only a curtain separating her from me and me punters. Or worse, still wandering the streets most of the night while I were working."

375

"Was she really about to be forced to sleep with men?"

"Aye. Scum, they are, the ones what want kids."

"It's appalling. I was completely unaware this sort of thing happened."

"No, well, you wouldn't be. I can see yer a lady, so you'd know nowt of real life."

Bella resisted the urge to tell the careworn woman that money and breeding didn't offer protection from pain and suffering. Because besides the struggle to survive, no doubt the impoverished also coped with the same losses and betrayals as the rich.

Instead, she said, "We'll get her away."

"Wi' you as her mam, Daph will have a better life."

Bella didn't know what to do. Should she tell Flo she wouldn't be Daphne's mother? But what if she then refused to assist them? Bella decided it was best to keep quiet.

"I never asked yer fella, but you don't live in London, do yeh? Daph will never be safe here. Moby doesn't like to be crossed, so he'll keep looking for her."

"No, we're staying at The Burlton, but home is well away from here."

"Thank Christ, 'cos the further she is from Crusher, the happier I'll be."

"Is he as bad as George says?"

"Worse. He terrifies me an' I've got to let the vicious lump o' muck have his way wi' me when I go back there. It won't be the first time by any means. As Moby says, it's the perks of Crusher's job to do any of us he fancies. But this time I've got to act like I want him."

"How awful."

"Aye. Folk think because us street girls go wi' men for

money, we've got no feelings. I get the odd decent punter, but most of them make me skin crawl."

Despite the few teeth that Bella could see, Flo bit into her pie, gravy oozing out and dribbling down her chin.

"Eat yours – it's good stuff. The filling might be the milkman's old nag, but it's tasty," Flo said.

"Is there no way you can get away and find a different job?"

"You mean well – I can see yer kindly – but look at the state of me. You wouldn't think I were only thirty, would yeh? Doing what I do ain't an easy life. At one time I had dreams, mind. When I were a kid, I wanted to work in a fancy tea shop or a millinery an' marry a decent fella, have a family of me own." Flo sighed. "It wasn't to be. Daph will have that chance now, thanks to you. She's bright, you know."

"Does she do well at school?"

Flo laughed harshly. "Never been a day in her life. As far as the authorities are concerned, she doesn't exist. That's why it's so easy for kids like her to be shipped abroad. Even though I won't get to see her, it'll be lovely to think of her learnin' her letters and doin' sums."

Bella wanted to bring this downtrodden woman some comfort.

"My sister and I are teachers – we own a school."

"Aww, smashin'. Daph will make yeh proud of her."

"Yes," Bella said, unable to think of another response.

"George is in the room wi' her, so things are going to plan."

"If they catch us, what will they do?"

"I'll not kid you. You've got yerself mixed up in summat right dangerous, duck. You're right pretty. I can see why

George wanted yeh. He might be handsome, but he's a bad lot. You'd only have to cock yer little finger an' you could have anyone. Why take up wi' him after what he did to Pearl and Daphne?"

"I'm not sure what you mean."

"His wife went with a few blokes 'cos he asked her to do it to pay the rent, but she was no tart. When he sold her to Moby, it devastated the poor cow. In the final days of her life, she spent most of her time locked in the cellar of The White Lion. I told her to behave an' do what the punters wanted, but she wouldn't. She just kept harping on about how her 'usband loved her and there must be some mistake."

Bella's stomach lurched. How could he do such a terrible thing? Was there no depth that George wouldn't sink to? The words caught in her throat.

"I-I didn't know . . . about Pearl or Daphne – any of it – when I met George. I fell in love."

"Aye, men – they make bloody fools of us all. Now, I'd best be quick an' get back over the road. Moby's arranged for three of us girls to go down the docks about ten when the pub trade is thinning out so we can service a ship's crew. The captain didn't want his men going ashore as they're only here for a few hours to take on food and water."

Bella knew she was gaping as she tried to hide how appalled she was.

"You're working all night, a whole crew?" she said eventually.

Flo seemed oblivious to Bella's horror. "Hopefully I'll be there until about five, then back in here for breakfast before I get some sleep. Now, about getting Daph away,"

Pearl said. "One of the other girls is in on what we're doing because she was planning on using the alleyway tonight with the fellas she picks up. If she saw you going down there on yer own, she might think you were trying to nick her pitch an' clobber yeh."

"George said no one else knew."

"I've not had a chance to tell him. She's all right – we can trust her. She doesn't want to see the little 'un get passed from fella to fella either. Now, I'd best get gone. I don't want any of the others seeing me wi' you." She gave Bella a small brooch. "Will yeh give Daph this to remember me by? The stones are only paste an' one of them is missing, but it's the only thing I own that means anything to me. It was me grandmother's."

"I'll make sure she gets it."

"Daph knows nowt about what's going on, other than he's her father. But I've told her to do whatever she's told wi'out asking questions." Flo stood. "Best of luck to yeh."

Left alone, Bella thought about George. Nothing he did should surprise her. But selling his wife made it clear he was a monster. What other wicked things had he done that she wasn't aware of? She'd been a fool to fall for a handsome face and some sweet words.

Suddenly realising it was nearly nine o'clock, she jumped up and made her way outside. Two things hit her hard: the biting cold and the urge to retch. She darted across the road, away from the lights of the café window. Leaning her hands against the brick wall, she vomited, splattering her boots and the Gladstone bag. Her whole body was trembling, her lungs straining to take in air. Agreeing to his scheme had been a mistake.

Startled, she jumped, straightening as someone behind

her tapped her on the back. She turned. A stubbled face was inches from her own. The stench of tobacco and beer assaulted her nostrils.

He smirked. "How much?"

"G-get away from me," she stammered.

"Waiting for a better customer, are yeh? I can pay as well as anyone."

"I don't do t-that sort of thing."

He laughed, swaying drunkenly. A hairy hand reached out and squeezed her breast. Instinctively, she dragged out her hatpin and jabbed it into his hand.

"Ouch! You effing bitch." He stepped backwards. "I'm not interested in you anyway." He spat in her face before staggering away.

Bella's tears mingled with the saliva on her cheek as she groped in her pocket for a handkerchief. After she'd rubbed the filth off her face and still clutching her hatpin, she moved into the alleyway. Above, a chink of light came from a curtained window. That must be where George was. The fog made it impossible to see the sloping roof he'd told her about.

She was quaking, yet her encounter was giving her courage. She'd defended herself. Cautiously, she inched forwards, praying that no one had followed her, using her fingers to feel her way further into the blackness. Then, pressing her back against a battered doorway opposite the faint light, she stilled. Her skin felt clammy and her teeth chattered from fear more than the cold air that whipped around her skirt.

As she waited, she told herself continuously that she was safe enough here. Yet, deep down she knew she'd count herself lucky if she survived the night without being molested by one of the singers of bawdy songs who passed the entry as they left the nearby hostelries.

When two shadowy figures came towards her, she tensed, hatpin poised until she realised one was a woman – probably the prostitute Flo told her about. Bella didn't move, barely breathing as they went by, and the woman gave her an almost imperceptible nod. Then, to her horror, Bella registered what was happening mere feet away from her and pressed her hands over her ears, but it didn't block out the distinctive sound of the couple copulating.

After what seemed an eternity, a husky female voice said, "Took you a while to get going there, me darlin'. Too much ale? Still, hopefully it was worth it in the end. Now, you get home an' no bothering yer wife for a bit of how's yer father. You've had yer fun for tonight. She'll be giving birth any day now and doesn't need your wanderin' hands."

As they passed again, the man was closer to Bella and she recognised him as the same one who had propositioned her. She was thankful he'd not noticed her as he adjusted his clothing.

Alone again, Bella waited anxiously, staring up at the window until eventually, the curtains opened, illuminating the roof below. The glass rattled in the frame as it opened and a silhouette appeared.

"Bella?" George hissed.

"I'm here."

Quickly, George lifted Daphne out and onto the ledge. Bella moved closer, hearing him whisper to Daphne.

"Be careful. Remember to be a brave girl. Everything will be fine. We're going to be a family."

Bella could just make out that he was holding Daphne's

hands, allowing her to work her way down as he stretched out of the small opening.

When he couldn't reach any further, he said, "You'll have to walk yourself. Steady now."

The child took one step, then Bella gasped as Daphne slipped on the icy tiles and swayed precariously, her bare arms flaying.

"Flo!" Daphne cried.

At the same time, there was a loud crash from behind George.

"Go!" he yelled before disappearing.

The child fell, landing on her bottom. Screaming, she slid down the roof, bringing slates with her. Bella jerked her head as one almost caught her as she reached out to grab Daphne.

The child slammed feet first into Bella's chest and the pair collapsed. Winded, Bella lay on the wet cobbles as crashes, shouting, banging and screams came through the open window. She heard Flo's voice clearly.

"Stop it, Crusher, yeh mad bleeder. You'll prise his eyes out."

There were more sounds of scuffles and then a shot rang out.

Chapter 38

Hands lifted Daphne off Bella.

"Get outta here, quick! They'll be out here any minute," a husky voice said.

Although dazed, Bella accepted the proffered hand of the prostitute who had nodded at her earlier and was pulled to her feet.

"For Christ's sake, leg it!" the woman urged, shoving Bella's sodden hat and the leather bag at her.

After steadying herself, Bella grasped Daphne's shoulders.

"Can you run?" Bella said, wheezing.

There was no answer.

Bella seized the child's small hand and ran blindly through the fog, dragging Daphne behind her without a thought for the direction of the tube stations. Terror spurred Bella on as they pelted down the road, darting down several side streets in the hope of making it difficult for anyone following, stopping only when the freezing air searing her lungs forced her to keel over, gasping. Not even as a schoolgirl playing lacrosse had she ever run so fast or so far.

Removing her hand from Daphne's, she pressed against the stitch in her side, fighting the nausea and dizziness.

Someone might already be giving chase. No matter how queasy she was, they must keep moving. George had told her that both stations were only a five-minute walk. They should have reached one of them by now.

"Where are we going?" a small voice said.

Bella looked at the shivering girl. "The underground railway."

"It's not this way."

"We're going to a different one," Bella said untruthfully.

Even if Daphne knew the area far better than she did, there was no way she was admitting to the child she was rescuing that they were lost. Daphne was ashen and blood was seeping from a gash on her cheek, but there was no time to deal with that. Bella dragged the coat out of the bag and hauled it up Daphne's arms. Next, she stripped off the girl's satin slippers, throwing them in the gutter, and pushed the boots on her bare feet. They were too big, so Bella pulled the laces tight.

All the while, her heart and mind were racing. She couldn't turn back – that would mean going closer to The White Lion. There was no choice but to carry on, putting as much distance between them and the pub as they could. If she found a busier road, she might flag down a hackney. They could even jump on an omnibus if they were still running this late.

"Come on – we have to go," Bella said.

"What about me new shoes?"

Bella looked at the ruined slippers. The only place for them was the bin, but they may well be the first decent thing Daphne had ever owned. She picked them up and shoved them in the bag. Then they set off again at a brisk walk.

Although she was rattled, Bella felt exhilarated. After tonight, surely nothing would ever frighten her again. She had no idea where they were going but hoped that eventually, they'd reach a better area.

They crossed a broad road and turned left, continuing until she noticed a tall brick building ahead through the fog. Despite the lateness of the hour, lights shone in several of the windows. She wondered if it was a hotel.

Outside, she could make out the inscription in the stone across the double doors. It was a hospital. She grasped the frosty iron railings while she caught her breath. Perhaps they could take refuge here. It might raise some questions from the staff, but it would be safer than trailing Daphne through East End streets all night.

It was then Bella heard hooves behind them. She tightened her grip on Daphne's hand, only relaxing as a voice said, "Do you need a ride?"

An elderly hackney driver, muffled against the cold, was smiling down at them.

"We've been visiting my husband in hospital. My daughter is distraught – can you get us to our hotel, please?"

"Aye, no bother."

This might be a trick. Perhaps they were both going to be dragged back to The White Lion to face Lord only knew what fate. She glanced at Daphne, who didn't appear to recognise the man. And not everyone in this part of London could be a fiend, Bella reasoned as she gave him the name of their hotel.

He climbed down and lifted Daphne into the cab, then produced a box for Bella to step on.

"I'll have you there in two ticks," he said as he closed the door.

"There's no need to be afraid," Bella whispered to Daphne as they pulled away.

Daphne snuggled into her side, her familiarity making Bella slightly uncomfortable. Realising the child had been through an ordeal, she held her close throughout the brief journey while her own mind worked through what might have happened in that room. Had George killed or hurt someone? What if they'd carted him off to prison? Should she go to the police? Most of Faredene's upper-class homes took the London papers. She mustn't allow herself to become embroiled in another scandal – it would ruin the school. What if he was lying injured somewhere? If he was, she doubted Moby would fetch a doctor to him. There was no way she'd ever forgive George, but she wouldn't want him to be hurt. She shuddered.

"What do I owe?" Bella asked as they alighted.

"It's on me. I'm heading home for the night now, anyway."

"I can pay."

"It's late to be out with a kiddy, missus, on a night like this. And you didn't get covered in mud on a hospital visit."

Bella mumbled her thanks.

"If your fella is chasing you, I hope he never finds you. Take care now," the man said.

In the foyer, the elderly night porter jerked awake, frowning. Pulling herself up to her full height and affecting a manner that she hoped would stop him from questioning their appearance, she said imperiously, "The key for room twenty-three."

In the room, Bella wrenched off her coat and gloves then turned to Daphne.

"Take your coat off – I'd best clean your face."

There was a small sink in the corner of the room and Bella wet one of her handkerchiefs and bathed the graze, seeing Daphne properly for the first time. Her face was angelic, beautiful – the image of George.

"Don't be afraid. You're safe now. My name is Bella and I'll look after you until George gets here."

When Daphne gave no response, Bella added, "Do you understand?"

"Uncle Moby will be right mad I'm gone."

"Your father will sort things with him."

"Is that tall, posh fella really me dad?"

"Yes," Bella said with certainty. The child looked so like George, there was no mistake.

"But you're not me real mam."

"No. No, I'm not."

"She's dead, but I can remember what she looked like. Uncle Moby told me she were working as a whore when she corked it. Flo looks out for me now."

Bella flinched. She didn't know the woman, but she felt obliged to defend her memory.

"Your mother didn't choose that life."

"Are we gonna be a family, like he said?" Daphne asked.

"Not me, but you'll live with your father."

"I thought you were his wife. He said you were gonna be me new mam."

"It's complicated. We're married, but we're not together."

"Why you here, then?"

"He asked me to help get you away from the pub and keep you safe."

"Uncle Moby said I weren't in no danger as long as I were a good girl."

387

"Daphne, you're too young to understand."

"No I ain't. I've seen what goes on. An' I was always told to stay away from men, but now Uncle Moby says I'm old enough to earn me keep, like Flo and the others. I'm gonna have a life of luxury if I do as I'm told. He says men will queue up to pay me attention."

Bella took Daphne's hands between her own.

"He's no relation to you whatsoever and he's wicked. What these men want to do to you is a crime – a terrible sin."

Daphne snatched her hands away.

"He's been good to me. Looked after me all me life an' fed me when he didn't need to, when me real mam got 'erself battered to death for not behaving and left me wi' no one."

That horrible man had totally turned her mind. How on earth did Bella explain the awful situation and the danger the child faced? Bella dug into her coat pocket, feeling around, hoping she'd not dropped the cheap brooch Flo had given her.

"Daphne, you trust Flo, don't you?"

"She says I'm her little ducklin'."

Bella held out the brooch. "Well, she gave me this to give to you. She wants you as far away from Moby as possible."

"She told me to do as I were told."

"Flo was helping us. And she tried to sneak you out the other night, didn't she?"

"Yeah, but she said we was goin' on a holiday. Crusher gave her a good pasting for it, so I don't think I'll get to see the seaside now."

"Flo was trying to get you away from London."

Daphne chewed the inside of her cheek as her mind worked. "Honest?"

"Yes. I met her tonight and she's afraid you're in danger from Moby." Bella didn't trust George, but for now he was Daphne's only hope. "Flo loves you. She hates working for Moby and wants you to have a better life than her."

"Can she come with us?"

"No, I'm afraid not. Flo didn't feel she'd be able to look after you."

Daphne took the brooch. "She always wears this on special days like Christmas. Will yeh pin it on me?"

"Shall I attach it to your new coat?"

"No, I want to wear it on me dress."

Bella secured it to the tartan dress.

"All right, let's get you ready for bed." After removing her boots, Bella said, "I'm sorry I didn't have time to put your stockings on. The boots have rubbed your feet."

"It doesn't matter. I like me new boots. Not as much as me slippers, but they're still nice."

Daphne made to climb in the smaller of the beds.

"You need to put your nightclothes on first," Bella said.

"What's them?"

Bella opened a drawer and held up a cotton and lace-trimmed nightgown.

"A frock for bed?" Daphne asked.

"Yes. What do you usually sleep in?"

"Not fancy stuff like I had on today but the dress I wear for cleaning an' running errands."

"Come on – I'll help you."

She undid the buttons of Daphne's dress, noting with disgust that apparently, Moby's idea of getting her dressed nicely didn't run to the purchasing of undergarments.

389

George would need to take care of such things immediately. It was going to be no straightforward task for him to raise the girl alone. But no doubt he'd persuade some woman to take them both on before long.

Bella removed Daphne's ribbon, brushed her blonde hair and plaited it before tucking her into bed. Normally, her instincts would have been to kiss her, stroke her head as she fell asleep. But she mustn't allow herself to become attached to George's daughter. Once he arrived, she'd leave to catch her train home – hopefully never seeing either of them again.

"I'll miss Flo 'n' Uncle Moby, but it'll be nice to have a proper dad. Do yeh think he might buy me a puppy?" Daphne said sleepily.

"He might. Sleep now."

Bella pulled the wooden chair George had sat on earlier in the day close to the window and settled her elbow on the broad ledge, her nose almost touching the glass as she stared out into the murky streets. What had happened back there? She hoped he'd get here soon.

Chapter 39

Bella must have nodded off, because she woke with a start when her head slipped off her hand. Rubbing her neck absent-mindedly, she wandered over to the bed and bent over Daphne, who was snoring softly. She wondered if the child she'd miscarried would have looked similar. Quickly, she turned away from Daphne, whose blonde hair curled around her face.

After washing, Bella changed her blouse, cleaned her boots and then tried to get the muck off her coat. It was stained but would have to do until she got home. She threw it back on the bed.

It was almost two in the morning when she accepted that George wasn't coming. Bella considered leaving London with Daphne in case Moby had people looking for them, but something had gone wrong and she needed to find out what. It would be too dangerous to take Daphne back to the café. The safest option was for Bella to go alone and get back before the child woke.

Dressed again for outdoors, Bella closed the bedroom door quietly, then spun round, startled, as she heard someone cough behind her. It was the night porter.

"Mrs Bristow, there's a woman downstairs who wishes to see you. I've asked her to wait. She's not, er, the sort of person we allow in the hotel, ma'am."

Realising instantly who it must be, Bella tore downstairs.

"Flo! You look exhausted. Come over here." Bella led her to a seating area that was far enough away from reception that they wouldn't be overheard. "George hasn't come back."

"I know, duck. He won't be going anywhere. That's why I pretended I was sick, to get away from the ship early. Nearly broke me neck rushing here before I go back to the pub."

"What have they done with him?"

"There's no point in my dressing it up like a pig's breakfast. I'm sorry for your loss, love, but he's dead."

"He can't be."

"Your fella knew it might be dangerous."

If anyone had asked Bella how she'd feel about George's death, many emotions would have gone through her mind. Numb wasn't one of them, yet that was exactly what she felt. She didn't love him. How could she when George was never the man she'd believed him to be?

"What happened?" Bella said.

"Even though I pretended I'd had a few too many gins and everyone knows if I have more than one it goes straight to me head, Crusher got suspicious when I started makin' eyes at him. Then he heard the window opening and the little 'un clattering on the roof, so he barged into the room. I thought he were gonna smash yer fella's skull an' tried to pull him off. While he were clouting me, George grabbed a gun from somewhere. Crusher dived at him. There was another scuffle and it went off."

"Poor Daphne."

"I'm sorry for yeh both. I can see yer shocked an' hate to leave you like this, but I need to get back to The White Lion. I don't want to give Crusher another excuse to use his fists on me."

"You're sure George is dead?"

"Certain. I had to clear up the blood while they got rid of the body."

"What do you mean got rid of it?"

Flo shrugged. "They might have taken it somewhere and burned it. Or dumped it in the river – it's where most of the bodies end up."

"We should go to the police."

"All that will do is get me, you and Daph killed, as well. Look, I don't mean to be hard on yeh. Moby's got men out lookin' for her. They can't cover the whole of London or even every station, so you've got to get away from here as quick as you can. Catch the first train."

"Do they suspect your involvement?"

"Not yet. Like I say, I were acting drunk and Moby got Crusher to dunk me head in the rain barrel to sober me up so I could clean up the mess in the back bedroom then get back out to work. Bastard nearly drowned me."

"Are you certain the café owner won't mention our meeting?"

"I can't be sure of anything. When I get back to the pub, they might slit me throat for all I know."

"What about the other woman, the one who was working in the alleyway? She helped us. Is she in danger?"

"No – she enjoys this life. Moby would never suspect her."

Bella knew little about Flo, but she was sure that despite the way she earned a living, she was a good woman.

"Then don't go back there," Bella said.

"I got no choice. Where the hell would I go? The only money we're allowed is a few coppers for bits of food. Some of us girls try to hold a few pennies back by making out we've had less punters. I mainly spent mine on Daph, but I had to be careful wi' that game. Nowadays, if Crusher thinks we're holding out on them, he takes his belt to the girl who makes the least."

"Surely you made enough tonight?"

"If the crew on that ship had paid me, I'd have done a runner wi' the brass, but Moby got the money direct from the captain. As it is, I need to get back now. I've already taken a risk coming here."

"Wait here, please. Just a few minutes . . ."

Once Bella was back in their room, she took several notes from her handbag and hurried back down to the foyer.

"Here – this should be enough for a couple of weeks. It doesn't matter where you go as long as you're safe. Try to find a job in a café. Start again," Bella said.

Flo's hand hovered. "There's enough here to keep me goin' for months. Are yeh sure?"

"Yes. Just go. Quickly."

Flo tucked the cash down the top of her dress.

"Daphne is right lucky to have you." She squeezed Bella's fingers. "Give her a hug from me."

George was dead and Bella was now responsible for his daughter. One thing was obvious – she needed to get Daphne out of London. Then what? She didn't relish the idea of taking her to Faredene. Apart from how her family would react, Daphne was the image of George and it pained Bella to look at her.

He was really gone.

Strangely, she felt free. Even after he'd run away with her money and his mother had told her that he was a bigamist, some small part of her had hoped, prayed that it was all a misunderstanding. It wasn't – George had been a deceitful, cruel man. She doubted she knew half of the bad things he'd done in his life, but at least he'd done one decent thing. He'd saved his daughter.

There was nothing she could do but tell Daphne the truth. She'd known her father for less than an hour, but still, it would be difficult for her to learn that she was no longer going to be living with him. It was too early to catch a train and Bella didn't want to risk hanging around on the platform, so she allowed Daphne to sleep.

When Daphne woke, Bella sat beside her on the bed.

"Is summat up? Where's me dad?" Daphne asked.

Bella held Daphne's hand as she spoke softly.

"Daphne, there was a terrible accident and George, your father, was killed."

"What's gonna happen to me, then? Am I going back to the pub?"

"No. It's not safe for you there. It was Crusher who killed your father. I'll take you to where I live. We'll sort out your future once we're there."

"Ta, but you don't want to be me mam, so I'd rather go back to Flo."

"She's gone. I spoke to her this morning while you were asleep."

"She's left me?" Daphne's tears pooled.

"Only because she wouldn't be able to look after you. I'll make sure you're safe and well-cared-for, I promise. Now come on – get washed and dressed. We'll have some breakfast and be on our way."

* * *

Bella steeled herself as Kate, her face livid, opened the door.

"How could you be so irresponsible! Have you lost your mind? You'd better have a good explanation, Bella, or I'll murd . . ." Her tirade faded as her gaze fell on Daphne, who was holding Bella's hand. "What . . . Who's this?"

"Let me get in, sis, and I'll explain," Bella said.

Feeling more in control than she expected, she shooed Kate out of the way and guided Daphne into the parlour, where her mother and father were seated together. Her mother's arm was in a sling, her eye and cheek purple and black. Bella dropped Daphne's hand and ran to her parents.

"Mother? What happened?"

"She was so worried about you, she fainted on the stairs while she was carrying Pierre," Kate said.

Her sister's voice was angrier than she'd ever heard it.

"I'm so sorry, truly I am. Is he injured?" Bella directed her question to her mother, who, like her father, was staring at Daphne in disbelief. When her mother didn't answer, Bella kneeled beside her and took her hand. "Mother, Father, I can explain everything. But please tell me you and Pierre are all right."

"We're both fine, Bella. But who is this child? Your coat is filthy. What on earth have you been doing? Not even a telephone call! Have you any idea how worried we've been?" her mother said.

"It's lucky Father didn't collapse, as well," Kate said harshly.

"Kate, don't shout – the child looks frightened," their father said. "Bella is home safe, that's what matters. Let's all calm down and hear what she has to say."

Bella crossed to the fireplace and pulled the bell. Doris appeared almost instantly.

"Doris, this is Daphne. Please take her through to the kitchens and ask Cook to give her some milk and something to eat." She turned to Daphne, who was stood with her back pressed against the sideboard, looking warily at them all. "Don't be afraid. I explained on the train that my family would be angry, but it's only because they've been worried about me. You go with Doris and I'll come through when we've finished talking."

Reluctantly, Daphne took Doris' proffered hand.

Bella sat down opposite her parents. They didn't look half as annoyed as Kate did, but Bella didn't blame her. In her place, she'd have felt the same.

"This had better be good," Kate said, joining her on the sofa but sitting on the edge, her body twisted so she was looking – or, more accurately, glaring – at Bella.

On the train journey, Bella had planned how she'd explain what had happened.

"George is dead," she began.

Over an hour later, Bella had told them how George had asked her to help him save his daughter from a life of enslaved prostitution. Skirting over the danger she herself had been in, she explained how they got her away with the help of Flo, who had also run away to begin a new life. To her amazement, no one interrupted or asked questions. In fact, they'd sat transfixed until she ended, "And so I've brought Daphne back here."

Kate was the first to speak, her face pained.

"Oh, sweet pea, I'm so proud of you, but you could have been killed." She squeezed Bella's knee.

"Bella, can you tell us more about the child?" her father asked calmly. "How old is she – five, six?"

"Eight, or so George said. Daphne doesn't know when she was born."

"Is she definitely his? Are you certain?" Kate said.

"No doubt about that – she's the image of him," Bella said.

"And she has no family?" her father said.

"No one as far as I'm aware. I don't think George believed he might die. It was probably part of some ludicrous ruse to make me admire his bravery, but he asked me to take her to an orphanage or raise her myself if anything happened to him."

"What do you plan to do with her?" Kate asked.

"I've not thought it through properly. One thing is certain – I can't send her to the orphanage, not after hearing from Doris how life is for the children in there. But raising her would be incredibly difficult – she has George's eyes."

"Perhaps we should enrol her here and she could be like any other pupil," Kate said, smiling encouragingly, clearly feeling guilty for being incensed earlier.

"She needs a family – deserves to have one. Besides, it'll be a long time before she can fit in here. Apart from her accent and manners, she doesn't even know the alphabet. I won't allow this to affect our school. You've worked too hard to build it up, Kate."

"Damn this place, Bella. If it's what you want, we'll sort it."

Bella smiled at her sister but said tentatively, "Mother, have you nothing to say?"

398

Her mother appeared to be choosing her words.

"Bella Caldwell, you may be a grown woman, but if you ever behave so recklessly again, you'll have me to answer to."

"I knew that's how you'd react."

"We listened to you, young lady, so now you will do me the courtesy of hearing me out."

Bella nodded.

"At my age, I thought I knew something of the seedier side of life, but what you've described has shocked me to the core. I'm livid that you never contacted your father and me. Of course, our priority would have been to protect you, but we'd have wanted to help the child, as well."

"I explained that involving the police would have put her in more danger," Bella interrupted.

"I haven't finished speaking," her mother said sternly.

Despite wanting to defend her actions, Bella knew she must allow them to express their annoyance. Nothing they'd said was unreasonable.

"Sorry – go on."

"Perhaps you're correct and police involvement would have made things worse. And despite the risk to yourself . . ." Her mother paused and glanced at her father. "Well, I'm sure your father agrees that we've never been prouder. Whatever you decide about the child, we'll give you our full support."

Bella sighed. It could have been worse.

Epilogue

25 June 1914

The young police constable turned away, covering his nose and mouth as his colleagues hauled a bloated corpse from the Thames. As the stench assailed his nostrils, he lost the contents of his stomach.

"Watch my bleedin' shoes," Sergeant Jones said. "First day on the job or not, you can't be bringing up your breakfast at the sight of a dead body. Come on, you soft git. You'll see worse than this by the time you've finished on the force. Check him for identification."

"Sorry, sarge. I need a minute," the young man mumbled before depositing more of his porridge on the quayside.

"There's nothing on him, sarge. No papers or anythink," he said a while later.

"It doesn't matter. He's not the pretty boy he was, but I can just about recognise him. He likes to be called the guv'nor, the arrogant bastard – though no one knew his real identity or where he lived. But he underestimated me. George Bristow, that's his name. Not that it matters now. It'll be a pauper's grave for him. Get the body slung on the cart before I put my boot up your arse," the sergeant growled.

The servants at Faredene Hall were laying out food on a large table. In the centre stood a two-tier birthday cake and another table nearby was stacked with boxes and packages tied with bright ribbons.

On the croquet lawn, Sean, threw his mallet on the floor as Kate's ball went through the hoop.

"No! How on earth do you manage to get every shot!" he cried.

"Talent," Kate said, taking a bow.

"I've come to realise my wife is remarkably skilled at everything, Sean," William said, smiling proudly. "Unless you're prepared to be thrashed with humiliating ease, I suggest you never play her at tennis."

Bella nudged Richard and whispered, "I think we may need to resort to underhand tactics if we're to have any chance of winning."

A light breeze whispered through the oak trees by the pond and sunlight filtered through the leaves onto the deckchairs arranged around the rug. Kitty was in a half-sitting, half-lying position as she made Pierre and Joshua's soldiers take part in a battle. The boys giggled each time she cried out as she caused one of the figures to fall to the ground. As another playful shout of protest came from the croquet lawn, Kitty jerked her head towards Harry, Albert and Edward.

"How can them three sleep through all that shouting?"

Victoria glanced fondly at her husband. "I expect they'll claim they've been awake all the time and only resting their eyes."

"Aye, well, I'll be giving Albert a nudge in a minute so he can take a turn entertaining these two," Kitty said as she stacked the bricks again.

"I'm glad you're down there, Auntie Kitty, and not me, because I'm getting so big, I doubt I'd be able to get up again," Jane said, rubbing her stomach.

"Twins! I can hardly believe it. I wonder if you'll have one of each like I did," Kitty said.

"We already have two boys, so girls would be nice, but I don't mind. Neither does Sean. If he has his way, we'll have a dozen."

"Let's hope Kate or Bella don't hit him with their mallet before he gets the chance to see the two you're carrying, because his sisters don't like to lose," Victoria joked.

"Kate was telling me that Bella's speaking to the Women's Guild next week," Jess said.

"That's right," Victoria said. "It's a good job Kate's Chairwoman, because while Bella's campaigning for a scheme to provide better food for nursing mothers and infants should be well received, Ethel would never have allowed the other topic even to be discussed. Now, with Kate's help, I've no doubt the project to help the fallen women of Faredene will get the support it needs. Bella surprised me by taking up Owain's cause so passionately. But I suppose she felt compelled after the things she saw in London – women forced into that life and the way they live—"

"Perhaps we shouldn't discuss fallen women in front of the boys," Jane said. "He might not be old enough to understand what they are, but since he got his hearing back, Pierre picks up on everything and repeats it."

"Bella should join the Guild," Kitty said.

"She won't have time – not now she's about to begin her training to be a nurse," said Victoria. "And even though she wants a long engagement, she and Richard will be getting married next spring."

"Aww, honey, before long you'll have even more grandchildren to fuss over," Jess said.

"The more the better," Victoria said. "As far as I'm concerned, there's no such thing as too many grandchildren. Children are so precious. It was such a good idea to give Daphne a party. Not knowing the real date doesn't matter, as long as she gets to celebrate her birthday."

"If any child deserves to be cherished, it's her," Jess said.

At that moment, a blaze of bright yellow frills came charging towards them, followed by Jake and Brian, all giggling as they ran.

"Can we have a ride on my new pony?" Daphne said, panting.

"Sure you can, baby," Jess said, pulling Daphne into her arms and smothering her with kisses. "You tell the grooms I said it was all right."

Daphne's little arms stretched around Jess.

"Thanks, Mam. I love you and Dad so much."

About the Author

Debra Delaney is a qualified coach, therapist and meditation teacher who is fascinated by what makes people think and behave in a particular way. Her understanding of people and their behaviour has helped her to build the interesting characters in her novels.

She lives in Shropshire with her husband, and between them they have a large family. Her biggest daily challenge remains juggling her many hobbies, spending time with loved ones and her passion for meddling in the lives of her characters.

Having completed *Beyond Deceit*, the third book in the saga, she is already developing ideas for new novels and hopes to be writing for many years to come.